Laurie R. King

Laurie King is a third-generation native of San Francisco Bay Area, but since her marriage to an Anglo-Indian professor she has lived briefly in twenty countries on five continents. She and her husband have two children. They live mostly in California, but also have a house in Oxford.

Laurie King's Sherlock Holmes and Mary Russell novels have been published to great acclaim, and *The Beekeeper's Apprentice* and *A Letter of Mary*, the first and third in the series, are also published by HarperCollins.

Laurie King has written three novels featuring detectives Kate Martinelli and Al Hawkin. The first, *A Grave Talent*, won both the Crime Writers' Association's John Creasey Award for Best First Crime Novel of the Year, and the equivalent Edgar Award in the US. She is also the author of the psychological suspense novel, *The Birth of a New Moon*.

By the same author

THE BIRTH OF A NEW MOON

Kate Martinelli novels

NIGHT WORK
WITH CHILD
TO PLAY THE FOOL
A GRAVE TALENT

Mary Russell novels

A LETTER OF MARY
THE BEEKEEPER'S APPRENTICE

LAURIE R. KING

A MONSTROUS REGIMENT OF WOMEN

HarperCollins*Publishers*

HarperCollins*Publishers*
77–85 Fulham Palace Road,
Hammersmith, London W6 8JB

The HarperCollins website address is:
www.fireandwater.com

This paperback edition 2000

1 3 5 7 9 8 6 4 2

First published in Great Britain by
HarperCollins*Publishers* 1997

Copyright © Laurie R. King 1995

Laurie R. King asserts the moral right to
be identified as the author of this work

ISBN 0 00 651494 4

Set in Goudy Old Style and Bodoni

Printed and bound in Great Britain by
Omnia Books Limited, Glasgow

for Zoe
τό φῶς τῶν ἀνθρώπων

The story between these covers is the second I have resuscitated from the bottom of a tin trunk that I received anonymously some years ago. In my editor's introduction to the first, which was given the name *The Beekeeper's Apprentice*, I admitted that I had no idea why I had been the recipient of the trunk and its contents. They ranged in value from an emerald necklace to a small worn photograph of a thin, tired-looking young man in a WWI army uniform.

There were other intriguing objects as well: The coin with a hole drilled through it, for example, heavily worn on one side and scratched with the name IAN on the other, must surely tell a story; so, too, the ragged shoelace, carefully wound and knotted, and the short stub of a beeswax candle. But the most amazing thing, even for someone like myself who is no particular Sherlock Holmes scholar, are the manuscripts. *The Beekeeper's Apprentice* told of the early days of a partnership heretofore unknown to the world: that of young Mary Russell and the middle-aged and long-retired Sherlock Holmes.

These literally are *manuscripts*, handwritten on various kinds of paper. Some of them were easy enough to decipher, but others, two of them in particular, were damned hard work. This present story was the worst. It looked as if it had been rewritten a dozen or more times, with parts of pages torn away, scraps of others inserted, heavy cross-hatching defying all attempts at bringing out the deleted text. This was not, I think, an easy book for Ms. Russell to write.

As I said, I have no idea why this collection was sent to me. I believe, however, that the sender, if not the author herself, may still be alive. Among the letters generated by the publication of *The Beekeeper's Apprentice* was an odd and muchtravelled postcard, mailed in Utrecht. It was an old card, with a sepia photograph of a stone bridge over a river, a long flat boat with a man standing at one end holding a pole and a woman in Edwardian dress sitting at the other, and three swans. The back was printed with the caption, FOLLY BRIDGE, OXFORD. Written on it, in handwriting similar to that of the manuscripts, was my name and address, and beside that the phrase, "More to follow."

I certainly hope so.

—Laurie R. King

For who can deny that it is repugnant to nature that the blind shall be appointed to lead and conduct such as do see, that the weak, the sick and the impotent shall nourish and keep the whole and the strong, and, finally, that the foolish, mad, and frenetic shall govern the discrete and give counsel to such as be sober of mind? And such be all women compared to man in bearing of authority.

> —John Knox (1505–1572)
> *The First Blast of the Trumpet Against the Monstrous Regiment of Women*
> (Published in 1558 against Mary Tudor; later applied to Mary Stuart. *Regiment* is used in the sense of *régime*.)

CHAPTER 1

Sunday, 26 December–
Monday, 27 December 1920

*Womankind is imprudent and soft or flexible.
Imprudent because she cannot consider with wisdom and reason the things she hears and sees;
and soft she is because she is easily bowed.*
                    —John Chrysostom (c.347–407)

I sat back in my chair, jabbed the cap onto my pen, threw it into the drawer, and abandoned myself to the flood of satisfaction, relief, and anticipation that was let loose by that simple action. The satisfaction was for the essay whose last endnote I had just corrected, the distillation of several months' hard work and my first effort as a mature scholar: It was a solid piece of work, ringing true and clear on the page. The relief I felt was not for the writing, but for the concomitant fact that, thanks to my preoccupation, I had survived the compulsory Christmas revels, a fête which had reached a fever pitch in this, the last year of my aunt's control of what she saw as the family purse. The anticipation was for the week of freedom before me, one entire week with neither commitments nor responsibilities, leading up to my twenty-first birthday and all the rights and privileges pertaining thereto. A small but persistent niggle of trepidation tried to make itself known, but I forestalled it by standing up and going to the chest of drawers for clothing.

My aunt was, strictly speaking, Jewish, but she had long ago abandoned her heritage and claimed with all the enthusiasm of a convert the outward forms of cultural Anglicanism. As a result, her idea of Christmas tended heavily towards the Dickensian and Saxe-Gothan. Her final year as my so-called guardian was coincidentally the first year since the Great War ended to see quantities of unrationed sugar, butter, and meat, which meant that the emotional excesses had been compounded by culinary ones. I had begged off most of the revelry, citing the demands of the paper, but with my typewriter fallen silent, I had no choice but crass and immediate flight. I did not have to think about my choice of goals—I should begin at the cottage of my friend and mentor, my tutor, sparring partner, and comrade-in-arms, Sherlock Holmes. Hence my anticipation. Hence also the trepidation.

In rebellion against the houseful of velvet and silk through which I had moved for what seemed like weeks, I pulled from the wardrobe the most moth-eaten of my long-dead father's suits and put it on over a deliciously soft and threadbare linen shirt and a heavy Guernsey pullover I had rescued from the mice in the attic. Warm, lined doeskin gloves, my plaits pinned up under an oversized tweed cap, thick scarf, and a pause for thought. Whatever I was going to do for the next three or four days, it would be at a distance from home. I went to the chest of drawers and took out an extra pair of wool stockings, and from a secret niche behind the wainscotting I retrieved a leather pouch, in which I had secreted all the odd notes and coins of unspent gifts and allowances over the last couple of years—a considerable number, I was pleased to see. The pouch went into an inner pocket along with a pencil stub, some folded sheets of paper, and a small book on Rabbi Akiva that I'd been saving for a treat. I took a last look at my refuge, locked the door behind me, and carried my rubber-soled boots to the back door to lace them on.

Although I half-hoped that one of my relatives might hail me, they were all either busy with the games in the parlour or unconscious in a bloated stupor, because the only persons I saw were the red-faced cook and her harassed helper, and they were too busy preparing yet another meal to do more than return my greetings distractedly. I wondered idly how much I was paying them to work on the day a servant traditionally expected to have free, but I shrugged off the thought, put on my boots and the dingy overcoat I kept at the back of the cupboard beneath the stairs, and escaped from the overheated, overcrowded, emotion-laden house into the clear, cold sea air of the Sussex Downs. My breath smoked around me and my feet crunched across patches not yet thawed by the watery sunlight, and by the time I reached Holmes' cottage five miles away, I felt clean and calm for the first time since leaving Oxford at the end of term.

He was not at home.

Mrs Hudson was there, though. I kissed her affectionately and admired the needlework she was doing in front of the kitchen fire, and teased her about her slack ways on her free days and she tartly informed me that she wore her apron only when she was on duty, and I commented that in that case she must surely wear it over her nightdress, because as far as I could see she was always on duty when Holmes was about, and why didn't she come and take over my house in seven days' time and I'd be sure to appreciate her, but she only laughed, knowing I didn't mean it, and put the kettle on the fire.

He had gone to Town, she said, dressed in a multitude of mismatched layers, two scarfs, and a frayed and filthy silk hat—and did I prefer scones or muffins?

"Are the muffins already made?"

"Oh, there are a few left from yesterday, but I'll make fresh."

"On your one day off during the year? You'll do nothing of the sort. I adore your muffins toasted—you know that—and they're better the second day, anyway."

She let herself be persuaded. I went up to Holmes' room and conducted a judicious search of his chest of drawers and cupboards while she assembled the necessaries. As I expected, he had taken the fingerless gloves he used for driving horses and the tool for prising stones from hoofs; in combination with the hat, it meant he was driving a horsecab. I went back down to the kitchen, humming.

I toasted muffins over the fire and gossiped happily with Mrs Hudson until it was time for me to leave, replete with muffins, butter, jam, anchovy toast, two slices of Christmas cake, and a waxed paper–wrapped parcel in my pocket, in order to catch the 4:43 to London.

I used occasionally to wonder why the otherwise-canny folk of the nearby towns, and particularly the stationmasters who sold the tickets, did not remark at the regular appearance of odd characters on their platforms, one old and one young, of either sex, often together. Not until the previous summer had I realised that our disguises were treated as a communal scheme by our villagers, who made it a point of honour never to let slip their suspicions that the scruffy young male farm-hand who slouched through the streets might be the same person who, dressed considerably more appropriately in tweed skirt and cloche hat, went off to Oxford during term time and returned to buy tea cakes and spades and the occasional half-pint of bitter from the merchants when she was in residence. I believe that had a reporter from the *Evening Standard* come to town and offered one hundred pounds for an inside story on the famous detective, the people would have looked at him with that phlegmatic country expression that hides so much and asked politely who he might be meaning.

I digress. When I reached London, the streets were still crowded. I took a taxi (a motor cab, so I hadn't to look too closely at the driver) to the agency Holmes often used as his supplier when he needed a horse and cab. The owner knew me—at least, he recognised the young man who stood in front of him—and said that, yes, that gentleman (not meaning, of course, a gentleman proper) had indeed shown up for work that day. In fact, he'd shown up twice.

"Twice? You mean he brought the cab back, then?" I was disappointed, and wondered if I ought merely to give up the chase.

"T'orse 'ad an 'ot knee, an' 'e walked 'er back. 'E was about ter take out anuvver un when 'e 'appened t'see an ol' 'anson just come in. Took a fancy, 'e did, can't fink why—'s bloody cold work an' the pay's piss-all, 'less you 'appen on t' odd pair what wants a taste of t' old days, for a lark. 'Appens, sometimes, come a summer Sunday, or after t' theatre Sattiday.

Night like this, 'e'd be bloody lucky t'get a ha'penny over fare."

With a straight face, I reflected privately on how his colourful language would have faded in the light of the posh young lady I occasionally was.

"So he took the hansom?"

"That 'e did. One of the few what can drive the thing, I'll give 'im that." His square face contemplated for a moment this incongruous juxtaposition of skill and madness in the man he knew as Basil Josephs, then he shook his head in wonderment. " 'Ad ta give 'im a right bugger of an 'orse, though. Never been on a two-wheeler, 'e 'asn't, and plug-headed and leather-mouthed to boot. 'Ope old Josephs 'asn't 'ad any problems," he said with a magnificent lack of concern, and leant over to hawk and spit delicately into the noisome gutter.

"Well," I said, "there couldn't be too many hansoms around, I might spot him tonight. Can you tell me what the horse looks like?"

"Big bay, wide blaze, three stockin's with t' off hind dark, nasty eyes, but you won't see 'em—'e's got blinkers on," he rattled off, then added after a moment, "Cab's number two-ninety-two." I thanked him with a coin and went a-hunting through the vast, sprawling streets of the great cesspool for a single, worn hansom cab and its driver.

The hunt was not quite so hopeless as it might appear. Unless he were on a case (and Mrs Hudson had thought on the whole that he was not), his choice of clothing and cab suggested entertainment rather than employment, and his idea of entertainment tended more toward London's east end rather than Piccadilly or St John's Wood. Still, that left a fair acreage to choose from, and I spent several hours standing under lampposts, craning to see the feet of passing horses (*all* of them seemed to have blazes and stockings) and fending off friendly overtures from dangerously underdressed young and not-so-young women. Finally, just after midnight, one marvellously informative conversation with such a lady was interrupted by the approaching clop and grind of a trotting horsecab, and a moment later the piercing tones of a familiar voice echoing down the nearly deserted street obviated the need for any further equine examination.

"Annalisa, my dear young thing," came the voice that was not a shout but which could be heard a mile away on the Downs, "Isn't that child you are trying to entice a bit young, even for you? Look at him—he doesn't even have a beard yet."

The lady beside me whirled around to the source of this interruption. I excused myself politely and stepped out into the street to intercept the cab. He had a fare—or rather, two—but he slowed, gathered the reins into his right hand, and reached the other long arm down to me. My disappointed paramour shouted genial insults at Holmes that would have blistered the remaining paint from the woodwork, had they not been deflected by his equally jovial remarks in kind.

The alarming dip of the cab caused the horse to snort and veer sharply, and a startled, moustachioed face appeared behind the cracked glass of the side window, scowling at me. Holmes redirected his tongue's wrath from the prostitute to the horse and, in the best tradition of London cabbies, cursed the animal soundly, imaginatively, and without a single manifest obscenity. He also more usefully snapped the horse's head back with one clean jerk on the reins, returning its attention to the job at hand, while continuing to pull me up and shooting a parting volley of affectionate and remarkably familiar remarks at the fading Annalisa. Holmes did so like to immerse himself fully in his rôles, I reflected as I wedged myself into the one-person seat already occupied by the man and his garments.

"Good evening, Holmes," I greeted him politely.

"Good morning, Russell," he corrected me, and shook the horse back into a trot.

"Are you on a job, Holmes?" I had known as soon as his arm reached down for me that if case it were, it did not involve the current passengers, or he should merely have waved me off.

"My dear Russell, those Americanisms of yours," he tut-

tutted. "How they do grate on the ear. 'On a job.' No, I am not occupied with a case, Russell, merely working at the maintenance of old skills."

"And are you having fun?"

" 'Having fun'?" He pronounced the words with fastidious distaste and looked at me askance.

"Very well: Are you enjoying yourself?"

He raised one eyebrow at my clothes before turning back to the reins.

"I might ask the same of you, Russell."

"Yes," I replied. "As a matter of fact, I *am* enjoying myself, Holmes, very much, thank you." And I sat back as best I could to do so.

Traffic even in the middle of London tends to die down considerably by the close of what Christians mistakenly call the Sabbath, and the streets were about as quiet now as they ever were. It was very pleasant being jolted about in a swaying seat eight feet above the insalubrious cobblestones, next to my one true friend, through the ill-lit streets that echoed the horse's hoofs and the grind of the wheels, on a night cold enough to kill the smells and keep the fog at bay, but not cold enough to damage exposed flesh and fingertips. I glanced down at my companion's begrimed fingers where they were poised, testing the heavy leather for signs of misbehaviour from the still-fractious beast with the same sensitivity they exhibited in all their activities, from delicate chemical experiments to the tactile exploration of a clue. I was struck by a thought.

"Holmes, do you find that the cold on a clear night exacerbates your rheumatism as much as the cold of a foggy night?"

He fixed me with a dubious eye, then turned back to the job, lips no doubt pursed beneath the scarfs. It was, I realised belatedly, an unconventional opening for a conversation, but surely Holmes, of all people, could not object to the eccentric.

"Russell," he said finally, "it is very good of you to have come up from Sussex and stood on cold street corners for half the night striking up inappropriate friendships and flirting with pneumonia in order to enquire after my health, but perhaps having found me, you might proceed with your intended purpose."

"I had no purpose," I protested, stung. "I finished my paper more quickly than I'd thought, felt like spending the rest of the day with you rather than listening to my relations shrieking and moaning downstairs, and, when I found you missing, decided on a whim to follow you here and see if I might track you down. It was merely a whim," I repeated firmly. Perhaps too firmly. I hastened to change the subject. "What are you doing here, anyway?"

"Driving a cab," he said in a voice that told me that he was neither distracted nor deceived. "Go on, Russell, you may as well ask your question; you've spent seven hours in getting here. Or perhaps I ought to say, six years?"

"What on earth are you talking about?" I was very cross at the threat of having my nice evening spoilt by his sardonic, all-knowing air, though God knows, I should have been used to it by then. "I am having a holiday from the holidays. I am relaxing, following the enforced merriment of the last week. An amusing diversion, Holmes, nothing else. At least it was, until your suspicious mind let fly with its sneering intimations of omniscience. Really, Holmes, you can be very irritating at times."

He seemed not in the least put out by my ruffled feathers, and he arched his eyebrow and glanced sideways at me to let me know it. I put up my chin and looked in the other direction.

"So you did not 'track me down,' as you put it, for any express purpose, other than as an exercise in tracking?"

"And for the pleasurable exercise of freedom, yes."

"You are lying, Russell."

"Holmes, this is intolerable. If you wish to be rid of me, all you need do is slow down and let me jump off. You needn't be offensive to me. I'll go."

"Russell, Russell," he chided, and shook his head.

"Damn it, Holmes, what can you imagine was so urgent that I should come all the way here in order to confront you with it immediately? Which, you may have noticed, I have not done?"

"A question you finally nerved yourself up to ask, and the momentum carried you along," he answered coolly.

"And what question might that be?" I did leave myself right open for it, but once launched in a path, it is difficult to change direction.

"I expect you came to ask me to marry you."

I nearly fell off the back of the cab.

"Holmes! What do you . . . How can you . . ." I sputtered to a halt. In front of me, the speaking vent in the roof of the cab was rising, and in a moment I could see two sets of eyes, dimly illuminated by the carriage lights and a passing streetlamp. One set was topped by a bowler, the other by a frippery gobbet of flowers, and they passed over us like two pair of roving spotlights, apprehensively examining the two men who were carrying on this lunatic dialogue above their heads.

Holmes lifted his hat and gave them a genial smile. I waggled the brim of my own and gave what I felt to be a look of criminal idiocy, but was apparently only slightly disconcerting. They stared between the reins at us, mouths agape.

"Sumfing Oi can do fer you, sir?" Holmes asked politely, his voice sliding down towards the Cockney.

"You can explain the meaning of this extraordinary conversation which my wife and myself have been forced to overhear." He looked like a schoolmaster, though his nose was dark with broken capillaries.

"Conversation? Oh yes, sorry, Oi s'pose it sounded sumfing mad." Holmes laughed. "Amatoor dramatics, sir. There's a club of us, rehearses parts whenever we come across one another. It's an Ibsen play. Do you know it?" The heads shook in unison, and the two looked at each other. "Fine stuff, but taken out of context, like, it sounds summat potty. Sorry we disturbed you." The eyes studied us dubiously for another long moment, then looked again at each other, and the hats sank slowly back into the cab. Holmes began to laugh convulsively in complete silence, and reluctantly I joined him. Some minutes later, he wiped his face with his filthy gloves, snapped the horse back to its trot, and took up a completely different topic.

"So, Russell, this gentleman and his lovely wife are going to number seventeen Gladstone Terrace. Kindly search your memory and tell me where it is to be found." It was an examination, and out of habit, I reviewed my mental picture of the area.

"Another nine streets up, on the left."

"Ten streets," he corrected me. "You forgot Hallicombe Alley."

"Sorry. This is getting far out for my knowledge of the map. I admit that one or two of the areas we've been through I've never seen before."

"I should think not," he said primly. Holmes tended to recall his Victorian attitudes and my gender at the oddest times—it always took me by surprise.

Holmes drew to a halt on a deserted side street and our passengers scurried for the shelter of their dark terrace house, not even waiting for the change from their coin. Holmes shouted a thanks at the closing door; his voice bounced off the disapproving bricks and scuttled off into the night.

"Jump down and get the rug, will you, Russell?"

When we were settled with the thing around our knees, he flicked the reins and the horse circled us back into the main road. We took a different route for our return to the stables, through streets even darker and dirtier than those we had come by. I was enjoying myself again, half-drowsing despite the continuous jolts, when Holmes spoke.

"So, Russell, what say you? Have you a question for me?"

It is difficult to pull away from a man when the two of you are compressed shoulder-to-shoulder and wrapped in a rug, but I managed.

"Come now, Russell, you are a great proponent of the emancipation of women; surely you can manage to carry out your intentions in this little matter."

"Little?" I seized on the word, as he knew I would. "First you place the proposition in my mouth, and then you denigrate it. I don't know why I even—" I bit back the words.

"Why you thought of it in the first place, is that what you were about to say?"

Before I could respond, a fast blur shooting out of a dark alley brought Holmes to his feet, nearly knocking me from my perch. A black shape was at the heels of the horse, snarling and snapping with a flash of white teeth as it dodged into the dim light from our lamps. In one smooth movement, Holmes wrapped the reins around his left hand and hauled back on them as he snatched the long whip from its rest with his right, and with considerable accuracy he turned the yaps into yelps. Sheer brute strength brought the horse back onto its haunches and kept it from bolting, but sheer artistry allowed it just enough of its head to resume progress. The animal's blinkered head tossed and fretted the reins from its shoe-leather mouth to the driver's arms, and its heavy and graceless neck gleamed with sweat, but it obeyed its driver. In a moment, still on his feet and with both hands now on the reins, Holmes resumed as if there had been no interruption.

"So, why *did* you think of it?" he pressed, his voice calm but with a finely honed edge to it. "Have I given you any reason to believe that I might welcome such a suggestion? I am fifty-nine years old, Russell, and I have long been accustomed to the privacy and freedom of the bachelor life. Do you imagine that I might succumb to the dictates of social norms and marry you in order to stop tongues from wagging when we go off together? Or perhaps you imagine that the pleasures of the wedding bed might prove irresistible?"

My patience broke. I simply could not sit and listen to another peace-shattering, friendship-threatening, and, yes, hope-destroying phrase. I tossed the rug up over him, pulled both knees up to brace my boots on the top edge of the hansom, then straightened my legs and flipped over the seat backwards, an acrobatic feat I could not possibly have performed had I stopped to think about it first. I staggered on the uneven stones, a jolt of pain shooting through my bad shoulder, but I was off the cab. Holmes shook his arm free of the rug and started to rein in, but the much-abused horse had the bit in his teeth now and fought him, kicking and heaving in the traces. I took three bent steps to the gutter, seized a gin bottle from the night's rubbish, and skipped it across the stones to smash at the horse's feet. It sent him onto his hind legs, the sting of a fist-sized bit of brick brought him down again, and at the third missile he bolted.

By the time Holmes got him under control again, I was gone, having fled through an alley, over a wall, around two corners, and into a sink of blackness. He never caught me.

CHAPTER 2

Monday, 27 December

A woman moved is like a fountain troubled,
Muddy, ill-seeming, thick, bereft of beauty,
And while it is so, none so dry or thirsty
Will deign to sip or touch one drop of it.
                    —William Shakespeare (1554–1616)

It was of no importance; I knew that even as I had gone off the back of the cab. Arguments were a part of life with Holmes—a week without a knockdown, drag-out fight was an insipid week indeed. Tonight's was hardly a skirmish compared with some of the vicious running battles we had indulged in over the five years I had known him. No, Holmes had been merely venting general irritation through a convenient, if unfortunate, blowhole. I had found him to be particularly irritable when a case was going badly, or when he had been too long without a challenge, and although I was not absolutely certain which was the circumstance that night, I should have put money on the latter. When we met again, it would appear as if it had never happened. On a certain level, it had not.

Still, just then I had felt more in need of a companion in bohemian abandonment than of a sparring partner, and when faced with intense verbal swordplay, I had decided to bow out. Rare for me—one of the things I most liked about Holmes was his willingness to do battle. Still, there it was, and there I was, walking with considerable stealth down a nearly black street at one o'clock in the morning in a part of London

I knew only vaguely. I pushed Holmes from my mind and set out to enjoy myself.

Twenty minutes later, I stood motionless in a doorway while a patrolling constable shot his light's beam down the alley and went his heavy-footed way, and the incongruity of my furtive behaviour struck me: Here went Mary Russell, who six months previously had qualified for her degrees with accolades and honours from the most prestigious university in the world, who should in seven—six—days attain her majority and inherit what would have to be called a fortune, who was the closest confidante and sometime partner of the almost-legendary figure of Sherlock Holmes (whom, moreover, she had just soundly outwitted), and who walked through London's filthy pavements and alleys a young man, unrecognised, unknown, untraceable. Not a soul here knew who I was; not a friend or relation knew where I was. In an extremity of exhilaration, intoxicated by freedom and caught up by the power in my limbs, I bared my teeth and laughed silently into the darkness.

I prowled the streets all that dreamlike night, secure and unmolested by the denizens of the dark. Two hundred yards from where Mary Kelly had bled to death under the Ripper's knife, I was greeted effusively by a pair of ladies of the evening. In a yard off what had once been the Ratcliff Highway, I warmed my hands over the ashes of a chestnut seller's barrel and savoured the mealy remnant I found in one corner as if it were some rare epicurean morsel. I followed the vibration of music and was let into an all-night club, filled with desperate-looking men and slick, varnished women and the smell of cigarettes and avarice. I paid my membership, drank half my cloudy beer, and escaped back out onto the street for air. I stepped over a body (still breathing and reeking of gin). I avoided any number of bobbies. I heard the sounds of cat fights and angry drunks and the whimper of a hungry baby hushed at the breast, and once from an upper room a low murmur of voices that ended in a breathless cry. Twice I hid from the sound of a prowling horse-drawn cab with two wheels. The second time launched me on a long and highly technical conversation with a seven-year-old street urchin who was huddled beneath the steps to escape a drunken father. We squatted on cobbles greasy with damp and the filth that had accumulated, probably since the street was first laid down following the Great Fire, and we talked of economics. He gave me half of his stale roll and a great deal of advice, and when I left, I handed him a five-pound note. He looked after me awestruck, as at the vision of the Divine Presence.

The city dozed fitfully for a few short hours, insomniac amidst the tranquil winter countryside of southern England. There were no stars. I walked and breathed it in, and felt I had never been in London before. Never seen my fellowman before. Never felt the blood in my veins before.

At five o'clock, the signs of morning were under way. No light, of course, though in June by that hour the birds would have almost finished their first mad clamour and the farmers would have been long in their fields. Here, the first indications of day were in the knockers-up with their peashooters aimed at the windows of clockless clients, the water carts sluicing down the streets, the milk carts rattling down the cobblestones, and the strong smell of yeast from a bakery. Soon certain areas vibrated with voices and the rumble of carts, wagons, and lorries bearing food and fuel and labouring bodies into London town. Men trotted past, dwarfed by the stacks of half-bushel baskets balanced on their heads. In Spitalfields, the meat market warned me away with its reek of decaying blood, pushing me off into neighbouring areas less concerned with the trades of early morning. Even here, though, people moved, listless at first, then with voices raised. London was returning to life, and I, stupefied by the constant movement of the last hours, light-headed and without a will of my own, was caught up, swept along by the tide of purposeful heavy-booted workers who grumbled and cursed and hawked and spat their way into the day.

Eventually, like a piece of flotsam, I came to rest against a barrier and found myself staring uncomprehending at a window into another world, a square of furious movement and meaningless shapes and colours, snatches of flesh and khaki, shining white objects bearing quantities of yellow and brown that disappeared into red maws, a fury as far removed from the dim and furtive London I had emerged from as it was possible to imagine. It was a window, in a door, and the slight distortion of the glass gave it a look of unreality, as if it were an impressionist painting brought to life. The door opened, but the impression of a two-dimensional illusion was curiously intensified, so that the rush of steam-thick, impossibly fragrant air and the incomprehensible babble lay against my face like a wall. I stood fascinated, transfixed by this surreal, hypnotic vision for a solid minute before a shoulder jostled me and the dream bubble burst.

It was a tea shop, filled shoulder-to-shoulder with gravel-voiced men cradling chipped white mugs of blistering hot, stewed-looking tea in their thick hands, and the smell of bacon grease and toast and boiled coffee swept over me and made me urgently aware of a great howling pit of emptiness within.

I edged inside, feeling unaccustomedly petite and uncertain of my (character's) welcome, but I need not have worried. These were working men beginning a long day, not drunks looking for distraction, and although my thin shoulders and smooth face, to say nothing of the wire-rim spectacles I wiped free of fog and settled back on my nose, started a ripple of nudges and grins, I was allowed to push through the brotherhood and sink into a chair next to the window. My feet sighed in gratitude.

The solitary waitress, a thin woman with bad teeth, six hands, and the ability to keep eight quick conversations on her tongue simultaneously, wove her way through the nonexistent gaps, slapped a cup of tea onto the table in front of me, and took my order for eggs and chips and beans on toast without seeming to listen. The laden plate arrived before my sweet orange-coloured tea had cooled, and I set to putting it inside me.

When she reappeared at my elbow, I ordered the same again, and for the first time she actually looked at me, then turned to my neighbours and made a raucous joke, speculating on what I'd been doing to work up such an appetite. The men laughed uproariously, saw the blush on my downy cheeks, and laughed even harder before they hitched up their trousers and left in a clatter of scraped chair legs. I eased my own chair away from the wall an inch or two and devoured the second plate with as much pleasure as the first, though with more leisure. I lovingly mopped up the last smear of yolk with the stub of my toast, raised my fourth cup of tea to my cautious lips, and looked out the window beside me—directly into a face I knew, and one which an instant later recognised me.

I signalled her to wait, threaded my way through the burly shoulders and backs, thrust a large note into the waitress's pocket, and fell out onto the street.

"Mary?" she asked, doubtful. "That is you, isn't it?"

Lady Veronica Beaconsfield, a lodgings mate in Oxford who had read Greats a year ahead of me, an unpretty person who guiltily loved beautiful things and invested vast amounts of time and money in Good Works. We had been close at one time, but events had conspired to cool her affection, and to my sadness we had not managed to regain any degree of closeness before she went down from Oxford. I had last seen her seven months before, and we had exchanged letters in September. She looked exhausted. Even in the half-light, I could see smudges under her eyes and a look of grimy dishevelment, foreign to her tidy, competent self.

"Of course it's me, Ronnie," I said, cheerfully ungrammatical. "What a surprise to see a familiar face amidst that lot."

I gestured with one hand and nearly hit an enormous navvy coming out of the café. He growled at me, I apologised, and he rolled his shoulders and strode off, allowing me to live. Ronnie giggled.

"You still do that, I see, dressing like a man. I thought it was just undergraduate high spirits."

" 'When we've got our flowing beards on, who beholding us will think we're women?' " I recited. "There's good precedence."

"Dear old Aristophanes," she agreed. "Still, don't you find

it a drawback sometimes, dressing like a man?" she asked. "I thought that man was going to punch you."

"It's only happened once, that I didn't have time to talk my way out of a brawl."

"What happened?"

"Oh, I didn't hurt him too badly." She giggled, as if I had made a joke. I went on. "I had a much rougher time of it once during the War, with a determined old lady who tried to give me a white feather. I looked so healthy, she refused to believe me when I told her I'd been turned down for service. She followed me down the street, lecturing me loudly on cowardice and Country and Lord Kitchener."

Ronnie looked at me speculatively, unsure of whether or not I was pulling her leg. (As a matter of fact, I was not, in either case. The old lady had been severely irritating, though Holmes, walking with me that day, had found the episode very amusing.) She then shook her head and laughed.

"It's splendid to see you, Mary. Look, I'm on my way home. Are you going somewhere, or can you come in for coffee?"

"I'm going nowhere, I'm free as the proverbial bird, and I won't drink your coffee, thanks, I'm afloat already, but I'll gladly come for a natter and see your WC—I mean, your rooms."

She giggled again.

"One of the other drawbacks, I take it?"

"The biggest one, truth to tell," I admitted with a grin.

"Come on, then."

It was nearly light on the street, but as we turned off into a narrow courtyard of greasy cobblestones four streets away, the darkness closed in again. Veronica's house was one of ten or twelve that huddled claustrophobically around the yard with its green and dripping pump. One house was missing, plucked from its neighbours during the bombing of London like a pulled tooth. The bomb had not caused a fire, simply collapsed the structure in on itself, so that the flowery upstairs wallpaper was only now peeling away, and a picture still hung from its hook twenty feet above the ground. I looked at the remaining houses and thought, There will be masses of children behind those small windows, children with sores on their faces and nothing on their feet even in the winter, crowded into rooms with their pregnant, exhausted, anaemic mothers and tubercular grandmothers and the fathers who were gone or drunk more often than not. I suppressed a shudder. This choice of neighbourhood was typically Veronica, a deliberate statement to her family, herself, and the people she was undoubtedly helping—but did it have to be quite such a clear statement? I looked up at the grimy windows, and a thought occurred.

"Ronnie, do you want me to remove enough of this costume to make it obvious that you're not bringing a man home?"

She turned with the key in her hand and ran her eyes over me, looked up at the surrounding houses, and laughed for a third time, but this was a hard, bitter little noise that astonished me, coming from her.

"Oh, no, don't worry about that, Mary. Nobody cares."

She finished with the key, picked up the milk, and led me into a clean, uninspiring hallway, past two rooms furnished with dull, worn chairs and low tables, rooms with bare painted walls, and up a flight of stairs laid with a threadbare, colourless runner. A full, rich Christmas tree rose up beside the stairs, loaded with colourful ornaments and trying hard, and long swags of greenery and holly draped themselves from every protrusion. Instead of being infused with good cheer, however, the dreary rooms served only to depress the decorations, making them look merely tawdry. We went through the locked door at the top and came into a house entirely apart from the drab and depressing ground floor.

The Ronnie Beaconsfield I had known was a lover of beauty who possessed the means of indulging herself, not for the desire of possession, for she was one of the least avaricious people I knew, but for the sheer love of perfection. Her uncle was a duke, her grandfather had been an adviser to Queen Victoria, there were three barristers and a high-court judge in her immediate family, her father was something big in the City, her mother devoted her time to the Arts, and Veronica herself spent most of her time and money trying to live it all down. Even while an undergraduate at Oxford, she had been the moving force behind a number of projects, from teaching illiterate women to read to the prevention of maltreatment of cart horses.

To her despair, she was short, stout, and unlovely, and her invariably unflattering hairstyle should have nudged the wide nose and thick eyebrows into ugliness had it not been for the goodness and the gentle, self-deprecating humour that looked out from her brown eyes when she smiled. That bitterness had been new, and I wondered when it had crept in.

This upper portion of the house was much more the Veronica I knew. Here, the floors gleamed richly, the carpets were thick and genuine, the odd assortment of furniture and objets d'art—sleek, modern German chair and Louis XIV settee on a silken Chinese carpet, striped coarse Egyptian cloth covering a Victorian chaise longue, a priceless collection of seventeenth-century drawings on one wall contemplating a small abstract by, I thought, Paul Klee on the opposite wall—all nestled together comfortably and unobtrusively like a disparate group of dons in a friendly Senior Commons, or perhaps a gathering of experts on unrelated topics trading stories at a successful party. Veronica had a knack.

The house had been converted to electricity, and by its strong light I could see clearly the etched lines of desperate weariness on her face as my friend pulled off gloves, hat, and coat. She had been out most of the night—on a Good Work, her drab clothes said, rather than a social occasion—and a not entirely successful Good Work at that. I asked her about it when I came out of the WC (indoor, though I had seen the outside cubicles at the end of the yard below.)

"Oh, yes," she said. She was assembling coffee. "One of the families I've adopted. The son, who's thirteen, was arrested for picking the pocket of an off-duty bobby."

I laughed, incredulous.

"You mean he couldn't tell? He's new to the game, then."

"Apparently so. He's not very bright, either, I'm afraid."

She fumbled, taking a cup from the shelf and nearly dropping it from fingers clumsy with fatigue.

"Good heavens, Ronnie," I said, "you're exhausted. I ought to go and let you have some sleep."

"No!" She did drop the cup then, and it shattered into a thousand shards of bone china. "Oh, damn," she wailed. "You're right, I am tired, but I so want to talk with you. There's something . . . Oh, no, it's useless; I can't even begin to think about it." She knelt awkwardly to gather up the pieces, drove a splinter of porcelain into her finger, and stifled a furious sob.

Something fairly drastic was upsetting this good woman, something considerably deeper than a sleepless night caused by an incompetent pickpocket. I had a fairly good idea what in general she wanted me for, and I sighed inwardly at the brevity of my freedom. Nonetheless, I went to help her.

"Ronnie, I'm tired, too. I've been on my feet—literally—for the last twelve hours. If you don't mind my disreputable self on your sofa, we can both have a sleep, and talk later."

The intensity of the relief that washed over her face startled me and did not bode well for my immediate future, but I merely helped her sweep up the broken cup, overrode her halfhearted protestations, and sent her to bed.

There was no need to disturb the chaise longue. She had a guest room; she had a marvellous bathtub long enough for me to soak the aches from both the shoulder and my legs; she had a nightdress and a dressing gown and a deep bed that welcomed me with loving softness and murmured soporific suggestions at me until I drifted off.

I woke at dusk, to complete the topsy-turvy day, and rose to crane my neck at the smudge of heavy, wet sky that was visible between the roofs. I put on the too-short quilted dressing gown that Ronnie had given me and went down to the kitchen, and while the water came to a boil, I tried to decide whether I was making breakfast or afternoon tea. Veronica's idea of a well-stocked kitchen ran to yoghourt, charcoal biscuits, and vitamin pills (healthy body, healthy mind), but a rummage through the cupboards left me with a bowl of some healthy patent cereal that looked like wood chips, though they tasted all right doused with the top milk from the jug and a blob of raspberry jam, some stale bread to toast, and a slice of marzipan-covered Christmas fruitcake to push the meal into the afternoon. After my meal, I washed up, went down for the paper, brought it up along with the mail, lit the fire in the sitting room, and read all about the world's problems, a cup of coffee balanced on my knee and a very adequate coal fire at my feet.

At 5:30, Ronnie appeared, hair awry, mouthed a string of unintelligible noises, and went into the kitchen. In lodgings, she had been renowned as a reluctant waker, so I gave her time to absorb some coffee before I followed her.

"Mary, good morning—afternoon, I suppose. You've had something to eat?"

I reassured her that I had taken care of myself, then poured another cup of coffee from the pot and sat down at the small kitchen table to wait for whatever it had been she wanted to tell me.

It took some time. Revelations that come easily at night are harder by the light of day, and the woman who had cried out at a minor cut was now well under control. We talked interminably, about her needy and troubled families and the problem of balancing assistance and dependency while maintaining the dignity of all concerned. She enquired as to my interests, so I told her all about the paper on first-century rabbinic Judaism and Christian origins I'd written for publication, and about my work at Oxford, and when her eyes glazed over, I probed a bit deeper into her life. At some point, we ate pieces of dried-up cheese from a piece of white butcher's paper and dutifully chewed at a handful of unpalatable biscuits, and then she opened a bottle of superb white wine and finally began to loosen up.

There was a man; rather, there had been a man. It was an all-too-common story in those postwar years: A friend in 1914, he joined the New Army in 1915, was sent virtually untrained to the Western Front, and promptly walked into a bullet; sent home for eight weeks' recovery, their friendship deepened: He returned to the trenches, numerous letters followed, and then he was gassed in 1917 and again sent home: an engagement ring followed; he returned yet again to the Front, was finally demobbed in January 1919, a physically ruined, mentally frail mockery of his former self, liable to black, vicious moods and violent tempers alternating with periods of either manic gaiety or bleak inertia, when all he could do was silently smoke one cigarette after another, seeming completely unaware of other people. It was called shell shock, the nearly inevitable aftermath of month after month in hell, and every man who had been in the trenches had it to some degree. Some hid it successfully until the depths of night; others coped by immersing themselves in a job and refusing to look up. Many, many young men, particularly those from this young man's class—educated, well-off, the nation's pool of leadership, who died in colossal numbers as junior officers—became fatuous, irresponsible, and flighty, incapable of serious thought or concentrated effort, and (and here was the crux of this particular case) willing to become involved only with women as brittle and frivolous as they were. Veronica no longer wore the ring.

I listened in silence and watched her eyes roam over her glass, the tablecloth, the mail, the dark, reflecting window, anywhere but my face, until she seemed to run down. I waited a minute longer, and when she neither spoke nor looked up, I gave her a gentle prod.

"It does take time, that sort of thing," I suggested. "A lot of young men—"

"Oh, I know," she interrupted. "It's a common problem. I know a hundred women who've been through the same thing, and they all hope it'll solve itself, and every so often it does. But not Miles. He's just . . . it's as if he's not there anymore. He's . . . lost."

I chewed my lip thoughtfully for a moment, and the image of those slick faces in the nightclub came back to me. *Lost* was a good word for a large part of our whole generation.

"Drugs?" I asked, not quite the shot in the dark it seemed,

and she looked at me then, her eyes brimming, and nodded.

"What kind?" I asked.

"Any kind. He had morphine when he was in hospital, and he got used to that. Cocaine, of course. They all use cocaine. He goes to these parties—they last all night, a weekend, even longer. Once he took me to a fancy-dress party where the whole house was made over to look like an opium den, including the pipes. I couldn't bear the smell and so had to leave. He took me home and then went back. Lately, I think it's been heroin." I was mildly surprised. Heroin had been developed only a couple of years before I was born, and in 1920 it was nowhere near as commonplace as cocaine or opium or even its parent drug, morphine. I had some personal experience of the drug, following a bad automobile accident in 1914, when it was given me by the hospital in San Francisco—it being then thought that heroin was less addictive than morphine, a conclusion since questioned—but an habitual use of the drug would be very expensive.

"Did you go with him very often? To the same house?"

"The few times I went, they were all different houses, though mostly the same people. I finally couldn't take seeing him like than anymore, and I told him so. He said . . . he said some horrid, cruel things and slammed out of here, and I haven't heard from him since then. That was nearly two months ago. I did see him, about ten days ago, coming out of a club with a . . . a girl hanging on his arm and laughing in that way they do when they've been taking something and the whole world is so hysterically funny. He looked awful, like a skeleton, and his cough was back. He sounded like he had when he was home after being gassed; it made my chest hurt to hear it. I do get news of him—I see his sister all the time, but she says he never visits his parents unless he runs out of money before his next allowance is due."

"And they give it to him."

"Yes." She blew her nose and took a deep breath, then looked straight at me, and I braced myself.

"Mary, is there anything that you can do?"

"What could I do?" I did not even try to sound surprised.

"Well, you . . . investigate things. You know people, you and Mr Holmes. Surely there must be something we might do."

"Any number of things," I said flatly. "You could have him arrested, and they might be able to keep him until the drugs have left his system, though it would probably mean hospitalisation, considering the shape he's in. However, unless he's actually selling the drugs himself, which sounds unlikely if his parents support him, he'd be let free in a few days and would go right back to the source. You'd have put him through considerable discomfort with little benefit. Or, you could have him kidnapped, if you don't mind great expense and the threat of a prison sentence. That would ensure his physical well-being, for a time. You'd want to let him go eventually, though, and then it would almost surely begin again." It was cruel, but not so cruel as raising her hopes would have been. "Ronnie, you know what the problem is, and you know full well that there's not a thing that you or I or the king himself can do about it. If Miles wants to use drugs, he will. If not heroin, then morphine, or alcohol. As you said, he's just not there, and until he decides to find his way back, the only thing on God's green earth you can do is make sure he knows your hand is there if he wants it, and leave him to it." I offered her a pain-filled smile. "And pray."

She collapsed, and I stroked her hair and waited for the storm to abate. It did, and when she raised her face, I felt a moment's pity for the man Miles, confronted by this red-eyed, dull-haired, earnest young woman with her Good Works and her small eyes set into an unfashionably round face of pasty skin, now blotched from her tears. For someone terrified of responsibility and commitment, Veronica in her present state would loom huge and hideous, the embodiment of everything his former life held to reproach him with. Despite my harsh words, for her sake I should make an effort.

"Ronnie, look, I'll see what I can do. I know a man at Scotland Yard"—this was a slight exaggeration—"who might be able to suggest something."

"You're right, Mary." She fumbled with her sodden handkerchief. "I know you're right; it's just that it's so damnable, feeling completely hopeless while Miles is destroying himself. He's—he was—such a good man." She sighed, then sat back, her hands on her lap. We sat together as if at a wake.

Suddenly, she looked up at the clock on her wall, and a curious look of shy animation crept onto her face.

"Mary, are you free tonight? I don't know what you had planned, but there's someone you might be interested in meeting."

"Yes, I told you I'm free. I had thought to go up to Oxford for a couple of days, but it's nothing that couldn't wait."

"Oh, good. I really do think you'd like to hear her, and I could introduce you to her after the meeting."

"Meeting?" I said dubiously. She laughed, her face alive again and the signs of the storm fading fast.

"That's what she calls it. It's a bit like a church service, but tons more fun, and she gives a talk—her name is Margery Childe. Have you heard of her?"

"I have, somewhere." The name brought with it an impression of disdain overlying unease, as if the teller (writer? in a newspaper?) had been uncomfortable with the woman and taken refuge in cynicism. Also a photograph—yes, definitely in a newspaper, a blonde woman shaking hands with a beribboned official who towered over her.

"She's an amazing person, very sensible and yet, well"— she gave an embarrassed little laugh—"holy somehow. I go to the meetings sometimes, if I'm free. They always make me feel good—refreshed, and strong. Margery's been very helpful," she added unnecessarily.

"I'd be happy to go, Ronnie, but I don't have any clothes other than that suit."

"There'll be some stuff downstairs in the jumble box that'll fit you, if you're not too particular."

Thus it was that scarcely half an hour later I, wearing an odd assortment of ill-fitting garments, followed Veronica Beaconsfield out of the taxi and across the wet pavement, under the sign that read NEW TEMPLE IN GOD, and into the remarkable presence of Margery Childe.

CHAPTER 3

Monday, 27 December

Women should keep silence in church; for they are not permitted to speak, but should be subordinate, as the law says. . . . It is shameful for a woman to speak in church.

I Corinthians 14:34–35

The service was well under way when we arrived and found two seats in the back. To my surprise, my first impression was more of a hall filled with eager operagoers than a gathering of pious evening worshippers. The room was a hall, rather than a church or temple, had tiered seating, and was larger than it had appeared from the street. On the raised stage before us stood a small woman, a diminutive blonde figure on the nearly bare boards; she was wearing a long, simple dress—a robe—of some slightly peach-tinted white material, heavy silk perhaps, that shimmered and caught the light in golden highlights as she moved. She was speaking, but if it was a sermon, it did not resemble any I'd heard before. Her voice was low, almost throaty, but it reached easily into all corners and gave one the eerie impression of being alone with a friend and overhearing her private musings.

"It was shortly after that," she was saying, "that I went to church one lovely Sunday morning and heard the preacher, who was a large man with a thundering voice, speaking on the text from First Corinthians, 'Let your women keep silence in the churches.' " She paused and gathered all eyes to her in anticipation, then her mouth twitched in mischief. "I was, as you might imagine, not amused."

The gust of appreciative laughter that swept through the hall confirmed her audience's—congregation's?—endorsement of her attitude and hinted at an admiration that edged into adoration. It was also overwhelmingly soprano, and I took my eyes from the laughing figure onstage and surveyed my fellows.

There were perhaps only two dozen obvious males in a gathering of some 350, and of the ones near me, three looked distinctly uncomfortable, two were laughing nervously, one was scribbling furiously in a reporter's notebook, and one alone looked pleased. However, on closer examination I decided that this last was probably not male.

The laughter trickled off, and she waited, totally at ease, for silence before starting again.

"I was grateful to that large and noisy man, however. Not immediately," she added, inviting us to chuckle at her youthful passion, and many obliged, "but when I'd had a chance to think about it, I was grateful, because it made me wonder, Why does he want me to keep silent in church? What would be so terrible in letting me, a woman, talk? What does he imagine I might say?" She paused for two seconds. "What is this man afraid of?"

Absolute silence, and then: "Why, why is this man afraid of me? Here am I, I thought to myself, barely five feet tall in my stockinged feet, where he's over six feet and weighs twice what I do; he has a university degree, and I left school at fifteen; he's a grown man with a family and a big house, and I'm not even twenty and live in a cold-water flat. So, can this man be afraid of me? Can he imagine I'm going to say something that might make him look a fool? Or . . . is he afraid that I might say something to make his God look a fool? Oh, yes, I thought about that for quite some time, I tell you. Quite some time. And do you know what I decided? I decided that, Oh my, yes, this big man with his big voice and his big God in the big church, he was afraid, of little, old, me."

Her eyes flared wide and laughter came again at her mock

glee. She held up a hand to cut it short and leant forward confidentially.

"And do you know something? He was right to be afraid."

A second storm of laughter burst through the room, led by the woman herself, laughing at herself, laughing at the absurdity of it, collapsing over a good joke with some friends. After some minutes, she wiped her eyes along with half the room and stood shaking her head slowly as the room settled into silence. When she raised her face, the humour had died in it.

"I didn't really mean it—you know that. Part of me wanted to stand right up and ask him a lot of uncomfortable questions and make him look foolish, but I didn't because, truly, it was too sad. Here this man is working with God, thinking about God, living with God, every day, and still he does not trust God. Deep down, he doesn't feel one hundred percent certain that his God can stand up to criticism, can deal with this uppity woman and her uncomfortable questions; he does not *know* that his God is big enough to welcome in and put His arms around every person, big and small, believers or seekers, men or women."

She walked over to a small podium and took a couple of thoughtful swallows from a water glass, then resumed stage centre.

"In the book of Genesis, we see two ways of looking at the creation of human beings. In the first chapter, God 'says,' and the power of the word alone is so great, it *becomes*. The word *becomes* light and dark, sun and moon, mountains, trees, and animals as soon as it leaves the mouth of God.

"Then in the second chapter, we see God in another guise, as a potter, working with this sticky red clay and shaping a human being." Her tinted nails caught the light as her child-sized hands shaped a figurine out of the air, then brushed it away. "Same God, just different ways of talking about His creation. But in either of them—just think about this now—does it say in either of them that God made man *better* than woman? The first account certainly doesn't: 'So God created man—humankind—in His own image, in the image of God created He him, *male and female* created He *them*.' Humankind, male and female together, is in the image of God, not just male humans. The verse nails it down to make sure it's absolutely clear."

There was a rustle of disturbance in the hall, and her voice increased in volume to cover it.

"And the other story, about God the sculptor? I'm sure you all know the saying"—her voice climbed and turned saccharin—"that woman was made from man's rib so she might stand beside him and under his arm for protection." She made a face as if she'd tasted something disgusting. "Have you ever heard such sentimental, condescending rot?" Her voice control was extraordinary, for she sounded as if she were speaking normally, yet the crack of the last word rose above the combined laughter and a handful of angry voices. "If you want to be logical about it, don't tell me that the woman was given to Adam as a servant, a sort of glorified packhorse that could carry on a conversation. Tell me what the story really said, that God realised creation was incomplete, so He divided His human creature up, and created Eve, the distilled essence of His human being. With Eve, humanity became complete. With Eve, creation became complete. Adam was the first human, but Eve . . . *Eve* was the crown of God's creation."

Now she was having to shout.

"That was what my loud preacher feared, to be told that he and his cronies had no more right to tell me that I couldn't speak in God's house than I had a right to tell the sun not to shine. But all that's changed now, hasn't it, my friends?" A great roar drowned out her words for the next moments.

". . . God's image, you have the God-given right to use your minds and your bodies. You are in God's image, and I love you. See you Thursday, friends."

Abruptly, she waved, and in a swirl of gold and white she was gone. The place exploded in hundreds of voices raised in shouts of argument, pleasure, friendship, and confusion. Ronnie leant over and spoke loudly in my ear.

"This lot will go and have tea and biscuits next door, but if you'll wait a few minutes, we can go back and say hello, if you'd like."

I would like. I was fascinated, impressed, more than a bit repelled, and altogether extremely curious. The woman had played her audience like a finely tuned instrument, handling nearly four hundred people with the ease of a seasoned politician. Even I, non-Christian and hardened cynic that I am, had found it difficult to resist her. She was a feminist and she had a sense of humour, an appealing combination that was regrettably rare, and she came across as a person who was deeply, seriously committed to her beliefs, yet who retained the distance and humanity to laugh at herself. She was articulate without being pompous, and apparently self-educated since the age of fifteen. Her attitude towards the Bible seemed to be refreshingly matter-of-fact, and her theology, miracle of miracles, was from what I had heard radical but sound.

Oh yes, I should like to meet this woman.

I followed Veronica against the stream of chattering, gesticulating women sprinkled with fuming men to an inconspicuous door set into the wall next to the stage. The large, uniformed man standing guard there greeted Miss Beaconsfield by name and tipped his hat as his eyes gave me a thorough investigation.

Behind the door, the atmosphere was closer to that backstage after a theatre performance than to a vestry following a church service. Swirls of dramatic young women were calling "darling" to one another over the heads of trouser-clad women hauling spotlights and cleaning equipment. Gradually, we insinuated our way through to the hindmost recesses, and as Veronica's face became more and more expectantly radiant, I became increasingly aware of the depth of her involvement and the degree of her authority in this organisation. We went unchallenged, followed only by envious glances directed at my companion, and these slid into frank curiosity when they took in the peculiarly dressed figure in her wake.

A door closed behind us and the cacophony shut off abruptly. The rough workaday backstage setting was left behind, and we walked through what looked like the corridor of some high-class hotel. A huge flower arrangement occupied a niche, dramatic orange-and-brown lilies and white roses, and

Veronica paused to break off two of the latter, handing one to me without a word. Around a corner, she knocked at a door. Muted sounds came from within—several voices—but no answer. She fiddled shyly with her flower, shot me an embarrassed glance, and knocked again more loudly. This time, it opened, to a stout, suspicious woman of about fifty in a grey maid's uniform, complete with starched white apron and cap.

"*Bonjour*, Marie," Veronica chirped merrily, and stepped forward in expectation of the door being opened, as indeed it was. The woman looked as if she wanted to shut it in my face but did not quite dare.

Margery Childe was holding court. At first glance, it seemed that she was having tea with a dozen or so women friends, but when the eye took in the sitting-at-her-feet attitude and the openmouthed smiles on the faces, waiting for the blessing of a word, tea was the very least of what these women were drinking in. She looked up at our entrance and a smile came over her face as her eyes raked me from head to feet with the thoroughness of the doorman but in a fraction of the time, and then she was greeting Veronica with genuine warmth and affection. Ronnie handed her the flower, laying it into her hand like an offering at an altar, and the tiny blonde woman held it to her nose for a moment before placing it with a tumble of other delicate blossoms that spilled from a low table at her side.

"I'm glad you came, Veronica," she said, her voice sweeter than in public speech but still remarkably low and throaty. "We missed you on Saturday."

"I know," Veronica said eagerly. "I tried to get here, but one of my families—"

"Yes, your families. I was thinking just this morning about that problem you were having with the young girl, Emily was her name? Would you come and talk to me about how she's doing?"

"Certainly, Margery. Anytime."

"Find out from Marie when I'm free in the next day or two; she knows better than I. And you've brought a friend tonight?"

Veronica stood aside and held back her arm for me to come forward into the circle.

"This is Mary Russell, a friend of mine from Oxford."

The eyes that looked up into mine were a curiously dark blue, almost violet, deep and calm and magnetic, and the only truly beautiful element in her face. She lacked the currently fashionable high bones, her lightly tanned skin was ever-so-slightly coarse beneath the professional makeup, her teeth, though not protuberant, were a fraction overlarge, and her nose had at some distant time been broken and inexpertly set. Her looks, however, served only to increase her appeal, to make her seem vital and interesting, where a conventional beauty would have seemed insipid. It was a face to watch and to live for, not one simply to adore. She was calm and sure and filled with a power beyond her years and, I had to admit, enormously compelling. The room waited for me to lay my rose at her feet and do my obeisance so it could get on with its courtly rituals.

Without taking my eyes from hers, I raised the flower with great deliberation and threaded it into a buttonhole, then stepped forward and extended my hand to her.

"How do you do?" I said, and smiled with noncommittal politeness.

There was the briefest fraction of a pause before she sat upright, and her eyes gleamed as she leant forward and put her neat, strong, manicured little hand into mine. Her shake was by nature of an experiment, marginally longer than was necessary, and she sat back with something that might have been amusement in her eye.

"Welcome, Mary Russell. Thank you for coming."

"Oh, that's quite all right," I said blandly.

"I hope you enjoyed the service."

"It was interesting."

"Please help yourself to tea or one of the drinks, if you like."

"Thank you, I will," I said, not moving.

"I think we may be seeing something of you," she said suddenly, a sort of pronouncement.

"Do you?" I said politely, making it not quite a denial. Our eyes held for a long moment, and suddenly hers crinkled, though her mouth was still.

"Perhaps you might stay on a bit after my friends have left? I should like a word."

I inclined my head silently and went to sit in a corner, much amused at the skirmish. This one might be as much fun as Holmes.

The next hour would have been excruciatingly boring had it not been for the undercurrents and interplay that I found absolutely fascinating. She played this room with the same ease that she had played the hall, though to very different purpose. Before, her aim had been exhortation, inspiration, perhaps a bit of thought provocation. Here, she was acting as spiritual counsellor, mother confessor, and guiding light to this, her inner circle, drawing them out and drawing them together into a cohesive whole around herself.

Fourteen women (excluding myself), all of them young (the oldest was thirty-four or thirty-five), all reasonably attractive, all obviously wealthy, intelligent, and well-bred, and all of them with that ineffable but unmistakable air of women who had not sat still during the war. I found out later that of the women present, only two had done nothing more strenuous than knit for the soldiers, and one of those had been saddled with invalid parents. Nine had been VAD nurses at one time or other, three of them from 1915 until the end, nursing convoy after convoy of dying young men in France and southern England and the Mediterranean, sixteen-hour days of septic wounds and pus-soaked bandages, a baptism of blood for carefully nurtured young ladies. Several had spent months as land girls, backbreaking peasant labour for women accustomed to jumping hunters across hedges rather than wrestling with a plough horse, twisting elaborate paper spills for the fireplace rather than planting potatoes in heavy soil. These were women who had lost brothers and fiancés in the mud of Ypres and Passchendale, who had seen childhood friends return armless, crippled, blind, destroyed, women who had joined their lovers in the glory of a right war, the pride and purity of serving their country at need, and been beaten down, one ideal at a time, until in the end they had been reduced merely to slogging on, unthinking. Fourteen blue-blooded, strong, capable women, the kind of people who invariably made me feel gauche and clumsy, and all of them willing, eager even, to lay the inbred authority and absolute self-possession of their kind, along with the hard-earned maturity of the past years, at the feet of this woman as they had their flowers. She questioned them in turn, she listened with complete attention as each spoke, she elicited comments from specific individuals, and she gave judgement—suggestions, but with the authority of divine power behind her. Each received her share of words with gratitude, clutching them to her with the hunger of a child in a bread line, and when Childe finally stood to indicate that the evening was at an end, each went away with something of the same attitude of skulking off to a corner to gnaw. Finally, Veronica and I were left with her. I was still slumped into my chair, watching. Veronica turned to me.

"Mary, do you want to come back with me tonight? Or you could take a cab later . . . ?" The evening had done her a world of good, I would give Childe that. She was again calm and sure of herself, though she, too, had something of the crust-in-the-corner look to her that made me think she might rather be alone.

"No, Ronnie, I'll go along to my club later, if that's all right with you. They'll give me a room, and I keep clothes there. I'll send these things back tomorrow—or shall we meet for lunch?" I offered. It amused me to ignore the woman standing in the background, as it had amused me in our earlier exchange to deny her the last word. I looked only at Veronica, but I was very aware of the other figure, and furthermore, I was conscious of her own awareness of, and amusement at, the undercurrents I was generating.

"Oh, yes, let's," Ronnie enthused. "Where?"

"The Elgin Marbles in the British Museum," I said decisively. "At midday. We can walk around to Tonio's from there. Does that suit?"

"I haven't been to the BM in donkey's years. That'll be fine. See you then." She took a deferential leave of Margery Childe and fluttered out.

CHAPTER 4

Monday, 27 December

The female sex as a whole is slow in comprehension.

—Cyril of Alexandria (376–444)

The door closed behind Veronica, and I was half-aware of her voice calling out to Marie and then fading down the corridor as I sat and allowed myself to be scrutinised, slowly, thoroughly, impassively. When the blonde woman finally turned away and kicked her shoes off under a low table, I let out the breath I hadn't realised I was holding and offered up thanks to Holmes' tutoring, badgering, and endless criticism that had brought me to the place where I might endure such scrutiny without flinching— at least not outwardly.

She padded silently across the thick carpet to the disorder of bottles and chose a glass, some ice, a large dollop from a gin bottle, and a generous splash of tonic. She half-turned to me with a question in her eyebrows, accepted my negative shake without comment, went to a drawer, took out a cigarette case and a matching enamelled matchbox, gathered up an ashtray, and came back to her chair, moving all the while with an unconscious feline grace—that of a small domestic tabby rather than anything more exotic or angular. She tucked her feet under her in the chair precisely like the cat in Mrs Hudson's kitchen, lit her cigarette, dropped the spent match into the ashtray balanced on the arm of the chair, and filled her lungs deeply before letting the smoke drift slowly from nose and mouth. The first swallow from the glass was equally savoured, and she shut her eyes for a long minute.

When she opened them, the magic had gone out of her, and she was just a small, tired, dishevelled woman in an expensive dress, with a much-needed drink and cigarette to hand. I revised my estimate of her age upward a few years, to nearly forty, and wondered if I ought to leave.

She looked at me again, not searchingly as before, but with the mild distraction of someone confronted by an unexpected and potentially problematic gift horse. When she spoke, it was in an ordinary voice, neither inspiring nor manipulating, as if she had decided to pack away her power from me. I wondered whether this was a deliberate strategy, putting on honesty when confronted by someone upon whom the normal techniques had proven ineffective, or if she had just, for some unknown reason of her own, decided to shed pretence. My perceptions were generally very good, and although it did not feel like deception, she did seem watchful. Hiding behind the truth, perhaps? Anticipation stirred.

Her first words matched her attitude, as if blunt honesty was both her natural response to the problem I represented and a deliberately chosen tactic.

"Why are you here, Mary Russell?"

"Veronica invited me. I will go if you wish."

She shook her head impatiently, dismissing both my offer and my response.

"People come here for a reason, I have found," she said half to herself. "People come because they are in need, or because they have something to give. Some come because they want to hurt me. Why have you come?"

Somewhat unsettled, I cast around for an answer.

"I came because my friend needed me," I finally admitted, and she seemed more willing to accept that.

"Veronica, yes. How did you come to know her?"

"We were neighbours in lodgings in Oxford one year." I decided I did not need to tell her of the elaborate pranks we had joined forces on, opting for a dignified enterprise instead.

"Ronnie organised a production of *Taming of the Shrew* for the wounded soldiers who were being housed in the colleges. She also hired a hall for a series of lectures and debates on the Vote"—no need to specify which Vote!—"and dragged me into it. She has a knack for getting others involved—but no doubt you've discovered that. Her enthusiasms are contagious, I suppose because they're based in her innate goodness. She even succeeded in getting me involved in one of the debates, and we became friends. I'm not really sure why." I was astonished, when I came to a halt, at how wordy I had been and how much of the truth I had given this stranger.

"The attraction of opposites, I see that. Veronica is softer and more generous than is good for her, which I doubt would be said about you. The hard and the soft, power and love, tug strongly at each other, do they not?"

It was said in a mode of casual conversation, and followed by a pull at her glass, but the devastating simplicity of her observations immediately raised my defences. However, it seemed that attack was not her intention, because she went on.

"That is the basis of our evening cycle of services, you might say." She reflected for a moment. "And of the daytime work, as well."

"A cycle?" I asked carefully.

"Ah, I see Veronica did not explain much about us."

"Nothing very coherent. A lot of talk about love and the rights of women."

She laughed, deep and rich.

"Dear Veronica, she is enthusiastic. Let me see if I can fill in the gaps." She paused to crush out the cigarette and immediately light another one, squinting through the smoke at me. "The evening services are what I suppose you might call our public events. Quite a few of our members came in originally out of curiosity, and stayed. Mondays, the topic is left general. I talk about any number of things; sometimes we have Bible readings, silent or guided prayer, even a discussion of some political issue currently in the news—I let the Spirit lead me, on Mondays, and it's usually a small, well-behaved group of friends, like tonight. Thursdays are different. Very different." She thought about Thursdays for a minute, and whatever her thoughts were, they turned her eyes dark and put a small smile on her full lips, and the magnetically beautiful woman I had seen earlier was there briefly. Then she reached down and flicked her cigarette over the ashtray and looked at me.

"Thursdays, I talk about love. It's a very popular night. We even see a fair number of men. And then on Saturdays, we talk about the other end of the spectrum: power. Sometimes Saturday meetings get quite political, and a lot of our hotter heads are given free rein. We don't get many men on Saturdays, and when we do, it's usually because they want a fight. Saturdays can get very exciting." She grinned.

"I can imagine," I said, calling to mind the shouts of the "quiet evening" I had witnessed. "And you have other activities, as well?"

"Oh heavens, the evening services are just the tip. Our goal, simply stated, is to touch everything concerned with the lives of women. Yes"—she laughed—"I know how it sounds, but one has to aim high. We have four areas we're concentrating on at the moment: literacy, health, safety, and political reform. Veronica is in charge of the reading program, in fact, and she's doing fine work. She has about eighty women at the moment learning to read and write."

"Teaching them all herself?" No wonder she was exhausted.

"No, no. All Temple members volunteer a certain amount of time every week to one or another of our projects. Veronica mostly coordinates them, though she, too, does her share of actual teaching. It's the same in each of the four areas. In the health program, for example, we have a doctor and several nurses who give time, but it's more a matter of identifying the women in the community who need help and putting them into touch with the right person. A woman with recurring lung infections will be seen by a doctor, but also by a building specialist who will look at her house to see if the ventilation might be improved. A woman with headaches from eyestrain will be given spectacles, and we'll see if we can find way to put more light into her working area—laying on gas, perhaps, or even electrical lights. A woman ill from exhaustion and nerves who has eleven children will be educated about birth control and enrolled in our nutritional-supplements program along with her children.''

"You haven't had any problems with the birth-control thing? Legally, I mean?"

"Once or twice. One of our members spent a week behind bars because of it, so we tend to give that information orally now rather than as pamphlets. Ridiculous, but there it is. It's getting easier, though. In fact, I understand that Dr Stopes—you know her, the *Married Love* woman?—intends to open a clinic here in London specialising in birth-control methods, sometime this spring. She's going to come speak to our members next month, if you're interested.''

I grunted a noncommittal noise; I could just imagine Holmes' reaction.

"And safety?"

"That was a branch off the health program originally, though now it's almost as large and certainly causes more headaches for us. We run a shelter—for women and their children who are without a roof or in danger from the father. It is appalling how little help is available for a desperate woman who has no relations to turn to. Violent husbands don't count as a threat in the eyes of the law," she commented, her voice controlled but her eyes dark, this time with anger, and I was briefly aware of her once-broken nose. "So two years ago when one of our members left us two large adjoining terrace houses on the corner, we opened them as a shelter and let it be known that any woman, and her children, of course, who needs a warm, dry, safe place is welcome.''

"I can imagine the headaches. I'm surprised you aren't overrun."

"We don't allow them to stay indefinitely. We help them find a job and someone to care for the small children, try to work something out with the husband—the shelter is not meant to be a permanent solution. There are still workhouses for that," she added with heavy irony, though the hardness of her face bespoke her opinion of the institution.

"Only women, then?"

"Only women. We occasionally get men, who think we're a soup kitchen, and we give them a meal and send them away. Men have other options. Women need the help of their sisters, and in fact, that to me is one of the most exciting things about what we're doing, when women of different classes meet and see that we share more similarities than differences, in spite of everything. We are on the edge of a revolution in the way women live in this society, and some of us want to ensure that the changes that are coming will apply to all women, rich and poor alike."

"Most of the women I saw here tonight, even in the service, seemed far from needy," I commented.

She refused to be baited, and smiled gently.

"My ministry is twofold. On the one hand are my poorer sisters, whose needs are immediate, even desperate, but relatively straightforward: spectacles, treatment for tuberculosis, warm clothing for their children. On the other hand are the women you saw tonight at the service, as well as those who refer to themselves as the 'Inner Circle'—young women like yourself who grew into maturity during the War, when it was common to see women doing work that would have been unthinkable ten years before, as well as older women who were running the country five years ago and are now made to feel harridans and harpies for pushing men out of jobs. My task is to bring the two hands together." She did not literally clasp her own hands, but the speech had the odour of ink about it, and I suspected it was normally accompanied by the theatrical gesture.

"Poor little rich girls," I murmured.

"Their needs are real," she said sharply. "Their hunger is no less acute for being spiritual rather than physical. In some ways, it is greater, because there is no cause to point at, nothing to blame but themselves. An empty cupboard is an inescapable fact; an empty heart can only be inferred from the life lived."

"And you say they lead empty lives," I said. I was irritated at the cliché, particularly tonight, with the smell of London's bleakest districts still in my nostrils. I wanted to push her into spontaneity, even if it meant ignoring my own opinions and playing devil's advocate to the full. "I should doubt that most of the women in this parish would agree with you. Most of them would be very happy to trade their empty cupboards for the trials of education, physical ease, and leisure. It's hardly 1840 we're talking about, it is? Or even 1903. This is nearly 1921, and nobody I know is about to be forced back into whalebone corsets and hobble skirts. Why, half of the women here tonight can probably vote."

"The vote was a sop," she snapped. "Granting individual slaves their manumission after a lifetime of service doesn't alter the essential wrongness of the institution of slavery, nor does giving a small number of women the vote adequately compensate the entire sex for their wartime service—to say nothing of millenia of oppression. All the vote did was break up the underlying unity of feminists and allow the factions to disperse. We allowed ourselves to be misled by a sop," she repeated. This speech was more personal and had its glints of spontaneity, but it was still ready-made—careful words, though with an angry woman behind them.

"So you use these women; you put them to work on your various projects in order to make them feel useful," I said.

To my surprise, far from taking umbrage at my words, she subsided with a laugh and winked at me conspiratorially.

"Just think of the vast amount of energy out there waiting to be put to use." She chuckled. "And no man will touch it. No male politician dares."

"You have political ambitions, then?" The newspaper photograph came back to me. A donation, had it been? To a Lord Mayor?

"I have no ambitions . . . for myself."

"But for the church?"

"For the Temple, I will do what needs to be done. Part of that may involve my entering the political arena."

"Using the vast resources of energy available to you." I smiled.

"Representing a large number of people, yes."

"And their bank accounts," I noted, but she did not rise even to that gibe. Instead, she put on a face as bland as anything Holmes could come up with.

"If you mean the funds our members make available to the Temple, it is true, God has been very good in meeting our needs. Most members tithe; others donate what they can."

My near accusation bothered her not in the least, and I had the distinct impression that she had searched her own heart on this question and felt certain of the truth in her words. She waited calmly. Her drink was only half-gone—whatever her faults, drunkenness did not seem to be one of them. I changed the subject.

"I was interested in your reading of the text," I began. "Tell me, was that a personal interpretation of the Creation Story, or was it based on someone else's work?"

To my astonishment, after all I had asked and intimated in the last few minutes, this apparently innocuous question hit her hard. She sat up, as amazed as if Lady Macbeth had interrupted a peroration to give a cake recipe, and watched me cautiously through narrowed eyes for a moment before an abrupt question was forced out.

"Miss Russell, what newspaper are you with?"

It was my turn to be astonished.

"Newspaper? Good heavens, is that what you thought?" I didn't know whether to laugh or to be offended—my only contacts with the profession had tended heavily towards the intrusive and ghoulish. It did, however, explain her odd façade of easy intimacy combined with formal speeches. She thought I was an undeclared journalist, using an unknowing acquaintance to get in and prise at The Real Margery Childe. I decided laughter was more called for, and so I laughed, apparently convincingly.

"No, Miss Childe, I'm not a reporter, or a journalist, or anything but a friend of Ronnie Beaconsfield."

"What do you do, then?"

I wondered briefly at the question, and realised that I didn't give off the same air of easy affluence that the rest of them had. It was a pleasing thought, that I was not recognisably of the leisured class.

"I'm at Oxford. I do informal tutoring, and a great deal of research."

"Into what?"

"Bible mostly."

"I see. You read theology, then?"

"Theology and chemistry."

"An odd combination," she said, the usual reaction.

"Not terribly."

"No?"

"Chemistry involves the workings of the physical universe, theology those of the human universe. There are behaviour patterns common to both."

She had forgotten both cigarette and drink momentarily, and she seemed to be listening to some inner voice, head tipped.

"I see," she said again, but I thought she was not speaking of my last sentence. "Yes, I begin to understand. You were interested in the way I read the stories of the Creation of woman. How might you read them?"

"In a very similar fashion, though I imagine we reached the point by rather different means."

"The means does not matter if the result is the same," she said dismissively, reaching down to rub the ash from the tip of her cigarette.

"You are wrong." She looked up, startled more by the edge in my voice than the blunt words themselves. She could not have known that to my mind sloppiness in textual analysis was absolutely unforgivable, far worse than the deliberate falsification of results from a slipshod chemical experiment. I forced a smile to take the sting out of my words, then tried to explain.

"Interpreting the Bible without training is a bit like finding a specific address in a foreign city with neither map nor knowledge of the language. You might stumble across the right answer, but in the meantime you've put yourself at the mercy of every ignoramus in town, with no way of telling the savant from the fool. Finding your way through the English Bible, you're entirely under the tyranny of the translators."

"Oh, for subtle distinctions perhaps. . . ."

"And blatant mistranslations, and deliberate obliteration of the original meaning."

"For example?" she asked sceptically.

"Deuteronomy thirty-two verse eighteen," I said with satisfaction. One single verb in this passage had occupied me and the librarians of the Bodleian for the better part of a month, and its exegesis was one cornerstone of the paper I had just finished and was due to present in a month's time. I was very proud of this verse. It took her only a moment to pull the words from her memory.

"Of the Rock that begot thee thou art unmindful, and thou hast forgotten God that formed thee." She sounded slightly puzzled. The passage was hardly controversial, being merely a segment of Moses' final exhortation to his wayward people, reminding them to turn from pagan practices, back to the Rock that was their God.

"That's not what it says," I told her. "Oh, it's what the Authorised translation says, but it's not what the original says. The final phrase, 'formed thee,' is nowhere in the Hebrew. The verb used is *hul*, which means 'to twist.' Elsewhere, it is used of the movement in a dance, or, as it is here, in childbirth. The verse ought to be translated, 'You have forgotten the Rock that begot you; you have forgotten the God who writhed in the effort of giving birth to you.' The purpose of the verse is to remind the people of the intimacy of God's parenthood, using both the male and the female forms."

Well, I thought as I watched her face, if the hardened academics react to my paper with even a fraction of her response, it will prove a memorable gathering.

She came out of her chair like a scalded cat, moved across the room, and pounced on a drawer, emerging with a worn volume of soft white leather. She flipped expertly to the place and stared at the words as if she'd expected them to have changed. They had not. She turned and thrust the open book at me accusingly.

"But that's . . . That means . . ."

"Yes," I said wryly, pleased with the effect my idea had on her. "That means that an entire vocabulary of imagery relating to the maternal side of God has been deliberately obscured." I watched her try to sort it out, and then I put it into a phrase I would definitely not use in the presentation in Oxford: "God the Mother, hidden for centuries."

She looked down at the book in her hands as if the ground beneath her feet had, in the blink of an eye, become treacherously soft and unstable. She turned carefully to the drawer, riffled the gold-edged India paper speculatively, and put her Bible away. She returned to her chair a troubled woman and lit another cigarette.

"Is there more of this kind of thing?"

"Considerably more."

She smoked in silence and squinted through the smoke. "Yes, I see," she said yet again, her eyes far away. In a minute, she jumped up again and began a prowl around the perimeter of the room, and so strong was the image of cat that I should not have been greatly surprised had she leapt up on the sideboard and threaded her way between the bottles. She came back to her chair and stabbed out her cigarette.

"I see now why you've come. You have come to teach me." I felt my eyebrow go up in a movement that was pure Holmes. "Could you teach me . . . to read the original, I mean?" she demanded urgently, as if ready to roll up her silken sleeves at that hour and begin.

"Neither Hebrew nor Greek is terribly difficult to learn," I said noncommittally, then added, "given time."

"You must show me this 'God the Mother.' Why don't I know about this?" Before I could answer, she went on. "It makes all the difference. There is more, you said?"

"It's no fluke. Once you're looking for it, it's everywhere. Job thirty-eight, Psalm twenty-two, Isaiah sixty-six, Hosea eleven, Isaiah forty-two. And, of course, the Genesis passages you cited tonight." That gave her pause.

"Yes, of course. But I never thought . . ." And there was the essence of it, I knew. She had absorbed the words, had hammered a few of them into a shape that suited her purpose, but it had never occurred to her to question the underlying themes, to look for patterns other than those handed down over the centuries, patterns that did not include the uncomfortable idea of the motherhood of the Divine. This woman was no deep thinker; the life of the intellect was foreign to her, and whatever her prayers and contemplations were, they were not analytical. Nonetheless, she was like a substance in a beaker, ripe for the transformation of a catalysing agent. And I had just dropped the first measure of that reagent into her quick, hungry mind. Time to stand back.

As if she had heard my thoughts, she raised her hand to stop me from withdrawing, then dropped it with a rueful smile.

"I'm sorry, I get too excited about things and want to have it all, now. You have your own work to do." The smile became wistful. "All the same, I'd appreciate any help you might give me. If there are any books. . . . You can see how important it could be to me, though I realise you haven't the time to wait around here and be my tutor."

I protested that I should be happy to help and that the term's responsibilities had not yet taken hold, and only when the words had left my mouth did I realise that her humility had trapped me as her authority could not, and her expressions of gratitude at my offer had an edge of triumph. Reluctantly, disarmed, I gave her my wry smile, and she laughed.

"I like you, Mary Russell. Please, do come and teach me. I think I shall learn a great deal from you. Even if it isn't about Hebrew or theology."

I laughed then, and she rose and pulled her shoes out from under the chairside table, and we walked through the now-silent maze to the entrance. She talked easily, mostly about flowers and the fact that she no longer had time for gardening, saying possibly that was why her friends (her followers) plied her with roses, though it still made her uncomfortable to accept them.

She was friendly and relaxed and self-deprecating, but I

could not feel entirely at ease with her. Precisely what it was about her that I found unsettling, I could not pin down. Partly, it was the childlike size of her, which made me tower awkwardly in my ill-fitting clothes. Partly, it was the way she walked so very close, her shoulder occasionally brushing my sleeve, so that I breathed in her not-unattractive aroma of sweat and hot silk and some subtle and musky perfume. Partly, it was the awareness of how easily she had found a weakness in my ready defences and made me agree to help her. Mostly, though, it was an intangible, a low, pulsing wave of fascination and discomfiture that continued, even now, to radiate from her like some fabulous tropical flower whose heavenly fragrance mesmerises the insects on which it feeds.

It was with relief that I wished her a good night. However, the relief was tempered by a certain wistful regret, and by the awareness that I had not entirely escaped the trap after all.

The impassive door guard got up from his chair and his yellow-back novel to unlock the wide door for me. It was raining still, and though the street was well lit, it was quite deserted.

I hesitated for a moment, half-tempted to telephone for a cab, but the image of Margery Childe as a carnivorous plant and a waft of disapproval from the guard came together, and I realised that despite the wet, I wanted to be out of the building, away from the provocative scent and into the clean shock of the night. I pulled my thin borrowed coat up around my neck, settled my hat low over my spectacles, and set out resolutely towards the brighter lights at the end of the street.

Halfway there, the cloy had rinsed away. The rain had also gained both my shoulder blades and the inside of my shoes, and I was occupied with mordant thoughts about the English climate and ambiguous thoughts about the woman I had left, when a surreptitious movement from inside the unlit doorway I was passing brought me whirling around in a crouch. A tall, indistinct figure loomed up, darkness in a dark place, with a pale slash the only indication of its face. It whispered at me, a sly and salacious hiss that oozed suggestively into the night, barely above the sound of the rain.

"Pretty young ladies like you have no business on the streets at this time of night."

I froze, but before the first immediate *frisson* of shock could pass on into gooseflesh, I straightened and began to laugh in relief.

"Holmes! Good God, what on earth are you doing here?"

He gathered his dark garments around him and stepped into the dim light, looking for all the world like some Byronic version of a vampire. (Thirty years before, I thought briefly, he'd have been run in, or strung up, for Jack the Ripper.) His face was largely in the shadow of his wide-brimmed hat, but one corner of his thin mouth was turned up in a familiar sardonic smile. When he spoke, his tones were half an octave lower than usual, which meant that he was feeling inordinately content with life.

"A whim, Russell," he said, and tilted his head back so I might see his eyes, crinkled in silent laughter. "Merely a whim."

CHAPTER 5

Monday, 27 December–
Tuesday, 28 December

Since private affairs are part of the human condition, as well as public ones, God has doled them out: All that takes place outside, He has trusted to man, all that is within the house, to woman. . . . This is an aspect of the divine providence and wisdom, that the one who can conduct great affairs is inadequate or inept in small things, so that the function of woman becomes necessary. For if he had made man able to fulfil both functions, the feminine sex would have been contemptible. And if he had entrusted the important questions to women, he would have filled women with mad pride.

—John Chrysostom

M

y dear Holmes, whatever it was and however you found me, we are well met. I was coming to see you tomorrow, in fact. I don't suppose you have an umbrella tucked beneath your assorted raiment?" I asked hopefully as a dollop of icy rain from the diabolically designed hat brim gushed down the back of my neck.

"You are dressed somewhat inadequately," he agreed unsympathetically, "and from the ill fit, I observe that the clothes are not your own. Perhaps another layer would not go amiss," and he began to undo the fastenings of the long, caped greatcoat he wore. I protested, but as he shrugged it off, I saw that underneath he wore a similar garment, in an unfortunate houndstooth check. He shook the coat free of half a gallon of water and dropped it onto my shoulders. It was enormously heavy but still dry inside. I straightened my buckling knees and fancied I could feel the inner layers of wool beginning to steam.

"Thank you, Holmes, that was most gallant of you. Precisely what I should expect of a Victorian gentleman. I don't suppose you have a Primus stove and teakettle in an inner pocket? Although an all-night restaurant with good radiators would do nicely."

"If your feet will carry you a mile in those shoes, I might offer you a greater degree of hospitality than a brew-up in a sheltered doorway."

"You have a room?"

"I have a hole-in-the-wall. You've not been to this one, I think, but it is one of the more comfortable."

"Any bolt-hole in a storm, Holmes. Lead on."

Although we began by walking side by side, he did in fact lead in the end, down several narrow passageways, up a fire ladder, across a roof, down another ladder, and through the crawl space beneath a large department store. We ended up at a blank wooden wall surrounded by blank brick walls. Holmes took out an electric torch and a key and inserted the latter into a tiny fissure in the wood. With a low click, one section of the wall lost its solidity. He set his shoulder against it, we slipped into the resultant dark space, and he pushed the door to and bolted it. With his torch, he indicated the way, undid and locked another door, led me up numerous stairs, then through a shadowy office and into a mahogany wardrobe hung with musty overcoats. We unfolded from the back of it into a space that smelt of coffee and tobacco and coal fire and the ineffable essence of books.

"Guard your eyes, Russell," he warned, and flicked on a dazzle of electric lights.

We were in one of his bolt-holes, the sanctuaries he maintained across London, each of them a small, self-contained, and invisible hideout equipped with the means of withstanding a siege (water, food, and reading matter) and an assortment of disguises, weapons, and the like that might be called upon in venturing out into a hostile city. I had been in two others, and this was the most elaborate, if not sumptuous, of the three. It even had paintings on the wall, something Holmes rarely bothered with: He preferred to use the space for bookshelves, corkboards, or target practice. I dragged off my sodden outer garments and looked for a place to drape them. Holmes held out a hand.

"Give them to me; I'll hang them in the airing cupboard."

He opened a narrow panel in the wall and took some

clothes hangers from the metal-lined space. I went to look over his shoulder, and found a vertical ventilation shaft about two feet across, into which he had set a length of metal pipe as a clothes rail.

"Emergency exit?" I asked, peering into the depths.

"Only in a considerable emergency. There is a bar forty feet down that ought to stop one from actually entering the furnace, although whether or not a person could remove the four screws from the access panel before being roasted or asphyxiated, I have yet to determine. I estimate that it is possible, but I have actually attempted it only when the furnace was cool. However, it is an eminently successful means of drying wet clothing." He closed the door. "Tea, coffee, wine, or soup?"

We decided on the last three, the wine splashed into the tinned soup to enliven it, and while he pottered with kettle, pan, and gas ring, I lit a fire and looked around, fetching up at one of the paintings, a large, too-perfect evocation of hills, trees, and sheep.

"This is a Constable, isn't it?" I asked him. "And who did the shipwreck?" This latter was a powerful, savage scene of pounding waves and drunken masts—like the Constable, very dated in its romanticism, but technically superb.

"That's a Vernet." His voice came muffled by cupboard doors as he shovelled about looking for edibles.

"Ah yes, your great-uncle."

"His grandfather, actually. Do you prefer turtle or cream of tomato?" he asked, emerging with two tins.

"Whichever is newer," I said cautiously.

"Nothing has been here longer than three years. However, a comparison of the respective dust layers would seem to indicate that the tomato is half the age of the other." He eyeballed them judiciously. "Perhaps eighteen months."

"The tomato, then. Did you bring everything in through the back of that wardrobe?"

"Hardly, Russell. I arranged the rooms, then bricked up the wall behind."

"It's nice, Holmes. Cosy."

"Do you think so?" He sounded pleased, and standing with

a spoon in one hand and a jagged-topped tin in the other, all he needed to complete the picture of domesticity was a lace apron. I was much taken aback by this utterly unexpected side of Holmes—I had never known him to be so much as conscious of his surroundings, save where they intruded on his work, and to have him admit to a deliberate choice and arrangement of household furnishings—well, I was taken aback.

"It was an experiment," he explained, and returned to his soup tin. "I was testing the hypothesis that one's surrounds influence one's state of mind."

"And?" I prompted, fascinated.

"The results are hardly conclusive, but I did find that after seventy-two hours here, I seemed to be less irritable, more rested, and had a higher threshold of distraction than after seventy-two hours in the Storage Room."

The 'Storage Room' was the first of his bolt-holes I had encountered, an ill-lit, ill-furnished, claustrophobic survival space in the upper floors of a large department store. Seventy-two hours in it would have sent me raving into an asylum.

"You don't say," I commented mildly, and shook my head.

"Yes, quite interesting, really. I intend to work the results into a monograph I've been writing, 'Some Suggestions Concerning the Long-Term Rehabilitation of Felons.' "

"Rehabilitation through interior decoration, Holmes?"

"There is no call for sarcasm, Russell," he said with asperity. "Drink your soup."

There followed a meal even odder than my breakfast/tea of eight hours previous, consisting of cream of tomato soup liberally dosed with Madeira, rock-hard water biscuits, two cold boiled eggs, half an orange that had begun to ferment, a slab of good crumbly cheddar, and the offer of a box of congealed after-dinner mints, which I refused in favour of a second wedge of the cheese. Holmes cleared the plates off onto a tray.

"Thank you, Holmes," I said politely.

He paused with a soup bowl in one hand, scowling down at the scum of dirty brown-red liquid that had been the result of wine meeting soup.

"Do you know, Russell," he mused, "I once earned an honest living for six entire months as a *sous-chef* in a two-star restaurant in Montpellier." He shook his head in self-reproach and rattled the dishes off into the cupboard-sized kitchen, leaving me to stare openmouthed at his retreating back.

Never, never would I get his limits.

He came back some minutes later with black coffee and a bottle of crusty port, handed me a cup and a glass, and lowered himself with a sigh into the other chair, feet towards the fire.

"So, Russell, are you going to tell me why you have suddenly become a church-goer, or shall I invent another topic of conversation?"

"If you knew I was there, you must know whom I went with. Did you find me through that amazing tea shop?"

"You left your philanthropic tracks across London like hob-nailed boots on a snowy hillside," he snorted in comfortable derision. "What on earth moved you to give that child five whole pounds? The entire parish was on fire before noon, though there was considerable disagreement over whether the series of gifts was, like lightning, a solitary occurrence or if it marked the beginning of a run of angelic visitations, and, if the latter, whether the better approach would be to wait calmly to be one of the chosen or to drag in benighted strangers from the streets and force food and drink into them. You may laugh," he protested, "but your little gesture has caused the whole of Limehouse to be overrun with beggars. Word got out that good meals were to be had, and hungry men from all over the city are now lurking under all the steps. Or they would be, if they weren't snatched up and fed before they had the opportunity to settle. At any rate, yes, after that, the general drift of your movements led me to the chestnut-seller who had found silver among the ashes, various elderly and unprosperous ladies of the evening, and finally to the denizens of the dockside tea shop. All except the chestnut seller remembered the inexplicable and unrewarded generosity of a bespectacled young man dressed for the country, and at the end, one of them knew the whereabouts of the young lady this singular young man finally went away with. Discreet enquiries proved that she was in the habit of going to hear the words of a certain woman of the cloth, if that be the right term, of a Monday night. That lady is not listed in Crockford, but I found her, and you. I had not realised you should be closeted with her for half the night, though. My bones protest."

"Come now, Holmes, your rheumatism only bothers you when it's convenient. Besides, you hadn't been there all that long."

"Why do you say that?" he asked, a spark of amusement in his grey eyes.

"The coat was damp, but the water was on the surface," I answered him unnecessarily. "If you had been in the doorway for very long, the water would not have shaken out so easily." He twitched his lips in appreciation and approval, and it occurred to me that since the term began, I had been either absent or preoccupied. Had he missed our exchanges, too? It was not something I could ask. I smiled back at him. "You might have saved your bones the discomfort by ringing the bell and asking the watchman to give me a message."

"And risk disturbing you at a case?" He sounded shocked, which meant he was making a mild jest.

"There's no case here—I'm sorry to disappoint you, Holmes. Nothing but my own peculiar interest in things theological. And yet, if you can set aside your instinctive response to these irrational matters, I should like your reaction."

"That is what you were coming to see me about?"

"In part, yes."

"Very well, let me get my pipe and I shall prepare myself to listen." To my amusement, in this place, his pipes were kept in a pipe rack, his tobacco not in a Persian slipper or a biscuit tin or beneath the nonexistent roots of an artificial aspidistra, but in a pouch, and his matches in a silver matchbox. Whatever would Watson say—or Mrs Hudson?

"I shall begin with Veronica Beaconsfield, rather than Margery Childe, not only because she led me into contact with Miss Childe but because she can be taken as the foundation upon which Miss Childe's movement is being built.

Without Ronnie, and women like her, there would be no Margery Childe."

I went over my day, beginning with seeing Veronica's face through the steamed-up window and ending with being let out into the rain by the night watchman, with considerable attention to detail, seeking to clarify my own thoughts as well as present the history of the matter to Holmes. I told him about Veronica's charitable deeds and her lost lover, about Margery Childe's magnetic speaking persona and her interaction with the women who came to her for comfort and strength. I was honest about my own response to the woman, both the attraction and the unthinking, almost visceral aversion to the control she held over her listeners, a reaction which had, in turn, prompted her finally to drop the pretence and give to me, a stranger, what was to all appearances her honest, unadorned self.

It was an indication of the similarity of our minds, or perhaps of the extent to which he had trained me in his techniques, that he did not interrupt me for clarifications during the hour I spoke. He refilled his pipe once and our glasses three times, but he made no remark aside from the occasional grunt and the noises of his pipe. When I finished and glanced at my watch, I was amazed to see that it was after 3:00 A.M.

"You are tired perhaps, Russell?" he asked, his eyes closed.

"Not really. I slept most of the day. Perhaps I'll have a brief nap before meeting Veronica for lunch."

"What is it you want of me, Russell? I agree this is all very interesting, from the point of view of the human mind, but why bring it to me?"

"I don't know. I suppose I thought that telling it to you might help me to clarify it in my own mind. It's all so— Why are you laughing?"

"At myself, Russell, at a voice from the past." He chuckled. "I used to say the same thing to Watson."

"Oh. Well, the parallel is not exact, because I truly do want your opinion, as a judge of humankind."

"I'm glad you did not say 'a judge of men.' "

"Not in this case. But what do you think, Holmes? Can she

possibly be genuine? Or is she a charlatan? On the surface, it has all the earmarks of chicanery, a subtle and high-class dodge. And yet, she herself rings true, despite her obvious manipulation of her followers."

Holmes packed his pipe thoughtfully, and I reflected that somewhere the room had good ventilation, or we should have suffocated long before this.

"You say there is considerable money involved here?"

"There were fourteen women in that room aside from myself. A third of them were related to men who sit in peer's stalls, another third have mothers whose surnames came from Boston and Wall Street. The cost of the clothing in the room would keep one of London's parishes in food for a year; the coiffures alone would feed a family for several months. Miss Childe owns the hall and the two adjoining houses. Her gown was a Worth, several pieces of furniture I saw would cause a Sotheby's auctioneer to croon, and her skin has been under sunny skies within the past two months. Yes, there is money behind her. A great deal of money."

"She may have lived in a cold-water flat when she was twenty, but not now, eh?"

"Far from it."

Holmes tapped his teeth with his pipe and stared into the fireplace.

"In my experience," he said thoughtfully, "the alchemists were wrong in assuming gold to be incorruptible. Religion and money form a volatile mix. I have had several such cases come my way. There was 'Holy' Peters, who put on the face of a missionary to lure lonely ladies and relieve them of their burdensome inheritances. Later, I met a certain Canon Smythe-Basingstoke, who gave such stirring public addresses concerning the poor children of Africa, complete with recordings of their voices singing and lantern slides of their pinched and winsome faces, before accepting donations to his valiant mission outpost. That case was too bald and uncomplicated for Watson to bother with, as I remember. And, of course, the case that brought Jefferson Hope to my door, although on second thought, that concerned a woman as well as money.

No, the path of God has often been diverted to lead to a human desire, the word of God twisted to suit human ambition. Were this lady living among the poor, I might be happier, but the tanned face and her silk Paris gown can only count against her sincerity. However, I am not telling you anything new, am I, Russell?"

"No, I had reached the same—hardly a conclusion. It's sad, in a way. I should greatly enjoy meeting someone who, as it were, talks with God. She is, however, very intelligent, and she is doing some fine work for the women of London."

"Time will tell," he said, and then he took his pipe out of his mouth and fixed me with a suspicious gaze. "Unless you were planning on a spot of independent criminal investigation?"

"No, Holmes. I told you, it's only mild curiosity—in my field, not yours."

"Another whim, Russell?"

"Another whim," I said evenly, and as our eyes came together, I was made abruptly aware of how alone we were and of the silence of the building around us. At that moment, something entered the room, a thing compounded of the memory of our argument atop the hansom, of the intimacy of the hour and the place, of my thin and clinging blouse and his long legs stretched out towards the fire and of my growing sense of womanliness. I suppressed a shudder and cast about rapidly for a red herring. "Speaking of criminal investigation," I said, reaching for my glass, "Veronica asked if there was anything I might do about her fiancé Miles and his drug habit. Have you any suggestions?"

"Nothing can be done," he said dismissively.

"He seems to have been a good man, before the trenches," I persisted.

"Most of them were."

"Surely there's something—"

He jumped to his feet and circled his chair, ending up back at the fireplace, where he leant down to smack his pipe against the bricks and send the still-alight dottle spraying onto the coal and the hearth. His voice was high and biting now.

"Russell, I am hardly the man to impose sobriety on another, save perhaps by my own wicked examples. Besides which, even discounting my unfitness for temperance work, I refuse to act as the world's nursemaid. If young men wish to inject themselves with heroin, I can no more stand in their way than I could stand in the way of a Boche shell in the trenches."

"And if he were your son?" I asked very quietly. "Would you not want someone to try?"

It was a dirty blow, low and unscrupulous and quite unforgivably wicked. Because, you see, he did have a son once, and someone had tried.

He rotated his head slowly towards me, eyes cold, face rigid.

"That was unworthy of you, Russell," was all he said, but the intonation of it brought me to my feet and to his side, and I laid my hand on his arm.

"Dear God, Holmes, I am sorry. It was cruel and thoughtless of me. I am so very sorry."

He looked at my hand, covered it briefly with his own, and turned away to his chair.

"However," he said, "you are right. It is irresponsible of me to say that I can do nothing, without having reviewed the case. If you would be so good as to give me the information on the young man, I shall think about what possible courses of action might be open."

"I . . ." I stopped, at a loss. "His name is Miles Fitzwarren," I began weakly, but broke off at his gesture.

"I know him," he said, and corrected himself. "Rather, I knew him. I shall see what can be done."

I might have been some tediously importunate client being dismissed with a scrap of comfort.

"Thank you, Holmes," I said miserably, and went back to my chair.

Out of the corner of my eye, I could see him, slumped down, chewing at the stem of his empty pipe. My red herring had performed its function, but I knew that this particular old hound would not be misled for long before backtracking to the main scent. For the moment, he sat staring blindly past the mended toes of his woollen stockings, into the glowing coals. I knew him, however. I knew every movement and gesture of the man, the lines and muscles of his face that were more familiar to me than my own, the mind that had moulded mine, and I knew that when his thoughts returned from the contemplation of that particular byway, he would fix me with his all-seeing gaze and with a few deft words unearth the topic I'd been trying so desperately to divert him from. It would happen in a minute, and when it did, the peculiar chilling awareness, a presence almost, that had already passed through the room would return tenfold, and it would not be dismissed.

I waited tensely for him to look up, feeling the quivering silence build in the space between us, and it was a shock, as if an adder had appeared in the bathwater between my toes, to realise that for the first time in my life I was uncomfortable in the presence of Sherlock Holmes. He did not look at me, and I took it as a judgement, and I was sore afraid.

But in the end, he did not fix me with a steely eye; he did not even glance at me. Rather, he moved, with a calmness that in another person would have meant a total unawareness of any untoward currents in the room. He bent forward and placed his cold pipe on the table, then reached for the salt-stained boots drying on the hearth and began to put them on.

"I must go out," he said. "I shall be back in three or four hours. You get some sleep, and I'll wake you by eight if you're not up already. It's good to be out of the building by nine, when the office workers begin to arrive." He finished tying his laces and stood up.

"Holmes, I—" I stopped abruptly, lost. What he said then made it apparent that he had not been unaware of the silence.

"It's all right, Russell. I do understand. The bed is in the next room. Sleep well."

He rested one hand briefly on the back of my chair as he went around it to the ventilation shaft, and one long finger brushed my shoulder. I wanted to reach up and grasp his hand and not let him leave, but I held myself still and allowed him to fold himself out through the wardrobe door. Then I sat and listened as a very different silence lowered itself onto the room.

The walls closed in, and the quiet was loud, and I was far from sleep. I went into the kitchen and did the washing up, wiped down the surfaces, made myself a cup of milkless tea, put his pipe on its rack, took a book from the shelves, and sat staring at the first page as the cup cooled. Sometime later, I remembered it and grimaced at the taste of the cold tannin, took the cup to the sink and dumped it out, washed it, dried it, put it away, and walked across the room to the internal door.

I looked at the bed a long time. In the end, I went back and took the throw rug from the back of the sofa, turned down the lights, curled up under the rug by the low glow of the fire, and wondered what the hell I was going to do.

CHAPTER 6

Tuesday, 28 December

How can woman be the image of God, seeing she is subject to man and has no authority, neither to teach, nor to be witness, nor to judge, much less to rule or bear empire?

—Saint Augustine (354–430)

I had met Sherlock Holmes at a time when adolescence and the devastating circumstances of my orphaning had left me with an exterior toughness and an interior that was malleable to the personality of anyone willing to listen to me and take me seriously. Had Holmes been a cat burglar or forger, no doubt I should have come into adulthood learning to walk parapets at night or concocting arcane inks.

Over the years of my informal apprenticeship, I had learnt his trade, while at the same time pursuing my own academic vision. No doubt it made an odder combination than the two topics Margery Childe had remarked on, but if detecting was what I *did*, theology was what I *was*. Chemistry served to take up the slack. There had been clashes between the two disparate demands, but so far a final choice had not been necessary. The two sides of me lived in friendly mutual incomprehension.

That bed, though . . .

In the course of various investigations over the years, Holmes and I had spent any number of nights within arm's reach of each other. He had slept in my bed, and I in his. Several times, we had even slept together in one bed, or whatever passed for a bed at the time. Never once had there been awkwardness over this. Two years before, at the beginning and at the end of a tense and terrifying case, we had each made a faint overture in the male-female dance, but later we had made the unspoken decision not to pursue that line of activity. We were intimate friends, but without the intimacy of the body.

Perhaps I ought to mention here that I was at the time not unaware of the entertainment value afforded by the reactions of one's body. The postwar years had brought large numbers of mature young men into Oxford, and one of them in particular, being possessed of a quick mind, a wry sense of humour, an inexplicable persistence, and an automobile, had taught me a great deal.

However, the mind is a most peculiar organ, and the simple fact was that until the night atop the hansom, I had never drawn a connexion between those bodily reactions and Sherlock Holmes. I had contemplated marriage, had even played with the idea of suggesting it, but until he had himself referred so sarcastically to the marriage bed, I had never actually pictured him in those terms. Now, however, the checks were off, the blinkers removed; since I had seen him emerge from the dark doorway into the rainy street, the physical awareness of his proximity and his being had hammered at me, unrelenting. When he passed behind me, I had felt like the victim of a child's balloon game, with static electricity causing the hairs on the arm to rise and follow the balloon's path back and forth above the skin—I had been almost painfully aware of quivering receptors following him about the room.

The only way to stop it had been to savage him and drive him away. That had bought me some breathing space, albeit brief and at a high price, but now I had it, I could not think what to do. Something would have to be done, that was obvious. I had not asked for this intolerable awareness, I did not want it, and I should have given a great deal to have it taken from me, but it had come, and I was in its grip.

I lay on the sofa long in what was left of the night, struggling with myself and my options, and in the end, long before dawn, I took the only possible action: I ran away.

I walked the streets until the sky was a fraction lighter than the rooftops, then went, shivering and wet through, to the door of the ladies' club that I had joined the year before. It was a small establishment with the cheerless and misleading name of the Vicissitude, but it did not allow its right-thinking feminist policies to interfere with the amount of hot water in its pipes or the quality of food that came from its kitchen. The old matron on night duty greeted me with horror and bundled me off to a hot bath, brought me a mug of something scalding and appallingly alcoholic, retrieved my stored clothes, and found a bed for me. I did not sleep much, but it was nice to be warm, and alone.

I was in the museum at the agreed time, ill-rested, unfed, and hastily dressed. At 12:30, Veronica had still not appeared. I decided to give her until one, and ten minutes before then, she came around the corner, as carelessly dressed as I, but pale, red-eyed, and half-focused. I greeted her with apprehension, wondering what new upheaval had tossed her here in this condition, but she managed a distracted smile and seemed to be trying to pull herself together.

"Mary, I'm so sorry. Something happened this morning, and I totally forgot the time until Margery reminded me that I had a luncheon date with you."

"Yes, I can see something happened." Her stockings did not match, her hair was perfunctorily combed, and she was wearing a dark green woollen dress with a black coat, an infelicitous combination. "You should have sent a message; I'd have understood. Was it something at the Temple?"

"No. Well, yes, in a way. Miles's sister died last night. She was a member. You met her, in fact—Iris. Tall, marcelled hair."

"Cigarette holder, red fingernails, small opal ring on her right hand. She had a terrible cold," I recalled. She had been one of those who had run a brief and disbelieving eye across my clothing and returned, politely amused, to the business at hand. Ronnie nodded.

"What happened?"

"She was mur—murdered." Her control slipped for an instant before it caught again, and she drew a shaky breath. "She left the meeting with the rest of us, just after eleven, but she never made it home. A bobby found her in an alleyway at four this morning, in the West End. She was . . . her throat . . . Oh God."

She gulped and put her hand to her mouth, and I grabbed her arm hard, putting a sharp twist into it to distract her, and hustled her out the doors and into the rain, down the steps, and through the gates. I kept pushing her until we had our seats in the restaurant. The owner knew me well and responded with alacrity to my demand for strong drink and food, and soon the greenish tones had faded from her face and she could begin to tell me about it.

"Iris's father telephoned me early this morning—about seven, I think it was—wanting to know if I had any idea where Miles might be. I said no, and he said if I heard from him that Miles should go home immediately. I started to say that it was unlikely that I should see him, but he just rang off. After I'd had some coffee I realised that he'd sounded terribly upset about something, so I telephoned back—it took the exchange an age to get through—and asked if there was anything wrong. That's when he told me Iris was . . . dead."

"And Miles was—" I started, but she spoke over me.

"We were never close, Iris and I. We were too different, I guess. But she was devoted to Miles, and very involved in her Temple work—it was through her that I met Margery. We will all miss her so much."

Her eyes filled, and I downed a few hasty mouthfuls to silence my hardhearted appetite before steering her with equal ruthlessness back from elegy to facts.

"When you spoke with their father, Miles was missing?"

She wiped her eyes. "Yes, but that's hardly unusual. Iris told me he often disappeared from his flat for several days at a time."

"What else did he say? Mr Fitzwarren, that is."

"Major. Just that she'd been killed and that his wife—Miles and Iris's mother—was under heavy sedation and wanted Miles. They had only the two," she added, and sighed into her untouched salad.

"Nothing else?"

"No. I told him I'd call later today, but he said I ought to telephone first, to see how Mrs Fitzwarren was feeling."

"Then what did you do?"

"I dressed and went to the Temple. I thought Margery ought to know, and I . . . I suppose I hoped she might tell me what to do. I wasn't thinking very clearly."

"Did she?"

"She wasn't in when I first arrived, so I went into the chapel for some quiet. She came in after a while, and I told her. She listened in that marvellous way of hers, and she told me to pray while she made some telephone calls. She brought together the Inner Circle, most of them, and reached a friend of hers at the *Clarion*, who gave her the news about where and when Iris had been found and how she'd been killed."

I interrupted briskly before the graphic remembrance could hit her. "Do you want to telephone the Fitzwarrens now and ask if they want to see you?"

"Yes, perhaps I ought to now. I get on well with Mrs Fitzwarren. I think she might like me to come."

She went off to Tonio's telephone while I paid the bill. When she returned, she was pale but composed.

"Yes, I'll go there now."

"Any sign of Miles?"

"None."

"How long has he been missing? Do you know?"

"Two or three days, I think. The major is furious."

Furious rather than worried, I noted, but I did not point it out. She had quite enough on her plate without that.

Tonio ushered us out the door and personally whistled up a cab. Veronica gave the driver the address and got in, and I leant on the door.

"I'll send you those clothes I borrowed," I suggested.

"The clothes? Oh, yes, those. There's no hurry; they're just part of the whatnot I keep for people to use. My families, you know."

"When are you seeing Margery Childe again?" I asked.

"Tonight or tomorrow, I suppose. It depends on the Fitzwarrens. Oh, that reminds me—she said to tell you she'd like to talk with you again, when you're free."

"Tell her I'll look forward to it."

"If you're still in town in a day or two, would you ring me?" She shuffled through her bag for a pencil and wrote two numbers on the back of a receipt from an antiquarian booksellers'. "I'll either be at home—the top number—or at the Fitzwarrens. Or at the Temple." She wrote down a third number, then gave me the paper.

"Good-bye for now, Mary. Thank you for everything."

"I'll see you soon, Ronnie. I hope it goes well. Oh, and Ronnie? Sorry." This last was to the taxi driver, who had slid the engine into gear and had to halt again. "Don't say anything about my friendship with Mr Holmes, please. It's a bother when people want to know all about him, so I don't tell them at first. All right? Thanks. 'Bye now."

I stepped back and slapped the roof, and the cab immediately slithered its way into the traffic. Veronica's chin was up, and I could not help but wonder how the Fitzwarrens would feel if they realised that they had just joined the ranks of the downtrodden unfortunates to whom Lady Veronica Beaconsfield ministered.

As I stood on the pavement, unaware of the rain, unconscious of the flow of people—faceless figures with dull, sodden coats, dark hats, and dripping black umbrellas—and the dingy buildings that hunched their shoulders over the noisy street, a second cab swerved dangerously across the wet road to halt at my feet. I obediently climbed in and sat, meditating on the oddity that Veronica had asked my help for an impossible task, that of breaking her lover's addiction, but not for the relatively straightforward problem of finding him, until the driver turned a face of exaggerated patience to me through the glass.

"Paddington," I mouthed automatically. Dear God, I must get away from this city before I suffocated from her complexities. Even before this latest blow, I had felt like a compass needle, oscillating wildly between the dangerous magnetism of a new and unexpected Holmes and the appealing cool feminism of Margery Childe. Just now, I wanted none of it. I wanted to draw in a deep breath of familiar, clean, unchanging air, in a place where challenge lay in the mind, where even the greatest frenzies of passion were woven into a tapestry of serene stability.

Four hours later, I was seated at my table in the Bodleian Library in Oxford.

CHAPTER 7

Tuesday, 28 December–
Thursday, 30 December

To the further declaration of the imperfections of women . . . I might add histories proving some women to have died for sudden joy; some for impatience to have murdered themselves; some to have burned with such inordinate lust that, for the quenching of the same, they have betrayed to strangers their country and city.

—John Knox

The remainder of the Tuesday and all of the Wednesday, I buried myself in my work. The paper representing my coming of age as a scholar, the first part of which lay in a neat stack of typescript on my desk down in Sussex, was from a piece of research I was doing on women in the Talmud. The initial stimulus had been a vigorous discussion (an argument, it would have been, had it not taken place in Oxford) on the mouldy old theme of "Why Weren't Women . . . ?" In this case, it was: Why were women so conspicuously scarce in Jewish literary records? Essentially, the question was: Can a feminist be a Jew, or a Jew a feminist?

I am a Jew; I call myself a feminist: The question was of interest to me. A week after the discussion, I had presented the topic to one of my tutors, who had agreed to work with me on it, and in fact he was looking towards a joint publication. He had already scheduled a public presentation of our finds to date, on the twenty-eighth of January. It promised to be a lively meeting.

The focal point of the essay's first section was a woman named Beruria, a remarkable member of the late first/early second century rabbinic community, a milieu in which were laid the foundations of what could be called post-Temple Judaism, as well as those of the separating sect of Christianity. Beruria was not, strictly speaking, a rabbi, that title being reserved for men. She had, however, completed the customary rabbinic training, and she was accepted first as a student, then a teacher, and finally as an arbiter of rabbinic decisions. Her martyred father and fiery husband were both prominent rabbis, which no doubt lent her a certain cachet for privileged action, but it was Beruria herself whom we glimpse in the Talmudic writings, not some clever pet. There can be little doubt that if her brilliant intellect, razor-honed tongue, voluminous learning, and profound sense of God had been placed in a man's body, the resultant figure would have rivalled Akiva himself in stature. Instead, she comes to us as an enigmatic and perplexing footnote, who tantalises with what is possible, while at the same time being the exception that proves the rule that the intensely demanding realm of rabbinic thought is an exclusively male dominion. Her prominence eventually proved too much for the sages who followed her, and a thousand years after her death, her memory was fouled by the medieval scholar Rashi, when he attached to her a scurrilous story of sexual misconduct, giving it out that she allowed herself, a married woman, to be seduced by one of her husband's students and then in shame committed suicide.

Through Beruria, I had been led back into Scripture itself, into (and here the reader will begin to see the point of this excursus) the feminine aspects of the Divine. Use of masculine imagery in speaking of God, of course, abounds: God takes the masculine gender in Hebrew, and the anthropomorphic imagery used in speaking of the Divine is predominantly andromorphic, from a hot-tempered young warrior to the wise, bearded gentleman depicted by Michelangelo Buonarroti on the ceiling of the Sistine Chapel.

Feminine imagery, such as in the passage whose (I was certain) correct translation I had given Margery Childe, does exist: Buried by redactors, obscured by translators, it is nonetheless there for the observant eye. The verses in Genesis which Margery Childe had called upon in her sermon had occupied me for three very solid weeks the previous October. I had taken the Hebrew to pieces, pounded the verses flat and resuscitated them, traced them through the rabbis and into the modern commentaries, eventually reached a tentative though solidly based conclusion, and finally written it up with voluminous footnotes and cross-references into part two of my paper. And then, two months later, to hear this untutored religious casually bringing out my laboriously formed hypothesis as something both self-evident and indisputable was, to say the least, intriguing.

With some pique, I went back to the Hebrew text and read it through, then again with care. It only took five minutes to conclude that she was right: Three hundred hours of sweat and eyestrain had gone into proving the obvious. I had reinvented the wheel. I shook my head and laughed aloud, to the indignation of my neighbours, and then flipped the pages over and got to work.

Oxford between terms is a delightfully peaceful place. At the time, I had rooms in a house at the north end of town, took the occasional meal with my landlady, a retired Somerville don, and walked or cycled in. That December was unseasonably mild, and my path to the library on the Wednesday morning took a circuitous route through the Parks. Other than that, I had blessedly few distractions, and I managed to get through a great deal of work that day, as if some quirk of the weather served to oil the wheels of thought: Requested books arrived promptly; my pen skimmed the pages smoothly; problems and conundra fell with gratifying ease before the sharp edge of my mind. I ate well, and, to my surprise and relief, I slept like an innocent both nights.

Then Thursday morning dawned, like an incipient toothache. I buried my head back in my pillow and concentrated fiercely on the suggestive implications of a certain irregular verb I had uncovered the previous evening, but it was no good. The soothing interval was over, and my vision of burrowing into Oxford until my birthday on Sunday began to shrivel before the cold, hard demands of responsibility. I had run away, for the third time in as many days, and the small voice that pled the demands of labour and the threat of public disgrace on the twenty-eighth of January stood no chance against the stern thunder of my higher self. I had obligations, and I was not meeting them here.

I rose and dressed for Town. As I rummaged irritably through my drawers for stockings without ladders and gloves without holes, the stern voice relented a fraction: Considering the duties I was about to take on, I needed something more acceptable to wear than my father's flannels and my mother's readjusted tweeds. I had not bought so much as a pair of gloves since the summer. While in London, my imperious self declared with gracious generosity, I might buy some clothes. I cheered up a bit, went down to swallow some tea and a handful of biscuits with my landlady, and left for the station. On the way, I sent off six telegrams—three each to Holmes and to Veronica at various locations, all with the message that I was going to be at the Vicissitude and would they please get into touch with me there. I boarded the train with a disgustingly clear conscience.

The morning I spent being measured, posed, scrutinised, and tut-tutted over by the married couple whose skills had clothed my mother before me and who had graciously permitted themselves to be saddled with me, one of their more wayward clients, on her death. They were a pair of elves, all brown eyes and wizened faces and clever fingers, and between her eye for colour and line and his touch with fabrics, when they dressed me, I was more than presentable. Over glasses of hot, sweet, smoky tea we decided that I had finally stopped growing and might now have real clothes. Out came the luscious thick woollens and cashmeres and the silks and linens, and she began to sketch long and dramatic shapes on a block of paper while he heaved various bolts onto the worktables, and the two of them carried on a nonstop pair of competing monologues and shook their fingers at each other until I made to escape. Whether it was, as they claimed, a period of doldrums after Christmas, or whether, as I suspected, my appearance so pained them that they wanted to know that I was properly clothed, or even if the challenge I presented caught at their imaginations, I am not sure, but they practically begged me to accept the first of my outfits on Monday morning, a symbolic beginning to a new life. I was more than happy to agree, whatever the reason.

I left the shop feeling dowdy and drab, and mildly apprehensive. The last time I had bought a wardrobe, it had ended up slashed to bits on the floor of a decrepit horsecab. To raise my spirits, I took lunch upstairs at Simpsons, where to my pleasure the maître d' greeted me by name. Finally, I took a taxi to my club.

A telegram awaited me, from Veronica, asking me would I come to her house at four, and would I care to go to the Temple that evening?

Upstairs, I contemplated the two dresses hanging forlornly in the wardrobe. One was a lovely rich green wool, but it was two years old, had been let down twice, despite the shorter hemlines, and looked it. The other was a very plain dark blue, almost black, and it was a dress I disliked enough to leave in storage fifty weeks of the year. I wondered which of the two was less unacceptable, then realised that neither went with the shoes available. I thought of the elves and sighed. Perhaps I ought to do as Holmes had done—arrange to leave half a dozen complete sets of clothing and necessities stashed about the countryside. After Sunday, I could afford it, if I wanted. It would certainly keep the elves amused.

I put both frocks and the decision back on the rack and went down a floor to the club's library-cum-reading room. I was not particularly interested in Iris Fitzwarren's death, save that it touched the lives of Veronica and Margery Childe, but out of habit, and perhaps out of respect for Ronnie, I thought it would do no harm to catch up with what the newspapers had to say. I went to the neat stack and dug down to the early Tuesday editions. However, I walked back upstairs an hour later with ink-stained hands but a mind little enlightened. Iris Elizabeth Fitzwarren, aged twenty-eight, daughter of Major Thomas Fitzwarren and Elizabeth Quincey Donahue Fitzwarren, had died as a result of knife wounds between one and three in the morning of Tuesday, the twenty-eighth of December. Scotland Yard had traced a taxi driver who reported dropping her outside an infamous nightclub late the night before, but intensive investigations had not yet succeeded in establishing when she had left the club or with whom—if anyone—she had been seen while in the establishment. Miss Fitzwarren was well known among the poorer classes (the phrase used by *The Times*), where she had worked to establish free medical services for women and infants. She had become interested in nursing during the War, had taken a course in nursing, and together with Miss Margery Childe, beautiful blonde directress (one of the more effusive afternoon papers) of the New Temple in God, Miss Fitzwarren had been instrumental in organising medical clinics in Stepney and Whitechapel. Miss Fitzwarren was survived by, and so on, and memorial services would be held, et cetera, et cetera.

In other words, I thought, scrubbing my nails, if the Yard knows owt, they're saying nowt.

I did my hair with more care than usual, dropped the plain dark dress over my head, and examined the result. The elves would tut-tut, I thought, but at least it was better than Veronica's jumble-sale clothes. I checked at the desk, but there was nothing for me, so I left a message with my whereabouts for the next few hours, to be given to Mr Holmes.

Veronica's courtyard looked even worse by waning light than it had by waxing. A handful of urchins lingered outside her door, no doubt waiting there until their mothers might allow them inside their own homes for tea. Two had healing facial sores, four went barefooted, and one had no coat. An incomprehensible but identifiable noise echoed across the yard, and after paying the taxi driver, I followed the sound to its source: Veronica's door was ajar and a pandemonium of voices came spilling out. I pushed my way gently through the children in order to lean my head inside, realised there was little point in knocking or calling a polite hullo, and walked in. The noise came from the second of the ill-furnished ground-floor rooms, in the back, and I stood at the door and tried to make sense of what was apparently a domestic squabble involving portions of at least four families, mothers with babies perched on their hips and sobbing children at their skirts, several bellicose men and male adolescents thrusting their chests out at each other, a matched trio of grandmotherly figures furiously casting anathema upon one another, and, in the middle, like a pair of crumbling rocks beset by a typhoon, two more people: Veronica Beaconsfield and another woman, small, squat, and foreign. A Belgian, I thought.

I stood at the back of the crowd for several minutes before Veronica's eyes, coming up from the deluge of words beating at her, latched on to me with unspeakable relief. I saw her lips move, saw her turn to the other target and mouth a phrase, at which the other woman's eyes went wide with something close to horror before she marshalled her forces and, with a motion curiously reminiscent of a prodded limpet, nodded at Veronica and put her head down against the storm. Veronica worked her way across the room, towards me, shaking her head and putting a hand up at the entreaties along the way, until she plunged out into the corridor.

"Do you have a cab?" she asked, ignoring the two women hanging onto her coattails.

"I doubt it; I didn't ask him to wait. Here are your clothes," I said doubtfully.

"Just toss them over there. Come on, we'll find one down the road."

I made haste to deposit the parcel on the shelf of the coatrack and reached the door just before the women. Smiling and nodding, I pulled it shut in their faces and scurried after Veronica, who had already rounded the corner.

"What on earth was that all about?" I asked. "And where are we going?"

"It's of no importance. I did something for one family, and the others now think they deserve the same. My assistant will sort it out. Or rather, they'll all get so tired of shouting at her, since she'll speak only French to them, that they'll go home. We have to go around to the Fitzwarrens'. Miles surfaced today." She shot out a hand and a taxi peeled itself from the pack. Once inside, she turned to me with an anxious line between her eyebrows. "Do you mind? Going there with me, I mean? Major Fitzwarren telephoned about half an hour ago and asked me to come, but I—do you mind coming with me?"

If she wanted to use me as a shield against Miles, I did not particularly care for the idea, but I felt quite strong enough. I told her I was content to go.

"Oh good. I don't know whether we'll have tea or a drink, but afterwards we'll go on for a bite and then to the Temple. Does that suit?"

"It suits."

"I'm so glad," she said, and to my astonishment she reached out and squeezed my gloved hand with hers. "Thank God you're here, Mary. I can't think how I could face this without your help."

"What?" I said lightly. "Is this the Veronica Beaconsfield who single-handedly holds together half of London?"

She flashed me a nervous smile and looked at her watch. We rode in silence through the gathering dusk to St John's Wood.

An elderly butler with the prerequisite long and lugubrious face admitted us into the marbled and gleaming entrance foyer and relieved us of our outer garments.

"Good evening, Marshall," Veronica said, handing him her gloves. "Mrs Fitzwarren is expecting me. This is Miss Russell."

"Good evening, miss," he said. "It is good to see you again, Miss Beaconsfield. I shall go and inform Mrs Fitzwarren of your arrival, if you would like to wait in here for a moment."

Veronica balked at the indicated door.

"Do you mind if we wait in the library, Marshall? I may be upstairs some time, and Miss Russell will enjoy looking at the books, I think."

An instant's hesitation was the only sign of a dilemma that would have undone a lesser man. Mere visitors were not normally given the run of the house, the hesitation said, but in the past Miss Beaconsfield had become more than a mere guest, and no formal announcement had been made to the contrary.

"Lieutenant Fitzwarren is currently in the library, miss," he said, further explaining his hesitation and giving the decision back to her.

"Miles?" she said, and it was her turn to hesitate before squaring her shoulders. "Well, I shall have to see him sometime. Perhaps you'd best warn him I'm coming, though. I'll show Miss Russell the drawing room, and you can come back for us."

This diplomatic solution met with his approval. He ushered us in and faded away, to reappear shortly, bereft of coats and paraphernalia. I was relieved that I was not to spend more of the evening in the austerely formal room, with its grey walls more suited to a summer's day and its collection of remarkably unsettling futurist paintings. The library for me.

Veronica's face was serious but not apprehensive; however, the spine that I followed down the portrait-lined passageway belonged to someone about to confront a firing squad. She took two steps inside the room, then stopped, and I looked past her at the figure by the window.

It took no great medical knowledge to recognise in Miles Fitzwarren a sick young man, and no great cleverness to discern his ailment. He moved as if gripped by the ache of influenza, but the torpid lassitude of that illness was replaced here by a jittery restlessness, an inability to settle into a chair or a thought, which reminded me of a caged zoo animal. It was painful to witness. To Veronica, it must have been excruciating, but there was no sign of it in her face or her voice.

"Hello, Miles."

"Evenin', Ronnie. You're certainly looking chipper," he burbled gaily. "Surprise to see you here, don't you know? It's been a while, hasn't it? Did you have a good Christmas? How are your parents—your father's sciatica, was it? Hope it didn't interfere with the shootin' this year. Oh, here, frightfully rude of me. . . . Come and sit down. You a friend of Ronnie's? Miles Fitzwarren. Pleased to meet you, Miss . . ."

"This is Mary Russell, Miles. A friend from Oxford."

"Another bluestocking, eh, Miss Russell? Or do you go around doin' good, too? How are the *opera sordida*, Ronnie?

Most awfully embarrassin', you know," he confided to me, "bein' surrounded by people who do good deeds right and left." His attempt at gay and tripping laughter rang hollow even in his ears, and the fuzzy remembrance that he was mourning his sister, or perhaps the tardy realisation that he was giving away quite a lot, hurried him on. "I've heard about this church lady of yours, Childe. Supposed to be quite the thing. Friend of mine in the City went to hear her about a week or two ago, said she talked all about love. Quite taken with her, he was, though I must say it all sounded positively loose to me, love in church. Still, she probably means well enough."

"Miles, I—"

"As a matter of fact, I saw her," he prattled on desperately. "A week ago. Someone told me who she was. Tiny little thing, should have thought she was a child if I hadn't seen her face. Suppose she is a Childe, though, isn't she—the name, d'you see? Still, good things come in small packages, they say."

I do not know what further revelations the man might have split, or what Veronica would have said, because the melancholy presence of Marshall appeared at the door and said that Mrs Fitzwarren would be pleased to see Miss Beaconsfield, if she should care to follow him.

Veronica stood up, bit her lip, took three impulsive steps forward to where Miles sat perched on the corner of a desk, kissed him lightly on the cheek, and turned to go. From his flinch, a person would have thought she was touching a burning coal to his skin. The look she flashed me held all her fear, her sorrow, and her hopelessness.

When she had gone, he seemed to forget my presence. He started to pace again, smoking furiously and stopping occasionally at the window to stare out into the dark garden. He was thin, a good stone less than when the suit was made (an exquisite suit, in need of cleaning), and something in his nervous hands reminded me of Holmes, and of Holmes' lovely lost son. The hands of this young man trembled slightly, though, as Holmes' never did, and the nails were unkempt. The handkerchief he pulled from a pocket was little better. He blew his nose and wiped his watering eyes, lit another cigarette, paced around the room, and ended up at the black window again, where I could see his reflection in the glass. (Sure sign of a disturbed household, I thought irrelevantly: curtains that remained drawn back after darkness has fallen.) He yawned hugely and looked for a long minute at his ghostly face in the glass before his hand came up and covered his eyes. His shoulders drooped, and I could see the moment of helpless capitulation come over him. I rose swiftly and moved two steps to stand, if only briefly, between him and the door, and when he turned around, he saw me and dropped his cigarette in surprise. He bent quickly to retrieve it and rub the sparks from the pile, and when he came up, the terrible brightness was back in place.

"Dreadfully sorry, old thing, you were so quiet—stupid of me, I forgot you were there. Awfully rude, I know. I'm not normally quite such a bounder—"

A bell rang. It cut off his drivel; it delayed my need to acknowledge that I had no right to keep him from his needle. Slow footsteps went down the corridor, the front door opened, and the heavy wood of the library door was pierced by the voice of a man, clear, high, and utterly unmistakable.

"Why, if it isn't Edmund Marshall. How are you, my good man?"

"Mr—Mr Holmes! Well, I never. It's been . . ."

"Thirteen years, yes. Is there a Miss Mary Russell here?"

"Yes, sir. She's in the library with Mr—with Lieutenant Fitzwarren."

The object of this sentence was frozen in the attitude of a hound listening for the faint trace of a horn. Or perhaps, rather, the fox at the sound of distant baying.

"Excellent. Here, take my stick, too, Marshall. This door, I believe?"

He was in the doorway, and his eyes immediately took in my position in the room and Miles Fitzwarren's physical and mental state—as well as the curtains, my hemline, and the chess pieces on the fireside table, knowing him.

He was wearing the dress of the natives, in this case a raven black suit of a slightly old-fashioned but beautifully tailored cut, with a sharp white collar and just the edge of brilliant cuff peeking out at the sleeve. Judging from the indentation in his hair, he had given Marshall a silk top hat. His trouser creases were like razors, his shoes mirrors, and he moved confidently into the opulent library with the politely bored attitude of a potential but unenthusiastic buyer. I subsided into a chair. He shot me an approving glance and strolled nonchalantly over to the chessboard.

"I must have just missed you twice this afternoon, Russell," he commented, reaching down to move a black knight. "First at your club and then at the home of Miss Beaconsfield, where a riot was just in the process of being quelled by a highly competent young Belgian lady. She told me in her tongue where you had gone." He pursed his lips and shifted a white bishop three spaces. "Your Miss Beaconsfield appears to have some . . . interesting friends." Another pause while he moved the black king to the side, and then he seemed to tire of it. He clasped his hands behind his back and continued around the room, his eyes examining the rows of leather-bound spines. At the window, his gaze dropped to the carpet, and he put out his left hand and began to run one finger slowly along the pleated back of the long maroon leather settee, then under the fringe of the lamp shade, across the space to the gleaming mahogany of the desk, touching its carved ivory pen holder lightly before he came to a halt before the rigid figure of Miles Fitzwarren, who was standing still for the first time since I had met him. Holmes stood in contemplation of the intricate crystal paperweight that had appeared in his hand, then slowly raised his eyes to those of the younger man, fixing him with a grey gaze that seemed to come from a great height.

"Good evening, Lieutenant Fitzwarren," he said with the voice of gentle Fate. The man jerked upright and tried to find his mask.

"Evenin', sir. I, er, I don't believe I've had the honour."

"We have met, but it was some years ago. The name is Holmes, Sherlock Holmes."

The younger man blinked his eyes rapidly and tried unsuccessfully to laugh.

"Awkward name, that, don't you find? People mistakin' you for that detective chappy? Magnifyin' glass and deerstalker and all that."

"I am that detective chappy, Lieutenant. And I have been in this house before, a trifling matter of some jewels, when you were but a lad. I expect you might remember if you turned your thoughts to it."

"Good Lord. I do. I mean, I thought it was my imagination, but I do remember meeting Sherlock Holmes." The awe had knocked out his silly-ass act, and he looked slightly stunned. "What are you doing here? I mean to say, is there anything I can do for you?"

"I came here to ask the same of you."

"I'm sorry, I don't understand. Do you mean about Iris? The police seem to be—"

Holmes held up a finger and cut him to silence.

"Lieutenant Fitzwarren," he said clearly, "you can be helped."

The young man gawped and swallowed. "Yes? Er, well, that's terribly kind of you," he began uncertainly before Holmes cut him off again.

"Young man, you have made the unfortunate and all-too-common discovery that the compound formed by the acetylation of morphia is highly addictive both physically and mentally. I cannot help you with your mental dependency on heroin, but I can help you rid yourself of the physiological one. It is not a pleasant process. You will feel as you do now for an unbearably long time, and you will for a shorter time feel considerably worse. At the end of it, you will feel weak and empty and filled with shame, and the craving for the drug will eat at your very soul, but you will be clean, and you will begin to remember who you are. If, as I believe, the desire for cleanliness and memory is growing in you, I can help. You, however, must make the decision."

"But . . . why? I don't even know you. Why should you . . ."

"For four years, you did for me what I could not, in the trenches, and this is the price. I have been in your debt since you set foot on the troopship. I can now begin to pay off that debt, by taking over a small part of the price that you paid. You need only say the word, and I am your man."

A clock ticked slow seconds. Half a minute passed, then a minute. I listened in agony for the approach of footsteps that would interrupt the two men (the one young and racked by the drug pulling at his nerves, the other implacable and utterly solid) and their wordless confrontation.

It was hard to say who moved first, but as the young man gasped for breath, his hand came up, and as Holmes took it, his other hand came around to seize Fitzwarren's shoulder in support and approval.

"Good man. Where's your hat?"

"My hat? Surely you don't intend—"

"I do intend."

"But, my mother . . ."

"Your mother will be infinitely better served by knowing that her son is returning to himself than if she were forced to be around him in his present state. She will forgive your absence at the funeral. Besides, if 'twere done, best 'twere done quickly." He took the elegantly clad elbow and politely but inexorably propelled his charge towards the door. "No, young man, you asked for my help, and as many have found, you must take it as it comes, inconvenient as that may be. Russell, you will make our apologies to the family and give out some explanation or other, will you? Also, would you be so good as to telephone Mycroft at the Diogenes Club and tell him that we are on our way to the sanatorium and please to inform Dr McDaniels that we shall meet him there."

The startled Marshall had scurried to retrieve the belongings of the two men, and Holmes took the hat from the butler's hand and slapped it onto Fitzwarren's head, jammed his own on, and gathered up the two proffered coats.

"Good-bye, Russell. You can reach me through Mycroft."

"*Mazel tov*, Holmes."

"Thank you, Russell," he said, and added under his breath, "I shall need it." Ignoring the hovering butler, he draped the young man's shoulders with a coat and shrugged into his own. The poor servant leapt for the door and held it until both men had been whisked away by the waiting taxi, and then he turned to me with a faint air of reproach.

"Does madam wish anything?" he murmured.

"Madam wishes only that that man can find a way out of his troubles," I answered absently.

He looked startled, but his training held.

"Indeed, madam," he said, only a fraction more emphatically than necessary.

I went back into the library, made the telephone call, and felt as if a heavy weight had been lifted from my shoulders. Only part of it was Miles.

CHAPTER 8

Thursday, 30 December

Woman compared to other creatures is the image of God, for she bears dominion over them; but compared to man, she may not be called the image of God, for she does not bear rule and lordship over man, but obeys him.

—Saint Augustine

With Holmes out of the way and Miles out of my hands, life looked somewhat more manageable. I played Holmes' game six moves to checkmate, poured myself a glass of predictably excellent sherry from a crystal decanter, and went to browse through the books.

I was twenty-three pages into a late-seventeenth-century Italian work on the doges of Venice when Veronica came back.

"Sorry to have been so long, Mary. Where's Miles?"

I closed the book over my finger. "Ronnie, your Miles is off taking the cure."

"What are you talking about?"

I told her briefly what had taken place.

"That was all? As simple as that?"

"A beginning, perhaps, nothing more."

She burst into tears and threw her arms around me, then flew out of the door and upstairs. I returned to the doges and was on page ninety-two (I found the archaic Italian slow going) when the door opened again. I rose, placed the book back on the shelf, and joined a happier Veronica Beaconsfield than I had seen since Oxford, with colour in her cheeks. I considered a warning, decided against it, and allowed Marshall to help me with my coat.

"I shouldn't be so happy," she said on the street. "Iris is dead, and I know that this hope for Miles is only a faint one, but I can't help it, I feel so very grateful to God that I happened to spot you that morning. Do you want to walk for a while, or take a cab to a restaurant?"

"Let's walk and see what we find on the way."

What we found was a corner stall run by a Sicilian that specialised in curry, flavoured buns and sweet spiced coffee. The food was odd, but eatable, and on the way to the Temple we found as well a deeper level of companionship than we had yet come to. Despite the cold and the knowledge that the Temple service was beginning, we continued to walk slowly, arm in arm, talking about our futures.

"And what of you, Mary? Will you become an archetypical Oxford don, or will you marry and have fourteen horrid and brilliant little brats?"

"I cannot envisage the latter, somehow." I laughed.

"It is stretching the imagination," she agreed, "although I can imagine you in almost any other situation."

"Thank you very much," I said primly.

"Oh, you know what I mean. None of the traditional choices really apply now, do they? Not for people like us, anyway. What about your Mr Holmes?"

"My Mr Holmes is nearly sixty. Rather late to break up bachelorhood." I kept my voice natural, humorous, mildly regretful.

"I suppose you're right. It's too bad, really—he's dreamy, in an impossible sort of a way."

I was startled. "You mean you find Holmes attractive?"

"Oh, yes, heaps of s.a. Why, don't you?"

"Well, yes, I suppose." Although I shouldn't have called it 'sex appeal,' exactly.

"But you sound surprised."

"I wouldn't have thought you—Why does he appeal to you?"

"Oh, he doesn't, not really. I mean, I'm sure he'd turn out

to be totally maddening, in reality. It's because he's so unavailable." She thought for a few steps, and I waited, intrigued. "You know, when I was fifteen—this was just before the War—someone at school had the bright idea of sending the top members of our form to Italy for the spring term. One of the girls had an uncle there, with a huge, dusty villa in the countryside not far from Florence, and the idea was that we hire a charabanc to transport us in every day to view the treasures. Of course, the thing broke down continuously, or the driver was on a drunk, or we rebelled, so in the end I think we spent two days in the city and the rest in the small town three miles from the villa.

"There was a priest in the village—there were several, of course, but one in particular—I don't know if it was the Mediterranean sun or our glands or just sheer deviltry, but all of us developed a Grand Passion for the priest. Poor man, it must have been so painful to have ten English misses on his heels, mooning about and bringing him fruit and sweets. He was good-looking, in a bony kind of way, very elegant in his black robe, but it was his air of unreachability that was so utterly electrifying. A challenge, I suppose, to break through that ascetic shell and set loose the passion beneath. Because one could feel the passion. My God, you couldn't miss it, in his eyes and his mouth, but it was under iron control. He kept it directed no doubt to his prayer, but you couldn't help but want to break his control and see what lay beneath." She reviewed what she'd said, then laughed in self-deprecation. "At least it seemed that way. He was probably terrifically repressed and scared to death of us, and no doubt he had all sorts of boring habits, as I suppose your Sherlock Holmes would prove to have. Repressed and cerebral, a deadly combination. Still," she said, blithely unaware of the shattering effect her words were having on me, "there must be plenty of unrepressed and agreeable older men around, the sort who mightn't normally expect to marry again but would allow themselves to be convinced. Doing their part for England's 'surplus women'."

"For heaven's sake, Ronnie, listen to yourself. What would Margery Childe say?"

"I know, it's terrible. But honestly, it's not nice to be alone . . . not forever. *Spinster* is such an appalling word somehow. You know, some of the women—" Her garrulity abruptly dried up, and I smiled to myself in the dark.

"Some of the women what?"

"Oh, you know, they say that the only true and equal love is Sapphism . . . marriage between women."

"Is Margery Childe a lesbian?" I wondered.

"No, I'm sure she isn't."

"How do you know? Is she married?"

"No. Although she may have been. Someone told me she'd lost her husband in the Somme."

"Who?"

"Who told me, you mean? Let me think. One of the early members, it must have been, who knew her before the war. Ivy? No—I know. It was Delia Laird. She was with Margery from the early days, when they used to hire village halls to preach in. Yes, that's right, Ivy's the one who told me she'd seen Margery with a gorgeous man in France a year or two back, all dark and Mediterranean and gangster-like. No, Margery's no lesbian."

"I didn't meet Delia Laird, did I? You said she *was* with Margery. Has she left the Temple?"

"She died, back in August. Drowned in her bath."

I stopped. "Good heavens."

"It was suicide. That is, the verdict at the inquest was accidental death, but we all knew she'd killed herself. Tablets and gin, in the bath; what else could it be?"

"But why?" I allowed her to pull me back into motion.

"Margery. Delia was one of those women who might have been a lesbian if she'd come from a less repressed background, or if she'd received any encouragement. As it was, she devoted her life to Margery. An unfortunate woman, from a good family but there was something indefinably wrong with her. Not to speak ill of the dead, but frankly, she was rather stupid. When the Temple began to take off a couple of years ago, well, Margery just sort of left her behind. She needed people who could run an organisation, not just hire halls and carry bags. Plus, she just didn't have the time to baby Delia any more. So Delia killed herself."

"Does Margery know it was suicide?"

"Oh no. I'm sure she doesn't. She was devastated."

"How sad."

"It was. Mostly it's sad Delia couldn't have made a match. She would have made someone an utterly devoted wife."

"Even if that someone was another woman."

"Well, yes."

"Would Margery have approved?"

"There are several woman couples in the Temple, she certainly doesn't seem to mind them. She seems to feel it depends on the people, that the love is the important thing."

We walked a few steps before I passed judgement.

"Strikes me as dead boring," I said flatly, and she started to giggle.

"I'd have to agree," she said finally, and then: "Are you a virgin, Mary? Oh dear, that sounds blasphemous," and she giggled again.

"Yes, I am," I replied. She looked sharply over at me.

"But only just?" she asked shrewdly.

"But only just," I confirmed. "And you?"

"No. We were engaged, after all."

"Don't apologise, for heaven's sake."

"Oh, I don't regret it, not at all. To tell you the truth, I've missed Miles terribly. Not having him at all is almost worse than having him drugged. I hope to God . . ."

She didn't need to say what she hoped. I put my arm across her shoulder and hugged her, thickly through all the garments, and we walked on in friendship to hear the words of Margery Childe.

As we approached the building, the air came alive with the vibration of voices raised in harmony. Ronnie smiled and quickened her step.

"Good, they're still singing. We haven't missed Margery. Come on."

She led me, not in through the ranks of double doors that opened into the back of the hall, but up a side stairway marked TICKET HOLDERS ONLY. The usher/guard nodded at our greetings and we hurried as the noise from inside came to an end. Amidst coughs and shuffles and the dying hum of speech, we entered a door marked PRIVATE. Inside was the Temple's Inner Circle, most of whom I had met the other night. They made room for us, a couple of them looking me over and dismissing me because of my clothing, and then the hall dimmed and fell quiet as all eyes went to the diminutive figure on the stage.

She was wearing a robe of darkly luminous silver-grey, and she seemed to glow. It took me some minutes to realise that she was in fact being followed by a spotlight only marginally brighter than the stage lights, and I smiled at the professionalism of the effect. However, I had to admit that not all the glow was an artifice. The magnetic pull I had begun to discount as my imagination was there, stronger than on Monday already and building as the evening—I cannot bring myself to call it a service—wore on. Her movements were languid, her eyes dark as she talked about the nature of love.

She waited for complete attention, for utter silence, before she dropped her first words into the packed hall, nearly seven hundred pairs of ears, I heard later, a quarter of them men.

"My friends," she said, her voice low and vibrant, "tonight's topic is love." Inaudible ripples ran through the room. She let them die down, then suddenly smiled. "On the other hand, love is hardly a topic about which we can speak. Love is the force behind speech. Love is the thing that speaks us. To quote my friend John, 'God is love.' A person who does not love does not know God. And, when one loves, one loves God.

"But, what does he mean by love? What do we mean by love?

"Think for a moment about another word: *light*. Light. If I were to take a stack of paper and give a sheet of it to each one of you and ask you to use it to describe what the word *light* means, do you imagine I should find even two pages that matched? I would get drawings: a lightbulb with its twist of filament, a gas fixture, a candle, the sun." She looked out into the audience, her head tipped attentively, the attitude of a schoolmistress listening for answers. "A bolt of lightning," she said, as if repeating what she heard for the benefit of the rest. "And—oh, yes, I see, a baby who doesn't weigh enough. And"—her eyes shifted—"a woman who wishes she weighed less. And a brilliant hot summer's afternoon when the sun bouncing off the street hurts the eyes. And the first gleam of sunrise, and the difficulties of an artist to capture the essence of a place in its light, and a man—" She did a double take, and her lips twitched. "A gentleman looking forward to igniting his cigar when this is over," and she smiled with the hall's laughter. " 'In the beginning,' " she chanted, " 'God created the heavens and the earth; And the earth was without form and void, and darkness was upon the face of the deep; and the Spirit of God moved upon the face of the waters; And God said, 'Let there be—' "

She stopped abruptly, holding the silence for several long seconds.

"If all these images can come from the word *light*, how many more from the word *love*, a thing invisible but for the movement it creates, a thing without physical reality or measurement or being, yet a thing which animates the entire universe. *God is love*. God creates, and when He sees His creation, He loves it and calls it good.

"The love of God, the joy God takes in Creation, is incomprehensible to us. We can catch a glimpse of it, at rare moments, and be left thirsting and alone, kept from the beauty and the power of divine love by the shackles of responsibility and weakness and doubt. But the soul thirsts, we thirst, and we look for the weak reflections of divine love where we might find them, that·if we cannot have our thirst quenched by a gushing, pure stream, at least we might survive on the water from ditches.

"The forms of love are many, the faces of God infinite. A

mother putting her baby to the breast is participating in the love of God. A child who finds a newly hatched bird under a tree and lays it back into its nest is participating in the love of God. A fox out in the moonlight stealing a chicken to take home to its young is a movement in the love of God. Two bodies in the night, moving in the dance we call love are, if the motive is pure, reaching for the reflection of divine love which they see in one another."

She waited calmly for another inaudible swell of reaction to die down, then went on.

"We are born in water, and we spend our lives thirsting. We are like a woman out hoeing her field, a woman who is hot under the sun, who knows where the stream rises up pure in the hills but who drinks from the slow-moving, weed-choked waters nearby because the source is so far away and there is weeding to be done and soon it will be time to go home for supper. Is the farmer wrong to settle for less? No, of course not. The weeds must be chopped or the children will starve.

"But once, just once, should not that farmer lay down her hoe and walk off into the cool hills to lie down with her face in the water and drink her fill, then go home after dark with her eyes aglow from the memory of that one perfect moment when her thirst was quenched absolutely? Will not that memory sustain her? Will she not taste the echo of its cool sweetness every time she draws from the muddied water and be strengthened? Jesus called it living water and said we would not thirst again.

"Once we have tasted the love of God, its sweet flavour persists in all the lesser forms of love that we come across as we work our fields. We taste it everywhere, in greater or lesser concentration, and we try to find ways of making it flow into us more fully. And that is when we discover that the flow of love, like the flow of a stream, suffers from being blocked up and kept to one's self. Water dammed up becomes stale, dank. Love not given out becomes dead and slimy. When we express our love, when we act as conduits for divine love, then the love within us is continually renewed, refreshed, restored."

Margery Childe spoke of love for a solid hour, holding her audience rapt until her final blessing. There is little point in presenting her homily in its entirety, because in print, without the dramatic pauses and husky thrill of her voice, the words lose their fizz, like warm champagne. Indeed, even as she was saying the words I found them absolutely maddening, an often ill-suited amalgam of personal sophistication and scriptural superficiality, mixed metaphors and rambling thoughts held together only by the force of her personality and pierced at a handful of unforeseen points by bolts of blinding perception. Her theology was rustic in its training (if training it could be called), sporadic in its development, and often wildly unsuccessful in its attempts at exegesis or midrash. For someone like me, with my background and my own careful passions, it might have sent me gibbering away into the night, but for one thing: Despite her unread, unsophisticated, raw, rude, and unlettered approach to Scripture, when it came to zeroing in on her target, she was dead-centre accurate.

It hit me about halfway through her talk (talk?—what an inadequate word for the woman's passionate display of exultation, despair, pity, joy . . .) what it was that I was hearing, and with that awareness I sat back in my seat with a jolt that startled my neighbours.

The woman was a mystic.

What I was hearing was an untutored woman singing to God in the only voice she possessed: a simple voice, unsuited to high opera, but not without beauty. With training . . .

I was disturbed. I was excited. I had told Holmes that I wanted Margery Childe to be someone who talked with God, someone actually doing what I and countless others had spent lifetimes scrutinising, and at that moment at any rate I was convinced that this was what I was witnessing. It was galvanic. Electrifying. I wanted to take notes. Yet it was also troubling, to see before me living evidence that the limpid stream I studied could become this crashing, unruly, primal force. It had the brutal effect of making me feel a trivialiser, as if I had confidently set out to analyse a minute section of a wall and stepped back from my completed work, only to find myself in the Sistine Chapel. It was depressing, but salutary. And quite fascinating.

She leapt and slithered through her discourse, losing her train of thought, shooting off into tangential metaphors, painfully misusing what I thought of as technical terms, and then, when all seemed lost, letting fly with the casual flare of illumination that left me stunned with its brilliance.

I have no great ear for music; I have only a degree more for poetry. What I do possess is a powerful and unerring sense for truth, particularly theological truth, and that night I heard it, ringing out clear and sweet in that unlikely hall from a woman who was working herself, and her audience, into a state that verged on erotic excitement.

She came back time and again to the concept of thirst, imbuing the word with a yearning that became ever more urgent. She called upon, inevitably, Canticles, but only obliquely, teasingly, and she shied away before committing herself to a full-blown orgy. (The Song of Solomon does become inordinately stimulating: "You are stately as a palm tree," it croons, "and your breasts are like its clusters. I say I shall climb the palm tree and take hold of its branches. . . . your kisses are like the best wine, going down smoothly, gliding over lips and teeth." And: "My beloved put his hand to the latch, and my heart thrilled within me." It is regarded as an allegory of the soul's desire for God, but the rabbis were forced to make strong injunctions against those who would sing it in taverns. It is, in a word, bawdy.)

She ended her talk, abruptly as before, with a phrase from Canticles: "Eat, O friends, and drink: drink deeply, O lovers.' " She smiled and gave a small bow. "Until Saturday, friends." And she was gone.

There was a certain breathlessness to the wave of voices that broke over the hall, and the Inner Circle around me, though they must have heard her any number of times already, stood up flustered and met one another's eyes with a defiant half embarrassment. Some of the gentlemen in the rows below seemed distinctly warm under the collar.

In the packed foyer, I could see a multitude of brightly coloured collection baskets, filling rapidly. Several of the circle picked up baskets and moved into the crowd, but to my surprise the others made their ways to the street doors. I turned and spoke loudly into Veronica's ear.

"Is there no gathering tonight, then?"

"No," she shouted back. "Not on Thursdays."

We streamed with *hoi polloi* out onto the cool and rational street and washed up, blinking, beneath a lamppost, ignoring as best we could the buskers and vendors who had anticipated the crowd.

"Why not on Thursdays?" I asked.

"Why what? Oh, Margery, you mean. She meditates, both before and after the Thursday meetings, always."

The contemplation of what the woman's thoughts might consist of during those meditations gave me pause. I came to myself with a start.

"Pardon me?" I asked.

"I said, do you want to go for dinner, or a drink?"

"Oh. Not a full meal, I think."

"A pub, then."

A pub it was, and since it was nearby, it was already populated with a large percentage of the night's congregation, laughing and merry and as unlikely a group of churchgoers as I had seen. We oozed snugly into two chairs at a minuscule corner table with our glasses and a plate of anaemic sandwiches from the bar.

"So, what did you think?" Veronica asked. I looked at her carefully, but there was no mischief in her eyes. And I couldn't even put her innocence down to virginal naïveté.

"I think that was the most amazing church service I've ever witnessed," I said, and then around a mouthful of cheese and pickle, I asked, "Was that her standard treatment for a Thursday night?"

"She was a bit subdued tonight, because of Iris's death. She wanted to devote the evening to a memorial service, but Mrs Fitzwarren absolutely refused to allow it. She's never liked it that Iris was so wrapped up with the Temple, and she blames Margery for the death."

"Blames her? How?"

"Oh, that's too strong. I ought to say, she isn't yet prepared to share her grief with anyone outside the family. Margery understands, but she's hurt, too—who wouldn't be? So she was, as I said, subdued. I've seen her so intense, the sparks fly."

"Must be against the law," I said under my breath. "Oh never mind, I was just thinking that if she becomes so . . . worked up, it's no wonder she can't sit calmly and drink tea at the end of it. I'd have to go for a brisk ten-mile walk."

"She says she depends on the energy that she gathers on nights like this, that when she meditates, she reintegrates it and is strengthened by it. She's an extraordinary person," she added needlessly.

"So it seems. Tell me, does she lead meditations, or prayer meetings, with you?"

"From time to time. She does what she calls 'teaching silence.' It's a way of listening to the universe—she calls it 'opening one's self up to the love of God.' Ask her about it."

"I will."

"You'll go and see her, then?"

"I think so. I had thought tonight, but . . ."

"Sorry, I should have explained. Do you want that other meat sandwich? Thanks. Why don't you telephone tomorrow and ask Marie when would be a good time."

"I will." I picked up the last triangle, something unidentifiable but vaguely fishy. Veronica was staring unfocused at the sandwich in her hand.

"She is truly extraordinary," she repeated. Her heavy eyebrows came together, and I waited. She glanced up and flushed. "Oh, it's nothing, just something I saw—or thought I saw. I suppose I could tell you about it, though you'll think I've gone loony. Maybe I oughtn't," she dithered. "Oh hell, why not?

"I was at the Temple one night, settling a woman and her two children into the refuge. I didn't realise how late it was, and I needed to talk with Margery about them, so I went to find her, not thinking. She wasn't in the sitting room—where we were the other night?—so I went on down the corridor to her private rooms, thinking that I'd find Marie at any rate. Well, I did find her—I stuck my head into the room Margery uses as a private meditation chapel and saw Marie sitting there, so I walked in. Before I could say more than 'Marie, have you seen—' she jumped up and grabbed my arm and started pushing me back out the door. Now, you probably could guess how most of us feel about Marie. I mean, she does her job and protects Margery from being eaten up, but she's hardly an easy person to get along with. Anyway, I stopped dead and said, 'Marie, what on earth is the matter?' and she hushed me and glanced across the room, the way you do when you want to make sure you haven't disturbed someone, so I pushed forward a few steps and saw Margery. She was kneeling, sort of sitting on her heels, and her shoulders were thrown back and her arms dangled down and her head was back, just rigid. She hadn't heard me. She looked as if she wouldn't have heard a bomb going off. I couldn't see her face very well, but her mouth seemed to be open slightly, and she looked . . . otherworldly, as if she weren't in the room. Marie snatched at me and started shoving at me—God, she's an irritating person!—and I let her push me to the door. I turned around when we got there, to look over her shoulder, and just then Margery sort of collapsed, like a marionette with its strings cut. Just went limp and folded into a huddle on the floor. Marie gave me a final push and bolted the door, and I could hear her walking—not running—across the room. I didn't mention it to Margery, or to anyone else for that matter. I don't know if she knows I saw her. It was a Tuesday," she added, somewhat irrelevantly.

Time had been called and the pub was quieting, but neither of us took much notice for several minutes, until the owner came and began pointedly to clear the tables next to us. We drained our glasses and put on our coats.

"Thank you for telling me, Ronnie," I said. "I agree, she's an interesting person."

"You don't think I've gone daft, then?"

"Oh, no," I said emphatically. "By no means."

I took to my narrow bed that night with a mind awhirl, plucked at by the plight of Miles Fitzwarren, the motives of Sherlock Holmes, and the spiritual life of Margery Childe. I did not sleep overly much.

CHAPTER 9

Friday, 31 December–
Saturday, 1 January

Let the woman learn in silence with all submissiveness. I do not suffer a woman to teach, nor to usurp authority over men, but to be in silence.

1 Timothy 2:11–12

I did ring the Temple the following morning, and after long delays and losing the connexion twice, I finally spoke with the churlish Marie, whose accent on the telephone was thick as marzipan. I shifted to French, but she stubbornly persisted with fracturing English, and at the end of the bilingual conversation, it transpired that Miss Childe was not able to see me that day for longer than fifteen minutes, that Miss Childe wished to see me for a longer period of time, and that Miss Childe therefore suggested that I dine with her the next evening, Saturday, at a half past six. I told Marie in the most florid of French that such an arrangement was entirely felicitous and unreservedly acceptable, then rang off.

I sat for a minute at the telephone desk, whistling tunelessly, and then picked up the receiver again and asked for a number in Oxford. While waiting for the trunk call to go through, I retrieved the morning paper. The day's article on Iris Fitzwarren stretched one meagre piece of news (that the nightclub she had been in was raided by Scotland Yard late Thursday night, with a number of deliciously scandalous arrests) into two columns, but despite the writer's efforts, it was obvious that nothing was happening. Had it not been for her name, the story would have been killed or relegated to the innermost recesses.

The exchange came up then with my number, and I spoke for a few minutes to the man on the other end, referring obliquely to certain debts and favours and describing the information I wanted, and said I would ring him back in an hour. Holmes would have done the matter by telegram, I knew, but I always prefer the personal touch in my matters of mild blackmail.

I went for breakfast and then returned to the telephone. My informant had the college address and private telephone number I needed, which I wrote in my notebook. I thanked him, took up my hat, gloves, and increasingly light handbag, and called a farewell to the concierge (such a grand name for that dried-up figure!). Taxis beckoned, but I resolutely turned my steps toward the Underground. Ridiculous as it seemed, after the depredations of generosity the other night to the East End poor, my purse was emptying fast, and no reinforcements were due until the banks opened on Monday. As I walked down the steps into the noisy station, a sudden thought made me laugh aloud: The cost of the clothes the elves were making for me amounted to precisely five pounds more than the total allowance I had drawn during my three years at Oxford, and here was I hoarding my last few shillings. Monday a ragged-coated philanthropist, Friday too poor for a taxi, and Sunday on the edge of being a millionaire (in dollars, perhaps, if the market was strong and the exchange rate very good).

In Oxford, I walked through a low drizzle and presented myself at the address in my notebook, where I was surprisingly well received despite the fact that I was obviously interrupting the great man's work. I spent an instructive two and a half hours and came away with a list of books and names. The former, I tracked down in the Bodleian, where I spent the afternoon skimming several thousand pages. I spent a few shillings on a stodgy pub meal, worked a while longer, and on my way out of the town centre stopped for a brief chat with the colleague (whom I had dubbed Duncan) with whom I was doing the public presentation in January. The brief visit turned into dinner and a lengthy consultation, and I returned late to my digs on the north end of town, read for another couple of hours, and slept fitfully.

Saturday morning, I rose early, made myself a pot of tea, and began to read Evelyn Underhill's massive (in scope, if not number of pages) treatise on mysticism. At a more reasonable hour, my landlady came in with a tray of coffee and buttered toast. Reluctantly, I closed Miss Underhill and picked up the material Duncan had given me the previous evening. At midmorning, I walked to his house, an amiable shambles of loud children and a wife every bit as absentminded as he, and after an hour's friendly argument, I took myself on a contemplative stroll through the Parks and Magdalen's deer park to a converted laundry in Headington, a building that smelt oddly of starch and scorched sheets when warm, at whose whitewashed front window passersby often drew up, startled at the noises coming from within.

Watson called this form of martial art "baritsu," for reasons best known to himself. (There was in his day a form of glorified grappling by that name, invented by an Englishman and dignified with an Oriental title, but had Holmes depended on it, he would never have survived Reichenbach.) That day, out of condition from weeks at my books and distracted as well, I called it torture, and I collected a handsome variety of bruises from my gentle and ever-genial teacher. I bowed to him gingerly and crept away to the train, reflecting on how salutary it is occasionally to put one's self in the hands of a ruthless superior.

I arrived at the Temple promptly at five o'clock, at the everyday business doors down the street from the meeting hall. As we had arranged, Veronica met me and spent the next hour showing me the workings behind the doors. It was an enlightening experience. We saw the Refuge, open to poor women in trouble, with long tables to feed them, a small surgery to treat their ills, and a tiny garden in the back with swings for the children. ("The only garden some of them have ever seen," commented Ronnie.) I saw the classrooms, with readers designed for children but used mostly, said Veronica, by grown women ("We're writing a simple adult reader"); the commissary, with its stores of food and clothing for the destitute; the secretarial training rooms, with a row of typewriting machines ("You probably know that if a woman refuses to take a job as a servant, because of the low pay, long hours, and lack of dignity, she may have her unemployment benefits cancelled," Ronnie said. I had to admit I did not); and a storage room with shelves of books, a future, dreamed-about library ("These people will read anything and everything, given a chance").

The next building, between the Refuge and the lecture hall, was the Temple's heart. On the street level were offices that handled communication for Margery—speaking engagements, business appointments, interested outsiders. These rooms resembled the offices of any prosperous business, without the heavy oaken dignity. What surprised me was the extent of what lay behind these.

Behind the front offices and taking up the entire basement was the Temple's political organisation. One room had nothing but telephones in cubicles and a large switchboard. ("We can get a response or put out information immediately—it also serves to train women while they earn.") Another had a round table nearly twelve feet across ("for making decisions on policies"). On the walls around it were a number of typed and hand-written notices and memoranda. "First reading divorce bill—March??" said one. "Remind Refuge workers that midwives get a shilling for each referral," said another. "If you know of any sympathetic journalist, give the name to Bunny Hillman." "Pamphlets for the Parliament demo will be ready midday 5 January." "Needed: more typewriters, bedding, children's shoes, eyeglasses." "Physical culture classes beginning 20 January; see Rachel." "Talk on 'Sex-Rôle Conditioning, Marriage Contracts, and the Age of Feminism,' Saturday, 22 January, St Gilberta's Church, W1." "NEEDED: country overnight lodgings for mother-infant outings this summer, preferably with forest or lake nearby. See Gertrude P." "LOST: shawl, mauve with dark trim; see Helen in the front office." "The next France tour leaves 18 February. Sign up now!! Remember: sensible shoes and be there early! See Susanna Briggs or Francesca Rowley." "Hymnbooks are disappearing at an alarming rate! Please remember to watch for them in the foyer after services and remind the member to return it to her seat!" "BOOKS WANTED for lending library, good condition, nothing too dreary. Veronica Beaçonsfield." We went on.

The next room was a study, with books on law and history; filing cabinets of articles, maps, and census reports; several volumes of jokes; and great piles of journals, from suffragette tractates to *Punch* ("This is where we draught the speeches"). There was even a print shop in the corner that could turn out broadsheets and pamphlets.

And to think, a week ago I didn't even know this existed, I thought, and then said it aloud to Veronica.

"You'd have heard of it before too long," she said, and I believed her. In my preoccupation with the religious aspects of Margery Childe's personality and message, I had been aware of the attendant practical manifestations of that message only as on the periphery. Now, moving around within the walls of the hive, as it were, I became increasingly aware that as far as Margery's followers were concerned, the thrice-weekly services might be Margery's way of infusing them with her energies, but here was where those energies were ultimately spent.

The Temple was a political machine, a highly efficient means of gathering in and laying out monies and giving the enthusiasm of every Temple member, no matter how lowly, a direction and a concrete goal. Canvassing, speech making, pamphlet printing; doctoring the poor and teaching the illiterate; feeding the hungry and planning assaults on the law of the land—all went on here, all directed by a member of the Inner Circle, and therefore ultimately by Margery Childe herself. A mystic, perhaps, but one quite aware of the need for works as well as contemplations. There was a groundswell of power within these walls, gathering beneath Margery Childe and carrying her—where? A seat on the local council? Into Parliament? The fifteenth-century St Catherine of Genoa was a teacher, a philanthropist, the administrator of a great hospital—and a mystic. A century before her, another Catherine, of Siena, advised kings and popes, played a key rôle in papal reformation, and ran a nursing order; she was also a visionary and a mystic ranked by Miss Underhill alongside St Francis in importance. So, why not Margery Childe in twentieth-century London?

We went back up the stairs to the ground floor, and Veronica was about to lead me into the side entrance of the hall when we were intercepted by one of the refuge workers.

"Oh, Miss Beaconsfield, I'm glad I found you. There's a Queenie something wants to see you, says her husband's gone off his nut. She's cryin' and carrying' on like anything."

"You go on, Ronnie," I said. "It's almost time for me to see Margery, anyway."

"If you're sure? I'll tell Marie you're here."

She scurried down the hallway and up the stairs, then returned within a minute, gave me a brief wave, and turned into the corridor that led to the shelter. I nodded at the women behind their desks, noting that their curiosity about me had increased when I had mentioned Margery, an indication that the Temple was now big enough to make its leader aloof from lesser mortals. I sat down and picked up a stack of pamphlets to keep me occupied, managing to work my way through *Diseases of Childhood*, *Treating Tuberculosis*, and *Women in the Classroom* before Marie appeared in the doorway, pronounced my name, and turned without another word. I followed at a leisurely pace and chattered away at the taciturn grey back in perversely cheery French as she led me up the stairs to, I was unsurprised to see, the corridor where Veronica and I had ended up on Monday night. Marie paused in front of the door opposite the Circle's meeting room, knocked once, waited for the response, and opened it for me.

Margery Childe was sitting in front of a fire, wearing an orange-and-grey shot silk dressing gown, a book in her lap. She uncurled from her chair and came to greet me, one hand out to seize mine.

"Mary, how lovely—may I call you Mary? Everyone calls me Margery. I hope you will. Do you mind an informal meal, here in front of the fire? I never eat very much before a service, and I have to go and dress and meditate in an hour. I hope you don't mind that, either. What a lovely colour of green that is; it does magical things to your eyes."

My responses consisted of Yes, of course, very well, of course not, I understand, and thank you, and I found myself giving Marie my coat and hat and being seated at a small table with two delicate chairs that I tentatively identified as Louis XIV. The place settings were luminous and paper-thin, the silver old and heavy, the glasses blown into an ornate and modern twist. I hid my twice-let-down hem beneath the table.

"Veronica has been showing you about, I take it?"

"Yes, it was most impressive."

"You sound surprised." From her expression, it was a common reaction.

"Mostly by the fact that I'd not heard of the Temple before Monday."

"We are working to remedy that. Wine?"

"Thank you." She poured from a cut-glass decanter into two glasses that matched those on the table, these with a twist of pale orange in the stem. "But it must be new," I noted, accepting the glass, "most of it. One of the presses in the print shop looked almost unused."

"True. Five years ago, we hired a pair of second-storey rooms once a week. We now own four buildings outright."

I wanted very badly to know more of just how the transformation had come about, but I held my tongue. It would have sounded, if not accusatory, at the least suspicious, and even if she did answer, I did not want that note to sound just yet.

"Very impressive," I repeated. "I shall make a donation to the library fund."

"A good choice," she said blandly, without so much as a glance at my tired clothing. "Veronica has great hopes for her free lending library." The bluestocking will be good for a couple of pounds, she was thinking, and with a rush of mischief, I decided to surprise her come Monday.

"I had also not expected you—the Temple—to be so politically active, somehow."

"Religion oughtn't dirty its hands, you mean? Without essential changes in the law, we will be operating soup kitchens and baby clinics until Doomsday."

"But don't you think—" I was interrupted by Marie, entering with a wide tray on which were several covered dishes. She unloaded it onto our table, removed the covers, and fussed with the arrangement of bits of cutlery for a moment, and then, somewhat to my surprise, she left. Margery served us, giving herself rather little and me rather a lot of the chicken slices in tarragon sauce, the glazed carrots, still firm, the potatoes and salad. She bowed her head briefly over her plate, then approached the food with neat concentration, chewing each mouthful thoroughly and washing it down with a sip of some pale herbal tea that had a slice of lemon floating in it. I drank a glass of fruity German wine. She ate a bite, then looked up at me.

"You were saying?" she enquired.

"I was wondering whether your identity as a, shall we say nonconforming religious leader might not count against you in the political arena."

"I think not. Some will take it as a sign of my dedication and will listen to me the more for it; others will see it as a mere eccentricity."

"I hope you're right." It was said politely, but she took it as a declaration of wholehearted support.

"That's very good of you. And actually, I have been thinking, and praying, a great deal about you and your offer." (Offer? I thought indignantly.) "And I have come to realise that my teaching has indeed been a very personal thing, and perhaps it is time to place it on a more universally acceptable plane. It came to me in the night that perhaps once the other projects are securely launched, we might think about sponsoring an academic project, research and discussions along the lines of what you were saying the other night. Invite the more prominent thinkers in the field. Perhaps even a journal . . . on the press you saw standing idle. What do you think?"

Damn it, was what I thought; then grimly, Does the woman imagine she can buy me? Something of the thought must have shown on my face, because she laid down her fork and leant forward.

"I'm not asking you to do anything you don't feel is right, Mary. I'm sure there are a thousand things I've said and done that you don't agree with. And I'm not about to say that I'll change. However, I want to learn. For my own sake, and for the Temple, I need to know how your world handles the questions that I grapple with alone. You say that you were surprised at our existence; it is nothing to the impression you made on me. I did not sleep at all Monday night. All I could do was think how blind and arrogant I'd been. I felt like some peasant who owned a pretty box, only to have someone take it and open it to reveal the jewels inside. I need your help, Mary. Not as a permanent commitment—I don't ask that of you. I'm not asking you to join the Temple. But I need you, just at the beginning, to start me on the road. Please."

How does one refuse such a request? I know that I was not able to. By the time Marie arrived with a second tray, coffee and strawberries (in January!) I found I had agreed to a series of informal tutorials with Margery and one lecture to the Inner Circle at the end of the month.

Having gotten what she wanted, Margery sat back with her coffee.

"Tell me a little about yourself, Mary. Veronica hints of dark secrets and exciting adventures in your life."

I made a mental note to kick Veronica when next I saw her.

"Ronnie exaggerates. I had to be away for over a month in the middle of my second year at Oxford, on some rather distasteful family business, and when I didn't talk about it later, rumours started." The truth was considerably more complex and deadly than that, but so far I had kept my name from the newspapers. "Then a couple of months later I was injured in an accident, and that seems to have changed the rumours to fact. You know how it works. The truth is, I'm just a student. Not an ordinary Oxford student, perhaps, but a student nonetheless. My mother was English, father American, both dead. A house in Sussex, a few friends in London, and an interest in feminism and theology."

"A long-standing interest. Tell me honestly, Mary: What do you think of what you've seen and heard?"

I started to give her a polite answer, then saw in her eyes that this was no light conversation on her part, but a very serious question. I put down my cup and frowned at it for a minute, putting together a response that was honest but not too revealing. She waited, and then I picked up the exquisite handspun glass that had held my wine.

"About ten years after the crucifixion of Jesus," I began, "there was born a Jew named Akiva. He was a simple man, a goatherd who didn't even learn to read until he was a grown man, yet he became one of Judaism's greatest rabbis. Akiva, like Jesus, taught best in brief epigrams and barbed stories. He also, incidentally, brought in a number of reforms regarding the status of women, but that is beside the point. I shall answer your question with one of his remarks. 'Poverty,' he said, 'is as becoming to the daughter of Israel as a red strap against the neck of a white horse.' " I put the costly glass down on the gleaming linen tablecloth and ate the last of my tiny, intense berries.

"You don't approve of wealth," she said.

"I'm not a socialist."

"In the Temple, then."

"I speak of the aesthetic beauty of poverty; you take it as a personal criticism."

"You feel uneasy," she decided, "at the misuse of funds. I do understand. Were it strictly up to me, I would take the gifts given me and feed my sisters. However, there is Biblical precedent for using the expensive oil rather than selling it, as Judas would have wished."

"Using it as an ointment to prepare the body for burial," I commented. "Not as a perfume for daily life. The parallel is faulty." She studied me intently, puzzled and more than a bit angry.

"It is a difficult thing," she said abruptly. "A certain amount of show and glitter is necessary, in order to be taken seriously by the sorts of people I believe we must reach. The image of ourselves as fanatics can only harm our cause. It is a balancing act—to walk proudly before men and humble one's self before God. Power and luxury are great temptations, Mary. Humility, discipline, self-abnegation are the only ways to remain pure to the cause."

Her words startled me, or rather, the way they were said. Margery Childe had seemed to me the soul of rational humanism, and although I had seen evidence of strong religious feelings, had heard Veronica's account of this woman's mystical trance, I had not been witness to such unbridled passion until now. For a brief and unsettling moment, her eyes gleamed with fervour and she sat forward as if to seize my shoulders; then it passed and she deflected an equally brief moment of confusion into reaching for the coffeepot and refilling our cups.

"You've touched on the topic for this evening, you know."

"Have I?"

"Yes. Power, we call it, but as that sounds so very aggressive, I often present the idea as 'eliminating powerlessness' when I speak to outside groups. You'll hear a great deal of energy, even anger, at our Saturday meetings. As I said to you the other night, the Vote is acting as a great deceiver, fooling women into thinking that the powers we took over for the duration of the War remain in our hands. In truth, the rights of women to own property, decide what their children will do, divorce themselves from a cruel or demeaning marriage, and a thousand other human rights held predominantly by males have developed little since the last century. We aim to see that changed. The suffrage movement is in disarray, aimless, splintered; I believe that we in the Temple can step in and pull the pieces together again."

"Through legislation?"

"Supporting proposed changes, yes, through educating voters and convincing members of Parliament. But we need women in Parliament—many women."

"You propose to stand for election yourself, then?"

"A seat is coming available in north London within the next two years. I have my eye on it, yes." Something in my manner must have communicated my doubts. "You seem dubious."

"I think you may be underestimating the misgivings the voting public will have with the idea of a 'lady minister' standing for office. In America, you might get away with it, but here?"

"I don't agree. We English are a sensible race, ready to overlook such minor foibles as an odd choice of religion or an inappropriate sex if the candidate is obviously the best one for the job. And after all, I've made a specialty of wooing sceptical males." She flared her eyebrows and I chuckled with her.

She talked a bit more about politics, about the coming march on Parliament and a bill concerning divorcement soon to come up for its first reading, about the as-yet-underexploited usefulness of newspapers for exposing gross inequities in a variety of laws, showing as they did the human face of the problems at hand, and about the challenge of building a public face and future constituency without compromising herself. She might well have lectured me all night had Marie not come in, looking, as usual, disapproving.

"Goodness," exclaimed Margery, "look at the time! Mary, I am sorry, but I must run. It was lovely to have such a nice long chat. I look forward to the next one. Will you stay for the meeting tonight?"

"Indeed."

"Good. Even if you're not politically inclined, you'll find it interesting. There are a number of very fine minds and hearts working in the Temple, and Saturday nights are their chance to speak out and be heard. However, I'm afraid it's time for me to excuse myself. Thank you for coming this evening. I look forward to our session on Monday. And . . . Mary? I'll keep in mind the red strap."

I went to the hall and took a seat in the back row, though Veronica would have welcomed me in the Circle's box, and I tried my best to make sense of the proceedings. I am not, however, as Margery had put it, politically inclined, and much of what was discussed so vehemently was more foreign to me than the politics of ancient Rome. I slipped away while the opposing packs were still in full voice, then, lost in thought, walked across half of London to my club.

I thought of Margery Childe and about the mystics I had

been reading about. I thought of Rabbi Akiva, and particularly about another dictum of his: that any nonessential words in a given passage must have a special significance, one not immediately obvious, yet of potentially great import. He was speaking of the interpretation of Scripture, but there was a broader truth in his dictum, one that Freud had recognised as well, and I could not help but wonder: Why had Margery so emphatically brought the ideas of discipline and self-abnegation into a discussion of poverty? The streets of London gave me no satisfactory answer.

CHAPTER 10

Sunday, 2 January–
Monday, 3 January

She wavers, she hesitates: in a word, she is a woman.

—Jean Racine (1639–1699)

Sunday dawned clammy and grey without, but it mattered not. Inside my head, the sun shone bright and hot. Birds sang. Today was the twenty-first anniversary of my birth, and I was free.

It cost me several expensive gifts to recompense my solicitor and the executors of the estate for going to the law offices of Gibson, Arbuthnot, Meyer, and Perowne of a Sunday morning, but the extravagance was worth it to me, and as they were all very familiar with my feelings concerning my guardian, and hers toward me, they were happy enough to oblige. They liked me, for some reason.

In deference to their sensibilities, I wore the sedate navy dress rather than one of my father's suits, and took a taxi. Upon reaching the gleaming door on the deserted street, I emptied the entire contents of my small purse into the cab-driver's hands. The last of my bridges having thus been burnt behind me, I reached past the spotless brass plaque for the equally spotless door handle, and entered my majority.

I walked out three hours later a wiser woman and a richer one, slightly tipsy from the goodwill showered on me and the glass of champagne somewhat subdued by the deluge of words and a precise knowledge of the responsibilities involved by my inheritance. I walked a short distance up the street and was hit by the realisation that I was also quite literally penniless. Feeling exceedingly sheepish, I went back and borrowed a few pounds from my solicitor. I also borrowed his telephone, but no message from Holmes had come to the Vicissitude in my absence.

I caught the next train to Sussex, and later that afternoon I supervised the gutting of my house. My aunt had left, at my instructions, taking her servants with her. Now on her heels, every stick of furniture, every carpet and curtain, every pot, pan, and picture was carried out and loaded onto an odd assortment of carts and motor lorries, some of it to be cleaned, some sold, but all to be purified: Of the entire house, cellar to attic, only my bedroom's furnishings remained untouched. When the last heavy boot climbed into its lorry and drove away, I flung open all the windows and doors to the night and let the sea mist scour the past six years from my house. My home.

Mine.

Half an hour later, chagrined for the second time that day, I was cursing myself for an utter fool and an idiot and hunting for something to boil water in, when I heard a voice calling from the front door.

"Miss Mary?"

"Patrick!" I clattered the coal scuttle back onto my bedroom hearth and ran downstairs to greet my farm manager. He was looking around the stark, freezing rooms dubiously, and I had to admit that the house had a ravaged look to it, all bare bones and flocked wallpaper. "Hello, Patrick."

"Evening, Miss Mary," he said, touching his cap. "They've made a clean sweep of it, I see."

"Precisely the words for it. The decorators come tomorrow and strip off the wallpaper, and then they'll start painting— top to bottom, front to back, everything clean and new. Except the outside, of course—that'll have to wait until the spring."

"It's going to be a different house."

"It is," I said in grim satisfaction. "Entirely different."

He looked at me, deliberate, phlegmatic, a friend. He nodded twice and pursed his lips.

"Struck me, though, what with everyone leaving yesterday, you might be a bit lacking tonight. Can I offer you a bowl of soup? Tillie sent it over, with a chicken and some of her cheese bread, if you're hungry." Tillie was Patrick's lady friend and the owner of the village inn, and her kitchen attracted patrons from Eastbourne and even London. I accepted with enthusiasm and walked with him down to his snug little house near the barn.

Later that night, warmed through and well fed, I reentered my house and stood without turning on the lights, listening to the faint shifting of 250-year-old beams, the whisper of the breeze from the kitchen window, the faint sensations of an old building adjusting itself to emptiness. I had loved this house as a child, our summer cottage before my entire family had died, killed by a car accident in California the year before I had met Holmes. I stood in the dark, wondering if I might coax back the shades of my mother and my father and my little brother, now that my aunt was gone, then walked up the stairs to stand in the door of what had been my parents' bedroom, a seldom-used guest room during my aunt's reign. It felt warmer in there, despite the swirls of mist. I smiled at my fancies, closed and latched the window, and went to bed.

In the morning, I rang Holmes, but Mrs Hudson had not seen him in some days. The house was miserably cold and damp and reproachful, and I abandoned it to the mercies of the decorators by returning to London.

Patrick drove me to the station in the old dogcart. When he had reined in, he dug into the pocket of his greatcoat and brought out a small wrapped parcel, which he thrust out in my general direction.

"Meant to wish you many happy returns, Miss Mary. Forgot to last night."

"Patrick, you didn't need to do that." Indeed, he never had before. I undid the wrappings, which looked as if they had been used a number of times before, and found inside a fine lawn handkerchief with my initials twining in one corner and a row of tiny purple-and-blue flowers chasing one another around the border. It was impractical, pretty, ridiculous, and touching. "How absolutely lovely."

"You like it, then. Good. Good. M'sister does 'em. Asked me what kind of flower you liked. Told her those what d'you call 'em, pansy things. Did I get it right?"

"Completely. I shall take it out and wave it in front of people all day and touch it delicately to the tip of my nose, and all of London will admire it. It's the nicest birthday present I've had."

"Get many, did you?"

"Er, no." Excluding the pounds, dollars, and francs, three houses, two factories, and a ranch in California, but those did not count as presents. "But I'm sure Mrs Hudson will have something for me when I see her."

"Mr Holmes not bein' one for gifts and all."

"The last present he gave me was a set of picklocks. This is immeasurably nicer," I said, waving it about. I leant over and kissed him on his bristly cheek, ignoring the furious blush this brought on, and dashed for my train.

I was outside the elves' shop when they put up the shutters, and I spent several hours there—expense I had expected, but I'd never have believed that clothing one's self could be so time-consuming! The two of them seemed oddly apprehensive when they ushered me into the room used for displaying the finished product (they used no live mannequins—in fact, the only people they seemed able to put up with having under foot were the two grandsons who tidied up after them, refolding the patterns, rerolling the strewn bolts of fabric, and sweeping up the pins and snippets). One glance explained their apprehension—the elves, confronted with a rail-thin woman nearly six feet tall in her stockinged feet who walked like a woodsman and hated frips and frills, had opted for drama, plain and simple.

The first piece, the only finished one, was not too bad, a suit of soft grey-blue wool with a wide band of Kashmiri-style embroidery, white and a darker blue, set into the jacket and the skirt. The fit was nearly as comfortable as my father's old linen shirt, for which I was grateful.

Then I caught sight of their idea of an evening gown suited to me.

One of the problems I have in clothing myself is a concern that never would have come up in my mother's day, but since the war, with dresses becoming ever more skimpy, evening wear was nearly impossible, and I had tended simply to avoid those few formal affairs I might have been tempted by. On Thursday, I had been forced to strip to the skin before Mrs Elf to demonstrate just why low necklines are not suitable: I do not care to have my fellows at table or on the dance floor offended by, or speculating on, my scar tissue. The automobile accident that killed my family when I was fourteen had left me just able to wear a cautious degree of décolleté, but five years later the bullet through my right shoulder put an end to any thoughts of bare flesh below the neck.

This dress, though—as a piece of pure engineering, it was fascinating; as a piece of evening wear, even in its present incomplete state, it transformed the padded torso on which it hung. High on the right shoulder, it dropped down to expose the left and continued down and yet farther down, the fabric barely meeting at the waist before it began a slit up the left side, where the hem angled down in a mirror image of the bodice line. The ice blue silk made it aloof—in any warmer colour, it would have been an incitement to riot.

I gulped, smiled feebly at Mrs Elf, declined her eager invitation for me to try it on, and turned to the other two half-formed outfits. One was a rich brown with slashes of crimson that looked as if they would appear and disappear with movement; the other was an intense eau-de-nil sheath with lots of little tucks and ruches that made the dressmaker's dummy look like the representation of a woman considerably more voluptuous than I. I clutched the fronts of my new overjacket and told them that I should have to return for a fitting soon, but I was not allowed to escape so easily. First I had to choose a pair of shoes from a huge stack they had caused to be delivered (I think they did not trust me not to wear mud-spattered brogues beneath their creation) and then Mrs Elf insisted on arranging her small cloche hat (matching embroidery, of course) on my hair, and even then I had to reassure them that I would remove my overcoat whenever possible.

I achieved the street, feeling like some child's costly doll. My toes were indignant about the unfamiliar shape they were being pushed into, and cloche hats always made me feel as if I were wearing a soft chamber pot. I was hungry and ruffled and not in the best mood to approach Margery and her Temple of women, and I stood on the street and said aloud the first thing that came to my tongue: "Holmes, where the hell are you?"

I was immediately abashed, particularly as neither the organ-grinder nor the pie-seller metamorphised into him, and even the man on the delivery wagon merely glanced at me and flipped the reins.

I had to admit it: I wanted to see Holmes, who, although one of the most peculiar individuals I had ever met, was none-theless the sanest and most reliable of men. Beyond that, I wanted to know what had been done with Miles Fitzwarren, four days ago. I had expected Holmes to be in touch before this. I stood undecided, until my eye caught on a POST OFFICE sign, and then I knew what I would do. I used their telephone, but no, the Vicissitude was holding no message for me, so, before I could reconsider, I wrote out a telegram and had it sent to five separate places, including his cottage in Sussex, if by some remote chance he had landed there. Each one said:

AM UNEASY NEED CONSULT
RUSSELL

I regretted it immediately the message had irrevocably left my hand. Perhaps he will not answer, I comforted myself, then took myself to Selfridges for something to eat.

My tutorial with Margery was for half-past four. Upon my arrival at the Temple, I sat down at a table and took out my chequebook, then handed the completed cheque to the star-tled secretary.

"This is for the library fund, which I believe Miss Beacons-field is in charge of. Would you kindly give it to her when she comes in?"

Communication within the Temple was excellent. Margery greeted me with all the naughts of my cheque in her eyes, al-though of course she did not mention it, and when she saw my clothing, the transformation was complete. I regretted it, but to have continued with her thinking me a bluestocking forced to mend the ladders in said stockings would have been too painful. I returned her greetings evenly, sat down, and pre-pared to teach her about her Bible.

We were interrupted only once, by a telegram for me, which read:

EIGHT OCLOCK DOMINICS
SH

It cheered me greatly. I folded it and made to thrust it into my pocket, only to discover that I had none. I put it instead into my handbag, turned back to Margery with a smile, and continued my brief overview of the history of Judaism and Christianity.

"So, we have the Hebrew Bible, roughly what you would call the Old Testament, composed of the Law, the Prophets, and the Writings; we have the intertestamental literature, or Apocrypha; and we have the Greek, or New Testament, com-posed of the four life stories of Jesus, called Gospels, the Acts of the early church, various letters and writings, and the Reve-lation of John.

"None of this was written in English. Now, that may sound ridiculous, but one gets so into the habit of thinking the Au-thorised Version as the direct word of God, that one needs to be reminded that it's only three hundred years old and was the work of men." I reached into my bag and took out two sheets of paper I had prepared earlier.

"I want you to commit these two alphabets to memory. This is Greek, for your purposes more necessary perhaps than the Hebrew. The letters are *alpha, beta, gamma*." I continued on to *omega*. "And these are the sounds they make, in this column. You'll see the similarities; that's because the alphabet we use in English grew in part from this one. Now, using the chart, sound out these three words."

She did it laboriously, but correctly. "*Anthropos; anēr; gunē*."

"Good. In English, we use the word *man* to translate both *anthropos*, "human being," and *anēr*, a "male person." *Gunē* is woman, the counterpart of *anēr*. Most of the time it is obvious which is meant, and occasionally one finds in Greek *anēr* when one might expect *anthropos*, and vice versa, but it is good to keep in mind, for example, the fact that Jesus is called the Son of Humanity, not the Son of a Man."

We worked on this for a while and I gave her a Greek Testament to use. We talked briefly about the difference between gender and sex, but since she was fairly fluent in French, I could pass lightly over that issue.

It was a stimulating ninety minutes, and I found, as I had expected, that Margery had a quick mind and an acute ear for theological subtleties, as well as having the determination necessary to overcome her lack of training. She might never compete with an Oxford scholar, but she might communicate with one.

That first session unavoidably served largely to point out to Margery her ignorance. She watched me slide my books into my case, a subdued and almost wistful look on her face.

"It's quite hopeless, isn't it, Mary?" she said with a rueful laugh. "I feel like a child who's just discovered sweets, standing at the sweet-shop window. I'll never have it all."

"It's hardly an all-or-nothing proposition, Margery. And remember Akiva—*you* can at least read."

CHAPTER 11

Monday, 3 January–
Saturday, 8 January

*Woman is the lesser man, and all thy passions,
match'd with mine,
Are as moonlight unto sunlight, and as water
unto wine.*

Alfred, Lord Tennyson (1809–1892)

I had to wait for a bath at the Vicissitude, and instead of the long, hot soak I had hoped to indulge in, I merely cleaned myself, jabbed the pins back into my hair, and dropped the embroidered suit back over my head. I was more fortunate with a taxi, which appeared only moments after I stepped onto the pavement, and it ducked and slid with ease through the lesser byways to the restaurant (which was not actually called "Dominic's," that being a pet name adopted by Holmes based on the proprietor's name, which was Masters.)

The maître d' recognized me (or perhaps he gave that impression to everyone) and escorted me to the table that had been reserved for Holmes. I declined his offer of drink and looked around me. The restaurant had suffered a brief period of popularity the previous year, but the tide had washed on, assisted, no doubt, by Masters's refusal to serve cocktails, provide dinner music, or offer unlikely foreign dishes on his menu.

Holmes came in, in one great shake shedding his overcoat, stick, hat, scarf, and gloves onto Masters's arms, and began to thread his way through the tables towards me. His bones were aching, I thought as I watched him approach, and when he came closer, the contrast between my mood and the gaunt grey exhaustion carved into his face hit me like a slap.

"Holmes," I blurted out, "you look dreadful!"

"I am sorry, Russell, that my appearance offends," he said dryly. "I did stop to shave and change my shirt."

"No, it's not that; you look fine. Just . . . quiet," I said inadequately. Only profound exhaustion, not just physical but spiritual, could so dim the normal nervous hum of the man's movements and voice.

"Ah, well, we cannot have that. I shall assume an air of raucous and disruptive behavior, if it makes you happy. However, I should like to eat first, if I may?" I felt reassured. If he could be rude, he was reviving.

He lowered himself into the chair and offered me a weary smile. "You, on the other hand, appear almost ostentatiously pleased with life." I sat under his unblinking gaze for a long minute and saw some of the lines in his face relax their hold. "Am I to take it that your majority agrees with you?"

"I believe it will. Holmes, where have you been?"

He held up a finger and half-turned towards the silent presence of the waiter.

"May we order our meals first, Russell? I have eaten irregularly since last we met and now find myself possessed of an immoderate preoccupation with the idea of meat."

We ordered a meal that even his obese brother Mycroft would have found more than adequate, and when we were alone, Holmes slumped back and prodded the bread roll on his plate.

"Where have I been, she asks? I have been on a passage through Purgatory, my dear Russell, into the abyss and halfway back. I have been a witness, a guide, and an unwilling participant in a young man's confrontation with the Furies, and in the process have been reminded of parts of my own history that I should have preferred to forget. I have been nursing, Russell—a rôle for which I am by nature singularly unsuited."

"You? You were caring for Miles? But Holmes, I never thought—"

"Your faith in my bedside manner is touching, Russell.

Yes, I have been helping to care for Miles Fitzwarren. Did you imagine I might draw him out of his house and habits only to deposit him in the hands of my medical friends and then wash my own hands of him? He would not have stayed, without me."

"So you . . . I am sorry, Holmes. I had no idea that I was getting you into that."

"No? No, I suppose you would not. It's quite all right, Russell; you needn't look so penitent. I've spent my entire adult life poking my long nose into the problems of other people; this is only a variation on that activity. Please, Russell, if you wish to be of some service, I beg you to remove that woebegone expression from your face. My old bones are much comforted by basking in the sight of your young radiance. That's better. A glass of wine?"

"Thank you," I said, speaking equally between Holmes and the discreet personage who materialised at the side of the table before Holmes could finish the phrase, poured, and faded away.

"How is Miles, then?"

"Ill. Weak. He is drained of self-respect, and filled with self-loathing. At least the worst of the physical reaction is over, thank God, and he's young and strong. The doctor foresees no immediate problems."

"So he'll be cured?"

"*Cured* is not a word one can use in this situation. His body will be clean. The rest is up to him."

Plates of food began to arrive.

"Well," I said when the waiter's arm had withdrawn, "I am most grateful, Holmes, though I hope it will not go on much longer."

He looked up sharply, a laden fork halfway to his mouth.

"Why? Has something come up?"

"Oh, no. No, nothing urgent, or I should have contacted you earlier." I concentrated on knife, fork, and plate. "I just . . . Well, it's odd, not having you there to consult, that's all."

147

I continued eating, and I was aware that seconds passed before his fork continued.

"I see," he said, and then added, "Would you care to tell me about your activities since Thursday?"

I would care, and proceeded to describe them. He ate with steady determination, and threw in the occasional comment and question. I told him everything, from my visit to the elves to the treatment I had given my Sussex home, and made him chuckle with an exaggerated account of boiling water in the coal scuttle.

Finally, over coffee, he sat back with the familiar unfocused gaze that signaled a massive rallying of forces beneath that thinning hairline.

"Whence comes her money?" he mused.

"Elijah's ravens did not bring him French hothouse strawberries on bone china," I agreed.

"My brother Mycroft's sources of information are better than ours for the purpose," he noted without emphasis.

I was absurdly warmed by his use of the inclusive plural, as if this were a case we were working, rather than a peculiar and individualistic interest of my own.

"She may have a supporter who holds the purse. It would be interesting to know. Politics makes for strange . . . partners, does it not?"

"You think it nothing more sinister than political manoeuvring, then?" he asked.

"Margery's money? Cynical as I may be, I cannot see her involved in anything more criminal than circumventing the labour laws. Of course, there's always sacrilege—that's a felony, isn't it? But not, I should have thought, an immensely profitable one. No, I think it's more likely someone was taken with her and decided to back her to the hilt. It would be very interesting to know who. A wealthy American dowager perhaps? A group of frustrated suffragettes?"

"Not an infatuated gentleman admirer?"

Extraordinary, how sensitive I was to the nuances of his suggestion. Or was he laying it on heavily for some reason?

"If so, he's very retiring. I've heard no rumours of her love life, aside from a gentleman in France."

"Yet she does not sound exactly aescetic."

"Hardly."

"Do you wish me to set Mycroft on the lady?"

"I think not yet," I decided after a moment of reflection. "Perhaps later, after the twenty-eighth."

"Ah yes, your great presentation. How does it progress?"

"Stunningly. Though poor Duncan is having cats because it seems a—what's the collective noun for a group of academics—a *gaggle*? an *argument*?—of American theologians are sweeping through on their way to a conference in Berlin and have announced that they will attend and have asked him to find them accommodation."

"It sounds as though you're being taken seriously." As usual, Holmes unerringly picked out the central issue.

"It's tremendously gratifying, and a great honour personally. I only hope that I feel the same when the sun comes up on the twenty-ninth."

"What about your plans until then? Are you finished with your coffee, by the way? Shall we walk? Along the Embankment? Or do you need to be back?"

"No, a walk would be lovely." After the business of putting on coats and the rest, we resumed outside, where the mist was creating cones beneath the streetlights.

"I can't very well go to Sussex; I'd freeze to death and either fret about how little the builders are doing or find I could not work because of their unending racket. No, the Vicissitude has a quiet reading room with three seldom-used desks. Not as good as Oxford, but I promised Duncan I'd go up every few days to placate him."

"Why stay in London? Margery Childe?"

"Well, yes, I shall see something of her. Why the interest in my plans, Holmes?"

"I fear I shall not be available as a consultant for a few days as you wished. I had a second telegram this afternoon in addition to yours. Mycroft wants me to go to Paris for a day or two and then Marseilles. Winkling out information from some none-too-willing witnesses in a large dope-smuggling case. Have you ever noticed," he added, "how Mycroft's metaphors tend to concern themselves with food?"

"You wanted me to go?" I was immensely pleased, although tentative about rebuffing his offer.

"I had thought you might enjoy it."

"I would, very much. But I can't. I'm not going farther from Oxford than London until after the twenty-eighth. If there's a blizzard or a rail strike, I can still walk there in time. It couldn't wait, I suppose?"

"I fear not. Another time, then," he said. He seemed untroubled, but was, I thought, disappointed.

"Another time, and soon. How long did you say you were to be away?"

"I shall leave Wednesday and return the following Thursday, possibly later if it gets complicated."

"Ah," I said, aware of a feeling of disappointment myself. "Well, perhaps I shall have something interesting for you upon your return."

He walked me to the door of the Vicissitude, and I wondered if I had imagined the faintly wistful turn of his wrist as he tipped his hat in farewell.

The next days went according to the schedule I had given Holmes: Tuesday in London, the morning at the British Museum with an expert in Palestinian and Babylonian antiquities, the afternoon with Margery, the evening at my club; Wednesday in Oxford; Thursday morning at the Bodleian, then back to London for an early-afternoon appointment with Mr Arbuthnot, my solicitor, followed by a fitting with the elves, from which I came away laden with dressmakers' boxes. I took them to the Vicissitude, where I found a parcel waiting for me, three books I had ordered for Margery. That I carried with me to Veronica's house, where we had, in her words, a "late tea or early supper" combined with a discussion about how best to arrange her lending library. We decided to leave early for the Temple, so as to examine Veronica's facilities there before the Thursday-night service. Another "love" night, and I admit I felt a degree of apprehension within the anticipation.

On the street outside the hall, I held up the parcel and told Veronica, "I'd like to give this to Margery before the . . . before her talk, or at least leave it with Marie. Is the main door locked?"

"I'm sure it will be, but I'll take you through the hall," she said. She led me through the back of the hall along the same route we'd followed ten days previously, although this time the final door was locked. She opened it with her key, and as I followed her up the stairs, she spoke over her shoulder at me.

"Margery is probably meditating, but we'll give it to Marie or else leave it in the common room with a note, where she's sure to— Marie! Whatever is the matter?"

I looked past her back, and there at the end of the corridor stood the phlegmatic maidservant, looking utterly distraught and wringing her hands as she stared at a door to our left. She did not respond until we were practically on top of her, when she whirled around and threw out her right hand at the door, more in supplication than in indicating the source of a problem. In the extremity of her emotion, both languages had abandoned her, and she just stood with her mouth working and her hand held out to the door.

"Margery? Is it Margery?" Veronica demanded. It had to be—nothing else would have this effect on her.

She nodded jerkily, found a few words.

"Madame . . . An intruder . . ."

"Marie," I said forcibly in English, to force her to think. "Is Margery in here?"

"*Oui.*"

"Is someone with her?"

"*Non. Elle est seule.* Alone, but . . . hurt."

"Margery's hurt? How?"

"*Il y avait du sang dans la figure.*"

"Blood on her face? But she walked in here by herself? And locked herself in?"

"Locked, yes, before I reach her. *Pas de réponse.*"

I lowered my head and spoke loudly at the door.

"Margery, if you're awake, please answer. You're worrying Marie and Veronica. If you don't answer, we're going to have to break down the door or call the police."

Nearly ten seconds passed before an answer came, her voice slow and low, but clear.

"No. Leave me."

I knelt down and put my eye to the keyhole, which, to my surprise, had no key in it. I looked, and stared straight into one of the most peculiar, dramatic, and inexplicable episodes I have ever witnessed.

What I saw and did next might easily have been rewritten by memory over the years. However, I have before me as I write these memoirs the letter I sent to Holmes the following day describing the events. So, in order to preserve the stark facts of what may or may not have happened, I shall copy directly from that letter:

> I saw the back of her head at the end of the room, before an altar. The rest of her was hidden by chairs, and her hair was in complete disarray, but its colour was clear and distinctive.
>
> "What room is this?" I asked Veronica.
>
> "The small chapel. Is she there?"
>
> "Yes." I stood up. "Stay here with Marie. I'll see if I can get in that other door, and if so, I'll come and unlock this one." I gave her no time to argue, but turned to the two doors that form the end of the corridor. The right one was unlocked, and when I looked in, I saw a connecting door. It, too, was unlocked, but when it came to the door into the chapel, I had to use my picklocks. I shot the bolt behind me, made my way around the edges of the chapel to the hallway door, and dropped my hat onto the doorknob so as to obscure the view from outside. There was an exclamation from the other side, which I ignored, and

went up to Margery where she knelt on the floor.

Holmes, she looked as if she'd been run down by a motor lorry. Her left eye was swollen nearly shut and the skin over the cheekbone had split, smearing blood down into her neck and back into her hair. Her mouth on that same side was thick and there were traces of blood on the lip, probably cut on the inside against a tooth. The rest of her was hidden beneath a woollen overcoat. She did not respond to my voice in any way, just stared unblinking at the Celtic-style cross on the altar.

I thought it best to determine the extent of her injuries before deciding what to do, and when I began to ease the coat from her shoulders, she made no more objection than a sleeping child. The coat was undamaged and clean but for some blood at the collar, but beneath it, her dress, in addition to the bloodstains from her face, was torn slightly at the neck and the right sleeve, and a line of lace along the front had been ripped free of its stitching. I unbuttoned the front of her dress—still no response—and found beneath it great red welts surrounded by areas of lesser bruising. From the shallowness of her breathing and the way she held her torso, I judged that her ribs were at least cracked.

She had been beaten, Holmes, by a man (or a powerfully built woman accustomed to using her fists) several inches taller than she, right-handed, wearing a heavy ring on his right hand. And no stranger, either, unless she had been walking down the street in January wearing only a thin woollen dress.

"Who did this to you, Margery?" I asked, but she was far away. I refastened the buttons, then took off my own coat and carried it over to drape across the second keyhole. I walked back to Margery and dropped to my knees directly in front of her.

"Margery," I said loudly, and repeated it several times. "Margery, you must answer me. You must see a doctor. I think you can walk, but if you don't respond, I'll have to carry you to your bed." The eyes in the ravaged face began slowly to return, and when they had focused on mine, I was relieved to see that the pupils were of an equal and normal size.

"No," she whispered.

"Margery, you've been injured. If you don't have your ribs strapped, every breath will continue to hurt you, and without stitches, that cut on your face will leave a scar. I'm going to open the door and let Marie help you to bed, and Veronica will have someone put out a notice cancelling tonight's service."

"No," she said again, more clearly but from a great distance, and it suddenly occurred to me that she sounded like someone speaking though the blanket of a hypnotic trance. I continued to look into her eyes, thinking. Unless her head injuries concealed deeper damage, the hurts she suffered were debilitating, but not life-threatening. (You will admit that I know something of injuries, personally and through my work at the hospital during the War.) No blows had landed lower than her rib cage, and the lack of cuts or swelling on her skull agreed with the evidence of her clear eyes. The hypnotic state, or whatever you wish to call it, was blocking the pain, and she wished strongly to be left alone. I nodded.

"I'll just have Veronica arrange to cancel the service, then. The doctor can wait until you feel ready."

"No doctor. No Veronica."

"You don't want the talk cancelled? Oh, come now, Margery. You're certainly in no condition to—"

"Go away, Mary," she said clearly. "Take them with you."

There seemed nothing to say to that. She was rational, an adult woman, and in no immediate danger. More than that, there was an urgency and command in her eyes that I did not care to go against.

While I was with her, the voices of Marie and Veronica had moved from the door where I had left them and followed my route through Margery's bedroom and dressing room, and Marie's key had rattled briefly but ineffectually in the lock. With a final glance at the woman's injuries, I left her, let myself out the hallway door—not a real lock, just a slim bolt on the inside—and called to the others. When I told them that Margery was not seriously hurt and that she wished to be alone, Marie immediately made to get past me to open the door. I stopped her, repeated her mistress's words, and shepherded them both down to the adjoining sitting room.

I gave Veronica a drink, offered Marie a glass of something and received a look of blistering hate, and set to wait.

At 7:30, I asked Veronica if there was anyone competent to take the service, were Margery to prove not up to it. (I did not tell them that I doubted that Margery should be able to creep onto the stage, even in heavy makeup, much less draw in enough breath to make herself heard even in the front rows, particularly without the services of a doctor's wraps and pain medications.)

"Ivy led it several times when Margery was away in December. Not preaching, of course, but hymns and readings." That did not advance us much, as Ivy was quite beyond the reach of mortal hymns. I asked her if there was anyone else.

"Rachel Mallory might do it." I sent her off to alert Rachel or whomever she might find of the possibility that her services might be called upon, then turned my warning gaze back on Marie, who subsided, muttering French curses that I wish I could have overheard more clearly, for the sake of my education.

The hall clock downstairs sounded the three-quarter hour.

"She will need me to dress her," Marie burst out.

"If she has not appeared by eight, you and I will go and see to her." The fury of her protests would have shrivelled a toad, but I cut them off with the curt remark to the effect that if Margery were to prove incapable of walking, Marie could hardly carry her without help.

The minutes ticked past. (Forgive the drama, Holmes, but I wish the account to be complete.) At six minutes before eight, I heard a door open and voices came to us, Veronica and another. Then they were at the door, both looking worried, and the other woman, Rachel, apprehensive and confused, as well. They stood in the doorway and Veronica started to ask me something, when her words were cut off by the sound of another door closing. Rachel turned to look, and she let out a short cry, and then Veronica, and Marie bolted past me, and to my utter confusion, the three of them were babbling a polyglot of relief and curiosity. Moreover, they were answered by Margery in a light, joking voice, and I still stood in the room when she came through the door with my hat and coat in her hands and held them out to me.

"You left these in the chapel, Mary," she said. "You'll need them later; it's chilly out tonight." And with that prosaic pronouncement, she turned and left, hurrying and apologising for being late. Before the door shut on them, I heard her laugh.

Holmes, there was not a mark on her. Her skin was whole and unbruised, the proud flesh subsided; she moved with her customary easy grace and had enough lung expansion to laugh. The only sign of what I had seen was the dampness of her hair on the left side of her face.

I searched her room, of course, and found no bloodied dress, but the collar of her coat had been scrubbed wet, and pressing the light brown fabric hard with a handkerchief produced a redbrown stain. From the coals in the fireplace, I sifted nine bone buttons and several metal clasps, all that remained of her silk undergarments and the damaged dress.

Marie found me on my knees before the fire and came close to attacking me physically. She berated me, called me seven kinds of a fool, and was silenced only when I poured the still-hot buttons into her hand and left.

Margery preached absolutely normally. She moved freely, projected her voice fully, seemed, if anything, more spirited and eloquent than she customarily was. She did not even end the evening any earlier.

I have seen people in an hypnotic trance ignore pain. I have even witnessed a hypnotised person hold his hand into flame and pass through undamaged, as the fire-walkers of the South Pacific are said to do. I have never heard of hypnosis used actually to remove existing injuries.

Your basic dictum in an investigation is, if faced by the impossible, choose the merely improbable. However, what does one do when faced with a choice between two impossibilities? I *saw* her face, Holmes, from a distance of less than a foot; I saw it afterwards up close, when she gave me my coat: There was not so much as a bruise, and she wore no more makeup than she had for previous performances: Furthermore, I am certain it was she, not a twin or double: She has two tiny flecks in the iris of her right eye, which cannot be duplicated. Either I have been the subject of a subtle, skilful, and powerful mental manipulation or I have been witness to what I should have said to be an impossibility: in short, a miracle.

I shall wait until tomorrow to post this, when I have seen Margery. Is it possible that she was moving under a deep hypnotic trance (prayer-induced?) which, when it breaks, will leave her with her cracked ribs and sore face? Will she show me a way to hide swollen flesh and cuts with invisible makeup? If so, I shall destroy this and feel exceedingly foolish. Still, I cannot help but wish that someone other than Marie had seen the damage, as well.

Yours, R

Postscript, Friday: I saw MC briefly this morning; by the mere fact that you have seen this, she is obviously in perfect health. Holmes, is this possible, or have you seen previous signs of madness in me and not mentioned them?

—MR

I was, as the letter reveals, badly shaken. I sent it to Holmes via his brother Mycroft, whose all-seeing eyes and octopus fingers would surely find him more quickly than the post office. Indeed, I received a reply the next day, a telegram that followed me from the Vicissitude to the Temple, where I was helping Veronica lay out shelves for her library. I opened the flimsy envelope with my dirty hands, read the brief note, then gave the boy a coin and told him that there would be no reply.

"What was it, Mary?"

I held it out for Veronica to make of it what she could.

"From Marseilles. '*Ab esse ad posse.*' 'From "it is" to "it is possible," ' " she deciphered, sounding none too sure of herself. "What on earth does that mean? Who sent it?"

"A wandering expert on early Rabbinic Judaism," I extemporized. "Someone at the British Museum came across a first-century inscription that seems to indicate that a woman was head of a synagogue in Palestine. I wanted to know if it was possible. Not a terribly informative reply, though."

"Odd," she said, studying the paper for hidden meaning. I distracted her.

"A better translation might be, 'If it happened, then it is possible.' A good slogan for the feminist movement, don't you think?"

"Surely not, Mary. The possibility must come first."

I plucked the sheet from her hand and pushed it into the pocket of my trousers.

"History is littered with odd happenings that were allowed to fade away into nothing, instead of being seized on as a new beginning."

The discussion moved away into Jean d'Arc, Queen Elizabeth, the women of the New Testament, George Sand, and on into the trackless wastes of theory.

That afternoon, I had a tutorial with Margery. Marie showed me in and then carried in the tea things, and without speaking or meeting my eyes, she managed to convey an attitude of scorn, superiority, and profound dislike. She had contrived to forget the state of her mistress's face, remembering only that I had tricked her and maltreated her and made a fool of myself. I sat and studied my hands until she had unloaded the tray and the door clicked shut behind her. I then looked across at Margery.

"What happened, Margery? How did you heal yourself?"

Amazingly, she laughed.

"You, too? Marie seemed to think I was on death's door the other night—why, I can't think. I'd have thought you have more sense."

"And you weren't."

"Of course not! I cut my finger on a broken glass and must somehow have rubbed it against my face." She held out her left hand. There was a plaster around the middle finger.

"Your dress was torn," I noted.

"Yes. I caught the lace on a rough spot on the bookshelf," she said evenly.

"Why did you burn it?"

"You are very inquisitive, Mary. I find the sight of blood repugnant, and bloodstains make me quite faint."

"May I see your finger, please?"

With a tiny shrug, she held out her hand. It was cool and quite calm in mine as I unfastened the plaster. The slice it concealed had been deep, had undoubtedly been made by a piece of broken glass, and had not been there on Thursday night.

There was nothing I could do, no one I could talk to. The only other person who had seen Margery's injuries was Marie, and she was firmly set on forgetting. If only I had allowed Ronnie to enter the chapel. With her as a witness, I might force an answer from Margery. As it was, mine had been the only eyes, and I was beginning to doubt them. I let loose her hand and she began to do up the plaster.

"It's very nice of you all to be concerned about me, but do save it for something serious like the 'flu." She turned her hand palm up to see that the plaster was neat, then paused, looking, I was certain, at the skin over her soft wrist that on Thursday night had shown a welt dotted with blood, where a ring worn by a clenched fist had slid across the ineffectual defence of the small hand. She stared at the spot as if mesmerised, and then she said, in a voice so low I could scarcely hear, "Occasionally, grace is given to the undeserving." After a moment, she turned her hand back, patted the plaster, and looked up at me, her eyes clear of anything but a slight amusement. "Now, Mary, you take your tea white and without sugar, is that right?"

We spoke that afternoon of one of her guide words: *love*. I talked about the earthy roots of the Hebrew *ahev* and *hesed*, *hashaq*, *dōd*, *raham*, and *rea'*, and the more ethereal Greek *agapē* and *phileos* (as well as *eros*, although it is not a part of the New Testament vocabulary).

I lectured, and she responded, but there was a distance between us. All I could think about was the ease with which she had lied.

As I gathered my books together, Margery stood up to fetch one we had left on her desk, and when she handed it to me my eyes were drawn again by the plaster on her finger. I decided to try one more time for an answer.

"You won't tell me what happened?"

"I did tell you, Mary. Nothing happened."

"Margery," I blurted out in a passion of frustration, "I don't know what to make of you!"

"Nor I you, Mary. Frankly, I cannot begin to comprehend the motives of a person who dedicates a large portion of her life to the contemplation of a God in whom she only marginally believes."

I felt stunned, as if she had struck me in the diaphragm. She looked down at me, trying to measure the effect of her words.

"Mary, you believe in the power that the *idea* of God has on the human mind. You believe in the way human beings talk about the unknowable, reach for the unattainable, pattern their imperfect lives and offer their paltry best up to the beingless being that created the universe and powers its continuation. What you balk at is believing the evidence of your eyes, that God can reach out and touch a single human life in a concrete way." She smiled, a sad, sad smile. "You mustn't be so cold, Mary. If you are, all you will see is a cold God, cold friends, cold love. God is not cold—never cold. God sears with heat, not ice, the heat of a thousand suns, heat that inflames but does not consume. You need the warmth, Mary— you, Mary, need it. You fear it, you flirt with it, you imagine that you can stand in its rays and retain your cold intellectual attitude towards it. You imagine that you can love with your brain. Mary, oh my dear Mary, you sit in the hall and listen to me like some wild beast staring at a campfire, unable to leave, fearful of losing your freedom if you come any closer. It won't consume you; I won't capture you. Love does not do either. It only brings life. Please, Mary, don't let yourself be tied up by the bonds of cold academia.''

Her words, the power of her conviction, broke over me like a great wave, inundating me, robbing me of breath, and, as they receded in the room, they pulled hard at me to follow. I struggled to keep my footing against the wash of Margery's vision, and only when it began to lose its strength, dissipated against the silence in the room, was I seized by a sudden terror at the nearness of my escape.

I made some polite and noncommittal noises, and quickly drew the session to a close. As I left the Temple precincts I tried to tell myself that Margery had not answered my question; however, I knew that she had.

CHAPTER 12

Sunday 9 January–
Thursday, 13 January

Man for the field and woman for the hearth:
Man for the sword and for the needle she:
Man with the head and woman with the heart:
Man to command and woman to obey;
All else confusion.

—Alfred, Lord Tennyson

I left the next morning for Oxford with a strong sense of brushing the dust from my boots. I would push it all from me, all the upset and confusion of Margery's apparent duplicity and, behind it, the impossible occurrences of Thursday night. Not for me the tugs and pulls of Right Action, the flattery of being Margery's personal tutrix, the courtly intrigue of the Inner Circle, the plotting and animosity of Marie. I did not feel any urge to take up my copy of *Mysticism* and find what Miss Underhill had to say about the physical side effects of mystical rapture, the bodily manifestations that could occur when the soul joined the Divine in a state of ecstasy. Like a child sick on too much chocolate, I wanted nothing more to do with it, and so I turned my back on London and returned to my own country.

The truth of it struck me as soon as I saw the spires of Oxford beginning to glimmer into solidity through the mist. This was, indeed, my home, as no other place was, or had been, or would be. I would buy a house here, I thought. What did I need with London? Or with Sussex, for that matter? Sussex could be for me what it had been for my mother, a summer cottage where I might play at farmer, but here, in this fold of earth between the rivers, this collection of buildings at once ethereal and human, was where my heart lay. Boar's Hill, perhaps, or Marston. Holmes did not need me; far better to take the initiative and remove myself from his irritated, and irritating, presence. I would speak to an estate agent—after the twenty-eighth.

I crawled into my books and pulled the pages up over my head, emerging only when I was thrown out of Bodley in the evenings. It was too dark to read by the light of the streetlamps, so I had a quarter hour or so of simple, mindless movement in the cold, wet, dark air to my rooms. In the mornings, I carried an umbrella, that I might read while walking back to the Bodleian, and each day I slipped into the library's miasma of old leather and damp wool with the incredulous relief of a caught fish being put back into its pool.

Even a fish must eat, however. On Wednesday, I rose briskly from my table to check a reference and was swept by a wave of nausea and dizziness. I grasped the edge of the table until it passed, and it dawned on me that I had not had a proper meal since—when, Saturday, Friday? And then, as if my body had been waiting for one sensation to push its way through to the surface, I was made immediately aware of dire thirst, the need to visit a WC, a stiff back, an incipient headache, and a corpselike sluggishness of all the muscles in my legs and arms. I dropped my pen and took up my coat and made straight for the nearest pub that served decent bar food: I couldn't even bear to wait while a proper meal was cooked.

The crowded pub was sprinkled with black gowns. I pushed my way in with determination, until halfway across the room a hand came up from the level of my waist and imperiously bade me stop. I focused on the people at the table and saw three familiar faces looking up at me with amusement at the grim set of my features, as well as with a flattering amount of welcome and bonhomie. I do not make friends easily, but these three were more than acquaintances.

"Mary, just the person! Reggie, go get her a pint," said Phoebe. The two of them were an unlikely pair, she big, brusque, and horsey, he small, neat, and quiet, but they were both brilliant in their shared field, which was cellular biology. I had met them two years ago in an anatomy lecture.

"Half a pint, thanks, Reggie," I said, reaching into a pocket for some coins. "And take these and get sandwiches, as well. Many sandwiches—I'm starving."

That half-pint was replaced by several more, and the sandwiches, though plentiful, did not go far in absorbing the alcohol. It was a merry lunch and a noisy one. Phoebe goaded me to the dartboard (which some tasteless undergraduate, if that is not a tautology, had stuck with a cardboard label printed ABSALOM) and after I had beaten every arm in the house, I played to the audience that had gathered, and I collected nearly two pounds in wages. An accurate throwing arm is perhaps the only truly remarkable skill I possess. It has, I admit, saved my life, but its chief benefit is parlour (and pub) tricks. I took in my winnings, used them to buy a round for the house, and sat down, glowing.

When we were thrown out for the afternoon closing, we stood blinking on the street, somewhat at a loss. The fourth member of the party, the one whose hand had so imperiously halted my progress, was a gangling young baronet, still an undergraduate, with a passion for both Einstein and a sweet-smelling blend of pipe tobacco, and an unexpected talent for brilliant puns and obscene limericks. I had known and liked him, as a friend, for eighteen months. This young man took a pipe from a tweed pocket, eyed it with mistrust, and put it back unlit.

"So, chaps. Back to the House to continue this mad debauchery, or some fresh air?"

We decided on both, a wide circle up through the Parks and down Mesopotamia, across the High and along the Cherwell, bleak and denuded of its summer wildlife of punters and ducklings, and down to the Isis, where darkness and a shower of sleet caught up with us almost simultaneously and sent us racing up the meadow to the shelter of the stairway. We burst into the warm rooms with an explosion of good spirits, coats and scarfs grew into a mountain on the floor, the baronet sent his scout off for hot drinks and poured us each a glass of cold fire, and we were all four of us brimming with an immense and inexpressible well-being.

It was Phoebe, inevitably, who gave voice to it.

"God, I'm so sick of work! I want to walk and walk until my fingers freeze and my feet blister and I fall into a room with a fire as if it were Paradise." Then, after hearing what she had said, she asked, "Why not? Why don't we?"

"Because it's raining out there, my dearest Phoebe," drawled the baronet. "And I want my tea."

"Not tonight; I don't mean tonight. But soon. Tomorrow? Why not tomorrow? Before term sets in again. Mary, shake away dull sloth, set an icy broom to the mental cobwebs. Just what you need."

Phoebe's irresponsible, imprudent, preposterous suggestion dropped into a ripe medium and bloomed brilliantly in my mind. With a flavour of throwing over traces and the logic of alcohol behind it, I agreed immediately, and the two genial men fell in. It was decided: A lengthy cross-country ramble was just the thing, for the four of us, as soon as possible. Tomorrow, in fact. We would meet at St. Sepulchre's cemetery, to set a cheery tone on our departure, at eight o'clock, walk up the river as far as our feet should take us, and stop the night at an inn or house, then walk back on Friday. If it rained, well, we should just get wet.

The next morning, I woke knowing I'd been a fool and knowing it was far too late to withdraw. I made haste to throw everything warm I owned into my worn rucksack and set off at a run to the cemetery.

We did get wet, but not disgustingly so. We followed the loops of the Isis upriver as it wound through the fields. In the afternoon, we came to a promising inn, ate a surprisingly good dinner, and drank too much. Phoebe and I tossed for the narrow bed, and I lost, but there were comforters enough to soften the floor. I fell asleep, beautifully tired and slightly drunk, and was awakened at three in the morning by a pounding on our door. I staggered across, wrapped still in a feather comforter, and peered out. My glasses were behind me in my boot, but I could make out the face of our host, irate and disheveled in the light of his lamp.

"Is one of you lot named Mary something?" he demanded. My heart tried to sink at the same time as it began to accelerate.

"I'm Mary Russell."

"That's it. There's a person outside, knocked me up at this gawdforsaken hour sayin' as how he absolutely had to talk to you, though why 'e can't wait for a decent hour I'm sure I—" I shut the door on his complaints and scrambled for clothing. Heavy jersey over my head, I stubbed my toe on my boots and rescued my spectacles, began to put on my woollen trousers and got them started back to front, but by that time, Phoebe, calm and efficient, had the candles lit and I could see.

"What is it, Mary?"

"Some kind of emergency for me. I'm going to see."

"Shall I come?"

"Good heavens no. No reason for all of us to climb into wet clothes in the middle of the night. I'll be back in a tick."

"Take your walking stick," she ordered. "A strange man, at this hour."

It was easier to obey than explain.

Mine host led me down the narrow stairs to the door—he had actually left my messenger standing on the step. It was raining again, but despite the garments, I did not think I knew the figure huddled there.

"Holmes?" I said doubtfully.

The man turned, and I did know him, but only just.

"It's Billy, isn't it?" Once an Irregular, then Holmes' long-ago messenger boy from the Baker Street days, and even now in middle age an enthusiastic assistant in London adventures. He looked completely out of place here.

"Yes, mum."

I reached out and hauled him into the inn, ignoring the splutters of the innkeeper. Billy peeled off his hat and woollen scarf, looked around for a place to put them and then dropped them on the floor, and began to unbutton his overcoat with blue fingers. I dug into my pocket and thrust a bill of some denomination or other into the innkeeper's hand. His protests cut off sharply.

"A fire, if you please. And hot drink, and food."

"Yes, miss. Right away, miss."

"Miss Russell, I have orders to take you to Town, immediately I find you."

"Speed will not be improved by your turning to ice," I pointed out, "and I have no boots on. Are you alone?"

"My brother's outside," he muttered, and finally succeeded in opening his coat. He groped into an upper pocket and came out with an envelope. I took it but did not open it.

"How did you find me?"

"They told me at your house you'd set off on a walking tour, planned on putting in for the night along the way. There were twenty-eight other places I asked before this one." The memory of twenty-nine sets of furious landlords was not, it seemed, a pretty one, and I was struck by the vision of two Cockneys hunting through the wilds of Oxfordshire in a London taxi, pounding on door after enraged door.

"Why didn't—oh, never mind. Here's something hot. I'll call your brother in. No, you dry out a bit." The envelope in my hand, I put my head out into the rain and gave a low whistle, and the driver of the cab was soon huddled beside his brother in front of the fire, drinking a horrid mixture of tea and brandy while their coats steamed. Only then did I put my thumb into the envelope and tear open the flap. I read, in Holmes' cramped and hurried hand:

> Veronica Beaconsfield had a nearly fatal accident on the Underground today (Thursday) at four o'- clock. Her doctor says she will recover. She's in Guys, room 356. I've dug Watson out to stick to her.

So much for my walking tour. So much for the resumption of my real life. I went up for my kit and followed Billy and his brother out to the incongruous, mud-spattered black taxi.

* * *

My friend Ronnie lay in her private room, bandage and plaster and a few inches of skin. The grizzled figure beside her bed looked up as the door opened, and I knew that under the coat lying across his knees there was an old Army revolver pointing at me. His face lightened immediately and he got to his feet, leaving the coat on the chair. I stepped back into the corridor so as not to disturb Veronica.

"Mary! I was beginning to wonder if the lad had fallen into the Irish Sea." "The lad," Billy, being old enough to be my father.

"Hello, Uncle John. It was good of you to turn out at this hour." I kissed his smooth cheek. He'd taken time to shave, which indicated that Holmes had stayed with Veronica himself for some time before asking Watson to report for guard duty. "Where is he?"

"Holmes? Don't know. Around somewhere. He'll probably look in towards morning. Any time now. How have you been, Mary? Did you have a good Christmas? And I missed your birthday, but I have a little something for you, brought it back from Philadelphia. Lovely town, that."

"Oh, yes? Er, thanks, and Christmas was fine." I couldn't remember Christmas just at that moment. "How is Veronica? Do you know what happened?"

"Seems to have fallen in front of a train coming into an Underground station. Elephant and Castle, was it? Or Borough? No, the Elephant and Castle station. Concussion, broken arm, lots of scrapes and bruises. Nothing bad, lucky girl. Shockingly easy to happen. Still, Holmes seemed to think it mightn't have been an accident, so I'm playing nursemaid for a few hours. Her people were here, and a young man with Holmes, but no one else, just the nurses. Until you, of course."

"Look, Uncle John, he was right. We can't take chances. Even . . . even the hospital staff. Keep a close eye, and if anything doesn't seem right—an unnecessary procedure, an injection—don't let them do it until you check."

"You and Holmes." He shook his head. "The two of you think I'm new to the game. I'm not about to let a stranger inject her with a lethal dose just because he's wearing a white coat. Me, of all people! Your Miss Beaconsfield is safe. Now run along and get yourself cleaned up before they catch sight of those boots and throw you out of here."

I decided that Holmes was right to trust Watson and that there was nothing I could do for Veronica here. I turned to go, but Watson made that noise beloved of Army colonels—which can best be transcribed as "harrumph"—so I paused.

"By the way, er, Mary, has Holmes brought up . . . That is, did he say anything to you about, aharrumph, well . . . fairies?"

"*Fairies?*" Holmes had many arcane interests, but nursery tales were a new one to me.

"Yes, you know, fairies, dancing, with wings and . . . you know, wings and things." He waved his hand vaguely and looked uncomfortable.

"I haven't seen a great deal of him lately, but when I did, he never mentioned them. Why should he?"

"You haven't seen it, then. It truly was not my fault," he burst out, "and if I had been consulted, I certainly should have objected. I have already complained strongly to the editors, but they say I have no recourse, since he's only my agent."

I seized on the last word.

"Are you talking about Doyle? What has he done?"

He groaned miserably. "I cannot bear to talk about it. Holmes was insufferably rude to me, said I'd ruined his career by getting mixed up with the man, said no one will ever take him seriously again."

"I'm certain he meant no such thing, Uncle John. You, of all people, ought to know how he is. He'll have forgotten it in a week." Whatever 'it' was.

"It's been two weeks; he was barely civil when he asked me to come here. Truly," he pleaded, "there was not a thing I could have done."

"I'll talk to him about it," I said soothingly, but if anything, his agitation increased.

"No! No, you mustn't. He's not rational on the subject, believe me, Mary. Say nothing about fairies, or Doyle, or *The Strand*. Or about me."

"Fine, Uncle John, I'll take care. And don't worry, it will come out right in the end."

Puzzled, I took my leave, and walked out of the hospital without, I think, any obvious haste. Even Watson, who knew me well, could not have guessed that the very sight of a hospital set my flesh to creeping. Even long days of VAD work during the war hadn't cured me. Such was my haste that the street sweeper outside the hospital had practically to trip me with his broom to catch my attention, despite the fact that I had known he would be there, in some guise or other.

He did not look at me, but dumped the frayed and much-mended broom into its slot on his trolley and ran a disgusting glove under his nose. I nearly missed his muttered "London Bridge Station, first bench on the right" before he began to cough, great rheumy coughs. I left before the act grew any more graphic.

The morning paper I bought outside the station had a small notice about Veronica's accident on a back page. I sat reading my way towards the front, noting the reports from the hunting field (the Prince of Wales had been out with the Warwickshire, and they'd taken three foxes. Brought from a zoo and loosed that morning, I thought sourly). A "Jurywomen's First Murder Trial" would see those good pioneers in the judicial world locked up for the night, alongside the male jurors, in an hotel in Aylesbury. Someone was using a live relic of the Boer War as a doorstop. The drawing of a light frock with an unlikely hat was entitled "Tailor-made for the Riviera." I had passed on to the ever-cryptic and often sinister messages of the agony column before a heavy and unpleasantly odorous body dropped beside me. I shook the paper in indignation and slid away, burying my face more deeply into its pages.

"You're back sooner than you thought, Holmes. Why aren't you in Marseilles?"

"Even I cannot productively interview dead men, Russell. Someone reached the three witnesses before I did."

I tried to look at him around my newspaper, which was fluttering uncontrollably in the breeze. I shook it upright in irritation.

"Is this subterfuge necessary, Holmes? I feel a fool. Next thing, we'll be establishing passwords."

"Perhaps it is not, but earlier there was a watcher at the hospital. He followed Miles Fitzwarren's taxi—don't drop the paper, for pity's sake!—so we shall have to move him, as well." Holmes' voice was slurred—from wearing a set of toothcaps, no doubt—and then became more so as he bit into a sandwich (bacon, from the smell of it—how could he chew bacon with false teeth?). "Miss Beaconsfield will be safe for a few days, but Fitzwarren and I shall go to her parents and convince them that she needs to be put into private care. That ought to clear the decks for action."

"What do you want me to do?"

"Go back to the Temple. The answer is there."

"What about the police?"

"What about them?"

"Shouldn't they be notified?"

"What an admirable citizen you can be," remarked the filthy, unshaven man beside me, around a mouthful of sandwich. "By all means, do go visit your friend Inspector Lestrade. He'd be terribly interested."

"For goodness sake, Holmes, be serious."

"You may be right," he said, to my astonishment. "Miss Beaconsfield cannot be moved for at least three or four days, and Watson will be wearing a bit thin by then. May as well put the official force at her bedside. One could only wish the Met weren't so confoundedly possessive about their crimes. They'll be very uncooperative when we refuse to divulge where we've spirited her away to. Still, it's no crime to aid a victim or investigate a church, not yet."

"What about Miles—" I started to ask, but was interrupted by a loud, meaty voice standing over us.

"Awlright, you," said the constable, "these benches aren't put here for you to eat your breakfast on. If you're not goin' in to buy a ticket, move along." Holmes obediently dropped the remainder of his sandwich into an unspeakable pocket, turned and lifted his hat to me (although I was still wearing my mud-encrusted walking gear), and shambled off to his cart. The PC turned his attention on me, and I hastily folded my newspaper around the thick envelope Holmes had slipped onto the bench, put it into my pocket, and joined the queue of early-morning workgoers to buy my ticket.

CHAPTER 13

Friday, 14 January

Women have in themselves a tickling and study of vainglory.

—John Chrysostom

At the cost of an apologetic smile and some feeble explanations, I achieved a room at the Vicissitude, and immediately the door was locked behind me, I took out the envelope Holmes had slipped me and spread it out across the bed. To my astonishment, it proved to contain a positive wealth of disparate information concerning the Temple, with snippets about finances interspersed with histories, some of them quite detailed, of a number of members, including Margery Childe.

As I read through it, and decided that Holmes could not possibly have assembled the documents himself, I gradually realised that the most interesting thing of all was not the information itself, but the way it was presented: The writing was that of one individual, distinctly a professional clerk; the ink and the paper were both uniform and fresh; the method behind the collection, although at first glance nonexistent, revealed a devious style of investigation I thought I recognised; and the sorts of information—interviews with chairwomen, the revealing contents of a dustbin, lengthy periods of following key members about—smelt of an investigator with machinations more subtle, and more extensive, than those of the official police.

It appeared that for some reason Holmes' brother Mycroft, whose title of "accountant" for an unspecified governmental agency referred to more than fiscal matters, had become mildly interested in Margery Childe's church several months earlier. He had begun to account for her movements, her resources, and the people she came into contact with, and when his brother had appealed for information, it was simply a matter of having a clerk copy the file. It would have taken Holmes and me weeks to duplicate the work here, and inevitably we should have missed things.

My diagnosis of a mild curiosity came not so much from the desultory nature of the information as from the actual gaps, which would never have happened had Mycroft turned his full attention to the question. There was a report of Iris Fitzwarren's death, for example, but not the details. The full report of the inquest held on Delia Laird's drowning the previous summer was included, but it only confirmed in greater detail what I had already learned from Veronica. The file contained various unimportant items, such as a mention of Veronica's flirtation with Socialism her final term at Oxford, but for the most part the information was thought-provoking, even in its incomplete state.

It was in the collection of financial data that Mycroft had dug deepest, and with the most disturbing results.

Delia Laird's "good family" that Ronnie had referred to was also a wealthy one. They were long-established manufacturers from the Midlands, and Delia herself had inherited a sizeable part of her father's estate when both her brothers were killed in France. She had left all her money to Margery. There was a great deal of money.

Iris had left less, a matter of ten thousand pounds. And there was a third woman, whose name I had not heard before: Lilian McCarthy. She too was moderately wealthy, she too had died—in a road accident, without witnesses, back in October. It seemed to have been her death that sparked Mycroft's interest. And she too had left a major part of her possessions to the New Temple in God.

Aside from that trio of suspicious deaths, however, Mycroft had found nothing concrete. There were rumours, for the most part about Margery herself, but none were substantiated and many were absurd, the sorts of wild accusations a figure like Margery Childe would tend to attract. Even Mycroft, who had never met the woman and who possessed an endless depth of suspicion, particularly when it came to females, had clearly discounted the tales of black rituals and witchcraft. She had no criminal record, she was generally well regarded even by people who detested her message, and she seemed to have solid alibis for the days all three women had died. I was interested to see that Ronnie's information had been correct, that Margery had indeed been married and widowed. In fact, this was the most devious thing Mycroft had been able to find about her: that she did not talk about having had a husband.

The Vicissitude had gone silent as my fellow club members dressed and ate and left for the day. With difficulty, I inserted the sheaf of papers back into the envelope and took it with me down the hall to the bath. I didn't actually think about what I had read, not with the top of my mind, at any rate. Instead I found myself thinking about Holmes as he had given me his brother's information, about his mania for privacy and his penchant for disguise. I lay in the bath and visualised him scuttling into one of his bolt-holes as an elderly newsboy and popping out dressed as a nun, into another with a street pedlar's tray of pencils and stationery and out again with mops and buckets, and I wondered, not for the first time, how one went about establishing even a single bolt-hole, where one might come and go, at odd hours and in odd attire, without exciting comment. One could hardly place an advertisement. In addition, a bolt-hole would lack a cook, and one could not expect to receive mail. The number of guests one could take in were also limited.

My mind wandered through the various and sundry drawbacks of the surreptitious life and, drowsing chin-high in the warm water, I became more and more bogged down in speculation about minor details: What if one needed a garment that was in another bolt-hole? If the building changed hands, did one arrive one evening like a rabbit finding its burrow dug up? And was there any way of rigging a telephone, and what if builders came through the wall in making improvements, or rerouted the electricity and cut one off? It was soporific and pleasant, and it was interrupted by a voice in my inner ear that came with the clarity of a divine pronouncement, the remembrance of the gentle remark made at parting by my solicitor, Mr Arbuthnot senior.

"You are now a very wealthy young lady, Miss Russell, who unfortunately has had little practical preparation for the experience. Please, if there is anything I or my partners can do to assist you, we should consider it an honour. We all had a great deal of respect for your parents." He had added, with a less official tone to his voice, "I was very fond of my cousin, your mother."

Precisely at ten o'clock, I was on the telephone to his offices. The haughty secretary immediately gave way to the senior partner.

"Miss Russell, how very good to hear from you," he asked politely.

"Mr Arbuthnot, I hadn't intended to disturb you with my enquiries, but you generously offered assistance the other day, and I need some help."

"Yes, Miss Russell?"

"I need a flat and a maid, and I don't want to spend days looking and interviewing. It occurred to me that someone in your offices—I shouldn't want to disturb you personally, but a junior member, even a secretary?—might guide me to some responsible agents."

"But of course," he said, relieved that my demands were no more outlandish than this. "Perhaps I might research the matter a bit and telephone you shortly?"

I gave him the number of the telephone I was speaking from, thanked him, and rang off. In ten minutes, the instrument rang, and I was listening to Mr Arbuthnot's smooth tones.

"Miss Russell, I believe I have just the man for you. His name is Mr Bell. Shall I put him on the line?"

I agreed, thanked him, and his voice gave way to a brisk young East End voice.

"Miss Russell?" he began. "The name's Freddy Bell. You're looking for a flat and a maid, Mr Arbuthnot said? Can you give me an idea of precisely what you'll be wanting, where, and how much you want to spend on it, so I can help you?"

"Yes, certainly. I don't need anything terribly large, five or six rooms. Plus quarters for servants, of course. The location is important, though. Not Bloomsbury necessarily, but not far away, if you take my meaning."

He caught it immediately, and my opinion of Gibson, Arbuthnot, Meyer, and Perowne went up a notch.

"A place where you can take anyone, no matter their station, without them feeling out of place, that the thing?"

"Precisely. Impressive, but not depressing."

"Right you are, miss. And the servants?"

"I had thought a maid who can cook the occasional poached egg."

"A housekeeper who does hair," he noted. "And a driver."

"I prefer to drive myself," I said firmly.

"For those occasional times when you need a butler, or chauffeur?" he persisted. There was a short silence.

"Are these relatives of yours?" There was a longer silence.

"Miss, I value my position in the firm. I hope to go far. I would not care to jeopardise it for the world."

"My apologies, Mr Bell. I shall consider it. And keeping in mind the fact that you value your position, I shall open myself up to being taken advantage of and say that at the moment, price matters much less than speed. I may not retain the flat for long, or the servants, but I require a working establishment quickly, practically overnight, in fact, and I realise that I must pay for that. Now, about the flat. Can you recommend an agency?"

"I am your agent, Miss Russell. Mr Arbuthnot asked me to do it for you. I shall make some telephone calls now, and if I might call for you this afternoon, I hope to have some flats to show you by then."

"So soon? That's very good. Three o'clock, shall we say? At my club?"

"The Vicissitude, isn't it? At three o'clock. Until then, Miss Russell."

What an unlikely conversation. Most "very wealthy young ladies" might have been offended at being fobbed off on the firm's Cockney, and indeed most partnerships kept a pleasant young man with a school tie for the purpose. Gibson, Arbuthnot, et cetera, was more imaginative than I had thought, and, I slowly realised, my mother's cousin had trusted me not to be misled by the accent. I looked forward to three o'clock.

The externals, for the moment, I could leave to our Freddy. Closer to home, I should have to take my own appearance in hand; however, I was not exactly certain where to begin. The elves had only four hands between them, and, too, I did not think their hallmark of subtle quality was precisely what I wanted here. An image a shade more brash perhaps; flagrantly expensive, instead of incidentally so—off-the-rack clothing, but top of the line. I went down to interrogate the concierge and manager, but those earnest and sensible ladies had even less of an idea where that sort of clothing was sold than I did. The other guests, however, were more helpful, and I soon set off to conquer the world of London fashion with a list of names and streets in one hand and a chequebook in the other.

The limitations of time were a disadvantage, but I and the shops struggled through. I arrived back at the Vicissitude, to find the entrance hallway stacked high with dressmakers' boxes, the concierge's desk buried under hatboxes, parcels of stockings and silk undergarments spilling into the next room, the corridor lined with boxes of shoes and boots, and the stairs blocked by a small escritoire, a silk carpet, and a lacquer birdcage. (The bird was to be delivered later, to the flat. I did not want it to die of neglect.) A delivery man in green livery was just leaving, and the concierge stood aghast, a large box in her arms which bore the august name of the most expensive furrier I could think of. Her face was pink with astonishment. I don't suppose anything quite like it had happened to that right-thinking club in its entire history.

"Miss Russell!" she squeaked. "Miss Russell, I really must—I must ask you what this is all about. We haven't room for these all, and really, for safekeeping . . ." She waved her hand and nearly dropped the heavy box.

"I know, Miss Corcoran, I do truly appreciate the trouble you've taken, and I promise to have everything out of the way before dinner." Freddy Bell would just have to cope. Prove his worth. "But just now I must go and change; I'm flat hunting," and snatching up a few boxes at random, I fled with them up the stairs, bruising my hip on my new escritoire.

Freddy Bell arrived punctually at three in a Daimler complete with liveried chauffeur. He blinked when he saw me—not perhaps what Mr Arbuthnot had led him to expect—and the club's concierge blinked when she saw the automobile. I smiled graciously all around and allowed myself to be handed into the car. However, I did not allow young Mr Bell to sit up with the driver; shouting through the window becomes tiresome.

"Miss Russell, good afternoon," said the young man as he settled himself beside me.

"Mr Bell," I greeted him.

"I have a list of seven possible flats. If you'd like to look at them, perhaps you might tell me what you like or don't like about each one. I've also set interviews with three maids and two married couples, beginning at seven o'clock at the firm's offices. Does this meet with your approval?"

"Very much," I said, and with a tap on the window, we eased sedately out into traffic.

The third flat on the list was ideal. It actually was in Bloomsbury, just off Great Ormond Street, a sleek and spanking-new building built on a piece of land cleared by a bomb from a Zeppelin in 1917. The flat was on the fourth storey, six large rooms and a kitchen. The owners were on an extended tour of the Americas, and they had furnished their possession in the latest brittle style, all angles and tubes, metal and mirrors and unnecessary drama, expanses of fawn carpeting and pale primrose walls and draperies. The bedroom contained a bed the size of a small luxury liner and a plethora of exotic fabrics draped across the walls, windows, and every surface. Perfect—horrible, but perfect.

"I'll take it."

"You will? That is to say, I'm glad you like it. There are also servants' quarters available, in the basement."

"I'll take them, too. You said this relative of yours can cook?"

"Oh yes, mum. Miss."

Glutinous puds and watery vegetables. Well, no doubt I should be taking my meals in restaurants a great deal.

"Fine. I'll sign the lease papers now, if you can find the representative, and then perhaps you'd send someone to the Vicissitude for my things."

"Certainly."

The servant question was settled as easily, when Freddy Bell's second cousin and her husband turned out to be a quiet, intelligent pair whose former employer had suddenly moved out to India, where servants are cheap, if maddening. Freddy and my new butler made several trips to the Vicissitude for my newly acquired finery and knickknacks while my maid-housekeeper investigated her new quarters downstairs.

While the two men were away on a trip, I prowled my new, if temporary, home, somewhat overwhelmed at the speed that is possible with the phrase "Cost is no object."

One of the few and, I hasten to add, completely inadvertent advantages given me by being under my aunt's care for the past six years was that I had come out of it quite unspoilt by money. My allowances were so small as to be miserly, and my pride kept me from appealing to the executors of the estate to remedy the situation of a wealthy young woman kept in penury. Although I knew that in theory I was probably one of the wealthiest women in Sussex, in practice I accepted that I had less pocket money than the butcher's daughter.

The only time I had escaped these fetters was the day two years earlier when, with a purse fat with notes borrowed from Holmes, I had indulged in a perfectly glorious orgy of shopping. On a much larger scale, today's profligacy had brought the same pleasure.

My rôle in the Temple investigation would be built upon the foundation I had already laid. My stunningly generous donation to the lending-library fund, my jumble-sale clothing replaced by couture would be followed by the entrance of the heiress come fully into her inheritance. By now, Margery would have seen the notice in *The Times* of the estate settled on one Mary Russell of Sussex. She would use me as her tutor, yes, but she would also woo me.

I had been standing for some time at the sheets of glass that formed the front of the flat, looking down through the bare branches of the young plane trees at the passersby, when the taxi drew up for its final time into the illuminated patch of wet paving stones below my window. Freddy got out and bent to take up an armful of parcels, and suddenly, shockingly, for a brief instant I was back on another street two years before, looking into a horsecab at the mangled, maliciously shredded remains of the clothing I had so happily bought during the day. Freddy crossed the pavement and disappeared beneath my feet. I shivered briefly at the inexplicably ominous feel of the night outside, closed the curtains, and went to let him in.

I slept that night in a costly flat, my wall cupboards bursting with ridiculously expensive clothing, my ludicrously vast bed emanating the ghostly presence of a man's cigars and a woman's perfume, my new walls all but bare, my bath bereft of towels or soap, my kitchen stripped to the dish-washing soap.

The entire game was marvellously entertaining.

My new servants were named Quimby. I called them Q and Mrs Q, and I have no idea how they looked upon such flighty familiarity, because I never enquired. I had asked them to be in the kitchen at nine, and they were. I plunked down in a chair at the tiny table and waved them to the other chairs. They looked at each other and went gingerly to place their backsides on the very edges of their seats.

"Very well," I began. "No doubt you've already guessed that I really haven't the foggiest what to do with you two. I'm twenty-one, I've just inherited a packet, and I decided to find out what might be done with it. It's no good pretending I'm used to a formal household; I've never had a ladies' maid, a chauffeur, or a butler, so I'm sure to step on your toes a dozen times a day, answering the telephone, picking up the mail, fixing myself a meal—everything I'm not s'posed to do. I'll drive you potty. If you're willing to put up with me, I'm willing to give it a try. What do you say?''

None of that was absolutely true, but it fit the image and laid a basis for my future behaviour, which was to do whatever I damn well pleased, and not to be ruled by my servants. They looked at each other again, then Mrs Q stood up and began to unpack the large basket she had brought with her, which I was pleased to see included coffee, and Q eased back a fraction in his chair.

"It suits us, miss."

"Grand. I'm sure we'll muddle along somehow. Now, first things first. Mrs Q, we need food. Fortnum and Mason knows me; just tell them I'm here instead of Sussex. Q, do you know a decent wine and spirits merchant?"

"Indeed, miss."

"Lay in whatever people like. Mixings for cocktails. You mix cocktails?"

"I do, miss."

"Yes, I know, it's a disgusting habit, but what can we do— people like them. And Q, if you'd rather wear a lounge suit, I don't mind."

For the first time, he looked disturbed, looked, indeed, as if I'd asked him to serve in a bathing costume.

"That will not be necessary, miss."

"You see?" I said, and saw in his eyes that he knew instantly what I was referring to. Perhaps this was going to work, after all. "I have a hundred things to do today. I won't take breakfast, but some of that coffee would be superb. I like it strong, by the way, with milk first thing in the morning but otherwise black. No sugar."

"I'll bring it in to you, miss," said Mrs Q. "Shall I draw your bath first and help you dress?"

"I think I can just manage that today, thanks, and I'm sure

you must have better things to do. Sometimes, though—do you do hair?"

"I started as a ladies' maid, miss, before I married. I don't know as how I'd be much of an expert with the short hair so many wear these days, but yours I can do, however you like."

"A woman of many talents. And Mr Bell said you cook?"

"Not what you'd call haute cuisine, miss, but I've produced the occasional formal meal in my day. In fact, the Vicerene of India asked for a recipe."

"Did she now? That's very good to know. I shan't be giving any formal meals for a while, though, so perhaps today you'd take care of getting the place running. Towels and things?" I spent a few more minutes explaining my preference in colours, my dislike of floral scents, and my convoluted dietary restrictions (I do not eat pork, if given the choice, nor shellfish, nor cream sauces on meat, nor half a dozen other things). We decided also that I was more apt to be out for meals than in, and if she had on hand the makings for omelettes and the like, I should be satisfied. I then sent Q out to hire whatever car he thought appropriate (which responsibility made him glow with a quiet ecstasy) and Mrs Q to buy the mountains of paraphernalia necessary for the establishment, then, managing manfully to dress myself, I shook myself free of domestic entanglements and took a taxi across the river to Guys Hospital. From there, I would go to New Scotland Yard.

CHAPTER 14

Saturday, 15 January

A woman's guess is much more accurate than a man's certainty.

—Rudyard Kipling (1865–1936)

Miles was with her, the two of them nearly concealed behind the heaps of flowers, fruit baskets, cards, books, and magazines. Neither of them recognised me. He rose warily, but politely; she looked up politely, and then her face beneath its bruises and bandages changed.

"Mary? Good heavens, it's you, Mary! You look marvellous!"

"The astonishment in your voice is so flattering, Ronnie. Oh don't be silly, I know I usually look like a dog's dinner, but if I don't spend some of this money, the revenue people will eat it all. Good afternoon, Lieutenant Fitzwarren. Sit down—I'm not staying." Of course he did not. "Ronnie, tell me what happened."

"I don't know, Mary, truly I don't. All I can remember is, it was such a crush—there'd been something on the line and the trains hadn't been coming in, something like that. And then it was cleared and I remember feeling the air moving down the tunnel, and then people started to push forward, and that's all, and I'm very glad I can't remember the rest of it."

"You didn't see anyone you know?"

"If my own mother had been there, I shouldn't have seen

her, unless she had been immediately in front of me. Why do you ask?"

I studied her carefully and decided her colour wasn't too bad.

"Because there's a possibility you were pushed, Ronnie."

"But of course I was pushed, I told you—now wait a moment, do you mean . . . ? You mean deliberately pushed, don't you? What a mind you have, Mary. Why on earth would anyone want to do that? It was an accident."

"Has it not occurred to you that there have been rather a lot of fatal accidents around the Temple recently?" I asked her gently.

"No, Mary! Don't be absurd. That's . . . No."

"Why do you think we haven't let you be here alone? First Holmes, then either Dr Watson or Lieutenant Fitzwarren."

That took most of the splutters out of her mouth, so that she lay there, as white as her sheets. Her hand sought Miles's, who looked, I thought, as ill as she did.

"I'm very sorry to do this to you, Ronnie, but something is going on in the Temple, and I have to find out what it is."

She looked at me for a long minute, her face growing ever more pinched. "Iris?" she said finally.

"She was part of it, made to look like some kind of warning from the drug world. And in October, Lilian McCarthy. And late August—"

"Delia Laird. You actually believe this."

"I don't know, yet. Ronnie, how much are you leaving the Temple in your will?"

"Twenty thousand. Why do you . . . No. Oh, no, Mary, you can't mean it."

"Ronnie," I said clearly and with all the honesty I could manufacture, "I don't think Margery is involved."

"How could she not be, if you're right?"

Good question.

"She could not have been personally involved with any of the deaths," I said. "She had alibis for all three of those periods of time."

"Someone else, then?"

"It's possible that someone close to Margery is doing it. Even if it's something Margery could do, I don't see that it's something she would do. I'm sorry, I'm not being very clear."

"Yes, I see what you're saying," she said eagerly. "Even if Margery could commit . . . murder, she wouldn't do it for money."

It was not quite what I had meant, but I left it.

"Then who?" asked Miles.

"Someone, as I said, close to Margery, someone ruthless, intelligent, and who either benefits somehow from Margery's wealth or who imagines he or she is doing Margery a service."

"Marie," whispered Veronica.

"Would Margery have gone to York without her?" I asked. Veronica's face fell.

"No. Probably not."

"I'll find out, but I doubt she has the brains for it. Who would know about the wills . . . who leaves what?"

"Margery, of course. Rachel Mallory, she supervises the office staff. Come to that, anyone with access to the filing cabinets. There's a file in there entitled 'Wills,' so we have a record of bequests."

Convenient. "Is the cabinet kept locked?"

"Oh, yes. But the keys are in Susanna's desk drawer, which isn't locked."

"So no more than two hundred people could have seen the file. That narrows my search down considerably: all I have to do is find someone who can read and who loves Margery. Easy enough."

"What are you going to do, Mary?"

"Make myself indispensable around the Temple and ask many chatty questions." And soon, I did not add, I would make suggestions that I was about to write a new will.

"Be careful, Mary."

"Me? Good heavens, there's no danger for me. You haven't said anything about Holmes, though, have you? That he's a friend of mine?"

"Not since you told me not to."

Oh dear. "And before?"

"I don't know. I vaguely remember saying something about the two of you, just a remark, such as 'I had rooms in Oxford with a girl reading theology who actually knew Sherlock Holmes.' Something like that."

"Whom did you say it to?"

"I can't remember, Mary, I'm terribly sorry, but there were half a dozen people, and I think I was at the Temple, but it might well have been a weekend house party."

She was getting upset, which would do her no good.

"Don't worry about it, Ronnie. If it comes to you, let me know, but something that vague—it's not likely to be of any importance. What is important is getting you well and keeping you safe. I don't think they'll try again, but I don't wish to lose a friend because I misjudged a madman. I'd like you to do two things for me."

"Anything."

"Listen to what they are before you agree," I suggested. "First, I'd like to inform Scotland Yard. They'll come and ask for a statement. You'll have to tell them about the will, and when they ask if you were pushed, all you need tell them is that you can't remember it but it might have been possible. They'll put a guard on your door until the doctor says you may leave."

"Is that it?"

"No. The second thing is, I want you to go away. Not for long, two or three weeks at the most, but thoroughly away. We'll tell everyone you're in a private clinic, recuperating. You can even go to one, if you like."

"I can't, Mary."

"You must. You're going to be out on home leave for at least three weeks, in any case. We'll just make you a home from home. Please, Veronica, I beg you. My eyes are going to be too busy to keep one on you."

"If I may?" Miles spoke up. "There's a lodge I use, in Scotland. A bit on the bleak side this time of year, but there's a large woodpile."

"Perfect," I got in before Veronica could say no. "You'll take Ronnie up as soon as the doctors here give her leave, and you'll stick to her like glue until I give you the high sign."

I completely ignored Ronnie's slow flush. Miles shot her a glance and retracted his hand, then scowled sternly down at her bedcover.

"There're servants there, of course," he said. "As chaperones. If you don't think—that is . . ."

"I can only see one possible complication, Lieutenant Fitzwarren," I said, and stopped there. He met my eyes, and his spine slowly straightened.

"There is nothing that need concern you, Miss Russell. While Veronica—while the safety of Miss Beaconsfield is my responsibility, you need not worry yourself as to my fitness."

"That is most gratifying, Lieutenant Fitzwarren," I said, and it did not seem odd to either of us that I, barely more than a girl, should stand in judgement concerning him. "Either Holmes or I will be here tomorrow, and we will arrange for transport and communication. In the meantime, you will, I hope, say nothing about this to anyone, even your families." They agreed, nervously. I turned to go, and my eye fell on the shaky pile of reading material. "Is there a *Strand* in there?" I asked, and without waiting for permission, I began to paw through the stack until I found the December issue, with the article I was looking for. "May I borrow this? Thanks awfully." I stepped forward and kissed the air above Veronica's cheek, a gesture that, combined with the form of the thanks, surprised me perhaps more than it did her. Hospitals did odd things to one's personality, even if one were only passing through.

Fighting the urge to wiggle my fingertips at them in farewell, I left them to their uncomfortable love. Two weeks or so in a Scottish hunting lodge would drive them either into each other's arms or at each other's throats.

I made my way to a public telephone and asked for Scotland Yard's number. While waiting for the connexion, I glanced through the article, "An Epoch-Making Event—Fairies Photographed," coauthored by Arthur Conan Doyle, to all appearances written in utter seriousness. It was illustrated, as the title said, by photographs of vapid-looking female children gazing right through the images of stiff fairy figurines, the artifice of which was so blatant that I should have taken it as a joke (a rather sophisticated one, considering Conan Doyle's usual heavy-handed style) had it not been for Watson's reaction. It seemed that the world in general did not regard it as a joke. Conan Doyle's fascination with the supernatural had been growing over the past years, particularly after the loss of his son in the war. Spiritualism had until now mostly been kept out of the stories he published about Holmes (with the occasional flight of fancy that caused the real Holmes to growl) but to have a piece of sensational literature such as the fairies article published, not only under the Doyle name, but in the very magazine the Holmes stories appeared in, was thoughtless, to say the least. Holmes blamed an American influence for the Doyle eccentricity, and as I read the article, I had to admit that his disgust had not been without justification.

The telephone crackled and the woman told me I was connected to Scotland Yard. It took a short time to reach the Criminal Investigations division, but once I was through, I put on a voice.

"*Good* afternoon," I cooed. "I should like to speak with Inspector John Lestrade, please. He's not? Oh dear, that *is* too bad. Could you tell me then—" I waited, and when the voice had stopped, I paused in silence for a moment, then applied a layer of ice to my voice. "No, there is not 'something you can do for me,' my dear man. The duke would not care for that in the least. Could you—" This second interruption I greeted with a lengthy silence, then dropped my voice and froze the man's ear. "Young man, if you wish to attain higher rank in your chosen profession, might I suggest that you learn to kerb what is obviously a deep-seated tendency towards ill manners? Now, *as* I was saying. Could you kindly tell me when the good inspector might be present to receive a telephone call? And before you are driven to ask—no, it would *not* be convenient to have him telephone me, or I should have suggested it in the first place."

The man on the other end cleared his throat and spoke in strangled tones. "Yes, mum. You'll understand, mum, I can't be positive about his schedule, but I know he has a meeting here in the Yard at four, and he'll for sure come to his office afterwards, around five."

"Very well. You will tell him to expect my call at ten minutes past five."

"Mum? If I could just tell him who's—" I gently rang off. Good. Five o'clock gave me plenty of time to dress myself, for Lestrade and for my debut at the Temple.

I spent the afternoon at the Turkish baths, being steamed, pounded, powdered, and perfumed, then manicured, plucked, coiffured, and dressed in clothing brought at my direction by Mrs Q, until finally, polished and gleaming, I was escorted carefully out to the pavement, a moving work of artifice, a monument to the skills of beautician and couturier. All I wanted was a brace of Afghan hounds. Taxis slavered at my feet.

I chose one whose leather work did not look as though it would put ladders into my stockings.

"Scotland Yard, please. And I'd like to approach it from the Embankment side, not from Whitehall."

"Right you are, miss."

I could, of course, have asked Mycroft to retrieve a more complete account of the police investigation into Iris Fitzwarren's murder, and in fact I did think about it, for perhaps five seconds. I had become involved in this whole affair through a friend, and if there was a case here, it was mine, not Holmes'. Veronica's safety was now a personal responsibility, and I had no intention of allowing Holmes to talk me out of carrying it through in my own way.

My goal for the evening was Inspector John Lestrade, the only person I knew to any degree within Scotland Yard. Holmes knew Lestrade professionally, had worked with his father numerous times in the Baker Street days, and I had met Lestrade two years before when he had been "in charge" of the investigation into the attempted murders of Mr S. Holmes, Miss M. Russell, and Dr J. Watson. (Needless to say,

Holmes and I had solved the problem; Scotland Yard took the credit.)

Unfortunately, Lestrade was not involved in the Iris Fitzwarren case. Even if he had been, I could hardly ring him up casually and expect him to answer my questions for the sake of some dubious old times. Indeed, considering the impression I'd left him with, I knew that if he were told that Mary Russell was waiting outside his office, he very probably would go out the back entrance. No, a subtler approach was required.

When the hideous building was in sight, I tapped on the glass and signalled the driver that I wished to stop on the river side of the road. He stopped beneath a streetlamp and came around to speak with me.

"Driver, we need to wait here for a few minutes. I wish to intercept a friend who will be coming out soon, but I . . . I cannot go in to meet him, his . . . colleagues might not approve. Do you take my meaning?" I met his eyes, and by the dim light, he gave me a grin, though not the knowing leer I was braced for.

"Yes, miss. Will he be expecting you?"

"My good man, you have a ready grasp of the essentials, I see. No, he is not expecting me. Would you mind awfully . . ."

"Just tell me what your friend looks like, miss, and leave it to me."

Something in my description changed his knowing expression to one of discreet puzzlement. (Lestrade's height, perhaps, compared with mine? Or was it the phrase "like a ferret, or rat"?) However, he took up his lounging position readily enough, and when Lestrade appeared (at 5:20, not 5:15, as I had estimated, but with the resentful irritation I had expected to see in his shoulders, from the ducal telephone call that had not come), the driver pushed away from the wall, looked towards the car for my white flag of confirmation, and dodged across the heavy bridge traffic to approach the inspector. Captions were unnecessary in the pantomime that followed, and it ended with Lestrade, puzzled and wary and still irritated, following the driver to the cab.

He put his head in and ran an experienced eye over me.

"Now, miss, what's all this your driver's been telling me about?" His eyes had reached my face again, and this time they stopped there. He leant forward, squinting, and then his ill-shaven jaw dropped. "My God. You're—Miss Russell, I never expected to see—is Mr Holmes—" He jerked his head back out the door, leaving his hat inside, but when the now frankly baffled driver failed to metamorphise into the *éminence grise* of a purportedly retired consulting detective, Lestrade looked back inside and cleared his throat.

"Why, Miss Russell, I doubt I'd have recognised you on the street. You've, er, you've changed." Such acuity had led Holmes to his renowned high opinion of the official police. I had to admit, however, that the colourful flapper in the dark taxi did bear only a passing resemblance to the gangly, ill-dressed nineteen-year-old he had last seen.

"Full marks, Inspector, although I believe that the first time we met, I was in evening dress. But I agree, it has been quite a while." I held his hat out to him.

He took it, glanced a last time at my silken ankles, and withdrew his gaze to my face and his thoughts to my presence.

"You wanted to see me, then?"

"I should like to buy you a drink, Inspector."

For some reason, this did not seem to meet with whole-hearted enthusiasm. On the contrary, his habitually cramped features tightened into open suspicion.

"Why?" he asked bluntly.

"Or dinner, if you have the time."

"Why?"

"You will become uncomfortably damp if you persist in that position," I commented mildly. It was drizzling.

"You're right. It's time I took myself home."

"Just one drink, Inspector, and a few questions. And, I may have some information in return."

"About?"

"Iris Fitzwarren."

"Not my case," he said immediately, his eyes sharpening.

"I am aware of that."

"Why me?"

"A drink, Inspector?"

His long day and a strong disinclination to put himself into my clutches battled with a simple curiosity, the policeman's innate desire for information, and other, more elemental urges, as well. With the circumspection of a male black widow spider approaching his beloved, Lestrade climbed in beside me. The driver stood waiting.

"Where to, miss?"

I looked to Lestrade for advice, and he in turn spoke to the driver.

"You know where the Bell and Bugle is?"

"I do, sir," he said, and climbed into his seat, fastened the rain cape over his legs, and we started up.

"But," Lestrade said to me, "I'll pay for the drinks."

The darkness hid my smile. I had thought he would.

I allowed Lestrade to hand me out onto the wet pavement, then arranged with the driver, whose unlikely name was Mallow, to wait for me. The man had definite possibilities as an ally, and I did not wish to lose him.

Lestrade had a pint of ale; I ordered a mixed cocktail, a monstrosity I normally avoided like the plague but which fitted my present persona. He swallowed a third of his glass at one go, put it down, and fixed me with a beady eye.

"Very well, young lady, what is this all about?" he demanded. I smiled pityingly, to tell him it hadn't worked, and began deliberately to remove my purple gloves, finger by finger.

"Ladies first, Inspector. Before I tell all, I need to know the things the newspapers are not saying about the Iris Fitzwarren case."

"What makes you think I know anything about it?"

"For pity's sake, Inspector, it's obvious you do. I should think you had a meeting with the investigating team just this afternoon." The ventured shot sank home, to my relief. I pressed on rapidly. "There was something strange about her death. What was it? What connexion did it have with the club? And why are you looking for Miles Fitzwarren?" His head came up fast.

"Do you know where he is?" he demanded.

I fluttered my eyes at him and complained prettily.

"You see? No one ever tells me anything. *I* didn't know you'd lost him. How could I? I don't know what you people *do* know—how could I possibly suspect what it is you *don't* know?" I ran one polished finger around the rim of my glass and looked up at him. "However, if you'd like to tell me what you do know . . ."

"Oh, stop that," he said irritably, and I laughed and settled back in my chair. "All right, but it'd better be worth it, and no one's to know where it came from."

"No one but Holmes," I agreed, and he nodded and drank deeply.

"You're right," he said in a low voice, "though I don't know how you guessed." He stopped and shot me a glance not lacking in humour. "Oh, right, I forgot. You never guess. How you deduced, then. Yes, there was something peculiar about her death. A couple of somethings, but most of all was the way she was killed. We've had three other deaths like hers in the last few months, two during the same night back in July, then one in late November. There was . . . a kind of mutilation common to all four, after death."

"Facial?" I suggested. He started to ask me how I had guessed, then visibly changed his mind.

"Yes. The earlier ones we knew about; the two who got it first had given us information concerning a certain importer, shall we say. The other one had a grievance against him, too."

"A personal one?"

"Yes. He was apparently not involved with the use of . . . the importer's wares, but his cousin, who was also his closest friend, was. The cousin died, he began to look into the death on his own, and five weeks later was killed for his trouble."

"Inspector Lestrade, I'm not a solicitor looking for evidence of slander. The man was, or is, I assume, importing drugs. He's killed three people who threatened to expose him, and he may have killed Iris Fitzwarren as well, for the same reason he killed the nosey cousin. What is his name?"

"Where is Miles Fitzwarren?"

"Safe. Unwell, but as safe as Holmes and several responsible doctors can make him. If you wish, Holmes can arrange that you or your colleague be taken to him. Now, the name?"

"Tommy Buchanan is the name he's going by at the moment. Heard of him?"

"No. Why do you connect Iris with him, other than the circumstances of her death? Oh come now, Inspector, I have to know before I can give you my information."

"Don't want much, do you?" He stood up and looked at my half-empty glass. "Another drink?"

"Thank you. The same." I lifted the glass as if to drain it, and when his back was turned, I took it from my lips and exchanged it for an empty glass from the next table. Its previous owner was deep in conversation with a young lady, and neither of them noticed, even when he absently picked up my lipstick-stained remnants and tossed down the strange contents. Lestrade came back.

"All right. But for Holmes' sake, it better be good. There was a note in her handbag, written on a corner of newspaper, that said, 'Tommy, the Poseidon, midnight.' The Poseidon being Buchanan's club," he added. "She got there about eleven-thirty, but Buchanan wasn't there that night; in fact, he wasn't even in town. He was having dinner with some friends in Surrey, spent the night there."

"Convenient."

"Yes, but verified."

"So he personally is off the hook."

"Exactly."

"Colleagues, employees, and henchmen?"

"Half a dozen of them. Nothing specific on any of them yet, but two of them have a history of knives."

"What else was in her handbag?"

He hesitated at the abrupt change of direction but could find nothing objectionable in it.

"Nothing out of the ordinary. Money purse, powder compact, lipstick, small mother-of-pearl penknife, handkerchiefs, key ring with the keys to her flat, to her parents' place, and one to each of her free clinics. A fifth one hasn't yet been identified, some sort of house key. She hadn't been robbed, there was money in the purse, and she had a gold bracelet and a small pearl ring on."

"Inspector, I should very much like to see a detailed list of what she had with her."

"I'm sorry, Miss Russell, that's going too far."

"I could possibly tell you where the fifth key goes."

He snorted. "You'd better tell me a lot more than that. How about starting with what your interest is. Was she a friend of yours?"

"Not at all. I did meet her, the night she died, in fact."

"Where? Not at the nightclub?"

"Unfortunately, no. At the Temple."

"*You?* Went *there?*" A curious melange of incredulity, amusement, and scorn swept across his tight little face. I ignored them all.

"Yes, I went there. Your fifth key almost certainly opens a door in there—if not an outside door, then to one of the offices."

"Fine, I'll tell—I'll let the investigator in charge know. Why were you there?"

"Business." I exaggerated.

"What kind of business? Last I heard, you were in your studies at Oxford."

"A client asked that I go there."

"A *client?* Oh, blimey, not you, too. Who's your 'client'?"

"I'm sorry, Inspector, there's a certain confidentiality involved that I'm not prepared to breach just now. There are other things, however, that I think might interest you." I looked around us. The smoke-filled room had become crowded and very noisy, and we had to raise our voices. "Not here, though. I want to go back to your office." Lestrade looked exasperated. "I know, but you wouldn't have let me come up if I'd just sent my name up, would you?"

"Why the—why on earth should I let you come up now?"

I leant forward to meet his eyes directly, then said clearly, "Fraud. Three women dead, probably murdered. Preventing a fourth woman's death."

We went to his office.

The room had not changed much in the two years since a marksman had come close to murdering me with a bullet through the window that overlooked the river. The dust was thicker, the walls grimier, but it was surprisingly neat, particularly when compared to Holmes' rat's nest of a study. I took the proffered chair, across the desk from him, and nearly quailed before his ferrety glower. Nonetheless, I had to see the list. I told him so, and he exploded.

"All right now, Miss Russell, I've been patient with you, God knows why, on a Saturday night when a Christian might expect to be at home. You keep hanging in front of my nose these little hints about how much information you have, but it's me who talks. Another little technique you learnt from your teacher Mr Holmes, no doubt. I'm beginning to think you don't know anything about this business at all."

"Would I do that to you?"

"Why ever not?"

"Would I do that to Holmes?"

That gave him pause, because it was obvious that I, a person whom Sherlock Holmes had called his partner, would not voluntarily put my partner's relationship with the police into jeopardy without very good cause.

"Please," I asked, "please, just let me see the list, and then I'll tell you all I can."

He did not notice that I had not said "all I know," but I thought he was going to refuse, anyway. However, in the end he went to his filing cabinet and withdrew, not a single sheet, but the entire file.

"God knows why I'm doing this," he grumbled, throwing it onto the desk in front of me. I knew why: It was because of Holmes. I said nothing, however, and opened it gratefully. He went off and I vaguely heard the rattle of kettle and cups while I rapidly scanned the pale carbon copies and committed to memory the details of Iris Fitzwarren's movements and possessions that last night of her life.

There was very little in it that was new, as Mycroft had given the information to Holmes, and Holmes to me. It was not politic to let Lestrade know this, however, and it was just possible something had slipped by Mycroft's source. I read, and at the end of the pages, I sat back and reached automatically for the cup beside me, which startled me by being cool. Lestrade was in his chair, his heels up on his desk, reading another file and making notes in a notepad. He looked up.

"Find what you were looking for?"

"I wasn't looking for anything in particular, Inspector."

"You were skimming through that pretty fast."

"I was reading. I have a couple of questions."

"Just for a change," he said sarcastically. He closed his file and put his feet on the floor.

"Er, yes. Did the beat constable make a regular round, or did he vary it?"

"It was regular. It is no longer."

"I see. Also, is this list of the articles in her handbag in any order? Or just a list?"

"Let me see that." He took it, glanced through it, handed it back. "It will be in the order he took the things from the handbag. The man who wrote the report is very particular that way."

"I see," I said again. The precise list had not been included in the oral information transmitted. I thought for a moment before I realised that he had spoken. "Sorry?"

"I asked you why it mattered, and if you do a Sherlock Holmes on me and tell me it's perfectly elementary, I swear, you'll never get so much as the time of day from me in the future."

"Oh, no, I haven't picked up that particular bad habit. I was just trying to come up with a reasonable explanation that would cover the facts. The constable wouldn't have gone through her handbag, searching for identification, would he?"

He spoke through his teeth, which I noticed were small and pointed.

"Miss Russell, the only person who opened her handbag was the man who wrote that list."

"Because, you see," I hastened to mollify him, "she had a head cold."

"Who?"

"Iris Fitzwarren. A bad cold. A terribly runny nose." I wasn't getting through to him. In a minute, he would hurl me out the door. I sighed to myself. "Inspector, why should a woman with a bad cold bury her handkerchiefs at the bottom of her handbag? There were none in the pockets of her coat, but two were underneath the compact and lipstick, and even underneath the paper with the name and address of the club. It's possible she had her handbag open and rummaged around for something—that might explain why the heavier items were on top—but she would never have put her only handkerchiefs away at the bottom. It was a very bad cold, and on a miserable wet night like that, she would have been blowing her nose almost continuously. Plus, there's the address, right on top. She didn't need it after she got to the club at eleven-thirty, but when she was killed, it was found on top of everything else. Unlikely if she'd put it in, but just where it would be if her murderer had emptied her bag of anything incriminating, shovelled the stuff back in, and then slipped in a note for the police to find, a note which would either explain her death in a satisfactory way or incriminate Tommy Buchanan, or both."

I watched his face covertly as I talked, seeing that although the significance of the handkerchiefs had escaped him, that of the note's placement had not. My estimation of the official investigators rose slightly. I continued.

"Obviously, if the note had been deliberately put there, it becomes extremely unlikely that Tommy Buchanan had anything to do with it, or his thugs. However, it would have to be someone who knew about Buchanan and also knew . . ." I fell silent for a moment, then resumed slowly. "Someone who also knew about the style of murders linked with him. I assume that various people know about that, newspaper people, for example, even if they were stopped from printing the details?"

"Undoubtedly."

"Does the *Clarion* have any women reporters?"

"Two, I believe." He was looking cross again, building up to another, no doubt final explosion, which I hastened to defuse.

"May I tell you a story, Inspector? It is not a long story, nor a pleasant one, and the amount of guesswork that has gone into it would horrify Holmes, but elements of it, I know to be the truth." He eased back into his chair with an "at last!" expression on his face.

"It begins with the war and the perfectly appalling numbers of young men who were killed and crippled during those four years. At the beginning of the War, there were around six million men in this country of a marrying age, between twenty and forty. By the end of 1918, nearly a million of them lay dead. Another two million were wounded, half of them so badly damaged, mentally or physically, that they may never recover. Where does this leave some two to three million healthy young women who would ordinarily have married healthy young men and spent the rest of their lives caring for babies and husbands? The papers refer to them—us!—as 'surplus women,' as if our poor planning left us here while the men were removed. The women who ran this country, and ran it well, from 1915 to 1919, have now been pushed from their jobs to make way for the returning soldiers. Strong, capable women are now made to feel redundant in both the workplace and the home, and no, Inspector, this is not just suffragette ranting; this is the basis of our case. . . ."

"Have you met Margery Childe?"

"I have. A woman who was staying in her church went home to visit her husband, and got herself murdered."

"What was your impression of her?"

"A nice woman, but strange."

"Strange how?"

"It was . . . She didn't seem to be listening to us. She answered our questions. She was polite, friendly even, but it was as if what we were asking weren't important. As if we had interrupted something and she had her mind still on it while she was talking with us—but, you know, I didn't get the idea that she was in any hurry to get back to anything specific. She was just . . . well, distracted, I suppose."

"Yes. And yet when one of her women comes to her with a problem, she listens with her entire being concentrated on that woman, because that is where her interest lies, because, quite simply, she has little time for the concerns of men.

"What happens, then, when this extravagantly charismatic, articulate, single-minded individual comes into contact with a segment of the population that is feeling unwanted, unimportant, and useless? What happens when some of those people are also very wealthy (remember all those young men whose deaths passed large parts of fortunes onto their sisters), when they are educated and come from powerful families and are so elated at being given a purpose, something of value in their lives, that they would give everything to the person who has given them back their dignity? Yes, exactly.

"You know that Iris Fitzwarren left money to Margery Childe. She left it to the New Temple in God, but it amounts to the same thing. Not all her money by any means, but quite a lot. Are you also aware that another young woman died last October, in an automobile accident, and left the Temple a small fortune? And a third drowned in her bath in August, leaving a larger one?"

Lestrade's eyes narrowed unpleasantly.

"I personally was not aware of that," he said carefully. "I will find out if Inspector Tomlinson knows."

"Perhaps at the same time you could mention that another wealthy Temple member was injured two days ago when she fell onto the tracks of the Underground, just as a train was coming into the station."

The big building was not silent, I thought in the minutes that followed, just sturdily built, like the opera house it had originally been designed as. Lestrade reached for the telephone, and in a minute he was speaking to a man who, his intonation implied, was marginally his superior, and something of a rival.

"Tomlinson? Lestrade here. I have someone in my office with information on the Fitzwarren case. . . . Because I was here, and she knew me slightly from a previous case. . . . Yes, I do think it's worth your coming in. I don't think I ought to give you her name or her information over the telephone. . . . Well, it's up to you, but if I were you, I'd give dinner a miss. . . . All right, twenty minutes." He laid the receiver into its cradle but left his hand on it. "If this other woman is in danger . . ."

"Her name is Veronica Beaconsfield—yes, of that family—and she's at the moment in Guys under the eye of Dr Watson or another of Holmes' minions, who would probably be happy to be relieved by an official guard. Miss Beaconsfield is, just to complicate matters, Miles Fitzwarren's fiancée. He has agreed to take her away from London after the doctors say she can leave, probably Monday or Tuesday, and keep her safe until we settle this. Holmes thinks Lieutenant Fitzwarren may be willing to tell you about his connexions with the drug world."

"Perhaps I should give one of our drugs men a ring, have him listen to you, as well."

"Not tonight. I must be on my way. No, truly, Inspector, I am more than happy to work with all and sundry on this, but tonight I have to be at the Temple for the evening service. I shall miss the first part of it as it is, but I need to be there when she finishes, because there isn't another meeting until Monday, and time is of the essence."

The police in 1921 were more restricted in their auxiliary use of civilians than they had been thirty years earlier when Holmes was at his peak; nonetheless, their concerns were primarily with the embarrassment of having incompetents endangering themselves or making a muddle of an investigation. With my background, and having received the spurious impression that Holmes was to be more or less constantly at my side, I knew Lestrade could be persuaded into supporting (however reluctantly) my proposed actions. On the principle that asking for a thing invites refusal, I simply told him my plans.

"So," I concluded, "there's nothing yet to justify a full, open investigation on your part, and there's a good chance it'd scare them off. I am already in a position to watch for anything odd, to take advantage of it. I can take care of myself. All I need is a way to set up an alarm for your instant response if I need it. If you put a watch on the Temple, or try to infiltrate, it would be duplicating what I already have, and it could easily put the investigation, and me, in danger." (I was saying, in effect, I've put myself into your hands; don't take my information and betray me with it. He heard me, though he did not care for it in the least.)

"At least stay until Tomlinson comes, let him hear what you have to say."

"I've given you everything of any importance, Inspector Lestrade. It's more important for me to be at that gathering of the Circle than waiting for your colleague."

"He may decide to arrest Margery Childe straightaway."

"If he does, then he's a damned fool and ought to be back pounding a beat, and you can tell him that Sherlock Holmes himself said that. Arrange a meeting tomorrow if you like. Or midnight tonight, for that matter." I gave him the number of the telephone that, along with the flat's other furnishings, was temporarily for my use.

He waited until I was at the door before he asked me the vital question.

"Do you think she killed those women?"

I was taken unawares by a sudden jolt of revulsion for my persona, my shoes, and the decision that had brought me here.

"Frankly, no," I said tiredly. "But I think you need to take a very close look at her. She is the common link between three dead women and a fourth who got lucky. She knows everything about her inner circle of followers. She knows that Veronica Beaconsfield and the others willed money to benefit the Temple. She has a friend on the staff of the *Clarion*, and this person would have known about the mutilations of the other victims. Margery has private rooms in the Temple complex, is often in retreat and unavailable, with a sharp-toothed maidservant to guard her doors, and very probably has some sort of private entrance. She is also embarking on a very expensive bid for public attention which will lead, she hopes, to a certain degree of political power. Clinics, literacy programs, and shelters can hardly be supported by the contributions taken in at the services. If you want me to tell you what your job is, I might suggest that a closer look at the church's finances would be in order, and a close scrutiny of the automobile and drowning accident reports. Inspector Tomlinson will undoubtedly have his own ideas. Now, I am away. Good evening, Inspector Lestrade. Thank you for the drinks."

I passed Inspector Tomlinson at the door, a tall and elegantly dressed figure perhaps a bit too aware of his own masculinity; not a characteristic, I reflected, that would help him on this particular case.

CHAPTER 15

Saturday, 15 January–
Friday, 21 January

*Woman must not depend upon the protection of
man, but must be taught to protect herself.*
            —Susan B. Anthony (1820–1906)

Beginning that Saturday night, I immersed myself in the Temple. Walking in just as the service was ending, I joined the Inner Circle as it made its way to the common room, oblivious of the raised eyebrows and shared glances, and announced to Margery my willingness to assume whatever of Veronica's duties I might be capable of, until she returned.

That was my entrée into Temple business. I could not, of course, fill Veronica's shoes administratively, but teach I could, and teach I did. I also ran errands, typed letters, answered telephones, fetched supplies, poked my nose into any available nooks and crannies, and in general offered myself up as anyone's dogsbody. With no particular discussion on the matter, from that first night I contrived to assume the position of fledgling member of the Circle, and in that rôle I contributed (in a deprecating manner) one or two ideas to a proposed political demonstration, helped print the tracts, took them around to the other Circle members, and on Tuesday stood on the pavement outside Parliament to distribute them. We were not arrested, fortunately; answering the police questions might have proven awkward, but the mere participation in the act bound me to their hearts more tightly than any amount of hard labour.

As the days passed, with the bustle of the Temple affairs and the continued friendly, open enthusiasm of Margery, I began to wonder if I had not imagined the strange episode of the night of the sixth. The Temple was about action, about helping and strengthening and changing the world one step at a time, and the thought of some miraculous healing going on behind its sedate brick walls seemed somewhat farcical, even tasteless. However, as Thursday approached, I was aware of a sense of anticipation.

In the end, the day went as any other Thursday, Margery disappearing into her study at five o'clock for a prolonged meditation, then, after her "love" talk, again retreating upstairs, alone but for Marie.

I spent a large part of all daylight hours in the Temple, and at night I worked late at my inadequate but ornate desk in the glass and steel flat. I did go up to Oxford on the Wednesday to consult with an increasingly agitated Duncan (who greeted me at his door waving a telegram from the Americans, who had blithely informed him that six European colleagues were to join us, as well), and I met Holmes twice in a clandestine manner, once on Monday and again on Thursday, after he returned from Scotland (where he had escorted Veronica and Miles to their lodge) and before his intended return to Sussex on Friday. The Monday meeting was with Lestrade and Tomlinson, and it ended with them disgruntled and me in possession of a telephone number—to which I promised I should report regularly and which they guaranteed would upon request produce an instant and surreptitious support force.

Life was schizophrenic, but not distressingly so, for I found myself enjoying my work in the Temple, discovered myself surrounded not by brittle aristocrats born with silver on their tongues and *Debrett's* in their veins, but by intelligent, hardworking women whose reserve hid shyness more often than it did condescension. It was a pleasure to work with quick minds, and one afternoon I joined in with glee when a speechwriting committee asked me for ideas. Several of my suggestions made their way into speeches given by Margery and others, particularly phrases from my childhood heroine, Abigail Adams: "All men would be tyrants if they could" met with great approval, as did "Arbitrary power [over wives], like all hard things, is easily broken." To accompany a speech on the idea that power corrupts, I suggested: "By taking our place in the thrones of power, we save the nation from the touch of corruption, men as well as women." For a speech to ecclesiastical wives, I suggested: "Drunk on power, and the grace of sobriety." And one Margery adopted for a Saturday night talk was: "Power without love is death; love without power is sterility." I had a grand time, found myself showered with dinner invitations, and wondered if I had found for myself a new profession in the world of speech writing, or perhaps advertising.

Friday afternoon found me in a stuffy, centrally-heated room with five beginning readers, their heads bent over the newly printed primers, fingers prising meaning from the marks on the paper, eyes squinting, lips sounding out each hieroglyphic before speaking it. Three grey heads, a brown, and a white blonde, bent down, laboriously giving birth first to one word, then the next, so slowly that any possible meaning was lost long before the sentence had reached an end. We had been trudging on for nearly an hour, my students and I, and I was craving the stimulus of tea or coffee or even fresh air when abruptly the brown head raised itself and I was looking straight into two startled eyes.

She looked back instantly at the page, removed her finger from the line, and, seizing the book in both hands, spoke in a single, flowing sentence.

"The boy has a cup of tea for his mother," she read, and repeated it, then looked up again and laughed, her eyes shining with the suddenly comprehended magic of the written word. Her teeth were mostly gums, she smelt of unwashed wool, her hair lay lank, and her skin wanted milk and fruit, but for the moment, she was beautiful. Veronica Beaconsfield knows what she is about here, I thought to myself, and took the work-roughened hand and squeezed it hard.

At 4:30, I went downstairs to the tearoom and drank a cup

with two of the circle who were waiting for their ride to a weekend in the country. They were exclaiming in irritation about the fog that had begun to close in and its inevitable delays, and I realised that I had been peripherally aware of the heaviness in the air. When I passed through the Temple offices on my way to Margery's tutorial, I glanced out of the window and saw the streamers that presaged an onslaught. Not bad yet, but I decided to miss the service that night rather than stumble across London to my flat. It would be thick later.

I went a few minutes early to Margery and told her about my happy experience with my beginning reader. She was genuinely pleased and interested, and again, as so often, I wondered what had actually happened that night two weeks before.

The topic I had set for the evening was the diatribe in Jeremiah against "baking cakes for the Queen of Heaven." We were twenty minutes into the session, deeply engrossed, when it came to an end with a brisk knock at the door and Marie's entrance. She held out a piece of paper to her mistress.

"Telephone call, madame. I thought you would wish that I bring this quickly." She ignored me completely, other than a scornful glance at the books on the table between us. Margery scanned the message, and it made her smooth forehead pucker slightly in consternation.

"Yes, thank you, Marie, you were quite right. Would you bring my things, please, and ask Thomas to get out the car?"

The maid nodded, and as she turned to go, she shot me a look of satisfaction and open dislike. Margery saw nothing, but I reflected on the woman's retreating back, thinking that if she was that jealous of her mistress's attentions, she must spend most of her time in a state of seething resentment. Unless, of course, it was merely me whom she disliked—or feared.

"I'm sorry, Mary," Margery was saying, "I'm going to have to excuse myself. That was an urgent message—but here, see for yourself."

I took the note and read, in Marie's French schoolgirl script, the following:

> Mlle Goddart has telephoned to say that she is embroiled in a severely unpleasant family affair and wishes most intently for your personal presence at your earliest convenience. The house is at 16, Norwood Place, number 3.

Marie returned with an armful of clothing and an uneasy expression on her face. "Madame, I regret to inform you that we are without an automobile. Mademoiselle Archer has not returned from her trip to Cambridge Shire, although she specifically informed me that she was to return by four o'clock. I have telephoned for a taxi, but they said it would take some time. There is a fog."

"Norwood Place is only a twenty-minute walk from here," I interrupted. "Probably faster than a car, given the fog."

Marie looked more sour than ever, but Margery seemed pleased.

"You know where it is?"

"I go right past it," I said, exaggerating slightly.

"Just give me the directions; there's no reason for you to go. Stay and have some dinner, or at least a drink."

"No, I'll go." Norwood Place was not in one of the more desirable neighbourhoods, hardly suitable after dark for a small woman in an expensive coat. The least I could do was to escort her safely to the door. "Could you find my coat, Marie?"

Caught between the desire to prise me away from Margery and her awareness that Margery would be safer with me than alone, Marie hesitated, then turned to Margery and began to protest vehemently. Margery held her ground.

"No, I won't let you go. Miss Russell is going that way in any case, and we'll be perfectly safe. It's not even five-thirty yet; I'm sure to be back by seven-thirty. . . . Very well, Marie, I promise not to walk back alone. When the taxi arrives pay him and, if Thomas is not back yet, have the driver continue to Norwood Place; he can fetch me back. . . . Yes, I shall ring if he's not there when I wish to leave. . . . No, there's sure to be a telephone nearby; Miss Goddart used one to ring here. . . . Well, whoever it was then. Marie, stop fussing me and get Miss Russell's coat. Sorry," she said to me under her breath. "She gets very like a mother hen sometimes. Hates it when I go out at night.

"Good, thanks Marie, see you later. . . . No, I'll not take time for a cup of tea. . . . Yes, yes, I'll telephone if I'm going to be late, but I won't be."

Marie held my coat for me, and even her disapproving hands could not take away the pleasure I felt in the luscious soft grey-blue vicuña with black sealskin collar and lining, new that very afternoon. It set off the richer blue of my dress, as if it had been made for it, as indeed it had. Margery looked at it closely.

"That's lovely, Mary. It's not a Chanel?"

I assured her it was not, then told her briefly about the elves.

"Ask them if they would consider doing some things for me, could you please? That hat is perfect on you, too, just the right shape for your face. My," she noted as we walked up the corridor to the front windows of the building, "it is rather thick, isn't it?"

It was full dark, but the lights from overhead and from the slow-moving vehicles illuminated the swirling yellow mist like a scene from a Wilkie Collins novel. Actually, it was not yet too bad, as London fogs went, and when our eyes had adjusted, we found we could see a good ten feet before the curtain thickened. At least we did not need to worry about tripping over kerbstones or walking into walls.

We walked slowly. The streets, as always in London, seemed to alternate between bustling thoroughfares and narrow pavements empty but for the occasional bobby; with the fog, the main streets were quieter than normal, and the mews and alleys echoed their desolation. Margery's heels clacked on the paving stones and my softer soles scrunched imperceptibly. The occasional horse and cart passed; cars and lorries eased by, their drivers leaning out over their doors and squinting through the windscreens. I consulted my inner map, turned us in the right direction, and decided it couldn't hurt to reveal my curiosity about Marie.

"You said Marie doesn't like you to go out at night. Is there any reason for that?"

"Not really. Just being protective. You're wondering why I put up with being bullied by my maid."

I laughed. "Well . . ."

"She has a good heart, underneath the prickles. She's a distant cousin; she came to me six years ago when the rest of her family was killed and her village taken by the Germans. It's important to her, feeling that I need her to care for me, and there's no doubt she makes life easier at times."

"Except when you wish to go out at night."

"As you say." She laughed.

"Do you get called out very often?"

"Not really, not anymore, although the Circle knows it can call on me whenever it needs to consult, like tonight. With so many others to—"

I never heard the end of her answer. As we walked, I had taken automatic note of our surroundings, more perhaps than usual because of the potential hazards contained in the all-concealing fog. When the quiet footsteps behind us broke into a run in the middle of a deserted patch of residences, I did not pause to think, just reacted. I shoved Margery hard from me and pivoted to meet the owner of these footsteps, who proved to be a slick young man with a narrow black moustache, dark eyes, and the gleam of a wicked sliver of steel in his bare right hand.

My unexpected response stopped him dead, and he eyed me uncertainly for signs of a weapon. When none appeared, he relaxed and took a step to one side, looking for Margery. She began to scramble to her feet.

"Don't move, Margery," I ordered. "Stay right where you are."

His eyes snapped back to me, and even in that light, I could see the evil smile of warm anticipation that crawled onto his face. For an instant, I froze, but when the knife came for me, my body moved of its own accord. The knife slid past my ribs, but he was fast, too, and recovered his balance in an instant, bouncing back out of my reach to reconsider while the tip of his blade flickered back and forth like the tongue of a serpent.

Had I been alone, it would have been simple, merely a matter of dodging out of his reach and not tripping over my shoes until I encountered something I could use as a weapon. However, I had no handbag, could not risk the temporary encumbrance of unbuttoning my coat, and I dared not move from my place while Margery was behind me. I reached up and pulled the hat from my head, to use as a shield for my hand at least, but when the knife flashed out again, I could not dodge far enough to avoid it entirely, and it sliced through vicuña and sealskin, wool and silk, and into the arm beneath.

It was like being cut with a razor, and I did not feel the pain at first, only the shock of violation. Without taking my eyes from his, I flexed the hand tentatively to reassure myself that it was still working, felt the burn of the wound mixed with a wash of cold air where none should be, and suddenly all I knew was fury. Yes, I was bleeding freely; yes, Margery and I were both in mortal danger, but just then the pain and the fear were nothing compared with the rage I felt at this wanton ruination of my beautiful coat and the sleeve beneath. I was damned if I would lose one more article of clothing to the knife, whether I was inside it or not. No slick-faced creature with a sharp blade was going to destroy my wardrobe again.

"You bloody bastard!" I shouted, and I don't know which of the three of us was the most astonished at the sheer fury in my voice. He hesitated, then came at me again, only this time, instead of dodging, I stepped inside his rush and turned, and at the cost of another nick (the sleeve would have to be replaced, anyway), I got both hands on his wrist. When he struggled, I reared back hard and felt more than heard the satisfying sound his nose made as it broke against the back of my head. The knife went skipping across the paving stones, and while he was distracted, I spun him around and locked his arm high against his back. I growled in his ear.

"If you move, something will break."

He did not listen (his kind never do), but wrenched his body violently away from me, and his elbow simply came apart. He shrieked, and when I dropped his wrist roughly, his screams doubled. I went to help Margery up. She had scraped one knee and would have bruises tomorrow, but for the most part she was only shaken, and that primarily due to the loud agony of the figure clutching his right arm with such exquisite care.

"My God, Mary, what did you do to him?"

"I didn't do a thing. I just let him do it."

"But he's hurt!" In a minute, she would be kneeling, with his head on her lap. I went over to the kerb and picked up the knife by its needle-sharp tip. Her eyes went wide, and I realised that she had not seen it before, as I had blocked her view as well as her body. She looked further and saw the rapidly spreading dark patch on my left arm and her eyes got even wider.

"He cut you," she said stupidly.

"He was trying to kill you, Margery," I said, more mildly than I felt. Had she been alone . . . I thought suddenly of Iris, and turned to look at the young assailant, so that I nearly missed the extraordinary expression that flitted across her face. It was momentary, preceded by shock and followed quickly by fear, but for a brief instant there was something else.

It looked like speculation—not at her attacker, but at something seen by an inner eye. She rapidly squelched it, and then there was only fear and the aftermath of shock, and by the time the bobby pounded into view, she was huddled, trembling, on a doorstep. I wondered just what it was I had seen.

Explanations took no little time, both there on the street and inside the police station. I accepted sticking plasters and ointment, refused a doctor (the cut was not deep, just long), and, after the leaks had been stopped, I spoke some private words with the inspector on duty. Telephone calls were made, and the general air of suspicious disbelief faded, replaced by one of respectful disbelief. My recommendation that the young knife wielder be arrested after his hospital visit sent one PC out the door to cling to him lest he disappear prematurely. My mention of number sixteen, Norwood Place sent another bobby scurrying out, though when he came back to confirm that there was no number sixteen, no families on either side, and no one who had heard of a Miss Cynthia Goddart, I was not greatly surprised. Margery was sent home under police escort, only a few minutes late for her dinner, and I was left alone in a cluttered police office before a stout, red-face chief inspector with a jolly demeanor but flint-like eyes. I smiled weakly, and he took me through each step of the evening yet again.

"So, Miss Russell," he said finally. "People in high places tell me you're to be trusted. Do you think I ought to trust you?"

I reflected, shrugged, and winced. I couldn't remember pulling my shoulder, but apparently I had.

"I don't know at this point whether it matters or not," I answered. He poked a stubby finger into the mound of paraphernalia on the desk blotter, things that had been politely but authoritatively removed from my person by a police matron. He chose one item—a set of picklocks—and examined it with expert fingers.

"Were there any injuries other than the scratch on your arm?" he asked politely.

"Nothing much. I have a bad shoulder."

He studied first my left shoulder, then the other, and though his jolly façade gave nothing away, I thought he knew quite well who I was and why my shoulder was bad. I had saved Holmes' life, and my own, at the cost of a shattered collarbone. Two years later, chips of bone continued to work their way to the surface with depressing regularity. He nodded.

"Some of these things are illegal," he continued conversationally.

"For the common citizen," I agreed. "And some of them

only become illegal when they are used."

"Hmm. And you're not a common citizen."

"If I wanted to commit burglary, or even murder, Chief Inspector, I should hardly need to resort to bits of machinery."

I met his eyes evenly.

"It wasn't an accident, then," he said after a moment.

"I told you it was not."

"But you didn't intend to break his arm."

"I warned him clearly what would happen if he moved. And he moved. If he hadn't attacked us with murder so obviously in mind, I might just have knocked him out. As it is, he'll not be knifing women for some long time. One more thing, and then I will leave. Scotland Yard is looking into the murder of Iris Fitzwarren. You might offer them tonight's little episode to chew on."

I stood up and gathered my belongings.

"We will need to have you sign your statement, Miss Russell."

"Tomorrow, Inspector. I'll come in in the morning. Just, please, don't let that man get away from you."

"No," he said simply. I felt a tiny flicker of warmth for the man. "Until tomorrow, then, Miss Russell."

"Good evening, Chief Inspector."

My reputation, or more probably that of Holmes, had followed close on my heels, and the path through the station was lined with curious eyes. At least there were no reporters to battle and outwit, and before I got to the front entrance, I knew there would be none waiting outside, either.

The fog had closed in. Such a mild monosyllable, *fog*, for London's own particular brand of purgatory, this greasy, burning, indescribably thick yellow miasma that seared the nose and fouled the lungs, rotted clothing and blackened buildings, caused hundreds of deaths by mishaps and brought the proud capital of an empire stumbling literally to its knees.

I made my way out the door and down the remembered four steps, patted my way down the front of the station a few feet, and allowed my shoulders to slump back against the bricks. God, I was tired, weary to the marrow of my bones. My right shoulder ached with the damp and the wrenching it had received, the two cuts on my left arm throbbed along with it, and my head pounded with the reaction of violence, received and committed, followed by two hours of verbal fencing with Inspector Richmond, with nothing in my stomach but sour Camp coffee. I leant my poor trampled hat back against the wall, aware of a trembling that threatened to surface from deep within my body, and tried to summon the energy to walk one and a half blind miles to my unwelcoming flat.

I always hated what Londoners called with such wry pride their "particulars," their "peculiars," their "pea soupers," like the beaming parents of some uncontrollable and pathologically destructive brat. Myopia is too close to a permanent state of fog to make for any entertainment in finding one's self groping through the streets with hands outstretched, with the additional irritant of having to be constantly wiping one's spectacles and wondering if it would not be simpler to dispense with them entirely until such time as the Thames deigned to melt back into its solid banks and its fluid state. Also, truth to tell, I have always been a bit of a claustrophobe, and the edginess that comes from suppressing an irritating and irrational fear, combined with my current far-from-irrational caution about venturing into a London bristling, for all I knew, with knife-wielding youths all too willing to pick up where their colleague had left off, made me regret that the chief inspector had not decided to keep me locked up overnight. Perhaps I ought to turn myself in, I thought in disgust. Fling my picklocks on the charge desk and myself into the burly hands of the sergeant on duty. I wiped my spectacles with my handkerchief and replaced them on my nose, then moved the white linen square slowly away from my eyes. Standing as I was directly under the entrance light of the station, at arm's length the handkerchief was only a vaguely lighter streak in the soup. From up the street came a heavy thud and a metallic screech, followed immediately by two frightened shrieks, one female and one equine, and two male voice began to curse each other hugely. Taxi and cart colliding, I diagnosed, and sighed.

In response, a voice spoke from the gloom on my right.

"Russell?"

I jerked and the handkerchief dropped from my hand, lost forever in the Stygian depths of the pavement, but had he been standing nearer than the ten feet or so that separated us, I believe I should have flung my arms about him and kissed him. As it was, I had to content myself with merely grinning— idiotic, considering the ambiguity of my feelings about the man over the past few weeks. But the lift in my heart could not be denied, as if the door to my own house had suddenly opened up before me on the street.

"Damn it, Holmes, how do you do that? I swear you must have psychic powers, or the best conjuring manual in the business."

I heard his footsteps come up to me as surely as if it had been a clear spring morning, and an impression of his face swam into view.

"Just a brother, with ears in many places. Mycroft reached me an hour ago with the message that the police had a dangerous young woman in custody. I came on the Underground, which is still operating, if slowly. Had you not emerged in another half hour, I should have gone to your rescue, but I thought it might be less complicated were I to let you talk your own way out. You were not injured?"

"Not seriously, either by the man with the knife or by the metropolitan police, thank you. What are you doing back in town? You said yesterday you were going back to Sussex for a few days."

"I never left, although town has seen nothing of Sherlock Holmes."

I had a sudden brief vision of Holmes moving crablike through the city, sidling through the background of scenes in first one guise, then another.

"Basil the driver?"

"Some of his cousins, perhaps," he agreed. "I decided that the experiments awaiting me were of less importance than the business I have here."

"And I am keeping you from it."

"You are it." Before I could consider whether to be warmed or forewarned by this, he went on. "You said you were going up to Oxford for a few days. Have you changed your mind?"

"Holmes, I can't change my plans. I promised Duncan."

"Quite. In that case, I shall assume the London end of the investigation until you return. Not, perhaps, inside your Temple, but nearby. Although, come to think of it, they may need a casual workman. Perhaps even a cleaning woman."

"Holmes, I'd rather you didn't."

"No? You may be right. It is, after all, your investigation. Is there some way I can be of service?" he asked politely, as if he might actually consider standing in the wings awaiting an invitation. I nearly laughed.

"At the moment, I fear, I am more in need of skills domestic than investigative. I am cold, Holmes, and I am hungry." I could not, of course, see his expression, but I did not think he smiled at my unintentionally plaintive words. He just turned and, tucking my right arm through his left one, began to stroll into the curry yellow night.

He did not even demand speech of me, but as we made our way—or rather, as he surefootedly steered me—through what my ears and nose told me were streets punctuated by narrow and unsavoury passageways, he told me a lengthy tale of a long-ago experiment into sensory deprivation—namely, living for eight unbroken weeks as a blind man, wearing completely opaque lenses and led about by the young urchin Billy.

At a conjunction of walls which, if invisible, had a familiar feel in its echoes, Holmes took out a key and the wall again opened. I greeted the Constable politely and the Vernet as an old friend, ate the food Holmes set before me, drank the brandy he pressed into my hand, and allowed myself to be pushed into the bedroom. The door shut behind me, and with neither qualms nor questions, I let the remnants of the elves' handiwork slither to the floor and sank with immense gratitude beneath the bedclothes, and slept.

CHAPTER 16

Saturday, 22 January

Remember, all men would be tyrants if they could. If particular care and attention is not paid to the ladies we are determined to foment a rebellion, and will not hold ourselves bound by any laws in which we have no voice, or representation.

—Abigail Adams (1774–1818)

I woke to find a valise containing clothing from my flat just inside the door. I scorned the silks for the moment in favour of a dressing gown I found in the wardrobe, so old that the thread had abandoned the quilted cuffs and collar, but quite long enough to cover my extremities. Holmes was seated in front of his fire, a cup at his elbow, a pipe in his hand, a book on his knee.

"Interior domestic," I remarked. "Portrait of an *amateur* at rest. What time is it?"

"Nearly ten."

"Good heavens, how sybaritic of me."

"Shocking," he agreed. "Tea or coffee?"

"Is there milk?"

"There is."

"All the comforts. Tea, and I'll make it. A scene as picturesque as the one you occupy must not be broken."

My arm gave off twinges as I reached for pot and canister, but nowhere near so much as I had anticipated. I hadn't realised Holmes was watching me until he commented.

"The cut is not troublesome, I see."

"No, happily enough. It burns, of course, but I was lucky."

"More so than your assailant. He is dead."

"*What?* But I didn't . . . Ah. Murdered."

"In his hospital bed, at four o'clock this morning. Not by the sword he lived by, I fear, and the hospital declares itself uncertain until the autopsy, but even they are aware that villains rarely drop dead of natural causes under such circumstances. Someone in a hospital coat with a needle or a pillow, no doubt while the constable was away fetching tea." He was annoyed rather than disturbed.

"Fast work. Inspector Richmond will be livid. Do you want a cup?"

"Yes, thanks. I'll cook your breakfast when you're ready."

He was quite the perfect host, producing on cue boiled eggs, toast and marmalade, tinned peaches, and coffee. Beyond that, he was the Sherlock Holmes of old, my friend and compatriot. We had not, I realised, had a great deal of time for simply chatting since I had gone up to Oxford at the beginning of the previous October, and we made up for some of the missed conversation that morning. His monographs and my papers took a solid hour, to say nothing of his bees, his chemical experiments, and the latest developments in forensic pathology, always an exciting topic.

There was actually little need for a conference with Holmes, and as he expressed little interest in what bits of hard information I had gleaned, I began to suspect that the reason for his presence outside the police station had been less the business he had claimed than—what was the alternative? Pleasure?

When eventually I rose to dress, I had forgotten about the rip in my arm and brushed painfully against the back of the chair. Holmes insisted on looking at it then. I hesitated, as beneath the dressing gown, I was wearing only my silk underclothing, but then I thought, Don't be stupid, Russell, he's seen you in a lot less than this. Still, I submitted to his ministrations with a heightened awareness of his fingers on my arm, although, for his part, he seemed unaware of a change, simply fitting a clean dressing across the rapidly healing cut as if the arm being serviced were his own.

I told myself firmly that I preferred it this way.

Certainly by the time we left the bolt-hole, we were friends again, which counted for a great deal.

The owner of the office building where Holmes had established his refuge was an enlightened employer, and the Saturday half day was so scrupulously observed that the place was all but deserted by two in the afternoon. I put a ladder in my stockings climbing out of the wardrobe (no wonder women got in the habit of allowing themselves to be handed in and out of places, with the sorts of clothing we have been forced to wear).

We returned to the station, where I signed the statement for Inspector Richmond and managed to slip away before he could question me further regarding a death I knew nothing about. That task completed, we strolled along to the nearest Lyons for coffee, a cheery place that struck me as an incongruous setting for Holmes until I thought of its anonymity. Outside on the pavement, he seemed oddly reluctant to part.

"You'll have that arm looked at in a day or two?"

"I said I would, Holmes."

"You're certain you don't want me to . . ."

"Holmes, it's only a week. Six days. Veronica is safe; I'm already entrenched in the Temple. I don't want you to dress up as a cleaning woman. As soon as I've finished with the presentation, I'll come back to work."

"I don't like it," he burst out.

"Holmes, hands off! You said yourself, this is my investigation—this side of it, at any rate. See what luck you have with solving the two other deaths. That should be a challenge even for you, deaths classified as accidents months ago. I give you a week, and then we can both tackle the Temple in an all-out effort."

His narrowed eyes followed a brewer's dray negotiating a turn into a narrow alleyway. He shook his head.

"I've never taken orders, from anyone," he muttered, almost too low to hear.

"High time then, Holmes," I pronounced with asperity. "I

may be in town Tuesday or Wednesday; otherwise, I'll see you on Saturday morning at the flat." I turned and walked away.

I had less success with Margery, who had regained what small amount of equanimity she had lost and now dismissed the danger. I reasoned, I pled, and finally I lost my temper and shouted at her, but without the slightest effect. She maintained that the attack had been a fluke and insisted she was in no danger; she would not restrict her movements or hire a bodyguard. I charged to my feet and loomed over her.

"I have not to this point considered you a stupid woman, but I am rapidly changing my mind. You obviously don't care about your own skin, but what about mine? I could have been killed. A quarter of an inch more and I could have lost the strength of my writing hand. What about next time? Who will be with you then? What will she lose? A pretty coat? Or her life? Margery, ask Inspector Richmond to recommend a bodyguard—only for a week or two, until they solve it. Martyrdom is great for the ego, but I personally have always considered it a waste."

She sat rigid, debating whether or not to have Marie throw me out, but she did hear my words, and after a while she wilted.

"I will think about it, Mary," she said quietly, and we finished the evening's lesson with no further furore.

CHAPTER 17

Saturday, 22 January–
Tuesday, 1 February

Nature . . . paints them to be weak, frail, impatient, feeble, and foolish, and experience has declared them to be unconstant, variable, cruel, and lacking the spirit of counsel and regiment.

—John Knox

Most of the passengers left the train in Reading. We sat for a few minutes in the station, carriage doors opening and closing several times, and then the train gave a shudder and we started up. I settled back with my book, eyelids heavy, although I was aware of a not-unpleasant blend of anticipation and apprehension as Friday's public presentation approached.

Ever since I had met Margery Childe, I had been torn, mentally and physically, and above all spiritually, between the London that she shared with Holmes and my own comfortable Oxford. For nearly four weeks, I seemed to have shuttled back and forth, in my mind and on this train, increasingly aware that a choice was being prepared for me to make. Now, however, whether because of the assertiveness I had shown to Holmes or the irritation I had felt with Margery, I felt considerably distanced from the problems the two of them represented. As the miles clicked by, I even began to reflect that, actually, one could almost look on the entire period since Christmas as a sort of holiday, an interesting and piquant interlude, possessed of an intellectual challenge, picturesque natives, a murder for spice, and the whole business tied up neatly before it threatened to trespass onto real life. I had renewed an old friendship and now cherished the addition of Margery Childe to my circle of acquaintances. Even the prickly state of affairs with Holmes had shown signs that the prickles were losing their more threatening points. Given time, and perhaps distance, that friendship might yet be maintained.

However, it was finished now—intoxicating feminists, doers of Good Deeds, and tutors with disturbingly male characteristics—an episode to be pulled out and remembered with fond amusement in the distant future. But now, Friday: a clear goal, known obstacles, all opponents out in the open, a hard challenge, but one I had been preparing myself for since I entered Oxford at the age of seventeen. Margery Childe, Veronica Beaconsfield, Miles Fitzwarren, and Sherlock Holmes were in a box labelled LONDON, and this short train journey should serve to close the top on it and place it, albeit temporarily, on a shelf.

Truly, honestly, I must never think these things.

Hubris was shattered without warning when my compartment door was calmly opened by a medium-sized man wearing a tweed ulster and an obviously false black beard, a disguise that effectively concealed the lower half of his face but could not hide the eyes. I did not need the gun barrel pointed at my chest to tell me what the man was, for I had seen such eyes before: This was a killer. Worse, there was intelligence there, as well as a distinct gleam of liquid pleasure. I sat very still. He closed the door behind him.

"Miss Russell," he said, very businesslike. "You have two choices: I can shoot you here and now, or you can swallow a mixture I have with me and become my prisoner for a few days. Obviously, the fact that I have not already used my gun indicates that I prefer the latter; bullets are unimaginative and do distressing things to human flesh, and the noise they make increases my personal risk of capture. That may appeal to you, but I assure you that you will be in no condition to feel satisfaction at my arrest. I suggest you choose the sleeping draught."

The unreality of his entrance and the melodrama of his

words robbed me of speech. I sat gaping at him for a long minute before I found my tongue.

"Who are you?"

"If I told you that, Miss Russell, I could hardly let you free again."

"Free me? I should drink your poison quietly and save you the trouble?"

"You choose the bullet, then? So very final, that choice. No chance of escape, of subverting or overcoming your gaolers, of changing my mind." He cocked the gun.

"No. Wait." It is very difficult to think with the end of a revolver in one's face. He was, quite clearly, a thug, with a heavy veneer of sophistication over an uneducated accent. Only a man who feared calloused hands spent time at a manicurist's. Still, there were brains alongside the brutality: not a pleasant combination. "What is in the mixture?"

"I told you: a soporific, standard medical issue, suspended in brandy. It's a decent brandy, too, if that matters to you. You will smell as if you were drunk, but you will sleep three or four hours, perhaps a little longer, depending on your sensitivity to the drug. You have one minute to decide," he said, and stood calmly just inside the door of the compartment.

"Why?" I asked desperately.

"We need you out of the way for a bit. We had thought merely to kidnap you, drop a bag over your head or put chloroform to your face, perhaps a needle in a crowd. However, your little demonstration yesterday night made us a bit wary of your skills at defending yourself. It was decided that the only options were those that kept us at a distance from you, while we were in public places where a prolonged struggle might draw attention."

Lies and truth mixed together. I thought he was telling me the truth about what the mixture contained; I thought he was telling the truth when he spoke of keeping me prisoner; I thought he was lying when he said he would turn me free. I also felt I knew who he was—not that I had set eyes on him before, but Ronnie had described just such a man. Although he did not strike me as "gorgeous" under the circumstances, I

243

had no doubt that this was Margery Childe's dark, Mediterranean gangster. I had never felt so alone.

"Thirty seconds," he said, without looking at a watch.

Perhaps, if I might get him to come closer . . . I nodded coldly and held out my hand.

His left hand went into an inner pocket and brought out a small decorated silver flask. He did not, however, bring it to me as I'd hoped, but tossed it onto the seat beside me. I put down my book and took up the flask, which was slightly warm from his body heat. I removed the stopper, sniffed it deeply: brandy, and something else. No bitter almonds, at any rate, or any of the other poisons that had an odour. I raised it to my mouth and wetted my tongue—again, no immediate taste of poison, but there was a familiar bitter undertaste, reminiscent of hospitals. I knew the taste; everything in me, body and mind, screamed against swallowing it. The thought of becoming unconscious in the hands of a man like this was intolerable, impossible. But would he use the gun, or was it a bluff? I looked into his eyes, and I knew with a certainty that it was no bluff. To fight in this small compartment would be suicide. Which, then, was it to be: a bullet or the chance of poison? I knew enough about poisons to be certain that the flask did not contain arsenic or strychnine, but that left a hundred others, from aconitine, which would kill with an imperceptible amount, to—

"Ten seconds."

It would have to be a poison that acted very quickly, because this train ended its run in Oxford, and if I were found alive, I might be saved; at the least, I would be capable of setting the police on his trail. The decision made itself, prompted, I think, less by logic than by the irrational conviction that he was telling me a degree of the truth, and that being a prisoner was preferable to death. I raised the flask at the same instant his arm was beginning to straighten out, then drank deeply.

"Drink it all," he said, and I did, coughing and eyes watering, then held it out upside down to demonstrate that it was empty. One drop fell to the floor, but his eyes remained on me.

"Put it on the seat and relax. It takes a few minutes."

He continued to stand with his back to the door. I continued to sit and stare at him, feeling after some miles as if this were one of the more avant-garde of the French plays that had recently become popular among the arty set. Perhaps this is the moment for me to make a forceful remark about my left toenail or the age of the sun, I thought flippantly, and then I felt the first quivers of impending unconsciousness as the drug began to descend on my nervous system.

A movement behind my would-be captor sent my heart thudding in wild anticipation, until I realised that the man looking in the door over the tweed shoulder also wore a false beard. Swooping disappointment made me peevish, and I opened my mouth to complain at the lack of imagination in their disguises, but to my consternation, what came from my mouth bore little resemblance to English. The newcomer looked at me and spoke from a great distance.

"She ain't asleep yet?"

"In a minute. She's not far—" And at his words, the compartment began to close in on me. My field of vision narrowed, from luggage racks and seats to the figures crowding the doorway, to two heads and a torso, and finally to the small scar that emerged from the false moustache and puckered the first man's lip, and the word *far* reverberated in my brain as FARFARFarFarfarfarfarfar and erased me.

When I woke, I was blind.

I was also violently and comprehensively ill onto the cold, hard surface I lay on, and when eventually I turned with a groan to escape the noxious stuff, I found that most of my body was in direct contact with the stones. Blind, stripped to my underclothing, and ill, I thought muzzily. Mary Russell, this is going to be very unpleasant. I laid my hot face back onto the cool stones and thought no more.

The second time I woke, I was still blind, still nearly naked, and felt just as ill. I did not vomit, although the sharp stink in the air made it a temptation and my mouth tasted unspeakably foul. I clawed my swarming hair out of my face, ran an automatic knuckle up the bridge of my nose to shove my absent spectacles into place, and then with an effort pushed myself upright. I wished I had not. My head pounded, my stomach quivered, and the darkness seemed to become denser, but I stayed sitting, and slowly I recovered.

I was alive. There was that. In the dark, in an unknown place, held captive for an unknown reason by an unknown number of enemies, clothed in nothing but knickers and camisole, without so much as my glasses and hairpins as weapons, but alive.

That I had lived was not in itself terribly reassuring. I sat on the stones, my head in my hands, and tried to think through the throbbing. After half an hour, I had come up with two small conclusions: First, my captor was a man of no mean ability, a remarkably intelligent, efficient, and daring individual who showed no signs of the gaol-bird in his manner and who was, therefore, among the more successful criminals. If one knew where to look, it should not prove difficult to find him—assuming I should happen to escape his clutches. Second, my mind seized on one chance remark: He had said that bullets were unimaginative. I could not help but reading into that choice of word the idea that he had something in mind for me, not just locking me in a hold. Not at all a nice thought.

He was no one I knew, personally or by reputation, which made for another question: Whom was he working for, or with? Who had arranged to pick me up so efficiently and ruthlessly and had me dumped into this hole? I assumed that it had something to do with the Temple, but I had to admit that there was no concrete reason for that assumption, that my life was sufficiently complicated to offer other possibilities. A voice from the past, taking revenge for something Holmes and I had done long ago? Or was I merely a pawn, captured to bring Holmes into a trap? My thoughts ranged and snatched at threads, meandering their way into the more remote reaches of reality. Marie hated me sufficiently to do this, although I had to wonder if she would not rather have merely crushed me beneath a lorry or had me shot. Perhaps I had been kidnapped by one of the Berlin-bound Americans, to keep me from presenting my paper. An academic rival, of Duncan's perhaps, set to ruin us both? Or—my aunt! Breaking the will by driving me mad, proving me to be incompetent, putting me and my father's fortune back into her hands . . .

That snapped me down to earth. My aunt was mercenary, but she had neither the brains nor the acquaintances to do this, and if I had seriously considered that, well, my mind was indeed in a fragile state. I shook my head to clear it, swore at my hag's mat of hair, and forced myself to my feet. Best to concentrate on the escaping side of things. Time to find out where I was.

The place I was in, other than being as black as a cow's stomach, was cool, but not dangerously so, paved in big uneven stones, and, I thought, large. To confirm it, I cleared my throat and said a few experimental words, more for the sake of the echoes than because I expected an answer.

"Hello? Hello? Is anyone here?"

The ceiling was not too high and the walls, some of them, not too distant. I got to my feet cautiously, found the pressure inside my skull receding, and began to shuffle forward with my hands waving about in front of me. I had no idea how much ground I had covered, with the dark pressing in on my face and eardrums like a silent cacophony, filled not only with mundane horrors such as cobwebs and rats (silent ones) but with lurking presences as well, hands reaching out to touch me. When my fingers finally stubbed against cold stone, I threw myself up against its upright bulk like a shipwrecked sailor on a beach and felt like embracing it.

The walls were fitted stone, my exploring fingertips told me, not brick: large, finely textured blocks. I turned left, changed my mind and turned right, and set out with my left hand bumping along the stone, my right hand out in front, literally inching forward until I came to another wall, joining the first at what seemed like a right angle. I patted this new wall for a bit as if it were a friendly dog and then turned my back on it, retracing the way I had come in order to pace the boundaries of my prison. My feet were just over ten and a half inches long, so that measuring my first wall toe-to-heel thirty-two times made this side a shade over twenty-eight feet. I continued left, and at seven and a half feet, I was nearly sent sprawling by a pile of something soft on the floor. It was not a body, to my mixed relief, but two large half-rotten sacks stuffed with straw. Cautious, searching fingers brought me to an odd, squat, smooth sphere that swayed when I touched it. I picked it up, explored it with my left hand, and removed the top. It was a gourd, filled with stale and infinitely sweet water. I stopped myself from gulping, but sipped, clutched it to my chest, and reached out again. After a couple of sweeps, my hand caught another smooth shape with a more familiar feel: a small loaf of bread. I settled back against the wall, my backside cushioned, nursing my riches in my arms.

After a few minutes I began to feel ridiculous. I drank another swallow and broke off a bite of the bread (heavy and tasteless, made with neither salt nor sugar) and forced myself to put down my treasures and resume the circumambulation. It was not easy to walk away from them.

When I had circled my prison, I found to my vast relief that my bed and supplies were precisely where I had left them, seven and a half feet from the second corner. My prison measured twenty-eight feet by sixty and a bit. There were no windows, even ones that had been filled in, as far up as my hands could reach, no breaks other than a door in the wall directly opposite my bed, a door as stout and immovable as the rocks into which it had been set. The ceiling overhead seemed to vary in height and was, from the echoes, stone or brick. A wine cellar fit my mental image of the room, with its constant temperature, lack of vibrations, and convoluted roof arches.

A wine cellar meant a large house, and I thought that if it were in the city, even a small city, the rattle of wheels and hoofs against paving stones would penetrate, if not as sound, then at least as low vibrations. So, I was locked in the cellar of a country house. Not much help, perhaps, but it was nice to know.

I also knew that I had not been locked here to starve. Food and water were not habitually given to a prisoner who was being walled up and forgotten. They would come for me.

Whoever "they" were.

Whatever "imaginative" torture they had in mind.

I curled up on the sacks, with one hand resting on my water gourd and the other clutching the bread, and slept for a while, and when I woke, still blind, the claustrophobic terror of being buried alive hit me.

I scrambled to my feet and groped my way to the nearest corner. I was becoming more accustomed to the blackness, because my ears told me when I was nearing the wall. Is this what Holmes had meant when he had practiced being blind in opaque glasses? With great deliberation, I squared myself against the wall and set off into open space, one foot's length at a time. Overhead, nothing; in front, nothing; on the floor, dust and grit. I straightened up and took the next step, felt around, then took the next.

When I reached my straw pallet again, I stopped for breakfast. I had found a half a dozen small pebbles, some chips of wood, and a couple of shards of porcelain and glass. These, I tucked against the head of my bed. I had also found the first of the pillars I had known must be there, supports to the ceiling over my head. There ought to be two or three of them—without interest other than for their possible use to hide behind. More interesting was the way in which my fingers had known the massive pillar was there a moment before I had touched it: For a vivid instant Holmes was leading me with sure steps through the fog.

I ate more of the tasteless bread, drank some water, continued my back-and-forth sweep. I found the second pillar, though no third one, and when I turned back to the bed, I found I had a sense of where it lay. Not precisely, and I did not have enough faith to drop my hands, but I could tell roughly where it was, and I went to it. My findings had accumulated, including now two walnut-sized knobs of rock, a handful of smaller ones, a horn button, and—treasure of treasures—a bent and rusty nail, about two and a half inches long. I tucked everything under my bed, then on second thought removed half of it and carried it over to one of the corners, pushing it into the lee of a slightly raised stone on the floor. I stood, pushed back my nonexistent glasses, and returned to my mat.

How long had I been in this place? The bearded killer had said the drug lasted three or four hours, but there was no way of knowing how many had been spent in transporting me here. Say, four hours drugged, and half an hour sleeping after I had been sick, then approximately four and a quarter hours in mapping out my surroundings. Between eight and ten hours, I thought, since I had drunk from the silver flask. It was Sunday morning; it felt much later.

How long before they returned?

I reached for the water gourd and felt a twinge, not from the knife cut, which seemed to have been given a fresh dressing, but from the inside of my left elbow. As I was fairly comprehensively bruised and aching, I had not taken much notice before this, but now I explored it with the fingertips of my right hand, and in a moment I knew that if the lights were to come on, I should see in the soft area over the veins a red welt with a pinprick in the centre—or rather, a needle prick.

Someone expert with a needle had either given me an injection, directly into the vein, or else drawn a blood specimen. The latter did not seem likely, but with what had I been injected? A second dose of sleeping potion? And if so, why into the vein? How long *had* I slept? What in hell was going on?

I was blind, in more ways than the one. It was something to do with Margery Childe—that much I could see; after that, the light faded. Was Margery herself doing this? Or was it part of another attempt on her life, removing me from hindering it? That could not be—I had already removed myself, by boarding the train for Oxford. Was I to be freed, as my abductor had told me, only to appear responsible for her death, or would there be two dead bodies, with blatant clues for the police force? Or, yet a third possibility: that I was to be freed but rendered harmless.

Unable, perhaps, to identify my captor?

Blinded perhaps?

The horror of the dark crawled over me then, and I knew that I was indeed blind, that my little farce of feeling all over the walls was lit clearly by an overhead bulb while observers in high windows watched the antics of a wretched, half-naked girl-woman with a madwoman's matted hair and scars all over her body, skirting not very successfully the pool of her vomit, hugging to herself a jug of water and a piece of stale bread, secreting a pathetic collection of stones in the corner of her—

I heard nothing, but there were vibrations where there had been stillness, in the stones beneath my feet and the air against my cheeks. I rapidly arranged the gourd where it had been, put near it the remainder of the loaf with the intact section of crust turned to the door, and threw myself on the floor in an attitude meant to suggest death.

A lock turned, then a bolt, and another bolt. Hinges groaned open and—light! Gorgeous, wavery, bouncing, blinding light. And an oath. I tried to ready myself to spring up, without visibly breathing. Tiny, quick breaths. Several feet at the door, entering.

"Close it." That was my abductor's voice, restricted still by the false beard.

Hinges groaned again; the door thudded; boots scuffed the stones. The light came closer, my eyelids reddened as it neared my face, and I came up running, hit the lamp from the man's hand and sprinted for the door, and had my fingers on the handle before my head jerked back painfully and I went down on my knees. I hit out and the man grunted, but he did not let go of the hold on my hair, and in a second they were all on me, and I was caught.

"Don't hit her," said the leader, and they did not, merely slammed me up against the wall. I winced away from the dazzle of his electric torch in my eyes.

"Hold her." I thought at first the obvious, but it quickly became apparent that it was a very different sort of invasion they had in mind. The man holding my left arm pulled it away from the wall, stretching my wrist out from my body while his other hand pinned my shoulder against the stones.

"Bring the other lamp." When I saw what my abductor was

pulling out of his pocket, I went berserk. I nearly freed myself, and it ended only when three burly men, bruised, bitten, and bleeding all, held me down on the floor and their leader put his hand over my nose and mouth and cut off my air. My frantic attempts to bite the man or free myself from his fingers exhausted my air; the room began to fade. When my air and my panic had both run out, he took his hand away, and as I gulped great draughts of air, he got to work.

I had never before experienced the sheer inexorable power of strong men. In utter humiliation and near abject terror, I could only look on as That Man knotted a silk scarf cruelly tight around my upper arm, took out a dark velvet case containing an already-filled hypodermic syringe, probed the hollow of my arm with knowledgeable fingers, and injected me directly into the vein. He slid his blunt fingers under the knot, loosed the scarf, and stood away.

And my body exploded. My every cell woke up and shouted in recognition of the substance being pumped through my veins, and a rush of pure, raw sensation flooded over me like a huge, slow electrical wave, leaving me quivering from the soles of my feet to the back of my head in what I can only describe as ecstasy. As it went through me, it seemed to shear my mind straight down the centre and split it, so that for perhaps a minute I experienced a sort of palimpsest of consciousness, a simultaneous awareness of events as they were now and as they had been six years and three months before.

I was aware of the stones at my back, the sharp smell of spilt paraffin, and the moan that issued from my twenty-one-year-old throat, a sound obscene even to my own ears and which caused the men pinning me down to cackle and joke among themselves as they stood away from my body and set about cleaning up the broken lamp and the old vomit.

At the same time, and every bit as vivid, was the hospital bed beneath me, the medicinal hospital stink of cleaning fluid and ether, the rustle of clothes moving, and voices: American voices. A man's authoritative American voice, but it was not my father's voice; never again my father's voice.

Mama? But the word was too far down in my throat to find

its way out. Words around me, weighty words that surfaced like bubbles from a murky pool from the vague noise I lay in: *doctor, infection, fever, dosage, weak.*

Someone was ill in this clean, bright room. Someone began to groan, a wavering sound that instantly cut off the words and replaced them with a more urgent rustle, a few curt commands. There was too much light in this room, terrible and harsh and white, and white shapes moving around me, topped with darker blobs—hair, heads, hands, touching me, a face coming into focus, emitting furry noises. I closed my eyes, felt the pain build like a demon, possessing me, hip and chest and head, building, and then another groan, higher in pitch, and hands, these ones cool and deft, and a brief flurry of angry sounds followed by a sharp jab in my upper arm, and then a wavering sensation as if the room were a celluloid film beginning to melt in front of the projectionist's bulb before it rippled and faded from view.

Back in the darkening cellar, I was sick again, this time into a canvas bucket I found in my hands. The clang of bolts echoed long in the cellar, leaving me on the cold and lonely stones in the darkness. When the echoes had faded, it was immensely quiet, apart from my laboured breathing and the heavy reverberations within my skull. I patted around me until I came across the straw pallet, moved over to it, and tried to grasp something that was me in the maelstrom. All I came up with was, appropriately enough, Job.

"I have made my bed in the darkness," I said aloud, and began to giggle dangerously. After a while, I put my head down, and I wept.

I was not at the time certain what He had injected me with, but it was similar enough to the painkillers I had known that I thought it might be morphine, or more probably the stronger derivative, heroin. His plan gained dimension in my mind: sure signs of drug use, the marks of the needle in my arm, the drug in my bloodstream. However, the same doubts as before still applied: Were these signs to be used to discredit some testimony of mine, or to explain my death? A third possibility occurred to me: Might He possibly believe that by a systematic exposure to heroin I would become inescapably addicted to the stuff, permanently corrupted to his nefarious purposes? Even in my muzzy state this seemed to me sheer romantic claptrap, a Victorian fancy akin to white slavery, but it was just possible that He might believe it. I should encourage the idea in his mind, I decided.

All this took some time to sort itself out. At first, I just lay and shivered and was sick again, into the bucket, but after a time my reasoning faculties began to return to me, although my body felt very peculiar.

Opiates leave one with a profound disinclination to do much of anything. It is not exactly difficult to go through the motions of life, or to think (other than the first half hour or so following an injection), but it is difficult to *want* to move, or eat, or think. One feels so very satisfied with life, the only improvement is actual slumber.

My only hope of salvation lay in my will, lay in contradicting the almost overwhelming desire to sit, and nod, and sleep, in refusing to submit to Lethe's seductive charms. I staggered to my feet and demanded that my disinterested limbs carry me around the walls of my prison, once, and again, and again, until I began to feel that my legs were my own again. The movement helped. Finding my way deliberately in the darkness helped. Thinking about the number of steps in a circuit and the number of circuits in a mile helped. Thirty circuits to the mile. I did two miles, ending at a jog trot and barely touching the walls, so that by the time I quit, my right shoulder hurt where I had scraped the wall a few times, and one of my toes was bleeding, but the soles of my feet knew the smoothness of the stones at the door, the slight rise that indicated the northeast corner (the door, I had decided, for the sake of argument, was to the south) and, had I been dropped down into the room, I could have differentiated the buckle in the stones beside my bedding from the one at the western wall.

I dropped onto my mat, feeling strange still, but not impossibly so, and drank some water and made myself eat, and felt the myriad of cells in my body return slowly to equilibrium.

The gears in my mind began to mesh again, and I sat back against the wall, and I thought.

I thought about Margery Childe's sermon on light and love. I thought about Miles Fitzwarren and what his true nature must be to inspire such loyalty in Veronica.

I thought of the odd and long-forgotten fever I had run all those years ago after the accident, the muscle cramps and the illness that had seized me after the healing was well under way and the medications were withdrawn.

I thought of Margery, and wondered if it were possible that she spent her love on this man, my captor; whether she quenched the thirst she had spoken of with this clever, brutal man who so obviously enjoyed causing pain.

I wondered about the rapture of mystics and the cost of that ecstasy, and how it compared to the everyday passion of simple human beings.

I thought of my early childhood, and of what my mother would think, seeing her daughter in the cellar, and how my father would rage, and how my brother would calculate methods of escape.

I thought of Patrick and Tillie, until the smell of Tillie's chicken cooking overcame the stench of paraffin.

I thought of Mrs Hudson, and her scones, and about how she had taught me to arrange my hair.

I drank again, deeply, ate half the bread, and found to my pleasure that a small and withered apple had been added to my cache, along with a second canvas bucket containing several inches of cold water and a scrap of face flannel. I ate the apple down to the stem, made good use of the water, and I began to feel like myself, strong and purified.

Two hours later, my captor returned, and it all began again.

Such was the pattern of my life for a long, long nine days, begun that Sunday and repeated some four dozen times. It became difficult to keep track of time. I knew just how many injections I had been given, from the growing pile of chips and stones I placed as markers in the southeast corner, but after a dozen had accumulated, I thought that my captor's visits were becoming more frequent, from approximately every six hours the first days down to five, or even four.

There was no telling the hours. My natural time sense, normally quite clear, was muddied along with everything else by the increasingly frequent and, I thought, increasingly powerful doses of the drug. Occasionally, his thugs brought with them definitive odours—eggs and bacon on the breath meant it was morning outside; beer defined the latter end of the day—but it was uncertain, and the variations in my own meals—the apple was sometimes a tough carrot, an onion, three dried apricots, twice a knob of cheese, and several times a cold boiled egg—followed no pattern.

Only once was I aware of the passage of time, and that was after some two dozen stones had accumulated, and it came to me with conviction and bleak resignation that in the meeting room in Oxford gowned men and women were coming together, and I was not there. After that, it no longer seemed so vital to keep the clock in my head ticking. It became more of an effort to do my sixty circuits after each injection, to keep my hair bound and my body clean. It became less of a pretence to hold my arm still for Him to inject me. Had He ever let down his guard and arrived without his three thugs, I should surely have attacked Him, but He did not, and I did not. The bread that was left for me soon lost all small interest it once had had, and I lived on water and the extras.

The only variations were in the food I ate and the thoughts I occupied myself with. At first, I drove myself to mental gymnastics, verb forms and recitations, mathematical problems and exercises in logic. I doubt that lasted more than a couple of days, however, before the engine began to run down. After that, I thought of many disjointed things. I recalled with crystalline clarity the first meal I had taken with Margery, the robe she wore. I tasted the honey wine Holmes had served me on a spring day in another lifetime. I thought of the way Watson beheaded his boiled eggs, and Lestrade drinking his beer, and the tea I had sipped with the maths tutor who had tried to kill me. Eventually, hunger, too, passed, and I thought mostly of Holmes.

Of Holmes, whom I loved. Stripped of dignity, sight, and probably life itself, I was stripped as well of self-delusions. I loved him, I had loved him since I met him, and I doubted not that I should love him with my dying breath.

But, was I "in love" with him? Ridiculous thought, instantly dismissed..The doubts and frenzies of a grand passion had by their very nature to wither under the cold, illuminating light of daily knowledge.

Love, though. Comfortable, interested, concerned, reciprocal love; was that perhaps a different matter?

And what rôle the physical? What place the body's passion?

I could never, I knew then, lose myself "in love." Margery had accused me of coldness, and she was right, but she was also wrong: For me, for always, the paramount organ of passion was the mind. Unnatural, unbalanced, perhaps, but it was true: Without intellect, there could be no love.

Since that moment on top of the hansom when the last lingering bubble of romanticism had burst, I had been looking for an alternative: freedom, academia, a régime of women.

Oddly enough, the very considerations that had made marriage impossible for him were mirrored in my own being: a rabidly independent nature, an impatience with lesser minds, total unconventionality, and the horror of being saddled with someone who would need cosseting and protection—the characteristics, come to that, that would have made it difficult for me to join Margery Childe, even without the rest of it.

Perhaps, though, the resemblance was not odd. Holmes was a part of me. Because of my age when we met, neither of us had erected our normal defences, and by the time I came to womanhood, it was too late: He had already let me in under his guard, and I him. Holmes was a part of me, and to imagine myself "in love" with him was to imagine myself becoming passionately enamoured of my arm or the muscles in my back. Yet in the same vein, it is not a part of Judaism to practice bodily mortification, to deny God's gift of a physical body. One accepts and appreciates this act of creation; one loves one's body, clumsy, inconvenient, and untidy as it may be. It was in this sense that I could love Holmes: Irritating as he could be, he was a part of me, and yes, I loved him.

Neither of us were domestic creatures. Holmes, by his nature and by the demands of his profession, had remained unfettered by domesticity, had never knowingly given a hostage to fate. The only woman he had allowed himself to love had been as jealous of her independence as he: Irene Adler had loved him for a time and then sent him away. And what of Mary Russell, a young woman as violently opinionated and as fiercely protective of her freedom as Holmes himself, and as competent as he at looking after herself?

It was, intellectually speaking, a pretty problem, and it occupied me for several days. By this manner, continuously interrupted by drugs and sleep and increasing befuddlement, I came tentatively to a point of balance with Holmes in his absence.

When thirty chips had gathered in the corner, I became aware of a new element in the cycle: anticipation. In another day or two, it degenerated into overt restlessness before his entrance, and there was distressingly little acting in the eagerness with which I stood, blinking and cringing at the light, to greet Him.

In the end, there came a third state, between the sweet horror of the poison flooding my veins and the body's craving for the next, a state of—I can only use the Christian concept—grace. For a brief time as the drug ebbed, I was granted a few minutes' respite. I ate, and to my mild surprise, one day I found myself speaking aloud the traditional Hebrew blessing over bread. After that, I used the time deliberately to do those things that returned me to myself. It was my nerves' calm eye, between the gale of quivering and the wind shift to restlessness, and after I had found it, Holmes was usually there, as a companion, beside me in the black and endless night. I strode up and down in my cellar, scorning the walls and avoiding the pillars as if I walked in the clear light of day, debating and arguing and reviewing the moves of chess games with Holmes, reciting psalms and the ritual prayers taught me by my mother, biding my time beneath a veneer of madness.

CHAPTER 18

Tuesday, 1 February

Thy husband is thy lord, thy life, thy keeper,
Thy head, thy sovereign; one that cares for
thee,
And for thy maintenance; commits his body
To painful labour both by sea and land . . .
Whilst thou liest warm at home, secure and
safe . . .

—William Shakespeare

Forty-five chips were in place. Restlessness for the forty-sixth had set in, and I was keeping busy sweeping up the débris from the rubbery boiled egg I had been eating, when suddenly I froze, aware somehow of unusual movement in the building above me. I had gradually, when I was in a state to notice, come to read the subtle vibrations in stone that transmitted distant footsteps, the faint sense of movement against one wall that I took to be water in pipes, and occasionally, rarely, a thread of hum that was human speech in the crack under the door. I swallowed the stub end of the egg and all but ran over to the most revealing wall. Movement there was; the stones fairly shuddered with it. Some emergency had hit the organisation. I backed away and turned to the door, thinking to press my ear to the crack, when I heard the familiar sound of feet on the stone steps. An injection was due, but those were not the normal footsteps approaching; this was a solitary man, and he was hurrying. Was this my death, coming for me?

I dove for the corner where I stored my larger rocks and scooped them up, flew to my bed and gathered the stones and the nail I had sharpened on the stones, and made the safety of the western pillar just as the key sounded in the lock. The bolts slid, and I prepared myself for a final defence. Light poured in with the opening of the door, more light than I had seen for days—an electrical bulb outside the door. I squinted desperately around the stones at the vague figure outlined there.

"Russell?" he said, and the breath congealed in my throat. "Russell, are you in here? Dear God, they've taken her." His voice went hoarse with despair, and he stepped back to shout, "Constable! Fetch one of those torches down here!"

"Holmes?" I said. The paltry stones of my defence rattled down around my toes.

"Russell! Are you all right? I cannot see you."

"I'm not certain you want to, Holmes," I croaked, and edged into the light, one hand out against the painful glare.

I could see nothing but a tall, dark shape, which made a strangled noise and took a step towards me, when the sound of constabulary boots on stones came from above. He whirled around and barked out an order.

"The torch won't be necessary, Constable. Resume your position at the top of the stairs." He paused, with his back to me for a moment, and when the footsteps had retreated up the stairs, he turned and walked past me into my prison. He stood first and contemplated my bed, the remnants of my food, and the gourd of water, spilt onto the stones in my final rush. Finally, reluctantly, he turned to me, and with no expression whatsoever, he looked at me, read the state of my pupils and my matted hair, my stinking rags. He reached for my arm. I flinched away from him as if he had lashed me, and he halted, then slowly put his hand out again and took my wrist, drew out my arm, glanced at the state of my veins, and let go. His only reaction was a brief spasm along the edge of his jaw. He looked back into my face.

"Will you be all right if I leave you here and go find you some clothes?"

"Leave the door open." My voice trailed upwards and cracked.

"Of course."

He ran light-footed up the stairs, and returned within three minutes, to find me cowering just inside the door like some timid beast afraid to seize its freedom. He held out a pair of trousers, a linen shirt, a pair of carpet slippers. I just looked at them.

"It will take me some time to locate your own clothing," he said, mistaking my hesitation. I reached for the things, avoiding his hand, and stepped back into the dark to dress. The clothes were my captor's. I could smell Him, feel the imprint of his body. A curious intimacy, but, oddly enough, not unsatisfying. I straightened my shoulders and stepped into the light, then walked out of my cellar prison and up the bright stairs, feeling like the mermaid granted feet.

Holmes escorted me up into the house, never touching me but guiding me with his physical presence, as substantial beside me as one of my pillars. In the main corridor, a uniformed constable came up to us, eyeing me with alarm before recalling himself and greeting Holmes.

"Mr Holmes, sir, Inspector Dakins sent me to ask you if the young lady would see fit to identify the men under arrest. He thinks there may be one or two missing, and it'd be helpful he says if the young lady could give us descriptions. If she's up to it, he says," the constable added dubiously. I straightened my shoulders again and felt the fingers of the restless shakes playing over my nerve endings.

"Yes, I'm quite fit," I said in an unfamiliar and far-off voice.

"Very good, miss. If you'd follow me."

Holmes stayed at my shoulder, close enough that I felt the heat of him, but never actually making contact. A part of me was disintegrating, not only because of the drug, and without him beside me, I could never have looked into the knowing, leering eyes of the thugs (easily recognised despite the absence of the false beards) and the curious, disapproving eyes of the police, could never have described my captor (two inches under six feet, thirteen and a half stone, black hair, small scars on his right lip and in his left eyebrow, Yorkshire-born, London-raised, with a fairly well-seated French addition to his accent, various moles, and the habits and abilities I had deduced), could never have made it out the door and up the stairs to the anonymous guest quarters and walked calmly in and waited while the constable brought in a tray with tea and biscuits and cheese and fresh plump apples and set it clumsily on a table. Holmes chased him out, poured a cup, and brought it to me where I stood with my face pressed up against the window, drinking in the glorious sight of a rain-swept hillside. The vibrancy of the green grass against the grey sky was almost frightening in its intensity; it certainly hurt my eyes. Holmes stood at my shoulder for a moment before putting the cup down on a polished table and reaching past me to work the latch and push the window open. Sweet, freezing air engulfed me, an almost tangible substance pressing against my face and in my hair.

"What time is it?" I asked him.

I heard the sound of his watch rubbing against the coin he wore on it, a faint metallic sound I had heard a thousand times before and had not thought I would hear again. "Twelve minutes past eleven."

For the first time in days I was anchored again to the progress of the sun through the heavens. Holmes took up the tea cup, put it into my hands, and then snatched it back to keep it from tumbling out the window. He carried it back to the tray, stirring in three spoons of sugar before bringing it back to where I stood. He held the cup to my lips, and I drank. When the cup was drained to the sugary dregs he gently closed the window and led me to a chair in front of the fire. I sat where I could see out of the window, and I managed to hold the second cup of tea on my own. The horrid iced biscuits he pressed on me were too much, and I told him so, my words ending in a jaw-cracking yawn.

"How long since you ate?"

"I don't know. Not long. I'm not hungry."

"Inspector Dakins will want to interview you when you've rested."

"God. Not today."

"He will insist, I'm afraid, unless you're unconscious in hospital."

"Perhaps we might arrange that," I groaned, and his face

lightened a trifle. For the first time, I noticed his appearance: gaunt, grey, and ill-shaven. Even his shirt collar looked tired, a highly unusual circumstance. Before I could rouse the energy to comment, he turned to go into the next room, where I heard the roar of the geyser starting up and the rush of water into the bath. He came out in a cloud of flower-scented steam.

"Can you manage?"

"Yes. I'm fine, Holmes, just feel a bit feverish, that is all."

"Shall I stay here, or hunt down your clothing?"

"I am fine, I tell you. By all means, find my clothes." I told him what I had been wearing. "And my specs. Just—don't lock the door."

It was an admission, but he did not comment, just said, "No."

In the bathroom, I agonised over the key, eventually forcing myself to close the door and leave it unlocked. I placed the key on the tiles below the bath, stripped and stuffed the filthy underclothes along with my captor's things into the waste bin, and eased myself into the hot, foam-covered water. I did not care to examine my body overclosely, but I did notice that the knife wounds, at least, received defending Margery in another lifetime, had healed to clean pink lines.

The heat helped, but I kept my eye on the door, and jerked when there was movement in the adjoining room.

"Russell? May I enter?" Of course: that was why he'd used such a liberal hand with the foaming bath salts. I was quite thoroughly hidden from view. I gave him permission. He placed some familiar garments on the dressing table, brought my glasses over and put them on a chair within reach, looked through some drawers and came up with a silver comb, which he put with my clothes, and turned to the door.

"Holmes? How long has it been?"

"You were taken from the train late on the twenty-second. It is now February first." He paused, to see if I had further questions, and then left.

He remained in the next room, although I knew he would rather be asking questions of the thugs and the servants and uprooting clues the officials were missing, if not destroying.

Twice, I heard a knock and a brief conversation at the corridor, several times the ting of a cup and saucer. I scrubbed my pores, washed my hair several times, until the tangled mass was at least clean, and ran hotter and hotter water in, but to no avail. I pulled the stopper, and as soon as I climbed out, I began to shiver. Familiar clothes helped. Putting my glasses on and having a world of bright, focused, everyday objects around me helped. But still I shivered. I took my borrowed comb into the next room. Holmes raised his eyes from a book.

"Do you think we might build up the fire?" I asked, teeth chattering. "Just until my hair dries?"

We soon had a blazing fire, but although I practically sat in it as well as wrapping myself in a blanket, I could not feel warm. Holmes carried over a small table with another cup of tea on it and sat down across from me. I took up the comb and set about pulling it through my snarled hair, but succeeded only in making it worse.

"Accusations are being made against you," he said abruptly.

"Accusations?" I said absently. "Damn, I'm just going to have to cut it all off."

Holmes stood up impatiently. "Give me the comb," he ordered, and standing behind my chair, he proceeded to tease the snarls out with none of the awkward jabs of the uninitiated that tangle a comb in long hair, but holding the heavy, wet mass in his left hand while the right stroked its way bit by bit towards the scalp with quick, expert movements. Not the first time he had done this, I thought, and felt myself shiver again.

"By the four men downstairs," he continued after a while. "They are claiming that you are a drug addict."

"I suppose," I said, "they have a point."

"That you came here as an addict. That you chose to inject yourself. That they didn't know their employer was supplying you. That you chose to lock yourself in an unused cellar occasionally, for unknown reasons."

"Oh, for Christ's sake, Holmes." I stood up and moved

away from his hands, wrapping the blanket more firmly about myself, walking aimlessly about the room. I dipped my hand inside the pocket of my skirt, found the handkerchief I'd put there ten days before, and wiped my nose.

"Of course. However, your behaviour over the last weeks has been notably unusual; you have taken to moving with a group of people of whom at least one is a known heroin user and addict; you have suddenly inherited a large amount of money and seem to have taken on yourself the way of life that often does go with experimentation with drugs. To the good inspector downstairs, knowing this as he does, the marks on your arm will be damning enough. When he witnesses the display of symptoms you are currently beginning to demonstrate, he will very possibly try to arrest you." I turned and stared at him, speechless. "Yours is a remarkably . . . advanced reaction, considering the number of days you have been away."

"After the accident, six years ago, they used a lot of it. It was thought to be less addictive than morphine."

"Yes. It was a very popular cough medicine. You would not, though, care to explain to the good inspector the sources of the predisposition that was then carved into your nervous system." His hand went inside his coat and came out holding the same long, narrow velvet case, loathsome and thrilling, that I had seen some four dozen times now. His eyes were completely without judgement as he held my gaze. Finally, as if in a dream, I began to pull up the sleeve on my blouse. He went to lock the door, then returned with a snowy handkerchief in his hand, which he whirled into a rope. I extended my arm, and he wound his impromptu tourniquet around my upper arm.

"Hold that," he ordered as he picked up the case. The syringe was already prepared, as I had always seen it, its plunger pulled back. Holmes examined it.

"He seems to have readied this just before we arrived. He usually gave you the full amount?"

"Yes." My voice slipped slightly. Holmes did not appear to notice.

"I shall give you half," he said, and brought up the syringe, felt for the vein, and inserted it impeccably under the skin. He slid the plunger down halfway, removed the needle, plucked the kerchief from my fingers, and pressed it against the tiny puncture.

I closed my eyes and could not control my reaction, the stiffening of pleasure and the shudder as it rushed up from belly to brain. In a minute, I exhaled slowly and opened my eyes into the grey ones of my dearest friend, and I saw in them the terrible reflection of fading pleasure and all the concern that the features did not reveal. I looked at him for a long minute, then down at the table, to the syringe that lay there. I picked it up, wrapped my fist around it, held it high, drove the point of it hard into the immaculate polish of the wooden table, and rocked it back and forth until the needle broke, then replaced it on the silken rest, closed the box, and held it out to Holmes. His face had not changed, but the worry had left his eyes.

Holmes finished combing my damp hair. I pinned it into a severe chignon, ate two biscuits and a piece of cheese, and went downstairs, with Holmes at my side. Inspector Dakins was interrogating one of the thugs, and my flesh began to crawl. Holmes did not give him a chance to speak.

"Inspector, do I understand that accusations have been made against Miss Russell to the effect that she voluntarily and repeatedly injected herself with heroin?"

"That is correct, Mr. Holmes," said the policeman carefully. "Mr. Bigley here was just telling me."

"Too right, I seen her all the time. Made no try to hide it, she didn't." The contrived innocence of his face and voice contrasted grotesquely with the leer in his eyes and the vivid recollection of the abuse he had thrown at me. I fought the urge to crawl behind Holmes.

"She was injecting herself, you say?" said Holmes sharply.

"In the library, I seen her, with this band wrapped around her arm, holding the end of it in her teeth. I didn't know what she was doin' at first," he said righteously. "Shameless, she was."

"The band around one arm and the hypodermic needle in the other?" Holmes enquired.

"Well, a'course. How else could she do it?"

Wordlessly, Holmes took my arm and unfastened the button of my left cuff. He pushed up the sleeve, tucked it so it stayed up, and turned my arm for the two men to examine. It looked worse than ever, nearly fifty puncture marks, several of them infected, the whole arm bruised and angry for a hand's breadth around it. The inspector looked repelled; Bigley looked smug. Holmes then took my right wrist and ran that sleeve up on an unblemished arm. He caught and held the inspector's eyes.

"Miss Russell is left-handed," he said with emphasis. "It is quite impossible for her to have repeatedly injected her own vein—a delicate operation, you will admit—using her right hand." He turned my left arm slightly and pointed to a greenish smudge which had not been there five minutes earlier. "However, these fading bruises on her arm are perfectly consistent with having her arm held down—which, knowing Miss Russell, I can say would have required several strong men, and may indeed have something to do with the marks of teeth on Mr. Bigley's hand—while her arm was then injected for her. Against her will," he added, in case the good inspector had missed the point. He had not, and I could almost see him beginning to bristle at the hapless thug. Inspector Dakins had perhaps been raised on tales of white slavers, I thought to myself, and rolled down my sleeves.

"You will wish a statement, Inspector Dakins?"

"Indeed," he said, and spoke to the uniformed PC. "Take Bigley into the next room. I'll finish with him in a minute."

I dictated my statement, giving but the briefest details of my captivity and leading him completely astray when it came to the effects of the drug on my system. Yes, it was seven or eight hours now since Bigley's boss had last injected me. No, I did not think I was addicted to the heroin, although that clearly was the intent. No, I had no idea why I had been subjected to the treatment. (The look of disbelief in the inspector's eyes drove into me, but I met it with equanimity. With Holmes there, and with the accent he heard coming from me, he did not press.) No, I was not feeling any ill effects, although, I admitted, I was quite exhausted and disorientated, perhaps from lack of adequate food, sleep, and sunshine. Holmes took the cue and stood up.

"I shall remove Miss Russell now, Inspector. She has had a trying time, and I have no doubt her doctor will require that she have some days of quiet. You may telephone her on Monday if you have further questions. Good day, and I wish you the best of luck with finding the other two men. Come, Russell."

To my astonishment, Q was outside with the car. The punctilious correctness with which he greeted me positively vibrated with relief and affection. The temporary strength I had gained from the needle was fading rapidly, though, and I allowed him to tuck a rug around me. Before Holmes could get into the car himself, though, there was a call from behind us. He straightened up to confer with the uniformed constable, then put his head back in, told me he would return in a minute, and went with the constable back towards the house. Q paused before closing the door and spoke in the general direction of my feet.

"He's been right frantic, miss. No sleep and next to no food. The wife thought he'd drop." He shut the door before I could summon an answer, then went back to his place behind the wheel. Holmes appeared a minute later, dropping into the seat beside me. He did look nearly as dead as I felt, I noted dispassionately.

"Dakins decided he needed my own telephone numbers as well, although I must have given them him at least five times," he explained. He looked at the side of my face and after a minute asked, "Sussex, or your flat?"

"Where are we now?" It was the first time I had thought to ask.

"Not far from Little Waltham, in Essex."

"The flat then, if you think it's safe."

"It will be," he said, somewhat ambiguously, and leant forward to speak to Q. I looked back as we went down the drive, and I saw a big, ugly, down-at-its-heels stone country house, like a hundred others. Nothing whatsoever to distinguish it, except the knowledge that I had left the remnants of my youth in one of its deserted cellars.

CHAPTER 19

Wednesday, 2 February–
Saturday, 5 February

*For nature has in all beasts printed a certain
mark of dominion in the male and a certain sub-
jection in the female, which they keep inviolate.*
                                    —John Chrysostom

The next days were tedious, but I had spent enough time recovering from various injuries to know that health would return eventually. It was less painful than most of the other convalescences I had gone through, rather like a case of the influenza that had ravaged the country the last two winters.

And yet, that is a lie. Not that the bodily discomfort was to any extent extreme: I felt shaky and feverish, cramped and aching and quite unable to eat, but no more than that. It was my soul that was ill, in a way I had never known and did not know how to deal with.

I first knew severe injury when I was fourteen, recovering from the automobile accident that had cost my family's life, an accident for which I felt responsible. Guilt ate at me then, and for some years afterwards. The second time was when I took a bullet in the shoulder, one that was meant for Holmes. In the aftermath, I had retreated emotionally, because the woman trying to kill us had been a person I respected and thought loved me, and because I could not blame Holmes for causing her death.

Now what I felt was shame, simple, grinding shame at my body's continued craving for the poison that had been fed me.

I wanted the needle, wanted it badly, and the desire was a craven one, and I was ashamed. For the rest of Thursday and all of Friday, I raged up and down in my locked bedroom, ignoring the entreaties of Mrs Q with her tea and her delicacies.

It was not simply physical addiction. Heroin does not turn a person into a raving dope fiend in a night, or a week. However, circumstances conspired against me, and the drug had acted more quickly than might have been expected. Normally, the man might have pumped me full of the stuff for a month and I still should have viewed the process with loathing; however, alone, undernourished, off balance in the dark, and with a history of prolonged use of a similar drug, I could not resist the only pleasures and stimulus offered me.

The desire wore down, of course; it was, after all, hardly a habit of any duration, and, like any addiction, it was mostly in the mind. However, the shame and the rage only grew, until I hated everyone: Margery, whose fault it somehow was; Veronica, who had put me here; Holmes, who had seen me in that despicable state and burnt me with his compassion. I refused to go to the telephone, had Q simply inform people that I was unwell and not to come by or send flowers. I did not read the growing pile of messages: from Margery Childe, from Mrs Hudson, from Duncan. I hated everyone, except, oddly enough, the true villain of the piece, the man I thought of as simply Him. After all, He had been an honest enemy, not a masquerading friend.

It was Holmes, I suppose inevitably, who pulled me out of this maudlin state. He came to the flat late on Friday. I naturally refused him entrance to my room. He entered anyway, by the simple expedient of sliding a newspaper under the door, poking a kitchen skewer through the keyhole to knock the key out, and briskly drawing back paper and key to his side. His shoulder proved stronger than my bare foot against the door, and I faced him in a fury.

"How dare you!"

"I dare many things, Russell, not the least of which is entering a lady's chamber contrary to her express wishes."

"Get out."

"Russell, had you truly not wanted me to enter, you would not have left the key so conveniently to hand. Put on your shoes and coat; you're coming for a walk."

Had I been less debilitated, he might easily have failed, but by dint of physical strength and verbal abuse, he got me into my coat, got me to the pavement, pushed and prodded and chivvied and distracted me until I found myself at the entrance to Regent's Park.

And there we walked. Up and down the paths we went, Holmes carrying on an endless and effortless monologue, beginning with the history of the park, the body once found in this hollow here, and the uprising plotted in that house over there. I then heard about the park's botanical oddities, the flora of northern India, the peculiar league of poison-eaters from Rajasthan, the embroidery of Kashmir, and the differences between Tibetan and Nepalese Buddhism, followed by a description of his recent monograph on the glass of automobile headlamps, another study on analysing the types of gin used in cocktails, his experiments with a recording of various automobile engines that he thought the police might find useful in helping witnesses identify unlit autos by night, yet another monograph comparing the occasional outbursts of mass hysteria in Medieval times with the current madness for dances with jerking and incomprehensible movements—

I turned on him.

"Oh come now, Holmes, that's absurd."

"Thank God!" he exploded, and dropped onto a nearby bench to mop his brow dramatically. "Even I cannot maintain a line of drivel forever." I stood over him and crossed my arms.

"Very well, you have my attention."

"Sit down, Russell." I thought about it, then sat.

"That's better. We must have walked ten miles tonight—I haven't seen so much of Regent's Park since Watson used to drive me out and force me to take exercise. For similar reasons," he added. "You are feeling better, I think?"

"Oh Lord, Holmes, isn't it dreary always being right?" I complained.

"You are quite right—it was not politic of me to point out that Uncle Sherlock knows best. I merely thought to enquire if you had an appetite yet."

"No," I said, and then amended it. "However, I admit that the idea of food is not quite so repugnant as it was earlier."

"Good. Now, shall we go to the zoological gardens and wax philosophical about the anthropomorphism of monkeys, or shall we talk about the man to whom you refer with a capitalised pronoun?"

"What about Him? Have the police caught Him yet?"

"You needn't fear, Russell, they have not. And will not, if you choose to do nothing."

We sat and listened to the noises of the park at night, traffic sounds mingled with distant jungle screeches. My hands were gradually regaining their steadiness, I noticed.

"Touché, Holmes. I am repaid for my thoughtless remark about your son."

"Hardly thoughtless. At times, a jolt is needed to get an engine moving."

"Consider my engine jolted. In which direction do you wish me to move?"

"In a most circuitous path, I think. We must not give the man a second opportunity."

"But what does he want with me?" I cried.

"Would it interest you to know," he asked, "that nine days ago Somerset House received, and registered, a will for one Mary Judith Russell, signed, witnessed, and dated the previous Friday? I thought it might. And perhaps you would also be interested to know that you chose to leave five thousand pounds each to your beloved aunt, your snivelling cousin, your farm manager, and your college; not a farthing, I was rather hurt to discover, to your old friend Sherlock Holmes. The bulk of your estate—the houses, the factory, the gold, the paintings, and the villa in Tuscany—went to the New Temple in God."

"Bloody hell," I muttered.

"As you say. The signature was quite good, by the way—a closer approximation than I could pen. I believe it to be the work of a forger who goes by the name of Penworthy. Poor Miss Russell." He sighed. "The sudden acquisition of riches drove her to a death of high living."

"I see now why He—why the man clung to me so closely. I had wondered how, if he is in charge of some criminal organisation, he could afford to remove himself from London for so long, but with something like my father's fortune at stake, I suppose he could not risk leaving the whole charade to a subordinate. Is there any link with the Temple, other than the will?"

"No proof of one, but it has to be with the woman herself."

"Oh God. It always comes back to Margery."

"It does." He started to say something, then changed his mind. We sat in another patch of silence, until another thing that had to be said forced itself onto my tongue.

"You were right, Holmes, Tuesday—at the house. Inspector Dakins would have seen only the addict's symptoms and not have listened to anything else. I hated that, having you give me . . . I hated it."

"You hated me."

"I suppose so. Yes."

"My shoulders are broad," he said easily.

"So, who is he?" I asked.

"He does not own that house. It was let, six months ago, to a man using the name Calvin Franich."

"Does Mr Franich have a small scar on his upper lip?"

"The estate agent said yes, he did. The interesting thing is, Scotland Yard knows of another gentleman with a small scar on his upper right lip and another in his left eyebrow. He calls himself Claude Franklin."

"Mr Franklin being . . ."

"A rather mysterious gentleman with fingers in any number of shadowy pies. He made a beginning, you may be interested to know, in convincing elderly widows to leave him a little something when they died. He disappeared from this country in 1912, as things were becoming a bit warm for him, and survived the war quite nicely by importing illicit goods to the Mediterranean. Recently, his name has been linked with drugs being smuggled into the south of France, and he seems to have slipped quietly into England some time in the last year. Very low-key, very clever, very dangerous, was Scotland Yard's verdict. They weren't happy to hear he's come home."

"I should think not."

"Has that restored your appetite?"

"Do you know, I believe it has. Not for great quantities, however."

"But an intensity of flavours. It is not your stomach that abhors the idea of food, if I may be allowed to mention that indelicate organ, but your palate. I have discovered a new establishment run by a chronically unsuccessful cracksman who was fortunately employed in the governor's kitchen during his last spell. He has found his calling. You shall begin with the prosciutto—no, not pork. Ah yes, the baked pear and Stilton, that ought to awaken your taste buds. And then a bowl of his onion soup—he makes it with a touch of garlic and a particularly interesting cheese grated on top—with a nice young Côtes du Rhône, I think, and perhaps if you're up to it a sole almondine with a glass of sparkling white wine—"

"You have convinced me. However, Holmes," I said gravely, "before we go any further, there is something I have to know. I realise this may not be the ideal time, but it is necessary that I ask, because my mind has dwelt much on the question while I was locked in the darkness, and if I do not bring it up now, I may never nerve myself up to it." I looked down at my gloved hands, choosing my words with care. "These last weeks, since Christmas, have been odd ones. I have begun to doubt that I knew you as well as I thought. I have even wondered if you wished to keep some part of yourself hidden from me in order to preserve your privacy and your autonomy. I will understand if you refuse to give me an answer tonight, and although I freely admit that I will be hurt by such a refusal, you must not allow my feelings to influence your answer." I looked up into his face. "The question I have for you, then, Holmes, is this: How are the fairies in your garden?"

By the yellow streetlights, I saw the trepidation that had been building up in his face give way to a flash of relief, then to the familiar signs of outrage: the bulging eyes, the purpling skin, the thin lips. He cleared his throat.

"I am not a man much given to violence," he began, calmly enough, "but I declare that if that man Doyle came before me today, I should be hard-pressed to avoid trouncing him." The image was a pleasing one, two gentlemen on the far side of middle age, one built like a greyhound and the other like a bulldog, engaging in fisticuffs. "It is difficult enough to surmount Watson's apparently endless blather in order to have my voice heard as a scientist, but now, when people hear my name, all they will think of is that disgusting dreamy-eyed little girl and her preposterous paper cutouts. I knew the man was limited, but I did not even suspect that he was insane!"

"Oh, well, Holmes," I drawled into his climbing voice, "look on the bright side. You've complained for years how tedious it is to have everyone with a stray puppy or a stolen pencil box push through your hedges and tread on the flowers; now the British Public will assume that Sherlock Holmes is as much a fairy tale as those photographs and will stop plaguing you. I'd say the man's done you a great service." I smiled brightly.

For a long minute, it was uncertain whether he was going to strike me dead for my impertinence or drop dead himself of apoplexy, but then, as I had hoped, he threw back his head and laughed long and hard.

Suddenly, without warning, I found myself turning to him, leaning into him until my face was buried in the lapels of his coat. "Oh God, Holmes. I was so frightened. Even now, the thought that He is out there somewhere paralyses me with terror." We stood together for a long moment, and he cleared his throat.

"There is only one solution, you know, Russell."

"Yes. I know." His white evening scarf was soft against my cheek, and he smelt of wool and tobacco. I sighed, and stood away from him, only peripherally aware of his hands falling back to his sides. "I seem to have spent the last few weeks running away from things. I can't very well do it now."

"You will not be alone," he said quietly. And indeed, from

that moment on I was not. I tucked my arm into his, and in amity we walked out of the park and caught a cab.

What the walk and the conversation had begun, the food finished, though what had helped most was having my anger redirected at its rightful target. After eating, we walked through nearby Covent Garden and then up to my flat, where I made coffee and we sat talking and I dozed off in front of the fire. Holmes woke me and sent me to my bed, where I slept, not for long, but deeply. I woke and put on my dressing gown to prowl the dark flat that smelt now of Holmes' tobacco, but the restlessness of the day before was controllable now, and the shame something to be acknowledged and not dwelt upon. I made myself some warm milk with a grating of nutmeg and stood at the window, watching the empty street below. After a while, the beat constable appeared, reaching for doorknobs, shining his light into corners, quite unprepared for any of the evil things that might befall him, but solidly, stolidly, reassuringly English. He passed on. I finished my drink and, walking past the smell of a pipe, returned to bed, and to sleep.

"Are you quite certain you feel up to it, Russell?" Holmes pressed.

In answer, I held my hand outstretched over the breakfast table. Steady as a rock, I noted proudly, and then noticed for the first time what Holmes was wearing.

"Where did you find the dressing gown, Holmes?"

"Lent me by the good Mr Quimby."

"Good of him. I was afraid they might be offended, an unchaperoned female and a male guest."

"I told the missus I was a bodyguard, and she had no further qualms. Women find me reassuring."

In the general run of things, Holmes was as reassuring as a shark, but I said nothing, applying myself to the eggs and the toast that tasted of actual food again.

"You wish to begin at once?" he asked again.

"Of course. We've no time to waste."

"Do not expect to be fully yourself for some days, Russell," he warned.

"I'll try not to fight off more than six thugs at a time. Joke, Holmes, only a joke. There isn't anyone in the Temple to fight, anyway, not at night. The guard is a drowsy old man."

"Miss Childe has taken on bodyguards, one or another of whom follows her about during the day." I looked up at him quickly, Mrs. Q's excellent eggs turning to pap in my mouth.

"And at night?"

"Apparently, she dismisses him after her services, earlier on the other evenings. However, you'll have to keep an eye out for the night guard, who prowls the Temple building itself."

"Thanks for the warning. I can't think she'd have him in the Temple overnight, though, and I'll be away long before he reports for duty in the morning."

"Take a gun."

"I will not. It would be found, and I'll not risk shooting a guard or even the tedious Marie just for the sake of your nerves."

He was not happy, but left it.

"You've decided how you will get in, then?" he asked.

"I can hardly borrow a child or two, so I shall go as an unfortunate and very young lady of the evening, at odds with her procurer."

"A prostitute beaten up by her pimp."

"I'll need foul teeth and a few fresh bruises. Which reminds me: What was it that you put on my wrist to make the fading bruises for the benefit of Inspector Dakins?"

"Algae from the water closet mixed with pipe cleanings. A pretty effect, is it not? I shall give you caps on two teeth and a yellow mouthwash I've been working on. It will stay on your tooth enamel even if you eat, although it won't stand up to brushing. The taste is pretty appalling, I'm afraid."

"I wouldn't have expected any less."

I rested during the middle of the day, and ate again. Holmes returned, given entrance by Q as I was scraping the last of the cheese from the plate. He deposited an armload of clothing and a stained and mottled canvas grip on the table with a fine disregard for propriety. I snatched up the underclothes and carried them away, then returned, to find him with a plate of his own.

"Thank you, Mrs Q," I called.

"Wig, or dye?" he asked around a mouthful of lightly curried chicken.

"Dye, for safety. I haven't been red for a while. A fiery redhead, that's the job."

The colouring was good enough to resemble a hennaed exaggeration of a natural red rather than a complete change in colour. Glasses, I should have to do without, carrying a pair in my pocket for the occasional peep. Skin lightened, two teeth capped and the rest stained with the revolting mixture. Mrs Q was seething with curiosity but said not a word. Holmes and I played chess and drank coffee all afternoon, and after a light, early supper, I went to dress.

The brassiere emphasised everything I hadn't thought was there; the dress was pathetic, particularly with the weight I had lost in the last two weeks. I overdid my hair, then pulled half of it into disarray. Holmes helped me with the bruises and reddened one of my eyes, and I stood back, waiting for his approval. His face, though, was as closed as ever I had seen it, and his jaw tightened briefly before he spoke.

"I suppose I shall become accustomed to this eventually," he muttered.

"I don't plan to wear this sort of thing regularly, Holmes," I protested.

"It's not the clothing you wear; it's the lion's dens you insist on walking into. You'd best go, before I'm tempted to lock you in your bedroom."

With a splutter of indignation, I thrust my arms into the sleeves of the ragged coat and slammed out the door. That the doorman did not immediately seize me and hand me into charge confirmed what I had begun to suspect of the building's bohemian ways.

* * *

I walked to the Underground station at Russell Square, occasioning a number of scandalised glances and the attention of several police constables, and rode the stinking depths to Liverpool Street. There, I emerged, to climb into an omnibus that took me into Whitechapel. The district was, as always, dreary and oppressive, and I was feeling queasy again and uncertain. I bought a hot pie from a vendor, but it did not help much, and I would have given the remainder to a starved-looking cat, but a child snatched it away before the animal could do more than sniff it.

I wandered up and down for the better part of an hour, cursed and driven away first from one corner and then another by their rightful occupants, approached by two separate men, both of whom lost interest when they heard my tubercular cough, establishing my presence in the neighbourhood and making quite certain that no one was following me. Eventually, I wound up across from the Temple's front entrance, along with the handful of buskers, acrobats, and pavement vendors who come out of the stonework whenever a crowd is about to pour out. This lot was considerably less skilful and affluent than their West End counterparts. The acrobatic midgets were stretching their backs as if to ease rheumatism while quarrelling violently with their musician, who held a violin case under his arm. The pie-seller's wares looked flaccid and misshapen. The two flower sellers chatted with a surprising camaraderie, considering the usually fierce territoriality of the breed. And here came another odd one, a massive woman whose full bust strained the bright yellow satin of her dress above the tray she bore, a selection of glittering geegaws. With the ponderous dignity of the profoundly intoxicated, she took up a strategic position across the street from the doors, and no sooner had they opened with the first of the released crowd than she burst into full-throated song.

" 'I'm called Little Buttercup—dear Little Buttercup, tho' I could never tell why,' " she warbled in a nearly accurate contralto, the jet beads on her primrose bonnet quivering with effort. She was remarkably successful, and one could imagine that the chief value of the baubles purchased lay in the story that would accompany its display—"You'll never guess where I bought this hideous thing. There was this creature, from the nineties, I swear, my dears. . . ."

When the tumult had subsided and the buskers were making off, I walked over to examine the dregs in Buttercup's tray. She had finished with Gilbert and Sullivan ("Sailors should never be shy . . .") and moved up in time to Al Jolson.

" 'It's time for mating . . .' " she gushed in a quavering Jolson tenor. " 'Anticipating . . . the birdies in the trees.' Buy a pretty, my pretty?" she broke off to trill at me with a gust of gin. I poked a scornful finger through the brooches and chains and found a ring, a chip of red glass set in a silver band that would discolour my finger before morning. I put it on.

"Loverly, dearie, a piece of real ruby that is. You'll treasure it forever."

"I doubt that," I said dryly, and haggled her down from her ludicrous price to a couple of farthings. I paid her, tucked my near-empty purse back into its pocket, and turned to look at the doors again.

"I shall stay on the street until you come out, Russell," said Holmes in his normal voice.

"As you know," I muttered with my hand over my face, "there is a good doorway up the street."

"If you find the path blocked, do not force it. We will return."

"Your singing voice is unearthly, Holmes, and the hat is ungodly. Nonetheless, I am glad you are here. I shall see you in a few hours."

"If you do not appear by dawn, I shall storm the city of women," he declared, but the jest was paper-thin. I drifted off.

Twenty minutes later, when the nearby pubs were calling for final orders, I eased into a dim corner for my final preparations. Makeup was all very well and good, but it would not fool a doctor, and I suspected that I would be examined in the shelter. I took a small wide-mouthed bottle out of my coat pocket, put it to my mouth, and sucked at it until it had attached itself firmly to my lip. I left it there for a minute, and when I broke the suction, I felt the flesh instantly begin to swell. I spent a few more minutes loosening my hairpins and pulling a small rent in the sleeve of my dress, stowing away my spectacles and running a layer of grime over face and clothes, then placed the bottle in a corner, peered cautiously out to be certain there was no eye on me, and stepped onto the pavement. I held myself as if my ribs pained me and walked up to Margery Childe's refuge for women.

CHAPTER 20

Saturday, 5 February–
Sunday, 6 February

*I, Fire, the Acceptor of sacrifices, ravishing
away from them their darkness, give the light.*
—Saint Catherine of Siena (c. 1347–1380)

The small brass plaque beside the door read:

NEW TEMPLE IN GOD
WOMEN AND INFANT TEMPORARY REFUGE

I mounted the steps and rang the bell.

There was as yet little activity in the shelter, as the pubs had just closed and the drunks had yet to reach the arms of their loving families. The woman in front of whom I eventually stood saw only a luckless prostitute in need of doctoring and reforming; she did not see the young heiress who had stood with her outside Parliament to distribute pamphlets and returned afterwards to dine in Margery's rooms. Ruby Hepplewhite looked up at me, polite, condescending, unseeing.

I twisted the tin ring around and around, tongued my nicely swollen lip, and tried to imagine myself into my rôle.

"Now, miss . . ."

"LaGrand, miss. Amie LaGrand."

"Miss . . . LaGrand. Is that actually your name?" she asked doubtfully. I twisted the ring furiously.

"Er, well, no, miss. It's Mudd. Annie Mudd. My—it was

given to me 'cause it sounded better, like."

"I see. Well, Miss Mudd—Annie. You understand that this is a temporary shelter for women and their children who find themselves without a home. It is not an hotel."

"I do know that, miss. I 'eard about you, on the street, the work you do. And when this . . . when I . . . I thought of comin' 'ere," I ended weakly. She took in the state of my face and clothes for the first time.

"I see. Sit down, Annie. How old are you?"

"Twenty-one, miss."

"The Refuge is run by the New Temple in God, Annie. One of the things we require is the truth."

"Sorry, miss. Eighteen, miss—on my next birthday. Come April."

"So you are seventeen. Where is your home?"

"Don't 'ave one. Not no more, I don't. I'm never goin' back there, miss. You can't make me. I'll throw meself into the river afore that, I swear before God."

"Calm yourself, Annie. No one wants to force you to do anything. Perhaps you'd better tell me everything. Why can't you go home? Did someone there hit you?"

"It was 'cause I said I wouldn't do it no more. He wanted me to go with that—" I searched for an unspeakable word, then, finding none, continued. "I said I wouldn't. Wouldn't never again. And so 'e, 'e slapped me round a bit and locked me in my room and I went out the window and down the pipe an' . . . and 'ere I am."

"You are speaking of your . . . procurer?"

"My wha'?" I was enjoying this.

"Your pimp?" she persisted gamely, thinking, no doubt, of how her mother would react if she were to hear the word spoken aloud.

"Oh. Yes, I s'pose."

"Where is your family, Annie? Do you have one?"

"Oh yair. Well, in a way. Mum's dead, but me sister, she lives in Bristol. That's where I thought I'd go, when I can get the money together."

"And your father? Is he dead?"

"By Gawd, I wish. Beg pardon, miss, but it was 'im what done this." I touched my distended lip cautiously.

She blinked and sat back slowly.

"Your father. Oh dear," she said in a weak voice. However, English breeding triumphed, and her forces rallied visibly. She stood up, told me to wait, and clacked off down the hallway. In rapid succession, I was given a brief medical examination (in which they were chiefly interested in wildlife and injuries, and not expecting a sophisticated form of drug abuse, so that by sleight of hand and an element of luck, I managed to keep the arm out of the nurse's sight), a bath, a change of clothing, a hot meal, and a bed in a curtained cubicle. By then, the evening's business was fully under way, and no one noticed as I purloined an assortment of pillows and blankets, which I pushed far back beneath the metal bed. I loitered about in the corridor outside the clothing dispensary until it was momentarily abandoned and then helped myself to a random frock and hat. They, too, went under the bed. The lights were still on—electrical lights, not gas—and the building was noisy with children and women, but I took off my shoes and lay on the thin mattress and closed my eyes. I did not think I would sleep, as my mind was taken up with unpleasant thoughts about the morality of what I was doing here and with the charged feeling one gets before embarking on a dangerous or illegal action. There are some means which no end, and no beginning, will fully justify; however, the dirty job of spying on Margery's privacy had to be done, and I was the best person to do it.

It seems, though, that I must have dozed off, a sure sign of the state I was in, because I heard the approach of footsteps and suddenly I was back in the cellar on my straw-filled sacks. I jerked upright and looked into Ruby Hepplewhite's startled face at the cubicle's curtain.

"Annie, what is it? What's wrong?" I pushed the hair out of my face.

"Nothing, miss. I was just dreamin'."

"Not a very pleasant dream, it would seem. I don't suppose you'll wish to swear out a complaint against your father, or the other man?"

"Go to the rozzers? Oh, miss, don't make me do that; 'e'd kill me for sure—"

"I told you, Annie, no one here is going to force you to do anything against your will. However, we will take you to the station tomorrow and put you on the train to Bristol, if you are certain your sister is in a position to take you in."

"Oh, miss, would you really? Oh, God bless you, miss. Yes, she wants me—she wrote to tell me to come when 'er baby was born, but 'e wouldn't let me. I'll save the money and send it back, miss. Honest I will."

"That isn't necessary. I will also give you the name of a woman in Bristol to go to, if your father appears or you have any problems. Now, I came to tell you that there is cocoa and bread-and-dripping in the dining room, if you'd like."

"Very much, miss," I said over the lurch of my stomach. "I'll just lace on me boots."

"I have other things to attend to, but I shall see you in the morning, Annie. I hope you sleep well."

"Thank you, miss." She left and I bent to put on my boots. As usually happened, the first fun had left the playacting, and I just wanted to finish my business here. I went down to the disgusting food, which I doubt I could have eaten even if I had been feeling strong, sat down near some children with large eyes, and shared my portion with them. After we had sung some cheery hymns, we were excused. In my cubicle, I wrote a note on a scrap of paper taken from a desk in passing, then turned off the light and lay on my bed until lights-out was called.

Eventually, feet ceased to pass up and down, voices were lowered, the last baby stopped grizzling, and a few women began to snore. I laced my boots on again (they had a new kind of sole, made of crêpe rubber, but no one had noticed that the waif walked the streets in silent shoes) and retrieved the pillows and blankets to arrange in a sleeping shape beneath the blanket. The frock, which was flowered and intended for a figure six inches shorter and four stone heavier, I hung on the hook over my coat to emphasise that the room was occupied, and I put the hat on the table. From the belt against my skin, a strip of flannel that I had succeeded in retaining throughout the bath and examination process, I took the two pieces of equipment necessary for the night's foray: my spectacles and a ring of picklocks. Holmes had advised a torch and jemmy in addition to the revolver, but I knew I would not be able to keep them from discovery. Taking care not to rattle the picklocks, I put them into the pocket that held such harmless objects as a small purse, cheap handkerchief, pencil stub, cigarettes, and a box of vestas, and took out the sop for my conscience: the note, written in a careful, half-literate scrawl:

> Dear Miss Ruby Hebelwite, thank you for your help, I will go to Bristoll with a frend who I remember is going, I will writ you from ther. Yours truly Annie Mudd PS this ring is for you its like your first name.

I wrapped it around the ring I had bought from Buttercup Holmes, tucked it under the hat, then cautiously pulled back the curtain and stepped into the corridor.

The shelter had only two connexions with the rest of the Temple: the main door on the ground floor and a lesser one on the second storey, used by cleaning personnel during the day and kept locked at night. The sleeping quarters occupied by the women and children were on the first floor, between the ground floor, which had offices, a kitchen, and a small surgery, and where there was almost always some activity, and the second floor, which was used mostly for storage and to house a few staff members. At one o'clock in the morning, the upper floor ought to be quite dead.

My crêpe-rubber soles whispered on the bare boards of the stairway, more noise than stockings would have made but less difficult to explain if I were discovered. Although how I should explain what a youthful prostitute was doing out of the dormitory with spectacles on her nose, the latest in patent shoes on her feet, and a set of picklocks in her hands, I did not care to meditate upon. Best not to be caught, Russell.

The upstairs door had a solid lock, but its security was nullified by the key hanging on a hook just out of sight inside the adjoining storeroom. I unlocked the door and put the key back in place, let myself into the Temple building, closed the door with exquisite care, and stood in the blackness, waiting for my eyes to adjust to the light that I knew must be there. In a moment, a rectangle swam into view, the end of this corridor as it was illuminated from the light below. I stayed where I was for another two minutes, then moved slowly forward, my left fingernails brushing the wallpaper.

In six steps, I had found my confidence. After ten, I stopped abruptly. Something? I put out my hands, felt only air, squatted, and my fingers came into contact with cold metal: a large tin bucket and a mop beside it, waiting for me to put my foot in it like some vaudeville turn. I exhaled, edged around them, and scuffled more cautiously towards the light.

A full-sized safe is not an easy thing to conceal. Freestanding, it tends to buckle floorboards, and hidden, it reveals its presence by the unnatural thickness of the wall. I was looking for something smaller, for personal items such as jewellery or, I hoped, deeds, contracts, or correspondence. I thought Margery would not have it in the ground floor, the public rooms; however, I hoped it would not be in her bedroom. Although I had once had a tutorial from a bona fide (and never caught) cat burglar who claimed, I think truthfully, that he had once varnished a sleeping man's fingernails, I did not relish the idea of examining a room with a sleeping occupant.

This house in which Margery lived and where downstairs the business of the Temple went on was a deep brick structure wedged in between the corner house next door, now the Refuge, and the Hall, originally built as a theatre. As with the Refuge, the top storey was used mostly for storage. Margery's quarters took up the first floor, and the ground floor and basement were given over to the Temple's offices, meeting rooms, and soon-to-be library. The stairs were at the back of the building; a wide corridor connected them with Margery's bedroom and dressing room, at the street end, and the other rooms: on the left side, the meeting room where the Circle gathered and then Margery's chapel; on the right side, first a small lumber room, then Margery's study, where she and I met for our tutorials, and finally the gorgon Marie's room, just before Margery's pair of doors at the end of the corridor.

I thought Margery would want her private safe in one of two places: the study or her dressing room. I considered the dressing room somewhat more likely, and although in cowardice I wanted to investigate the study first, I should have to go past that door and pray that neither Margery nor Marie were insomniac tonight. A light burnt directly over Margery's two doors, and the only escape, if someone came into the corridor from the stairs, would be through Margery's dressing-room window onto the street below.

The building was silent, but nothing in London is ever entirely still. There was movement, but not close, perhaps even on the street outside. I eased down a few stairs and peered into the still, bright corridor, with its apricot wool carpet on the floor, the watercolour landscapes on the walls. The paint gleamed quietly in the brightness spilling from the pieced-glass lamp shade, colours of apricot and orange in a twining pattern that reminded me vaguely of Margery's wineglasses. I walked down a few more steps and around the newel post, then stood for a long moment with my heart in my throat and fifty feet of waiting corridor stretched out in front of me, looking like the maw of a carnivorous plant, waiting for me, its insect prey.

My soles scrunched immensely on the deep pile, and as the doors of Margery's rooms approached, I was made aware of how very bad my nerves were: I was convinced that both Margery and her Marie stood waiting, to leap on me the moment I turned my back.

It seemed a very long time, but was less than half a minute, before I was beneath the light. Without turning my back to the opposite doors, I reached down for the knob to the chapel door and found it open. The eternal candle burnt over the altar, lighting my way to the connecting door into the dressing room. This one was locked.

It was not, however, a very good lock, and it gave way to my probes in a short time. That alone warned me what further scrutiny confirmed: The room contained nothing more valuable than the clothing in the wardrobes (admittedly expensive enough, mostly Worth and Poiret, with a few Chanels adding a modern note). The prices of these clothes would make the elves' place look like a pawnshop.

A slow, intense circuit of the room revealed nothing, except that Margery's taste in underclothing was remarkably exotic and that she snored. I let myself out through the chapel, locking the dressing room door behind me, and went back out into the light.

The study door was locked, and this lock was a good one. By the time it opened, I was blinking sweat from my eyes and muttering silent but emphatic imprecations against all the locksmiths I knew and Mr Yale in particular. It took me twelve minutes to conquer it, and for every one of those 720-odd seconds, I fully expected Marie's door to fly open and send me sprinting for my life. The damned thing finally clicked, the wire pick rattled slightly against the brass, and the knob in my greasy palm squeaked minutely when I turned it. I slipped inside, closed the door, eased the knob to and flipped the simple latch I had remembered from this side, and waited, breathless, counting off three long minutes before I relaxed into an irritating shakiness. The gorgon slept.

When my eyes had adjusted to the light easing in from under the door and the low glow from the fire, I could see that nothing much had been moved since my last tutorial with Margery. I reached out to the back of the sofa, picked up the thick cashmere shawl kept there, and went back three steps to lay it along the bottom of the door. The shawl would block any light from inside the room, and I then stuffed the end of my handkerchief into the keyhole. It was now safe to turn on the electric lights.

The familiar room came into view. There were three good

possibilities for hiding a safe, as I remembered, and I found it at the second one: a block of the decorative supporting cornice at the fireplace. It slid away, revealing a solid eight-inch-square slab of iron with a handle on one side and a combination dial in the centre—a combination dial, not a key.

I sat down on the arm of the sofa and stared at it bleakly. I was a fool not to have let Holmes do it. This safe was of the best quality; it would not fall for any of the clever tricks taught me by Holmes' pet safecracker (*not* the one who had opened a restaurant on his release). Despite the popular image of a burglar with a stethoscope, safes are broken not by hearing, but by touch. Steady nerves, infinite patience, and slow, painstaking, concentrated labour results in what our Eton-and-Balliol cracksman had called "that moment of indescribable giddiness" when the tumbler falls into place. However, steady nerves and slow concentration were precisely the qualities I lacked most just at the moment. Five days before, I had been locked in a cave, half-starved and stupefied with drugs: I could not do this. The safe was not going to open for me, not in the time I had.

Tell it to Holmes, nagged a voice. Watch his brief flare of irritation give way to sympathy, understanding. Live with that, will you? If you don't get it open tonight, there's tomorrow, isn't there?

I carried a chair over, flapped my hands about vigorously to wake them up, rubbed my fingertips firmly against the brickwork to increase their sensitivity, and then bent my entire body and mind to the problem of opening that safe.

I was soon dripping wet, more from the tension than from the coals at my knees. In half an hour, the quivering of my back muscles had spread to my hands, and I had to break off and do a series of noiseless calisthenics.

An hour crept past, then two, and still I bent with my cheek against the fireplace, my eyes shut, my whole being concentrated on the square inch of skin that caressed the dial. By this time, I could work only for ten minutes before the trembling of my muscles made it impossible to continue, and for two minutes I would stand, stretch, lie limp on the sofa, exercise violently, and then return to my work. The thought of Holmes' sympathy drove me back at first, but later it was simply mindless determination, and I suppose I should have still been sitting there when Margery walked in, but that at 5:20, three hours and six minutes after I had begun, the giddy sweetness seized the dial and the mechanism opened itself to my shaking hands.

I sat back and scrubbed my face with both hands, and neither face nor hands felt connected to the rest of me. I took my spectacles out of my pocket and put them on, then carried the contents of the safe over to the desk to examine them.

Margery Childe's secrets were few, but they were potent. My visual memory is normally excellent, but I could not trust my mind in its present state, so I took a piece of paper from the desk and, using Margery's pen, wrote down the details of her hidden life. In chronological order they were:

> A marriage certificate, to a Maj Thomas Silverton, 23 May 1915.
>
> A Military Cross with its purple and white ribbon.
>
> A telegram beginning, WE REGRET TO INFORM YOU, dated 3 November 1916.
>
> A second marriage certificate, this one in French, dated 9 December 1920—just less than two months ago. Margery was listed by her maiden name alone, no mention of Silverton. Her husband was named Claude de Finetti, with an address in London. His given occupation was the French equivalent of our *gentleman*.
>
> A will, autograph by Margery and witnessed, on 19 December 1920, by Marie and another whose name was unfamiliar but whose writing was that of an uneducated woman. In it, Margery left one half of everything she owned to her husband, the other half to the maintenance of the New Temple in God.

Another will, written by the same hand that had

> signed the wedding certificate as Claude de
> Finetti, dated and witnessed as Margery's was,
> leaving everything to his wife, Margery.

I looked long at the man's writing, at the signatures of a name that was not his own, at the script of an opportunist and a sensualist and an expert at deceiving the world, at the amorality in his *m*'s and the deception in his *t*'s, at the cruelty and the self absorption in his upswings and his loops, and I knew, without a fragment of doubt, that I was looking at my captor. Claude, I thought, we have you now.

There were also four brief letters addressed to "My darling wife" and signed just "C." I glanced at the first, and jerked back as if burned. My immediate impulse was to throw them onto the fire, my second to put them away unread, but I obviously could do neither, and so I reluctantly ran my eyes across his pen strokes. They were, one might say, love letters, were one to grant the word *love* the broadest possible definition. I made dutiful note of what few pertinent details they contained ("last Thursday"; the name of a play; a restaurant) and folded them up with hands that felt dirty. They did, however, serve to explain Margery's oddly fervent references to self-abnegation and discipline.

It was now 5:37, and I made haste to tidy up. I put everything back as it had been, wiped my fingerprints from the safe, on the remote chance I had disturbed something without noticing, replaced the chair, and placed her pen back in its holder. I needed to be gone, but the opening of the safe had restored a small degree of life to my brain, and another question had presented itself: How had Margery entered this room, bleeding and disheveled, without being seen on the street?

On earlier thought, I had tentatively decided that it must be the wall of bookshelves that gave way to a hidden opening, but on closer examination, there was no seam. I looked at the cornice that hid the safe.

Marie's room. I stood up quickly and stared at the adjoining wall on the side of the fireplace opposite the safe. Only

Marie would say nothing, were she to notice an odd chunk out of the floor space between the rooms.

Beside the fireplace was a series of shallow fitted shelves, holding an assortment of photographs and bric-a-brac. On the stray chance that the man who had fitted the secret compartments was as symmetrical as his fireplace surround, I prodded at the decorative bit that matched the safe's covering. There was a low click, and the wall moved.

As I stood looking proudly at my handiwork, there came another noise down the corridor. I reacted instantly. I dove for the door, undid the lock, slapped the light switch off, ripped the shawl from the floor, yanked my handkerchief from the keyhole, tossed the shawl over the back of the sofa, ran silently to the secret door and pulled it open, stepped in, and then leapt out again and retrieved my notes from Margery's desk, turned off the desk light, and groped my way back to the door. Once through it, I pulled it closed on its well-oiled hinges, and it clicked shut just as the light went on in the room. A pinpoint beam cut a path through and split onto my shoulder. I put my eye to the peephole.

Margery came in the study door, tousled and puffy with sleep. The way she moved inside the shimmering dressing gown confirmed her forty years; nonetheless, she was, if anything, more beautiful than her formal self. Feeling like a *voyeuse*, I watched her go to the fire and scrabble some coals onto the remains, then scratch her scalp and drop onto the sofa. After a moment, she tucked her legs underneath her, and to my great relief, she reached absently behind her and pulled the shawl across her shoulders, without noticing its disarray.

I was safe, for the moment at any rate: Margery was not about to follow me into the passageway (for the breath of air on the backs of my legs informed me it was not merely a hole), nor was she about to begin work at her desk, where the heat of the light could hardly fail to alert her that it had recently been on.

She sat and stared blankly into the fire. I could hear movement behind me in the room Marie occupied: water running, a door closing. In a few minutes, she came in, combed and starched in her grey uniform dress, carrying her tray. She greeted Margery formally, then laid out the tea things, built up the fire properly, and left Margery to her thoughts, and me to my dilemma.

I had originally thought to go downstairs and slip past the night guard through the front door, trusting that the mystery of an unbolted door, without signs of burglary, would soon be dismissed. Now, however, I was trapped.

Unless . . .

No. I'd had quite enough of dark places. I was happy to wait.

Until Holmes tires of watching for me and comes in? Oh, curse the man. Why choose now to become a solicitous male? He would rescue me, if I wished it or not.

No. No, thank you, there would be cobwebs and steps and hidden latches at the other end, and me with one small box of vestas.

One thing, though: I'd learnt skills in the dark.

Absolutely not. I will wait here until she goes to dress, and then I will sneak out. The place will be nearly deserted, of a Sunday morning.

How long? Two hours, three? Your bladder will burst, thanks to the refuge's tea.

That, unfortunately, was true, and truth to tell, the fear of having to do something about it in the passageway, all too reminiscent of my time in the cellar, drove me down into the dark more than anything else.

It was a long, long passage, tortuous and utterly unrelieved by light. The vestas I clutched as talismans against the night. I lit each one with care, scurried along until it began to burn my finger, then groped my way down the passage for a few more feet, considerably more disorientated than if I had remained in the dark. I knew that if I gave my senses a chance, they would guide me, but in craven cowardice I clung to my feeble lights, and I still had three in the box when I reached the end.

There was a door, a narrow one, and it opened easily onto an equally narrow passageway that was, glory of glories, open to the sky. I sidled between two buildings, stepped out onto a street, and stood breathing in the early-morning air.

The street seemed to me a foretaste of paradise—the morning mist was the breath of God; the early pedestrians, angels. I had come straight through the block of buildings onto the next street up from the hall, so with a wary eye for constables and Temple members, I made my way around the two corners until I found Holmes (Buttercup long discarded for the costume of an indeterminate labourer). I seized his hand, which surprised me as much as it did him. What is more, I did not release it until we reached my flat.

CHAPTER 21

Sunday, 6 February

[Thy husband] craves no other tribute at thy
hands
But love, fair looks, and true obedience—
Too little payment for so great a debt. . . .
Even such a woman oweth to her husband;
And when she's froward, peevish, sullen, sour,
And not obedient to his honest will,
What is she but a foul contending rebel,
And graceless traitor to her loving lord?
                                    —William Shakespeare

That silly demonstration seemed to convince Holmes that I was at the ragged edge, either physically or mentally. On reaching my flat, he insisted that I undress, bath, and take Mrs Q's breakfast in bed, where he sat scowling horribly at me until I had pushed the last of it down. I was taken aback, as Holmes normally treated my infirmities as his own—that is, he ignored them. Perhaps, as Q had hinted, the previous days had been as hard on him as they had been on me, if for different reasons. I looked at him over the rim of my cup and dutifully recited all I had done and found within the Temple buildings. He sat on a pink satin boudoir chair, his labourer's boots propped on the foot of my Brobdingnagian bed, his fingers steepled, his eyes shut. I reached an end, then waited, but there was no response. I suspected he was asleep. I put the cup noisily on the tray, and his eyelids flashed open.

"I never asked you, Holmes. How did you find me . . . in that house in Essex?"

He leant forward and busied himself with the coffeepot, and I thought at first he was not going to answer. However, renewing his scowl and transferring its focus to his cup, he said. "My career has been sprinkled with glittering examples of incompetence, Russell, normally buried under the verbiage by Watson, but rarely has my stupidity had such potential for truly calamitous disaster. I did not even realise you were missing until Friday morning."

"When I didn't show up for the presentation. But didn't Duncan miss me sooner than that? We had planned to spend Wednesday together—Holmes! You went there, to the presentation?"

"I was there, properly gowned—my own gown, too, mind you, not from a costume box. I walked into the hall, to find utter panic, of the Oxford variety: tight voices, careful polysyllables, a certain amount of wringing of hands. Margery Childe was there, too, incidentally. I found your colleague Duncan and he controlled himself long enough to tell me that no one had seen you that week. I sought out Miss Childe and she confirmed that you had not come to the Temple during the week, as you had halfway promised, but she had assumed that you were busy. After your landlady assured me that you had indeed not been in your rooms for nine days, it took me the remainder of Friday to confirm that you had been on the late Saturday train and to assemble an investigatory team, half of Saturday to locate a stationmaster who remembered a party of drunken Londoners, which included a totally unconscious woman, and then the trail went dead. Your abductor took to the minor roads in a Ford automobile, and the number of farmers who remembered hearing a Ford go by in the wee hours of Sunday, in opposite ends of a county at once, could not be believed. By Monday, I was reduced to quartering the countryside, with—"

He broke off at the sound of the telephone. I obediently allowed Q to answer it, then waited until he came to the doorway to pick up the instrument at the side of my bed (installed there, no doubt, for the convenience of ladies who sleep until noon). When I put it to my ear, all I heard was a wild gabble of male voices.

"Stop!" I ordered. "I cannot understand you. Who is this?"

"Miss Russell, oh Miss Russell, it's Eddie here, she's off, is

Mr 'Olmes there, he said I should ring if she came out onto the street, my cousin's following her, but he said to tell you and Mr 'Olmes, is he there—"

"Eddie, where are you?" I said loudly. Holmes went rigid.

"Around the corner from the Temple building, miss, she's making for the river, Billy's on her tail, she and that maid of hers came out and had a blooming row and she ended up shoving the old grouch on her backside in the street, and then she just took off."

"Stay where you are, Eddie. We'll be there in five minutes." I slammed the receiver down, cracking off some of the gilt decoration, and threw myself out of bed. Holmes was already at the door.

"Russell, you're in no condition to—"

"Oh do shut up, Holmes. Fetch us a taxi," I said, and began to remove the few clothes I had on. He made haste to disappear.

Instead of a taxi, I found Q behind the wheel of the car, Holmes beside him. I jumped in and the car was moving away before the door had shut. We were soon driving past the Temple, deserted on the Sunday morning, and around the corner a lanky sixteen-year-old waved us down from the door of a newsagent's. I held the door for him, and he climbed cautiously in. He bobbed his head at me and greeted Holmes with the same excitement he had demonstrated on the telephone.

"Mornin', Mr 'Olmes, sir. Billy said he was doin' just like you said. There's a string of us left behind where she goes. He's stayin' with her," and then he began to repeat himself in slightly different words, several times. There were indeed a string of them, the youngest a girl of six, the oldest a gaffer bent over a cane, each of whom we gathered up into the car. I had shaken the hands of eight of Billy's multitudinous relatives when Holmes' sharp order came from the front seat.

"Down!"

Ten of us collapsed onto the floor and seat while the car drifted sedately past first Billy and his current cousin and then Margery Childe, turned into a side street, and pulled up to the kerb. Holmes and I extricated ourselves.

"Q," I said, "I want you to return these good folk to their homes. If you can find a tea shop open, give them breakfast first. I'll reimburse you." Despite protests, I closed the door firmly in all those faces and Q drove off. Holmes and I pressed ourselves into a doorway and waited for Margery to pass on the adjoining street; then we walked out to intercept Billy and tell him to drop back.

She was making for the river, that was clear. She looked back twice, but both times Holmes seemed somehow to anticipate her, and she did not see us. Other than those two backwards glances, there was no attempt at subterfuge, no urge to take to wheeled transport, and she went straight south to Tower Bridge. We followed her over the greasy, cold river, staying well back until she had gone off of it going east, when we trotted to catch her up. She took to the dockyards on the south bank of the river, the dirty warrens where the sun never penetrates, and we alternately strolled and sprinted in her wake.

We were, it seemed, nearly to Greenwich when, hurrying up to a corner, we peered forward and caught the glimpse of a disappearing cloak.

"Gone to earth, by God. I thought she'd walk to Dover," muttered Holmes. "You stay here. Follow if she reappears. Drop crumbs or something. I'll place Billy on the corner back there, in case of a back door." He faded into the background.

A conscientious bobby can be one of the most irritating things on the face of London. One such found me after less than five minutes, took a look at my young man's clothing and long henna hair, and began to give me a hard time. I took my eye off the street, fixed him with a condescending stare, and spoke down my nose in my most imperious of plummy tones.

"My good man, I should inform you that you are speaking to Margaret Farthingale Hall. Lady Margaret Hall. What you see before you is the tail end of a long and not terribly amusing party that Jeffie Norton—the American film star?—held yesterday night. A costume party, as you can see. I suppose I ought to be gratified that you find my costume so intriguing, but I am beginning to find the game just the least bit tedious, and I fear the costume is proving less exotic than I had anticipated. My escort for the evening, when last I saw him, had the more interesting costume, a nineties number with feathers and sequins—too, too Folies Bergère, don't you know? You haven't seen him, I don't suppose? No, that's too much to hope for. Knowing him, he is waiting around the corner until you leave. He's a dear boy, but so conservative without champagne to keep up his nerve. So, if you'll just run along, I shall see if I can coax him out of the woodwork." I turned a dismissive back.

An older constable might well have persisted, but I had intimidated this one into believing the voice and the attitude rather than the clothing, and after issuing a stern warning, he left me to my vigil.

After ten minutes, I was beginning to wonder how long my constable's rounds took him. After fifteen, Holmes' head appeared unexpectedly, protruding from the doorway into which Margery had gone. I hurried forward and slipped inside.

There was a body just inside the door, bound and gagged.

"The only guard?" I whispered.

"There was another at the back. Help me carry this one out of the way."

I picked up his feet, then nearly dropped him as I saw his features.

"Holmes, this was the other man from the house in Essex."

"Good," was his only remark, but he showed no gentleness when we dumped the body in an adjoining office room.

"She's upstairs," Holmes whispered. "Second floor, by the sound of it. The place seems almost deserted."

"Perhaps they've all gone to church."

The building was a warehouse, which seemed to contain little but great coils of rope and bales of rag. Two lorries stood near the gates, but as a business, it seemed none too prosperous. There were voices coming from upstairs, wordless but angry. As we went carefully up, they sorted themselves out into a man's rumble and a woman's shrill, and closer still, I knew them both. The woman was Margery, although I'd never heard her sound like this. The male voice was that of Claude Franklin: my captor; Margery's husband.

I flushed, hearing him, and felt abruptly how very ill and tired I was. I must have sagged slightly, because Holmes' hand was on my elbow.

"Take the revolver," he said, holding the thing out to me. I reached for it automatically, then pushed it back into his hand.

"You keep it, Holmes," I whispered. "I'd shoot my own foot."

He slid it back under his belt and we began to creep up the stairs until we were on a level with the arguing voices. They didn't hear any of the creaks the old stairs made, and there seemed to be no other people in the building.

"—could you possibly think I wouldn't find out, Claude?" Margery was saying. "I suppose I've been incredibly stupid, but when I heard Friday that Mary was held captive, and then her will— That's why you've been away, all this time, isn't it? Were you planning on . . . Would you actually have killed her? For her *money*?" Her voice rose with incredulity.

"You stupid bitch. Why do you think I married you? Why do you think I wait around in this godforsaken hell-hole every Thursday night? For your bloody conversation?"

Had we heard any movements from the room during the lengthy silence that followed, we should have moved to intervene, but there was nothing but silence. Finally Margery spoke, calmly, in a voice I'd heard her use during our lessons.

"That boy with the knife; he was from you, wasn't he? I thought for a moment he might be, that you'd decided the beating wasn't enough, but I couldn't believe it. But he was. And he died. Did you arrange that, too? You must have. You wanted me dead so you could have the Temple's money. My God, what kind of an animal are you?"

I glanced at Holmes, and knew that the look of strain on his face was duplicated on my own. "He's going to kill her," I whispered.

"That may be what she's after," he said.

"Which means," Margery continued, slowly putting together an incomprehensible picture in her mind, "that you would have killed Mary, once you heard about her will. Why are you laughing?"

"Jesus, you really are stupid."

"Why?"

"She didn't write a will. I had it written for her."

This silence was shorter, as if she were becoming accustomed to a new and foreign mechanism. "You decided to kill me for my money. She saved my life. You then kidnapped her, forged a will, and would have killed her if the police hadn't found her. I assume you would have then made another effort to have me killed. You aren't human, Claude. Your own wife, in order to inherit—" She stopped, and when she spoke again her voice, for the first time, was low with horror. "Iris. My God, you killed Iris. Is that what gave you the idea? Her leaving me some money?"

"Margery," he said, with what could only be affection in his voice, "I've been putting this together for months now, since last summer. Long before I married you."

"Delia?" She groaned. "Oh, no, no."

"Look," he said, and I heard the sound of a chair scraping back. "I have to leave. I don't want to hurt you, Margery. I liked you, I really did. It's all gone to hell now, anyway. A year's worth of work and that Russell female will have the police on me, damn her eyes. I'll have to lie low for a couple of years at least—I could never risk making a claim on your estate."

"I'm not going to let you walk out of here, Claude."

"You don't have any choice, Margery."

"If you shoot me, Claude, you will die."

Conviction rang out in her voice, not fear, but Holmes and I were already moving, and we hit the door a split second before the shot rang out. The old wood crashed open before our joined weight and we entered fast, Holmes high with the gun in his hand and me rolling low, as pretty a joint effect as if we had rehearsed it. Franklin was standing behind a heavy oak desk, with the gun still pointing at Margery. He brought it around and got off two quick shots that overlapped with a third from behind me. I came to my feet in a crouch, in time to see Franklin stagger and go down. There was a swish and a heavy thud behind the desk. Holmes, holding the gun out, took three quick steps to the side, and then his jaw dropped and he gave vent to a brief oath.

Franklin had vanished.

I stared briefly at the floor, empty but for a smear of blood, before I gathered my wits and turned to Margery. Holmes began to run his hands over the floor, feeling for the hidden panel.

"How is she?" he asked over his shoulder.

"She'll do. It went through her below the shoulder joint, but it looks clean."

"There's no hope here," he said, getting to his feet. "He bolted it from the back."

"I should have known there would be a secret passage here, too."

"Would have made no difference if we'd known," he said briefly. "Can you leave her?"

"Yes."

We thundered down the stairs, leaving all doors open, circled the corner at a run, and swept straight into the arms of the constable.

"What's all this now?" he said predictably. Holmes dodged his hands and flew on; I danced out of the constable's reach.

"There's a woman on the second floor wounded; she needs medical attention. We're after the man who shot her. Can't wait." He was, naturally enough, not pleased, and he followed heavily on my heels. Unfortunately for Billy, Holmes' assistant chose that moment to join the chase, and he was captured while I continued, despite leaden legs, to gain slowly on Holmes. I finally caught him up when he ran out of land; I found him standing beneath a crane on a pier surrounded by coal barges. He pointed out into the river, chest heaving and momentarily speechless.

A small skiff with its oars shipped, empty and drifting free, was being pulled by the current from the side of a sleek launch that lay slightly upriver. As we watched, the boat coughed and emitted a ragged burst of smoke. I looked grimly about for a boat we could steal, but Holmes threw off his coat with determination and bent to his bootlaces. Arguing all the while, I began to do the same.

"I see a boat up on the next wharf, Holmes. We can have the police telegraph ahead and have him cut off before he reaches the sea. Holmes, we can't hope to swim it in time."

"You will swim nowhere. In your current condition, you'd probably drown, and then where should I be?"

"Of course I'm going with you," I said, and bent to my second boot. My vision faltered for a moment and then recovered. Holmes stood still at my side, watching my efforts.

"You're not," he said, and then something immensely hard hit my head and I collapsed instantaneously into the darkness.

I came to in stages, as if I were hitching myself up the side of a cliff. I finally gained the top and raised my spinning head from the boards that stank of tar and horse dung and rotted fish. I had been stunned only for a minute or two, for the launch was still there, running smoothly now and beginning to turn downstream as its mooring came free. A stocky figure with black hair moved back down the deck towards the wheel. As the boat continued to turn, a second figure came into view, a long, thin man clinging like a spider to the side of the hull, his lower half in the water. The stocky figure walked by the second one without noticing, and the instant he was past, Holmes hauled himself up and over onto the deck and lunged at him.

He was a split second too late, or too slow; perhaps Franklin was simply too fast. Holmes did manage to get his hand on Franklin's gun, and the two figures stood grappling on the deck while the boat continued to turn lazily and the other boats working the river came and went unawares. With the boat facing downstream and the two men invisible, there came a shot across the water, and another, but when the launch turned again, they were still there, still upright and grappling. Franklin was strong, but Holmes was taller, and the barrel of the revolver was now facing the deck. A third shot echoed across the water, and then the boat turned again, only now there was a sailing barge in its way, heavily laden with horse dung. I heard shouts as the crew tried to warn the launch off, but it was too late. The launch hit her broadsides.

I never knew if the third bullet punctured the launch's petrol tank, or whether something ruptured the tank when the smaller boat hit the barge, but when I looked at the launch in the instant following the collision, the smoke from its stack had already changed character. In another instant there were sparks coming out, and then flames. Soon there was a dull crump; in thirty seconds, the launch was engulfed in flames, and the voices of the barge crew could be heard even above the roaring in my ears. They succeeded in pushing her off with poles and holding her there.

It only took two or three minutes for her to burn to the water, and then she sank.

I had not realised I was on my feet and at the very edge of the pier until my knees collapsed beneath me and left me sitting on a great mound of rope, watching the sudden scurry of activity before me, men on boats of all kinds, shouts, people running, cursing, gesticulating, a police boat. The men on the barge were standing in a row, staring down into the water over their side, subdued, with the attitude of those who have witnessed death.

I stared at the fragments of burning planks and unidentifiable smouldering things, the remnants of what had been an expensive launch, and I felt nothing. There was nothing inside me to feel. How curious. I watched the boats gather, waited for the horror to overwhelm me, waited for the urge to fling myself howling into the river, or into insanity, but I felt nothing but emptiness.

After a long, long time, a stir came in the water below my feet. I looked down and saw floating there a white oval topped by a scrawl of iron grey and coated with scum and débris. It spoke to me in the drawl of a Cockney.

"Give us an 'and, laidee."

"Holmes?" I whispered. I knelt. I put a hand down to the water and hauled back a dripping, scorched caricature of a man in shirtsleeves, barefoot, missing half the hair on the back of his head, covered in oil and filth, and exposed to half the diseases of Europe. When he was upright, I flung my arms around him and put my mouth to his. For a long minute, we were one.

Rational thought returned in a flood. I pulled back, and I hit him—nothing fancy, just a good, traditional, lady's open-handed slap that had all the muscles of my arm behind it. It rattled his teeth and nearly sent him back into the river. I glared furiously at him.

"Never, never do that again!"

"Russell! *I* did not—"

"Knock me out and leave me behind—Holmes, how could you?"

"There was no time for a discussion," he pointed out.

"That is no excuse," I said illogically. "Never even think of doing something like that again!"

"You'd have done the same, if you'd thought of it."

"No! Well, probably not."

"I do apologise for making your decision for you, Russell."

"I want your word that you'll never do anything like that again."

"Very well, I promise: Next time, I will allow the villain to escape while we stage a debate on who is to do what."

"Good. Thank you." He stood fingering his jaw; I reached up to explore the knot on my skull. "My head hurts. What did you hit me with?"

"My hand. I think I've broken a bone in it," he added thoughtfully, and, turning his attentions to that part, he flexed it gingerly.

"Serves you right." I reached out and brushed a strand of rotted straw from the side of his face, peeled a scrap of oil-soaked newspaper from the charred remnant of his collar. He pulled a dripping handkerchief out of his trouser pocket, wrung it out, and unfolded it, then ran it over his face and hands and hair. He held it out and glanced at its transformation into a mechanic's rag, then dropped it over the side of the pier and turned back to me, his face unreadable.

"A bath and some inoculations are called for, Holmes," I said, or rather, started to say, because on the third word he stepped forward and wrapped his arms around me and his mouth came down on mine with all the force that the side of his hand had used earlier on my skull, and with much the same effect on my knees.

(How could he have known? How could he know my body better than I did myself? How could he foresee that a thumbnail run up my spine would—)

"By God," he murmured throatily into my hair. "I've wanted to do that since the moment I laid eyes upon you."

(—arch my body against his, close my eyes, stop the breath in my throat? That his lips on the inside of my wrist and on the hollow of my jaw would concentrate my entire being, every cell in my body—)

"Holmes," I objected when I could draw breath, "when you first saw me, you thought I was a boy."

(—on that point of joining? That his mouth at the corner of mine was so excruciating, so tantalising, that it would arouse me more—)

"And don't think that didn't cause me some minutes of deep consternation," he said.

(—than a direct kiss, would ring in my body the desire for more?)

When he held me away from him, it was fortunate he left his hands on my shoulders. He spoke as if continuing a discussion.

"You do realise how potentially disastrous this whole thing is?" he said. "I am old and set in my ways. I will give you little affection and a great deal of irritation, though heaven knows you're aware of how difficult I can be."

"And you smoke foul tobacco and get down in the dumps for days and mess about with chemicals, but I don't keep a bull pup."

"What?"

"Never mind. Holmes, is this a proposal of marriage?"

He blinked in surprise.

"Does it need proposing?" he asked. "Would it please

some obscure part of your makeup if I were to get down on one knee? I shall, if you wish, although my rheumatism is a bit troublesome just at the moment."

"Your rheumatism troubles you when convenient, Holmes," I remarked, "and I think that if you're going to propose marriage to me, you'd best have both your feet under you. Very well, I accept, on the aforementioned condition that you never again try to keep me from harm by hitting me on the skull, or by trickery. I'll not marry a man I can't trust at my back."

"I give you my solemn vow, Russell, to try to control my chivalrous impulses. If, that is, you agree that there may come times when—due entirely to my greater experience, I hasten to say—I am forced to give you a direct order."

"If it is given as to an assistant, and not as to a female of the species, I shall obey."

These complicated negotiations of our marriage contract thus completed, we faced each other as a newly affianced couple, reached out, and shook hands firmly.

POSTSCRIPT

Being deceivers, yet we are true;
unknown, yet well known; dying, yet, behold we
   live;
punished, yet not killed; sorrowful, yet always
   rejoicing;
poor, yet making many rich;
having nothing, yet possessing everything.

                              2 Corinthians 6:8–10

There is no precise end to a tale such as this one, and yet, a line must be drawn. For the sake of those who wish to look beyond the boundary, however, I shall recount two conversations I had that spring.

The first was held six or eight weeks after the final events of this story, when Veronica rang me in Sussex. Miles had set off for a tour across America some weeks before, but she had just received a telegram from him sent from Washington, D.C.

"He's turning home early," she said. "He's coming back to me, Mary."

"Did he say that?"

"His exact words were, 'What am I doing here query. Bounderhood piled on bounderhood.' He's coming home."

"I'm very glad, Ronnie. I only hope you don't reciprocate my example of rudeness and stage a secret elopement."

"Not a chance, with our families. There probably won't be a ball, because of Iris, but that's just as well. Miles is almost as clumsy on his feet as I am."

They married in a cloud of white roses. She had him for three years and one child before losing him to a sniper's bullet in Ireland in 1924.

The other conversation took place a few months later. The

first of the court cases set off by the charred body of Claude Franklin/Calvin Franich/Claude de Finetti eventually wrangled its way to a close, leaving two members of the Inner Circle, Susanna Briggs and Francesca Rowley, serving time in prison for their parts in his smuggling operations. Other cases were pending, capital cases against the men taken in the London warehouse and in the house where I had been held in Essex, but in none of them was Margery Childe charged. There was no evidence that she knew of her husband's smuggling or of his murderous plots involving inheritances; after the conversation Holmes and I had heard, even Lestrade had to agree that she had been blind, but not criminal. She was not charged, not by the authorities. However, she brought against herself a verdict of guilty, and as penance stripped herself of everything. The monies she had inherited were returned to the families of the murdered women, the remains of the Temple turned over to those of her Circle who were still faithful, and Margery took herself, with all her considerable charms and abilities, to the west coast of Africa, where she did great good and was much loved until her death in a cholera epidemic in 1935.

I went to see her the night before she left, in the run-down boarding house where she was staying in Portsmouth. She wore a tweed skirt and a woollen cardigan, and her drab, uncharacteristic clothing seemed the most substantial thing about her. She poured me tea from a flowery chipped pot, as we sat in the landlady's dusty drawing room, rain slapping drearily against the windows.

"I thought I was doing God's will," she said in a voice as light and lifeless as the ashes of a fire. "I thought I knew God's will. I thought, even, that there were times when He talked with me. Pride, the most deadly sin. And you, who seemed filled with pride, who I thought believed more in some interesting psychological condition than in the divine person of God, it turns out you were right, and I was wrong. I don't understand, at all."

She sounded merely puzzled, not resentful or even hurt.

My heart went out to her, for truly, her only fault had been her pride. "Margery, there's a story rabbi Akiva tells, about a king who had two daughters. One was sweet-tempered and lovely to look at, and whenever she came to her father with a request, the king took his time before granting it, so he might enjoy her great beauty and her musical voice and her sparkling wit. Her unfortunate sister, on the other hand, was a harridan, coarse of face and tongue, and no sooner would she appear before the king than he would shout at his ministers and servants, 'Give her whatever she wants and let her leave!'"

It took her a moment for her to understand, but then she laughed. For the last time I heard Margery's stirring, oddly deep laughter, and I was glad that it could end this way.

"You go tomorrow?" I asked her.

"To the boat, yes. We sail during the night."

"I have instructed my solicitors to place two hundred pounds each month into the mission accounts. If you need more, write to them, or to me."

"That is too much, Mary."

"I'm not giving it to you. I dare say Africa can absorb any amount of gold one can throw into it."

After a moment she dipped her head, a familiar gesture of regal acceptance. We drank our tea, and I could not resist the urge to ask her a final time.

"Margery, tell me. The healing. Did I see it?"

"Of course you did, Mary."

"Why wouldn't you admit it?"

"I did. I told you that God can touch us. Grace is sometimes given, even to those of us who do not deserve it."

I left a short time later. In the doorway, Margery went up on her toes and kissed my cheek. I never saw her again.

And yes, Holmes and I married too, and although it may not have been a union of conventional bliss, it was never dull.

Let still the woman take
An elder than herself: so wears she to him,
So sways she level in her husband's heart;

For, boy, however we do praise ourselves,
Our fancies are more giddy and unfirm,
More longing, wavering, sooner lost and worn,
Than women's are.
                              —William Shakespeare